Seasons of Truth

Other Books by Scott James Magner

Hearts of Iron

Blood and Ashes

Homefront

Seasons of Truth

Book One of the Hunters Chronicle

Scott James Magner

Produced by Scott James Magner

Edited by Marti McKenna, Bridget McKenna

Cover and interior art © 2015 by Roberto Calas

Seasons of Truth/ Scott James Magner. – 2nd edition.

ISBN 978-0-99630-592-1

ARUS Entertainment, Seattle, WA

For information on this, and other titles by this author, visit

www.arusentertainment.com

For my family, both biological and acquired. I wouldn't have made it here without your faith and support.

For my Brothers. All of you. For being there to pick me up when I fell, or for promising to do so should the need arise.

For those who protect us from the evils of the world. Lest we forget.

And for you, the reader. Because someone has to keep the dream alive.

WINTER

5 JANUARY, YEAR OF OUR LORD 1197

"...having extracted what we could from the beast, we took him up into the tower. Knowing what manner of demon it contained, we threw back the shutters, and the cleansing light of day shone full upon his face.

He would kill no more."

Your Grace has been most helpful and encouraging in my research. I only wish I could reward your patronage with more solid results. I find little that explains the acts of these Moorish "inquisitors," and they themselves were taken by violence soon after recording the verdict. No record of their final rest is made, simply a notice of passing.

I search further for the records of their lives. As always, please find a copy of my efforts in the accompanying pages...

AS THEY PASSED THROUGH THE SMOLDERING REM-nants of the village, Carlos longed for the secure, safe confines of his cell in the city and another commission for the Duke of Barcelona. On most days, he would already have searched records of the recent and distant past for heretofore unknown facts and prepared his findings for Matthieu or another one of the brothers to deliver to their patron.

On most days, he and Matthieu were not shaken awake before prayers, told to collect their belongings, and then loaded onto a rickety wagon to ride many miles under a too-bright sun that did nothing to heat the frozen ground. Carlos had suffered each impact of the wheels against the cracks in the ancient road in his bones and still had no idea as to why they were being sent away.

Three years ago, their journey from Toledo to Barcelona had been shortened and made pleasant by Matthieu's constant stories of the city and her splendors. Today his friend spent the journey up the hill to the monastery of Sant Cugat du Valles in silence. Neither boy had been given any reason for the relocation, and Carlos couldn't shake the feeling that they may have been an afterthought of some grander plan.

What possible use could there be for a researcher here? What mysteries might a scholar uncover in the crumbling stones of a backwater abbey or the ramshackle village accompanying it?

The fire had touched most of Ruri's buildings in some fashion, and several were no more than blackened outlines. The monastery's walls showed no signs of damage, but as the wagon clattered up the final slope to its gates Carlos saw only hints of its storied past.

This hardly seems like the site of the miracle of Saint Severus. Of course, Caesar rewarded him for that with ten nails in his head. Saint Medir and his companions fared little better, flogged, dragged, and then killed with swords on the same cracked stones that rattle our wagon. And just past these gates is the spot where Saint Cucuphas and his followers were martyred.

The courtyard didn't look like a holy site. It was just another frozen patch of dirt, and were it not for the monks coming to claim them, it could have been part of any city noble's house.

As the wagon rolled to a stop, Matthieu nudged him with an elbow, and Carlos turned back to see what his only friend wanted. Matthieu's eyes were wide in wonder, and Carlos didn't know what could possibly interest the other boy in this unwarranted exile.

Even though the garrison is long gone, the Romans and their dead still rule here. There is no life in this place, and the sooner we can leave it, the better.

Carlos began climbing over the side of the wagon, but one of the horses started at something and took a step forward, causing him to lose his balance and fall. Carlos hit the ground hard, much faster than he'd expected. The long miles of dusty road in his mouth were joined by a fresh infusion of cold dirt. Gasping, he tried to rise on tender elbows, face hot with shame. This was no way to present himself, and his awkward, undignified arrival was sure to embarrass the Bishop.

A calloused hand filled the space in front of his eyes, and Carlos followed it up until it became a wiry arm covered by a coarse, black cassock. Struggling at last to his knees, he raised his own bruised hand to meet it, aware of the small stones pressed into his skin as their palms met in a firm grip.

There was strength in that hand, and with a quick tug Carlos found his feet almost as quickly as he had the cold courtyard. His gaze followed the cassock's sleeve until it covered broad shoulders, then gave way to a weathered smile and piercing blue eyes beneath a smooth, hairless brow.

"Given the size of you and that hair, you must be young Carlos. I am happy both to find you in one piece and to learn of your skill at kneeling."

Carlos' mouth worked like a gasping fish, but he could not make it form any words. He snatched away his hand, leaving a small smear of blood on the palm of his benefactor.

"That he is, Father." Carlos shifted his eyes from that remarkable face toward Matthieu's familiar voice. His friend exited the wagon with no difficulty, carrying not only his own bundle, but Carlos' and the crate of scrolls and records the Bishop had sent with them. Somehow he shifted all three parcels so that his hand was free and clasped arms with the older man.

"Carlos is very eager to begin his duties here. It was all we could do to keep him in the wagon up from the City, so great was his desire to reach our new home."

Carlos stared at his friend, so animated now in conversation with a stranger. Why had he been silent all this time, only to come alive in the presence of this man?

"Well then, if he is Carlos, then you can be no other than Matthieu. There is plenty of work for both of you, and we can begin at once. Brother Mark can see to your things while we walk."

It took Carlos a moment to realize that the conversation

had shifted from the Latin in which he was greeted to the variant spoken in the northern regions of France. Carlos had heard Matthieu speak it for most of his life, but rarely had his friend smiled so widely as he did now.

Their accents are a perfect match.

"I am Frances, as you have surmised. What we do here is not so different from the duties you have known, but since our order is a small one you will also do many tasks you previously ignored or witnessed performed by others."

Father Frances delaMonde, the Abbot of Sant Cugat du Valles was the name attached to those eyes and hands. Carlos could not have picked a worse person in front of whom to fall, and he had yet to even introduce himself properly.

This day could get worse, I suppose. And surely will if I do not catch up to Matthieu and the Abbot.

Frances walked with Matthieu, ignoring Carlos' wide-eyed stare. Quickening his steps, Carlos caught up to them as they moved through the courtyard.

"...and you will find that the work itself is a reward greater than those sought after by the priests in the city. No, do not try do deny it my son, I have spent years at this post, but also many in other places.

Carlos' objection died on his lips, stilled by the Abbot's slight turn of the head and lowered eyes. It was as if the Abbot could read his thoughts and everything he did was wrong. His face burned with shame, but still he could not find his words.

"But do not think I do not want to hear what you have to say. All the brothers here have a voice, and the right to speak their minds."

Emboldened by this invitation, all the things Carlos wanted to say tried to come out at once.

"Your Grace...it is...I mean to say..."

"Carlos, we do not use such titles here. I am a brother like any other, and when the brothers named me their Father, it was all the honor I needed. You and Matthieu have a place here now—this is your home as much as ours."

"I...Father...we have come at the instruction of the Bishop, who told us you have a need. But I...we do not know of it, only that we are to report to you…"

Frances examined Carlos with ice-blue eyes, the warmth of his smile at odds with the intensity of his stare. His gaze shifted to include Matthieu, whose own smile had faded when Carlos voiced the concern both young men shared.

After several heartbeats and one long breath, Frances motioned for the pair to follow. The sound of his bare feet on the hard-packed earth carried clearly to their ears, although Carlos heard the motion of other monks in the distance.

Ahead of them was a long, low building constructed of weathered wood. A hanging oilcloth covered a splintered doorway, and piles of white cloth were stacked outside the structure. Frances indicated with an outstretched arm for the pair to enter.

Matthieu and Carlos exchanged looks of confusion, then Carlos heard another sound—one he knew all too well. He moved forward, entering the building carefully so that the harsh light of morning did not disturb those he knew were inside.

The smell hit him first. Sweet, sickly, with undertones of smoke. Inside, moaning and bandaged men occupied cots lining the walls, attended by monks applying clean cloths to burned skin.

"The fire within the skin may be raised by repeated application of clean, damp cloths. Take care to use only fresh bandages, so that no further insult is carried to the patient. Always remember there is a man present, whose soul is as important as his substance. When finished, remove the cloths and wash the skin thoroughly, then apply a paste of honey and lavender to the area. You wrote those words, did you not, Carlos?"

Carlos turned to regard Frances, whose clear, strong voice had transitioned to Greek. Matthieu looked at them both, eyes wider than ever—it was a language with which he was not familiar.

Carlos' response shifted back to the language of Matthieu's childhood, an unspoken plea for assistance and support.

"The words are not mine, Father. I am only an instrument of he who first recorded them. It is the task that I performed for the Duke and the Bishop and before him for our instructors in Toledo."

"No, Carlos. Those words are yours. Galen and Avicenna recorded the treatment and symptoms respectively, but centuries apart, and centuries before you were born. Those instructions are yours—I reviewed them last night after the stables in the village below collapsed and burned, and these men were brought to our care."

"Perhaps, Father, if you could be more specific regarding our duties." Matthieu's voice was tight, and only by dint of their long years of association could Carlos detect his anticipation and desire.

"As I said, I have been long in this post, but longer elsewhere. I am too old to be the only medicus in this abbey. Had I sent these men to Barcelona last night, they would have died before reaching the first bridge. Were I to have cared for them with no knowledge of the proper treatment, they would have lasted until the morning but not long after.

"You wrote those words seven years ago, Carlos. You were only a boy and Matthieu not much older. Had I known you were in Barcelona these last three years, you would have been sent for long ago. It is time that you two became proper healers instead of skulking about, watching while others give aid.

"We will find uses for your other talents as well, but as soon as these men return to their homes, we three will tear down this building and replace it with a larger, more complete xenodochia."

Carlos could only nod, acknowledging the desire in his own heart that matched the need in Matthieu's eyes.

We will be men of medicine now, not just faith.

"Good, then. Now help me with these sheets. They are not going to wash themselves, and we are sadly lacking in effective solvents."

Carlos followed frances outdise, while Matthieu moved further in to the building to give aid. this place could become a home after all, and the young man who was once a young boy could not not imagine wanting to be any other place.

...also, in the chronicles of His Eminence, Achard de Saint-Victor, there is mention of a man named Karl Outrikos. Little more than his name is recorded, which in itself is odd. If this man caught the attention of the church, one would think that there would be more recorded of him than "...a thick, cloying scent, such as that described in the matter of dark Karl Outrikos.

But the context is unmistakable. Some part of this man's life has been hidden from those of us who search for truth. Was he a priest, a doctor, or perhaps a victim of the disease Achard records, so similar to that we see here in Catalonia?

Moreover, why is he described as "dark?"

It is my hope to petition the University in Paris for access to their sealed records from his time as Abbot there. With your permission, I should like to have similar records from Seville sent here, as well as...

THE DAY'S DUTIES COMPLETE, CARLOS WALKED WITH Frances delaMonde in the late afternoon sun. Cold air and pending storms had no effect on the construction of the walls around them—the men of Ruri labored according to the plans and architecture set down by Rome and also Rome's schedules.

"And with the records held in France, I may learn more of this Karl and earlier outbreaks of pox. There may be similarities to accounts I studied before coming here—references to odd trials conducted by the Moors. If you sponsor my letter to the Bishop, surely the request will be approved."

This morning, Matthieu had brought Carlos dispatches containing part of a private collection uncovered in a vault outside Palermo. They were so similar to those Carlos once translated from the cities of Toledo and Seville that Carlos had a hard time understanding why they were not found together as part of a greater chronicle.

A disease of the skin and lungs was recorded in all three cities 200 years past. A strange malady afflicting travelers and citizens, taking or sparing lives indiscriminately. Also recorded were reports of madness and civil unrest as well as non-disease related deaths that should not have been remarked upon in such documents.

Seeming coincidences, but nothing suggested conspiracy. However, all three accounts mentioned individuals connected to Paris, and Carlos hoped that with the assistance of scholars in that city, other links would surface.

"My son, I will instead arrange for you to travel there directly and bring the records back to us. It is time you left for a while, Carlos. Eight years under my tutelage have given you all I have to teach."

Carlos did not quite know how to respond, although many years of listening told him the statement was intended for review and did not require an immediate answer. Instead, Frances kept walking, indicating that Carlos should follow.

Soon after he and Matthieu arrived at the abbey, the two boys had begun walking with the older man. "Physical Faith," Frances called it. An alignment of body and spirit, motion and emotion.

"A healthy body breeds a healthy mind." And with that philosophy Frances delaMonde had remained active well past the age when most men could barely dress themselves.

In warmer seasons, they spent this time tending the vines and crops the abbey relied on for survival, but in winter they either circled the courtyard or pulled alongside Alejandro's horses to draw water or mill grain harvested in months past.

The Abbot had been a man of the world once, a soldier and scholar who lingered in the East after his time in the

Crusades, gaining much from the knowledge of the Greeks. No longer French, never fully Spanish, the Abbot came to faith late in life, though he now lived fully in the Lord's grace and had done so since before Carlos was born.

Carlos' life was one composed of faith, and he wished for no adventures to complicate it further. The abbey was his world, with enough outside stimulus to occupy his curiosity.

"Father, I should not leave here just now. My duties are too important for personal distractions..."

The remainder of Carlos' statement was silenced by a tightening of Frances' smiling eyes.

"My Son, you must consider all aspects of the situation before you say such things." The Abbot's warm voice could fill a room, but it now held a cold edge. Only their long years of association emboldened Carlos to even this small dissent—one not normally afforded to a subordinate monk.

Frances was reminding him subtly, gently, that when the Abbot instructs, the Brother obeys.

"I have no choice—no voice here, do I?"

"No, my Son. You always have a voice. But you have a duty to God that transcends your work, no matter how skillfully you perform it. To grow—to expand your abilities—you must travel and gain experience. Our order is one of service, but also of study and discovery."

"I shall not debate you, my friend. But I also do not relish months without our talks." No lies, no wasted words between the two monks. "Father" was the address the older man preferred, but as the Abbot, and a true Bishop in his own right, he was due greater reverence.

Being first among equals, the Abbot was not permitted favorites, though Carlos' duties put him in more frequent contact with him than most.

"As shall I, my son. And when you go, you will leave me at the mercy of your followers. No, do not deny it. You young men are brothers in spirit, if not blood. You have done good work here, but at this time, they must grow as well. A tree that stands in shadow, even one as unassuming as yours, cannot grow as strong as it would in the light. It will be a good thing, this journey of yours. Through it, we will know the truth of your studies."

The older man's smile matched his eyes and words. Friendly, warm, honest, and as always offered without reservation.

Carlos and his mentor continued their discussion of the pilgrimage he was to take as they walked. Carlos kept up his part of the conversation, but his mind worked also on understanding the older man's earlier statements. The long miles of road would keep his body fit, but aligning it with his spirit might take all his learned discipline and strength of faith.

Carlos considered Frances a friend without reservation, and the fact that aside from Matthieu he had few others within the abbey was troubling. He'd formed bonds with all of the abbey's brothers, and tried to spend time with all of them as he moved throughout his day. They were his family—more so than the parents he had never known. But after almost a decade, Carlos' deep attachment to the Abbot was much more than that required in a community of monks. He'd come to regard his mentor and friend as a father in fact.

Frances was as important to the archivist's life as the "brothers in spirit" he named: Matthieu, Carlos' former ward Alejandro, and his current apprentice Robere. Daily life without these men would be a cold and lonely place.

Will I miss the others as much, or as keenly?

He should. He would, rather. The brothers at Sant Cugat were as much a part of him as his arms and legs. Every hand that lifted a bundle was his, and every hurt they suffered pained him. If his heart was reserved for only a few of them, that was a secret shared with no one but God.

Another reason for travel, perhaps. Time amongst strangers might recenter me on my life here.

"Your followers," Frances had said. Carlos did not think himself particularly interesting. He spent his life resurrecting echoes of the dead through the words they left behind. Collecting knowledge from their lives and comparing it to newer wisdom, and the word of God.

After his arrival in Sant Cugat, Carlos had devoted what spare hours he had to texts from doctors, healers, laymen, and priests from all ages. As boy, he discovered the Greeks, and Aristotle's words and practices had fired his young imagination. To continue learning from the past, he dutifully copied and translated all pages given to him, and his understanding grew with each manuscript so handled.

The ancient world was far away, though traces of it lingered still in the kingdom of Aragon. It had been very real to Carlos the student, and each new philosophy he acquired expanded his world.

A life in books could be indexed and filed. But Faith? Faith must be shared and spread. And despite their recent work in that area, such a task might be beyond his apprentice's capabilities. Robere was not growing in the Lord here, he was stagnating.

"Father, might Robere also benefit from the travel ahead of me? I know I have come to rely on his insights and abilities a great deal in the last year. If I am to gain value from a quest for knowledge, surely he would as well."

"Do not worry, Carlos. I shall continue the boy's education according to the path you have set for him. I assure you, when you return he will look us both in the eye." At the thought of Robere standing tall, Carlos returned the Abbot's wide grin.

"And among my followers, do you number Alejandro?"

Ahead of them in the sun, the stable master's broad back strained, muscle and sinew pulling at feedbags for the abbey's animals, two at a time. The young boys assisting him were two to a bag, and Carlos could not help but be envious of his ward's transformation from a starving child to a jovial giant.

Alejandro had grown strong in the Lord, with a faith mirroring his body. He was no monk, but fit the abbey so perfectly that he might have been there for hundreds of years like the walls surrounding them. Carlos did not worry for the man; he was as uniquely in his place as the moon in the night sky.

With me gone, his life will change not at all.

"Yes, 'little' Alejandro is definitely one of yours. You have done good work there, Brother. God's work: Charity and Grace. We will all be diminished in your absence, but still we must walk apart for a while. Sit with me a moment, Carlos. These old bones require rest."

The Abbot indicated one of the low stone benches near

the practice area, where Matthieu and two local men-at-arms were sparring. Also nearby was Robere, watching the three men move with eager eyes.

Carlos could certainly understand why. His oldest friend was large and well-muscled, similar in body to Frances. Even wearing a simple cassock and armed with a staff, he towered over his opponents.

While Carlos could compare himself to Matthieu's strengths, in Robere he saw his life reflected in a still pond. It would not take much imagination to place the boy's thin, weak face and body composed of angles and awkward motion among the students at the Toledo academy where he and Matthieu had spent their early years.

Matthieu's opponents were a pair of young men, newly called from Ruri to serve the Duke of Barcelona. They were lightly armored and wielded wooden practice swords approximating the heft and balance of the steel counterparts resting against another of the courtyard's benches.

While somewhat skilled, the young men fought singly, not pressing as a pair against their foe as would trained knights. Matthieu, laughing, used their reticence and inexperience to his advantage, drawing them into his circle and herding them into positions of imbalance.

He was a spinning blur, his simple staff at first a wall, then a striking snake, then a lever lifting and propelling him from the ground to divide his foes. Upon landing, he threw his staff horizontally and with force, cracking against the practice swords and sending all three weapons flying. Disarmed, the exhausted recruits signaled surrender.

"You see, my friends?" Matthieu's Catalan was slow, but precise, and more than sufficient to impart a lesson to the spent swordsmen. "You are stronger—better armed than I. But you allow me to take your strength and use it for myself. Tomorrow, you will tell me how you would fight the heathens, who know much more than I the ways of war. They will not grant you a second chance, nor offer comments as to your skill.

"But for today, shall we discuss why you lose to an inferior opponent?"

Inferior? Hardly. Matthieu was the most skilled fighter in the abbey, and in another life could easily have led an army on a crusade of faith. In fact, he had been offered a place with the Teutons during their last campaign, not only for his strength and faith but also for his skill at healing.

Matthieu flatly refused. Such things were present enough here when local soldiers returned home to die. Carlos knew a part of his smiling friend died with each patient they lost. Whatever advantages the life of a warrior might give him, that other life was far away and involved a much different man.

Carlos guarded these borderline heretical thoughts carefully. The Cathars spoke of such things—of return and rebirth. And the Hindi, with their many-armed gods and cycles of life. Carlos much preferred his soul where it was, thankful that men such as Frances, Matthieu, Alejandro, and young Robere enriched it. He would miss them in the months to come.

Frances was staring at Carlos, and with a flush of embarrassment the younger man realized he'd been asked a question.

"I'm sorry, Father. My thoughts gather wool, instead of your wisdom. What was that again?"

"What avenues of research will you follow regarding this Karl? The records you compile are certainly of interest, but they are neither conclusive nor canon. Part of being a teacher is knowing how to learn, and I must confess a desire to know the end of this mystery myself."

"Once I have access to more accounts, I shall..."

A flash of speed and a whisper on the wind made Carlos pause. One of Matthieu's students was down, a fletched shaft protruding from a lifeless eye. Another swift sound, and Matthieu clutched at another arrow embedded in his shoulder.

"To arms. *To arms!* Defend yourselves!" The Abbot's voice filled Carlos' ears as Frances rose, commanding attention from everyone in the courtyard. His strong legs quickly crossed to collect the soldiers' swords from their resting places. Neither man would need them now—the second of Matthieu's students lay bleeding in the dust with a third arrow transecting his spine.

Where? From what vantage do they assault?

Carlos looked around his home, searching for things that did not belong. Bandits had attempted such attacks before, hoping to find easy prey amongst the peace-loving monks. And if there was one unifying theme he'd learned while studying accounts of war, it was that the first strike was often meant as a distraction.

There.

The abbey's bell rang out an alarm, and the Abbot tossed Carlos a scabbarded sword. The older priest moved forward, marshaling the monks and workmen toward the gates. Strangers held them open while dusty riders charged in from the road. Carlos moved to follow them, but a shuffling sound from the left drew his attention.

Flames leapt from the stable's roof and an ill-dressed ruffian led several horses past the prone form of Alejandro. The big man's shaved head showed the impact of the bloody rock on the ground beside him, and Carlos had seen enough injuries like it to know his friend would likely die without immediate attention.

Carlos shook the sword free from its scabbard and turned toward the stables. Any unseen archers would have to wait while he saved Alejandro's life.

Again.

29 DECEMBER, YEAR OF OUR LORD 1200

C ARLOS FORCED HIS WAY AGAINST THE WIND, CHASING a sound he couldn't identify through rapidly falling snow. He was late, too late—the Brothers had surely begun the evening office without him. He couldn't hear their voices over the howling wind, but the routines he followed each day were as accurate as any candle.

The translations were important, but not so much so that he could ignore his other responsibilities. No amount of mystery 200 years past could excuse his tardiness, nor would he attempt to explain how cleverly he'd linked letters from Rome, Aachen, and Paris to thrice-copied records of ancient Barcino, on which Barcelona now stood.

Almost linked, that is. Similar was not same, and his curiosity could only be indulged so far. He and Matthieu were allowed their time in the scriptorium, but in addition to their primary roles as healers also had to attend to less elevated duties. Tonight, after prayers, he would need to help prepare the morning meal as well as endure another dry lesson from Brother Joseph on how to manage the abbey's funds.

Thankfully, no patients in the xenodochia required urgent care, though Master Jeremiah would remember his missing toes all the more for the stinging hot bath Carlos gave his feet. Even the most dedicated of monks wore heavy boots this season and made sure both the leather and the wool stockings inside were whole and dry before venturing out into the snow.

Frances and Carlos were able to save the man's feet, but

had he mentioned one of the horses trodding on them a day earlier, he would not now be limping along with a permanent memory of those small, frozen breaks. And the abbey's other residents certainly would not be shouldering his duties until the amputations healed.

There it is again. The howl of the wind and the white of the driving snow was less to his left than it should be. Carlos had heard and ignored something earlier while hurrying from his records to his patient, and now that he moved back over his footsteps, already filled with freshly fallen snow. His sixth winter here along the coast was far colder than the previous five, and the snow piled high each night only to settle into hard packs by morning.

Carlos paused, listening with closed eyes to both the wind and the damp edges of his cassock slapping the bare flesh underneath. He was sure that a voice other than that of the storm was speaking.

"...p...p..."

...please...help...

Words, soft and desperate. But from where? Carlos opened his eyes onto a wall of white, lost in the storm save for his own awareness of his location. Fifteen paces forward and three to the left was the entrance to the stables. Two to the right and twenty forward was the scriptorium, and forty behind him was the xenodochia.

Carlos left his familiar footpath, moving through hip-deep snow at half his normal rate. With each labored step, he measured the length of the triangle separating him from that voice.

...please...help...them...

He thrust his hands deep into the hard snow, ignoring the knives of ice tearing at his fingers as he dug. When he found a cold, frozen shoulder, his numb fingers cleared away white frost from a boy's face. He shouted for help, but the words were carried away by the wind, lost in the night as he willed this new patient to live.

Thin, too thin. Hardly any flesh on his bones, and nearly as cold against my hands as the storm on my face.

The torn rags pretending to be clothing were not nearly

sufficient to cover the boy, so Carlos bundled him as best he could against the heavy black wool of his cassock. The part of his mind not immediately concerned with the next five minutes of the boy's life wondered how, why, and when he had come to take shelter against the sagging walls of the stable.

The part that was cared more about the where, specifically the inside of the structure rather than the walls that framed it. Closing his eyes again, memory guided his steps as he battled the flying ice between him and the building's door. He reached out, but grasped empty air where a securing wooden bar should be and fell forward through this unexpected opening.

As he rested briefly with his back against the open door, Carlos found the darkness where the glow of a coal burner should have been more chilling than the icy body of the boy he'd pulled from the snow.

"p...please...no...they will...f...freeze..."

The sound from within the monk's cassock was as thin as the boy who made it, but it proved there was still life in his frozen form. Carlos pushed the door closed as best he could against the gathered snow, grunting with the effort as he shoved with all the strength he could spare. When it refused to move further, he eased the boy to the ground.

Away from the warmth of Carlos' chest, the boy began shivering. Carlos pulled straw from an empty stall that should have housed a horse to cover him. The thief might have killed all the remaining animals in his carelessness, had he not left behind a boy with more compassion than sense. It must have happened in the last three hours; surely Matthieu would have discovered this scene after he left to attend to the evening baking.

Carlos' attention moved quickly from stall to stall, counting the shivering animals by their labored breathing. Two sets of lungs were missing, meaning that three horses had been left behind to die. In the darkness of fifth stall, he heard something unexpected. The horse there was kicking repeatedly against something soft, and even over the heavy scent of horse the young healer knew the smells of death.

Whoever he was, or had been, at least one thief had already received judgment for his actions.

Carlos approached the stall with caution, carefully coaxing the frightened animal out and across the dark room, mindful of the boy at his feet. As the horse passed by, it seemed to calm down, pressing into the monk as if to herd him toward the freezing child. Jeremiah's chagrined lessons about this animal had been clear—he kicked and bit when angered, and the quickest way to rile him up was to push him against his will.

Counting the seconds of the boy's life down, the monk gave the horse its head. Keeping one hand on its muzzle, he backed ahead of it until he stood next to the straw-covered boy. The animal's head kept pushing against his palm, so he took a step back, then another. Incredibly, the horse knelt, gently resting its back against a thin and shaking hand barely visible in the cold darkness.

Carlos spared little time marveling at this miracle—the horse had bought the boy some number of extra breaths—time the monk could use to search the stall. Carefully stepping around the pair, he crouched and felt forward for what he suspected must be there.

His fingers found a fold of cloth, overlaid with slick leather of some kind. A doublet perhaps? Expensive garb for a thief, but anyone desperate enough to venture out on a night like this had already left behind reason and propriety.

Carlos grabbed at the fabric and pulled, trying to move the body. His worn boots slipped where hooves would not, and the monk's back slammed hard into packed earth, straw, and dung. There would be a bruise later, but his pain was not the issue. Taking a stronger grip, he pulled hard at the bulk of the dead man. Something cracked in front of him at the same time a knife of hot fire stabbed through his shoulder. Both body and monk sailed out of the stall to land hard against the opposite wall.

Pinned to the stable between the solid weight of a corpse and what felt like a hand cart, Carlos cursed his stupidity while sucking cold air through tight lips against the agony in his arm. He had either dislocated or torn something in his shoulder, and should have expected that the thief's corpse might not be easy to move. As Carlos had so dutifully reminded Jeremiah, blood was not immune from freezing in this weather. Within or without the body, it was a liquid like any other, and when frozen could turn as hard as stone.

With only one arm, precious moments passed before he could extricate himself from the corpse. The hand cart at his back was out of place, but once he was free of the body, it proved useful in gaining his feet. Arranging the body in the cart as best he could, Carlos stumbled to the boy, trying to distinguish his breathing from that of the much larger horse.

"...tha...that's right...you...you will be safe...now...do...do not worry...."

All sounds but the monk's heartbeats seemed diminished, distant. The boy had not stopped shivering, but his voice was stronger now. The animal beside him blew some comment, one echoed from two other stalls. Moving forward, the horses shifted in the darkness at his approach.

Focus, Carlos. Focus. Unless you survive, all these lives are lost.

Kneeling beside the boy, his good hand felt clammy, shivering skin beneath the straw. Even with the horse's help, the boy was far too chilled to last much longer.

Without hesitation, Carlos removed his cassock and draped it over both the boy and horse. The night air pricked at his flesh, biting cold even in this sheltered space. The twenty-eight paces to the kitchen were all he needed to cover, so his boots and the smallcloth around his waist would have to be enough.

If not, we are all dead.

Gathering his resolve for the frozen hell outside, Carlos drew what strength he could from both the animals and the boy who may have used his last breaths to call for their protection. Their unspoken faith in him was a bonfire more than sufficient to help him cross the courtyard. Imagining that feeling folded into thick blankets around his bare skin, he let go of his pain and fear, pushing out into the white wind toward where his brothers raised their voices to the Lord.

He had no other choice but to succeed...

HALT! I OFFER YOU MERCY, SHOULD YOU YIELD."
Carlos' voice betrayed no hint of the unease he felt. To kill a man, even in defense of others, was a thing not to be taken lightly. He had training with both staff and sword—Matthieu had seen to that. But outside the practice field, those skills had never been tested.

"Kill him." A second bandit spoke as he exited the blazing stable. Cruel scars and a purple bruise twisted his face, giving it an almost inhuman appearance. While the young man holding a train of frightened horses seemed unsure, this one's dead eyes offered no hope of mercy or surrender, and the curved sword he carried with an odd, over-sized hilt promised neither.

In your name, I take up arms.

The silent prayer gave Carlos strength as he approached. The horses were important to the abbey, but not nearly so much as the profusely bleeding man who cared for them. He needed to end this quickly so that he could attend his friend.

The younger man, really no more than a boy, was the weaker opponent. The temptation to deal with him first was strong, but the true danger was the veteran bandit, who surely did not receive his scars in peaceful pursuits.

Longer reach, a better weapon, and time were all advantages he held over the less experienced monk. As if reading his mind, the scarred man drew his strange sword and gripped it in both hands. The longer handle now made sense to Carlos; wielding the blade like that could generate a dangerously powerful attack.

Carlos had skill and speed, but no way of knowing this opponent's skill. His familiarity with his own weapon was all he could count on in this fight. The shorter sword in his hand was the most traditional of designs. Two sharpened edges, tapering to a point. A sword that won an empire and the template for three thousand years of war.

Carlos had trained with similar weights for many years and could use it to disable, or if necessary, kill. With keeping part of his attention on the younger bandit, he advanced on the second man.

The swordsman betrayed his attack with an overhand swing. Carlos danced inside the overpowered chop, drawing a line of blood across his opponent's right arm. Not deep enough to cripple, but a painful distraction.

"Surrender. Again I promise clemency if you will but lay down your sword."

The outlaw's answering snarl of rage was only partly directed at the monk. Carlos noted and dismissed the departure of the second man, who left behind the stolen horses. One less thing to worry about, and another advantage lost to his opponent.

Carlos deflected a sweeping slice from the curved sword with his short, sturdy blade. He felt its force in both arms and knew that he would lose if the fight continued much longer. His only hope was to press the attack.

A quick slash, and another line of blood joined the first, this time a deep cut in the meat of the arm. With the cut, a swath of cloth tore away from the man's ragged sleeve, revealing discolored skin covered in blisters.

The Pox. Another problem to address, when there is time to think.

The bandit retreated a step from Carlos' attack, but had somehow lost track of his surroundings. His back brushed the burning stable, transforming his filth-infused clothes into an almost unreal white halo of flames. His snarl transformed into a scream, and he dropped his weapon to bat away fire from his face. He ran, flailing and fanning the flames rather than rolling on the ground to extinguish them.

Carlos could spare him no further thought. His injured

friend was in similar danger, despite less flammable clothing. Groaning with the effort, he dragged Alejandro a short distance from the blaze.

His friend lived, but Alejandro's breathing was shallow and weak. The pulse in his veins was slow, and there was altogether too much blood on the ground. Carlos examined the wound on his head and hastily applied an improvised bandage torn from his cassock.

Carlos turned to offer care to his opponent, but it was too late. The fire had finished the job the pox started, and the smell of burned flesh joined that of seasoned wood and dry straw rising in black clouds of smoke. The unnatural color of the flames consuming the man's body was disturbing, but not as much as the actions of the horses.

Contrary to everything Carlos expected them to do, the animals did not move away from the flames, but instead stood guard over their caretaker. Judging his friend's safety more important than the mystery, Carlos again took hold of Alejandro's shoulders, and necessity gave strength to his tired arms.

Lifting him half off the dusty courtyard, Carlos backed away, each step followed by a team of horses both familiar and new. The abbey's sturdy animals were joined by several saddled horses scarred by war. They moved as a team in harness, hooves falling in time and pulling an unseen wagon away from the burning structure until men and beasts alike were safely free from the flames.

The slow, muffled cadence stopped, and when the last hoof fell into place the world snapped into focus. Sounds he had not thought absent rushed at him in a wave, nearly causing him to drop Alejandro's too-light form.

From someplace behind him, Matthieu's strong voice was joined by that of Frances, and both were accompanied by ringing steel. Carlos turned his head to see fighting at the gates—the monks surrounded and outnumbered by the bandits who'd thought Sant Cugat an easy target. The stunned and bleeding outlaws on the ground around them were proof enough of that mistake.

Both allies and enemies rallied to the fighting, bare feet

and boots alike moving across the courtyard as the abbey's bell went silent. Carlos laid his burden down gently—his friend was as safe as could be under the circumstances, and Carlos was needed elsewhere.

Leaving Alejandro in the "care" of the horses he loved so well, Carlos returned to the burning stable for his discarded weapon. The intense heat assaulted him as fiercely as had the bandit, as orange flames trailed upwards until black smoke mingled with gathering storm clouds.

The light of the blaze was brighter than the late afternoon sun, and looking away to search for his sword, images of the flames stayed in Carlos' field of vision. He closed his eyes for protection, calling up a memory of the scene over lingering outlines of red and blue.

He advances on the bandits. The boy is standing there, and the scarred man near the entrance. A while-hot blaze marks his body's position in both memory and the inside of his eyelids.

There is the rock used on Alejandro, glowing blue. The sword should be...

Carlos' searching fingers touched cool metal, slick with blood. His hand tingled as if he were touching a ringing bell, and the heat was suddenly gone. A cool breeze washed over him, carrying the scent of some tantalizingly familiar flower.

His eyes opened onto a conflagration burning as bright as ever, but one no longer painful to look at. The white image of the bandit's body was gone, replaced by a smoldering pile of black ash.

And in his hand was not a dull iron blade with a handle wrapped in leather and wire, but instead a mirror-bright piece of sky containing a wave pattern that followed the elegant curve of the metal.

It was lighter in his hands than he expected, much more so than the crude, thick bar with which he had harried his opponent. The balance was perfect, as if made for his hands. The edge shone with reflected fire, and Carlos could detect no counterparts to the deep notches their brief combat had made in his own sword. From the tip of the smooth blade to the sharp relief on the carved handle, the bandit's sword looked as if it had never before been used.

Carlos took several swings to get its measure as he charged the gates, trying not to think of the wounds he saw on both friend and foe as he ran. The sword sang through the air, a rich tone like the wind across chimes. But the beauty of its construction was not nearly enough to blot out the ugliness around him.

War, however small, had come to his home. He held a sword in his hands—hands that were covered with the blood of an innocent man. And if Carlos was to save not just Alejandro, but any man wounded here today, this battle must end.

As he drew closer to the gate, Carlos saw several of his brothers down and bleeding and the laborers of Ruri staggered back against the wall. They were joined in defeat by six bandits, but that many men still stood against his friends.

Matthieu and Frances were the abbey's only defenders still on their feet, and each now had three opponents looking to reduce that number further. Their singing was strong and proud, and Carlos drew what strength he could from it as he moved toward the fight.

With each step, Carlos' resolve grew. He was ready to do what must be done—to take life, so those he loved might live.

Be the petal on the water. Become the wave, and flow around the stones of the river.

What?

The words were a memory, spoken in a voice both his and not his. Carlos tightened his grip on the carved bone handle, and its raised edges pressed hard into his palms. His hands shifted, moving apart and into a position of balance that felt natural and right.

Familiar.

The sounds of battle echoed in Carlos' chest and with each word Matthieu sang his arms grew stronger. With each motion of Frances' arm, Carlos' legs pumped faster, until he stood at the Abbot's shoulder and his Brother's back. A hole closed behind him in the ring of swords, and some part of his mind adjusted the number of opponents downward by one.

When his lightning fast swing stopped a blow aimed at Matthieu's injured shoulder, Carlos was surprised to feel the blade absorb the blow and push it back like a spring. His opponent was similarly shocked, unprepared for a counterattack as the blade flew forward with the barest movement of the monk's arms.

His hands shifted again, and Carlos spun, reaching out to his right to meet a sword aimed toward Frances' head. Lightning struck a second time, and the count fell again.

Carlos, Matthieu, and Frances each took a step to the left, rotating around an axis of Faith until each had a new opponent. Three swords came up against four, and two lines of blood formed on men standing in front of Carlos.

The fading light of afternoon dimmed as the cool breeze became a cold, wet wind. His chest vibrated in time to the song behind him, filling his lungs, pumping blood through his body. His hands felt both farther away and closer, more present than he had ever known.

…be prepared to dig two graves…

Carlos' vision narrowed to a single point of light surrounded by a tunnel of dark. On the other side was a man whose pale, blotched face twisted in a snarl as he shoved home his sword.

The filth-covered thug's face shifted from anger to surprise, unprepared to drop his sword when the hand still holding it landed at his feet. There was a moment of silence before the screaming started, and Carlos stopped his swing just short of the next bandit's neck.

Three.

"Yield."

The word came from somewhere outside himself, and Carlos felt the world snap back into place at the sound of his own voice. The singing stopped, replaced by the sound of dropping swords, this time by hands held high in surrender.

Carlos lowered the blade, heavier now that the rush of battle had ended. The carved designs on the long handle pressed into his throbbing hands, still wet with Alejandro's blood.

I am a falling leaf, blown by the warm winds of autumn. This, too, shall pass.

His left shoulder fell away, as the support of Matthieu's arm slid down. Feet, hooves and shouts come from outside the gates as help arrived too late to assist in the abbey's defense.

The time of killing was over.

Time now for life, and death, as willed by God.

R OBERE, ROBERE! HOLD HIM. WE MUST STOP THE BLEED ing now, while there is still time!"
Carlos pulled the cord tight, hands slick and wet with red. His raised voice was not alone in the hall; the screams of the wounded and dying were everywhere, including the young man they treated now.

"*Frere* Carlos, I...I..."

Robere's words were a choked whisper, and despite his love for the boy Carlos had no time for the tears in it. He fought to keep his own voice calm and strong, and was so tired only the urgency of his task was keeping his eyes open.

"Robere, if you do not hold him, he is lost. Work now—grieve later for your friends." With one hand holding the cord tight, he pushed down on the boy's chest as best he could while Robere stared numbly.

Under the pressure of his hand, Carlos felt a shudder and a sharp inhalation before one last heartbeat forced blood past the binding under his clenched fingers.

Too late. Timothy, the cooper's son was gone, and no amount of wishing would bring him back.

Releasing the twisted twine around the corpse's leg, Carlos covered the dead boy's eyes with his hand, closing his own and saying a brief prayer. There would be time later for a proper rite, but for now the boy's soul waited with his father's at the Master's feet.

Timothy was not exactly Robere's friend, but was of an age with his apprentice and had stood as tall as any soldier at the gate. The damage to his leg was severe enough that had he lived, the boy would never stand straight again.

Robere's inaction had denied him that chance, or at least enough time for a surgeon to arrive from Barcelona.

And if they were very lucky, his pox would not spread. The heavy copper scent of blood mixed with sharp odor of pus from broken blisters and those of other bodily fluids they'd discovered when removing the boy's sodden trousers. Too many men here showed the same signs, too many friends and neighbors who had ignored headaches and fevers despite Carlos' continued warnings and instructions.

Carlos took two heartbeats to center himself, regaining the detachment necessary to continue treating those he could still save. In those heartbeats, he heard Robere's sandaled feet and now-unchecked sobs withdraw.

This is no time for weak hearts. If Robere cannot collect his thoughts, he has made the right choice.

Carlos stepped back, pulling a red-soaked sheet over the body. More men needed his care, or the hungry ground out-side the abbey's walls would claim his failures. Two fewer hands to work with was another difficulty to overcome to-night—one only remedied by action.

Sant Cugat du Valles had stood on this hill for many years, burning, rebuilding, and rededicating often. Associated with this latest incarnation were not only the monastery under perpetual construction and the scriptorium in which Carlos spent most of his time, but also the xenodochia where he and the other monks now worked without prejudice, healing friend and foe alike. Even Matthieu, with his wounded arm bound tightly against his chest, gave aid to his attackers as he would to any other injured man.

Heartbeats became minutes and hours, the sound of the wind out-side marking time as well as any guttering candle. The storm grew stronger, but eventually every wounded man had been seen at least once. Robere did not return, and after many hours of treating others Carlos was at last free to sit with the most seriously injured of the abbey's residents.

"Carlos?" Alejandro's voice was weak and his head wound still troubling. Frances had cleaned all dirt and other material from the cut, but the blow had also cracked the bones of his skull, an injury few escaped alive.

Carlos moved to his side, checking the heat in his head and the speed of his pulse, both of which were elevated from normal levels. Alejandro looked small laid out under the white sheets, diminished from his normal health and vigor.

"I am here, my friend. Please rest yourself. Tomorrow, you will feel much improved."

Years of practice had given Carlos the ability to lie with the truth. His friend would certainly feel better with the coming of dawn…if he survived the next few hours. But it was far more likely that he would be laid to rest beside Timothy and the abbey's other honored dead.

"Carlos…I will miss you, when you leave us. But…go… with no regrets. Our…my life here, it is enough for me. I am happy here. This…place is all I need."

A weak smile belied the pain the man must have felt. Carlos allowed its twin to grow on his face; apparently Alejandro was aware of Frances' plans.

It was also likely that the big man was hallucinating—a possible symptom of his injury. One of these circumstances the monk could examine later, the other he could only witness to an inevitable end.

The cracked skull was not Alejandro's only injury, although it was certainly the most serious. When he first moved the big man away from the burning stable, Carlos had thought the pool of blood completely sourced from the gash on his head, not noticing the puncture low on his back. A knife from behind had likely been his first warning of attack.

Carlos could almost see the confrontation play out in his mind…

Alejandro is feeding the livestock from the bags he stowed earlier. He welcomes his attackers to the stable, thinking them more volunteer laborers. A sharp pain in his side, and the big man whirls on his attacker, his fist impacting a scarred jaw. The younger bandit grabs a small fragment of a mill stone and uses it to subdue the larger man…

Carlos felt no guilt over allowing the boy to escape. God

would judge him according to how he lived the rest of his life. And if his health was similar to that of his compatriots, that reckoning would come sooner, rather than later. Forgiveness was Alejandro's to give but doing so benefited him, and him alone.

"Alejandro, do you have anything you wish me to hear? Please speak to me for as long as you can." Carlos applied a cool cloth to the wounded man's brow. Equalizing his temperaments would assist in the healing, as would the calming sound of a friendly voice. Another not quite "accepted" treatment, but one that Carlos had used to great effect in the past.

"I am fine, Carlos." The big man's voice was a whisper, one too soft for the monk's liking. "Is Matthieu well? I saw his shou...shoulder, before the torches grew too dim to see."

With the sudden blow, the stable master's brain, that most delicate of places, had bounced within his head. The blindness accompanying such an injury was temporary, but disorienting. His vision might return in stages, but for now there was darkness. The injury could also cause a deep drowsiness—one from which the sufferer could not rouse. Keeping his friend's mind active and alert while his body healed was critical to his survival.

"Yes, my friend. Matthieu is fine and hale." Carlos looked to his brother, barely standing on his own, but still tending to the needs of others. He wished he could change places with him—that the other monk would attend Alejandro. He couldn't bear to hear what might well be his friend's last words or to prepare his patient for the journey into God's loving arms.

His friend...

"Alejandro, can you hear me?" The big man's closed eyes and shallow breathing were a bad sign. "Alejandro, you are a strong man, much stronger than I. Remain here with us, we need such strength if we are to rebuild our stables."

Carlos leaned close, holding Alejandro's hand tight as if he could keep his friend alive by pure willpower. Alejandro's cool, clammy skin and weak heartbeats were nothing compared to the heat and pounding pulse of his own body.

Live, Brother. Please, live.

Alejandro gasped, a hard, forced sound. His eyes came fully open, and Carlos knew at once that his vision had returned. Their eyes met, and a thin, pained smile rewarded his prayer.

This—this is our reward for service. This warmth, this love is why we live—and keep living. **Stay with me, Alejandro. Stay.**

"I...will...stay, Carlos. I want to...stay..." The reply was soft, barely above a whisper. Standing over a wounded monk at a nearby bed, Matthieu shook his head, lifting a simple wooden cross to his lips as he mouthed a silent prayer.

"Matthieu is here. Speak to him now, I shall return soon." Carlos moved aside as Matthieu came to hold Alejandro's hand, standing nearby as the two men spoke.

Matthieu, Carlos, and Alejandro were three young men without fathers, learning together that the abbey was all the family they needed. While the youngest of them, Alejandro was by far the strongest, and they would need that strength to rebuild the abbey.

When I am gone.

There was much work to do before that day came, but Carlos was resolved now to the truth of the Abbot's words. This was his home, but every son, every brother must leave security and family behind at some point to appreciate the gifts they have been given.

That time approached faster than Carlos wanted—even in this very long night, there was too much left to accomplish.

It is time to deal with Robere.

During the attack, his apprentice had hidden inside the monastery, and the shame of that inaction now weighed on his soul. It didn't matter that Robere had no combat training; the boy was too fixated on the faces of dead men whose names he knew. The boy's problems separating his feelings from his duty made him a liability for this sort of work, and returning him to confidence would take a different kind of specialized treatment.

Carlos stepped into an alcove to exchange his blood-soaked cassock for a fresh one. It was the third time he had done so since the attack, and like the last two, it would have to be burned.

Someone will need to go through the abbey's stores for replacements; the men covered in coarse sheets behind me have no further use for their spare garments.

The first step outside was like plunging through river ice. Every inch of Carlos' skin tightened against the cold, and he rubbed his chest to keep his core warm. Fall had loosed its lingering grip on the hillsides, and Winter had finally come to Sant Cugat.

Tomorrow, I will need to have someone check on the vines and their covers. When I have an accurate count of the abbey's survivors.

A last patch of gray evening clung to the courtyard, refusing to surrender to night. The wind whipped around his ankles and caused the abbey's ancient bell to ring softly as it swayed. Carlos saw no men walking in the courtyard but smelled something cooking within the main building.

His feet moved in familiar paths, taking him toward the scriptorium at the edge of the square where he hoped to find Robere. To get there he passed the ruins of the stable, and the charred skeleton of Alejandro's domain was an ugly reminder of the afternoon.

The structure, along with the wagons it held, was completely destroyed. That the bandits had emptied it of horses before firing it was a blessing. But those horses—and the bandit's mounts, now unsaddled and bare—searched the charred ground for scraps of straw and grain, shivering against the wind.

Most of the raider horses were smaller and leaner than the animals the abbey kept for pulling carts, and by the scars and sores visible on their bodies, had been worked considerably harder in their lives. These were mounts bred and trained for war, but to see them standing meekly alongside the cart horses, the line between soldier and servant was almost invisible.

Alejandro would ease them into gentle retirement when he recovered. He would weep over their cruel treatment, promising them better lives free from pain and war. But tonight Sant Cugat's stable master was near death, and whatever hands had unsaddled the new animals were now occupied with some other task.

These, too, are my patients. They require aid as much as the men within.

Food, shelter, warmth, and companionship were needs shared by all living things, and the horses had been offered little of any in the battle's aftermath.

Carlos approached the line of animals carefully so as not to alarm the newcomers. He spoke softly, announcing his presence and intentions as he walked.

"There now, friends. I am Carlos, and I must apologize that Alejandro is not here to greet you properly. He would know your names by now and have seen to your needs. But as you can see, we have been busy today and are not prepared for visitors."

The largest of the new horses was his goal: a beast whose back started above Carlos' eyes and had deep brown flanks that seemed to be made of shadows. It stood apart from the others, and the abbey's horses followed its movements with their eyes. There was a rope tied around its neck, apparently used to secure the animal on the other side of the courtyard. The horse must have pulled loose from the improvised picket, leading the others here to find food.

Carlos held his hand out, moving closer until he was but inches away from large, brown eyes and flared, quivering nostrils. He did not flinch as a mouth of heavy, yellowed teeth nuzzled his open palm. A horse's bite could wound as quickly and severely as a sword, but he had no fear of or for this creature.

Whatever faults the bandits carried here with them, they had chosen, or stolen, good horses. Carlos moved his hand to the animal's face, gently stroking the muzzle before moving carefully to the side of its head. It answered his wordless murmuring with a snort but did not shy from his touch.

Carlos cradled the animal's head as he had seen Alejandro do many times before. He whispered into the horse's alert ear, laying his cheek against the side of its long face and feeling its breathing slow and calm.

His hands were warm against its skin, and the chill of the coming storm was forgotten. For a moment, the last rays of sun fought free of the gathering clouds, outlining all the horses in golden fire. Carlos closed his eyes, trying not to think of Alejandro's terrible injuries, envisioning instead how much his friend would want to be here in this moment.

"Come then, my new friend. Let's see you taken care of."

With a hand on the big brown's shoulder, Carlos walked toward the kitchens and retied the picket line, grateful for the warmth and sounds within. Under the light of some nearby torches, he examined the horses more thoroughly. Finding no fresh injuries, he went inside to arrange for their fodder.

The oats to be boiled for tomorrow's morning gruel would serve just as well as fare for horses tonight. Not only were there fewer men to feed now, but the surviving brothers would not begrudge the shortage. Blankets would come from the same source as the extra rations, and the long porch used to dry firewood for the bread ovens would serve as a good enough stable for the night. Tomorrow, he would arrange for the animals to be sheltered in Ruri, just as Ruri's horses had been sheltered here when he first came to the abbey.

When each animal was contentedly chewing oats mixed with barley set aside for a mid-winter ale, provided with a supply of fresh water drawn from the cistern, and covered with a thick blanket, Carlos felt at least one of his duties complete. But another hour had passed, and there was still no sign of Robere.

Those laboring in the kitchen did not remember seeing him, and Carlos was starting to worry. His apprentice needed as much care as these animals—as much as had Alejandro himself, at their first meeting. Carlos let his gaze linger on the ruined stable, remembering the ramshackle structure that preceded it.

We have come so far together, my young friends. Please, do not leave me now...

EVENING BLED INTO NIGHT AND NIGHT INTO EARLY morning. Carlos had not slept, nor did he think he would any time soon. There were things yet to do and too little time in which to address them. He stopped to close the eyes of Brother Joseph, who like Alejandro had been among the first of the abbey's wounded.

Of the twenty-six permanent residents of the abbey, fifteen now occupied beds in front of him. The rest would be buried later today, when more healers arrived from Barcelona to assist the wounded.

Brother Joseph's smile and kindly eyes would not be there to meet them; his time on Earth was finished. With his passing there was now one fewer healer to assist the other patients in their recovery. Other than Robere, only Carlos and Frances had escaped any serious injury during the attack, and their skills were now taxed to the limit.

The building Carlos and Matthieu had helped raise that first summer was well made, with thick walls of treated wood that had kept out the worst of the night's chill. His scholarly hands had been bruised repeatedly in their construction and through all the seasons since they had stood inviolate. Frances was as able a carpenter as a cleric, and when Alejandro was strong enough to help, the two of them would apply those skills to the now burned and ruined stable.

When he recovers, we will build it again, as many times as necessary to protect the animals from the predations of small-minded men.

The interior of the xenodochia was kept clean and ordered by both monks and the lay healers who frequented it, and even though much blood had been spilled during the night, it was once more a place of rest. Light filled the room from high openings sealed with oiled cloths, and although this season had been milder than most of the winters Carlos had spent here, a fire burned in the central hearth to keep his patients warm under heavy wool blankets.

The doors of the xenodochia had no locks; no one needing assistance was ever turned away. The sick, the wounded, the poor—all were welcome. At one end of the building, bandaged villagers with grim faces scrubbed and cleaned sheets in boiled water, using the rough, gray soap that was Sant Cugat's most profitable money-making occupation. The wine, bread, and beer produced from the fields were of little use to those without coins to spare, but the Bishop made it very clear to his wealthy patrons that clean hands and bodies were more favorable to God than dirty ones.

Carlos wondered what they would think if they learned the soap was free in the villages, or for any willing to trade labor for the abbey's goods. Even in the best of years, few could offer payment for the services of healers, even if the monks had been inclined to charge for them. But the church did have needs beyond the faith, and individual enclaves were expected to contribute some local funds toward their operation. Making soap was one of the ways the abbey met those needs, supplemented by coins earned from Carlos' translations and the products of its harvests.

And Joseph handled the xenodochia's accounts. One more thing the others will need to learn to do once I am gone...

Over the long night, Carlos instructed the hands still able to help in how to perform the basic tasks of a medicus while he struggled to save the lives of their friends. The instruction was more for their protection than edification—there was additional reason for diligence. Of the dozen or more men that had invaded the abbey, four had been captured alive, and the nameless youth who had abandoned the stables rather than face Carlos was not among them.

All of the bandits were diseased, with black blotchy skin, blisters, and free bleeding. Their bloodstained clothing carried a foul odor, requiring immediate disposal by burning. The smell was only partly filth and soil—the men themselves reeked, as if rotting from within.

One simply died after the battle, coughing out his life's blood before he could even be restrained. The bandit Carlos maimed had gone over into God's hands in the early evening. Like Timothy, his wound passed too much blood before it could be addressed, and never stopped bleeding once bandaged. The disease had simply progressed too far for his body to handle the additional insult of a severed hand.

The remaining two captives were in little better shape. Neither was much inclined to talk, but as a precaution the monks had secured them and made them as comfortable as possible. Only their roped wrists and ankles distinguished them from others with signs of disease on their bodies.

All too many had come here with these same signs in previous months, and too few had survived the experience. Most were penniless, friendless, and afraid to stop working to seek medical care until it was too late. What meager sustenance they could scrape from lands impoverished and left abandoned by the church's Crusades was further taxed by these slowly dying bandits, who chose to take what they needed from others rather than work or ask for it.

Now, all resources were in short supply. The sick bandits needed separation from unaffected patients, and additional care some would say was better spent on men who would live long enough to repay the kindness.

Avicenna's lessons, even once removed, were very clear on the topic of infection. Those afflicted must be kept apart from patients not exhibiting signs of corruption and kept as clean and comfortable as possible while treatment is applied. Tonight this meant keeping murderers close to their intended victims, but it couldn't be avoided.

Further complicating the situation is that while the Church practiced forgiveness, the Duke was far less understanding. As soon as they were well enough to travel, the bandits were to be brought before the magistrates and held accountable for whatever other crimes they may have committed.

Men such as these seldom engaged in honest acquisition, and the effects—and clothing, soiled though it had been—of soldiers were unmistakable. In addition to being murderous thieves, the bandits were deserters. Each crime had the same penalty, and the bittersweet irony of saving lives simply to have a vengeful noble take them away soured Carlos' mood.

Many of the wounded here were innocent of any crimes and suffered the same fate as their attackers despite the desperate efforts of the healers. Carlos' anger had too many targets and not enough uses; negative emotions had as devastating an effect on treatment as the presence of foreign bodies.

Carlos looked up from his tempered temper at Robere, now chastened and returned to his duties. He did not ask where the boy had run to, nor did Robere mention it. Robere had set his own private penance, the strain of it showing in his reddened eyes. He now worked at changing bandages and supervising the wounded workers and villagers who could still stand and help.

Timothy should not have been sick, certainly not to the level and progression of symptoms they discovered on his person. He received the same instructions on proper hygiene as all who came to the abbey—well before the time when he first would have developed signs of pox.

Ignorance was an enemy almost as deadly as the swords of bandits. But willful ignorance was a crime, whose victims were the very ones inflicting the insult. As long as they were endorsed by the Church, the faithful of Ruri followed routines they did not find overly inconvenient. While Carlos despaired of ever instilling the practice of daily bathing among a populace afraid of demons in the night's chill, he was at least able to impress upon his patients the need to wash clothes to drive away vermin and to change their bedding regularly.

Vermin. Carlos was reminded of another passage, not from his medical research, but from his spiritual training. From the Books of Moses and the tale of the Exodus.

"Then the magicians said unto Pharaoh, This is the finger

of God: and Pharaoh's heart was hardened, and he hearkened not unto them; as Jehovah had spoken."

Here, it was not Pharaoh's heart that hardened, but the minds of a populace that had never known the words of Moses or the deeds of Aaron. To them, the Finger of God was a tale to frighten children and the meanings of the plagues affecting the brothers' oppressors lost entirely. Pharaoh was long dead and far away.

But the people of Ruri had lived through other dangers enumerated in the book of Exodus. Flies and pestilence affecting their livestock. Boils and rashes on their bodies. The deaths of children. These things required little imagination. In the Catalan hills, people had no need to guard against the evils of intolerance—they practiced them. And although it pained Carlos to admit it, faith could only provide so much in these times. The people needed to believe, but they also needed to listen—to learn.

To Know.

Today, he healed the sick. Tomorrow, if God willed it, he would make them well.

Carlos watched his apprentice at his tasks, wondering what future might best suit him. Over time, Robere might come to have compassion for all and have the makings of an excellent doctor, but he was no man of the people. The life of a priest was not one he'd come to love, simply one he would endure.

Earlier in the day—no, yesterday now—Robere had been all smiles and happiness. He'd followed after Matthieu with the day's dispatches stuffed into a heavy satchel, trying desperately not to trip over the hem of his cassock.

Unlike Carlos and Matthieu, Robere Marcel was not a forgotten orphan raised by stern and unforgiving priests. He was the youngest son of a French knight. Somehow, the nobleman obtained one of Carlos' translations and sent his son to the source of that document so that he might learn something useful when it became apparent he would never be a warrior.

An apt pupil with an open mind and an inquisitive nature

that some researchers needed a lifetime to develop, Robere could someday become an excellent instructor. However, on this day, in this time, he was but an apprentice.

Time, then, to clean the slate.

"Robere. Please attend me when you are finished there. I have today's lesson prepared for you." Carlos had never forgotten the care and patience the brothers of Sant Cugat devoted to both himself and Matthieu upon their arrival, guiding them to the lives they now led. If he could give even half as much help to his student, he would count himself a very lucky man indeed.

Robere washed, straightened his robe, and joined Carlos by one of the too-few empty beds near the front of the room. Carlos motioned for the younger man to sit, watching him for several long, slow breaths while determining the right words to say. The previous afternoon's lesson on the brevity of life had been difficult enough for the young man, and what Carlos had to say now would be no easier.

Robere gave no sign of being uncomfortable under this scrutiny. In this solid composure, he had already exceeded Carlos as a student. Now it remained to the teacher to push those boundaries just a bit further, while still leaving enough room for the student to grow into a comfortable adult life.

He made his decision. As he did often, Carlos relied on wisdom given him by Father Frances. The Abbot's words were, as always, appropriate.

"Honest and direct. Never hide the truth, for in doing so you only show the lie."

Best to ask the question now, rather than have him suffer in years to come.

"Robere, is a life of service one you truly want for yourself?"

Carlos watched his student process the words behind open and trusting hazel eyes.

"To be a doctor? I enjoy the work, *Frere* Carlos. I enjoy giving health back to those who are ill and infirm. There is a truth to be found here, akin to that we achieve though the translations." Robere's speech lacked confidence but more than made up for it in precision. His passion was clear, if not complete.

From some portion of the room he could not identify, Carlos heard Father Frances speaking to constables up from the city, relating once again the details of the attack. He flushed to hear his actions described in such glowing terms; he never sought praise, only to serve. The Abbot was quite animated in the telling of his protégé's competence and of the abbey's ability to handle the aftermath of the attack.

Carlos paused the lesson briefly, wishing he was half as competent as the man Frances described. Hoping the example he was setting for Robere would turn out to be a good one.

Wishing he could sleep, or more accurately, that he might wake from this nightmare.

It occurred to Carlos that Frances was doing more than simply repeating the details of the attack. He was arguing that the surviving bandits be left in the abbey's care for a longer time than the constables felt necessary. By stressing the abbey's skill at dealing with the conflict, he also minimized the threat the prisoners posed.

He was saving lives, possibly more effectively than the bandages used by Carlos and Matthieu. The infected bandits were probably doomed in either event, but would have far a better chance at life if they remained where they were.

It is another skill Robere would need later in his life, and one which Carlos also sought to master.

"Robere, to truly heal, a medicus must suffer along with his patients. They cannot be regarded as something so ordinary as a full bed or ailing villager. Each sick man is the whole of humanity incarnate; the mission of a medicus is the one handed down from Christ our Savior, who came to give life and to give it in abundance. When you walk in this room, you are not their doctor. You are their neighbor—their friend. You are also the conduit of God's love, understanding, and charity to all."

"Yes, teacher. I believe I understand."

"When you choose this life, you choose God. You take him into yourself and begin a collaboration to heal the sick. Our mission, like those who came before and those who will come after, is to give service. Physical harm, or an insult to the body such as this pox we labor against, imprisons the spirit and in turn overpowers the body. To truly do good, you must accept this as part of yourself. It will become your identity."

He hoped his student was evaluating the lesson, and then applying it to himself. It was hard to read the boy in this mood—shoulders set, thin face impassive. In this regard he was very much like Carlos the younger man, struggling to hide his emotions and never sure when to ask a question.

Yes, I know that struggle very well. It's hard to see the path to happiness when stuck in that place.

"For me, there was no other path. The Lord called me to him from the moment I first drew breath. He showed me the truth of his ministry in the actions and faith of those around me, and to serve him in all things is all I have ever desired.

"When you came to us, Robere, you wanted to learn. You desired an understanding of God but also of the words and deeds of those who have gone before. I can show you a path—my path, but to follow it, you must realize that for me the destination was reached when I first placed my foot on it."

Carlos watched his young apprentice with a thoughtful eye. If he still harbored any confusion, Robere hid it well. Carlos did not know whether his silence meant the message was getting through or the boy was still punishing himself for his earlier fears.

"Think on this as you rest and make notes on yesterday's translations. Before all of this happened, Matthieu asked for news of the past, and I would hate to disappoint him."

"I will, teacher. Thank you for my lesson. I will think on your words and attempt to understand them, and the truths you provide."

No, not a priest. But a doctor he may yet become. And by facing his fears with an open heart, he will certainly become a Man.

Carlos dismissed his apprentice to his duties. While they had saved lives through the long night, the task would never truly end. Containing the pox was more important than any personal concerns and only the first part of the process. The patients' souls must be healed as well as their bodies.

If the pox could not be cured, it could at least be pushed

back and possibly survived. If they could find the cause, perhaps even prevented. The Moors never found one but neither had they stopped looking. From what they reported down through the years, it ran in cycles like any other, affecting segments of the population seemingly at random and then passing to other parts of the countryside.

Anyone could be laid out on one of the beds here, and there was little the monks could do to address the situation and halt its progress. The bandits had it, the villagers had it, and Carlos could not imagine two more different lifestyles.

The bandits' motives were as troubling as the nature of the pox. The abbey had nothing of real value to such men; the closest things to treasures here on the grounds were the scrolls and manuscripts in Carlos' care. So why had they come? What reasons could they have had for coming here, of all places, when there were other villages outside Barcelona's walls with much more to offer?

Dwelling on the issue longer wouldn't make the answer any more apparent. As soon as prisoners could stand, they would answer questions, the answers to which would determine the rest of their lives. Carlos needed to give his thoughts to the problems facing his greater community.

In a few hours, those villagers who could walk on their own would probably return to their homes. Carlos would need to visit them often in the next few weeks to ensure that their condition did not worsen away in the absence of constant care.

But for now, his world was here, surrounded by wooden walls and wounded men. Carlos began changing the prisoners' dressings, the only task he had left before retiring. The strong scent of lye and ash mixed with lavender masked only some of the foul odor emanating from their blackened and blistered skin.

Despite both Frances' and Carlos' efforts, they would not stay in Sant Cugat long. The abbot had obtained for them at most one more day of freedom. The bandits might not enjoy the time remaining to them, but at least it would not be spent in chains.

Carlos paused to regard Matthieu, now singing softly to

Alejandro. The two men had their eyes closed, and Carlos watched the stable master's mouth moving along with the Latin he did not understand.

There is another patient to be seen after all.

Matthieu's voice did not falter as Carlos unwound his bandage to examine the wound, nor did his grip on Alejandro's hand tighten as Carlos replaced the cloth with a fresh dressing.

Carlos' eyes met Matthieu's as his eyes opened, seeing in them the tears he had held back for so very long. Matthieu's smile was all the payment Carlos could ever ask for his services—Matthieu's friendship was already the greatest gift he had ever received.

Frances is wrong. Matthieu is the hero of this day. I can only hope to equal his example.

Moving out into the new day beyond the xenodochia's walls, Carlos felt relief grow inside him as pure sunlight shone on freshly fallen snow. The previous day's violence was all but erased by a pristine blanket of white, the last reminder being the sight of Frances ushering mounted guards away from the gate. They took with them testimony and dispatches for two rulers of the area, the Duke and Bishop of Barcelona.

The snow did not conceal familiar paths from Carlos' feet, and they carried him quickly to his cell and the sleeping shelf he had too long neglected. He closed his eyes and tried to imagine a world with no violence such as he had seen in the last day. His place of peace and sanctuary, had been invaded, and though he knew the pain of this day would fade over time, too much had happened to simply dismiss the memories from his mind.

Father Frances had once been a soldier, and though he fought now for souls, he'd once wielded a sword as skillfully as he did words. Carlos had seen a glimmer of that earlier man yesterday, and the skill with which his own hands had killed was troubling.

In the end, it would be words that brought about the world he dreamed of—words he would need to learn and remember. When all men were willing to lay down their swords, no men would need them.

Surrendering at last to his exhaustion, he prayed that he could someday see such a place here in the physical realm; one he might share with friend and foe alike.

"Carlos? If you are able, we have more work to do."

Frances' voice came from the hallway, calling the tired monk back from the edge of peace.

"Yes, Father. I am at your service."

"Good. Collect some fresh parchments and sharpen your quills. We do not have much time left to bear witness."

Carlos sat up on his shelf, willing himself back to full alertness. There was only one reason for such urgency. His skills as a healer were no longer needed, and he was again an archivist in the service of the Lord.

Deus Vult.

On this day, the Twenty-Fifth of February, in the Year of our Lord 1205, Frances delaMonde and Carlos de Roja, Brothers of the abbey at Sant Cugat du Valles, do affirm and attest that all accounts given here are true and accurate.

We sit in witness to the last testament of…

CARLOS STEADIED HIS HAND ABOVE THE PARCHMENT. The quill was fresh and sharp, the ink mixed and ready. Two candles illuminated the page, and he was far enough away from the bed that their light did not trouble the patient's sensitive eyes.

Or was "patient" the proper term to use? "Prisoner" no longer applied; no earthly chains or laws could hold him now. The bandits' condition had worsened far more rapidly than either healer anticipated—even as Frances had sent away the duke's men, the first of them had died. The new dawn seemed to accelerate their decline until only one remained.

Out of respect for the man's former life as one of God's soldiers, Father Frances offered the last bandit both extreme unction and forgiveness if he would but tell his tale and that of his associates. Soon enough he would join them in the next world, and Carlos sat ready to record his final words.

"What is your name, my son?" The Abbot was a veteran of many such interviews, and his voice was cool and calm. Frances' quick mind and sharp perceptions paired well with his years in the world, and he had a reputation for being difficult to deceive. It was this, more than any charity, which finally convinced the Duke's men to allow the dying bandits to stay here.

If they would not speak to Frances, only an inquisitor would be able to shake loose the truth. And though he was clearly a criminal, even the act of attacking an abbey did not make this man a heretic.

The irony of the situation was not lost on Carlos. Not so long ago he had sat at his desk reading of just such an interview. The deaths of his friends and neighbors, as well as the man who'd killed them, were the cost of gaining more direct experience.

Too much. Too much to pay by far.

"Why do you care, priest? You'll not save us—we are all cursed men."

The bandit spit foul wind through rotting teeth. His eyes stared blankly ahead, fixed on some point in the curtained alcove that included neither Carlos nor Frances.

"Perhaps not, but I would like to know it anyway. I prefer to look a man in the eye, to speak to him as a friend, or at the very least, not as an enemy. My name is Frances, and despite what you may feel, we bear you no ill will. We are your friends, and are here to help."

In the years of their acquaintance, Carlos had never heard the Abbot raise his voice in anger or use it to hurt or deceive another. When he spoke, those around him smiled or at the very least stopped scowling. It was effective in this case as well.

"Ramon. My name is Ramon. It is the only one I claim. My brothers and I left all else behind in the war."

The bandit's staring eyes moved, and in the dim light it looked to Carlos as if he was watching another scene entirely. Whatever he saw, be it his memories or possibly dementia, it clearly terrified him.

"Tell me of the war, Ramon. Of your Crusade. I went to Constantinople myself many years ago. My own brothers and I spent much time in service to the Lord, and we came back stronger for the journey."

Carlos lifted the quill after recording Frances' words, thinking about all the times he and Matthieu had listened to Frances' stories of the road and the battles he had fought. Even knowing that Frances would never lie to them, they could tell that he held back much of the power of those tales, and that they could never truly understand what their mentor had gone through unless they were unlucky enough to go to war on their own.

Today Carlos understood. The tiny sliver of war he'd seen was enough to shake his life from its solid foundations of faith, but it paled in comparison to full-scale battles between armies and ideologies. Frances delaMonde knew both, as did Ramon. And while Frances had grown strong from his experiences, the dying man they interviewed had chosen a different path.

"What do you know of strength, Frances? Have you seen your brothers killed over a crust of bread as their bodies betrayed them from the inside? Have you given the order to charge while your brothers' lives pooled around your knees?"

Frances was slow in responding, and Carlos took the time to refine the point on his quill.

"I have seen these things, my son. I have seen all you describe and more. I have wielded both the sword and the shovel on the battlefield and prayed long to find the strength to bear that weight." There was a touch of sadness in Frances' words, and for the first time Carlos had a sense of the true length of the Abbot's life.

"You were with Phillip?" Ramon's demeanor softened, and his breaths came easier.

"No, my son. I was with Louis. When Phillip called, I was too old to answer. Others took up our banner then and returned to the temple we had held so long."

This new bit of information surprised Carlos. Not Frances' true age—he'd known that Frances had gone to war almost 50 years ago and that upon his return from the East had given up the sword and taken vows of ordination. What the young monk had not pieced together from the Abbot's stories was that he'd been one of the Knights Templar. His stories had indicated a military background, but never one so illustrious.

"You do not sound like a man old enough to be my father, Frances. But I believe you. I have nothing left to lose. Ask your questions, then."

"You are young enough to have been my grandson, friend Ramon, if ever I'd had time for a family. And old enough to have ridden with Philip yourself on his second attempt, twenty years ago. Is this true?"

From there, the interview wandered far from the story

Carlos had expected to hear, and as his quill danced across the page, he wondered whether he'd brought enough parchments to record it all. The person answering the abbot's questions was a much different one than the man who had attacked the abbey. Not a bandit, but a believer. A patriot, and a man of honor who had responded not once, but twice to the call of his king. But Frances had not forgotten the purpose of the interview and before long returned his questions to the matter at hand.

"Ramon, we need to talk about why you came to the abbey. Many men died during your attack, both your brothers and mine."

Ramon's face hardened, and his words lost their pleasant seeming. With the return of his anger also came a bloody, hacking cough that made the candles flutter, casting a momentary red glow over the corner.

"Those men were not my brothers. They were the remains of us—what was left after the war."

Carlos laid down the quill, preparing to ease his patient's suffering, until Frances' upraised hand stopped him. The Abbot leaned forward, taking Ramon's wasted hands in one of his own and using the other to wipe bloody spittle from the bandit's mouth with a clean cloth, before carefully placing it aside for disposal.

"I am sorry to have upset you, my friend. Please forgive my assumption. Are you able to continue? It is important that we know so that we can prepare you for the next world."

"I have already told you, Frances. I am cursed. We all are, and none of your prayers will change the disposition of my soul."

Carlos came to the end of the page and set it aside to dry. There was no time to sand it, and he hoped that the spots of blood from Ramon' cough could be safely cut free without changing any of his testimony. While the abbey had many fresh sheets onto which it could be copied later, it seemed a shame to waste this one, true record of what was transpiring.

Frances waited for him to sharpen the quill again before speaking and then continued as if no time had passed.

"Never doubt the power of prayer, my son. Faith can move

mountains, will allow you to overcome any obstacle, defeat any foe. My faith has allowed me a long and full life—a second life rich in service."

"Faith. Let me tell you about faith, priest. My faith died long ago, on the fields of Bosporus. It sickened on the road out of Rome, and as the miles passed each night, it lost all power to move us. Our captain drove us relentlessly, and whatever fire burned in his soul replaced whatever dreams we had of holy retribution on the faithless."

Ramon's words now held none of their earlier warmth, and Carlos was surprised when Frances seemed momentarily at a loss. It did not last long, but he had the distinct impression that the abbot wanted to change the subject. His internal debate didn't last long though, and his next words were a direct challenge to Ramon' statement.

"Let us speak of that, then, before we return to your recent motives. Your captain—you do not speak of him well."

"He was a changed man after Rome. He was not the leader who brought us out of France. We left the main force, abandoning all supplies and traveling fast and hard each night for the eastern shore. We rested during the day, and at night we took what we needed—the only one of his strategies that worked. That was why we came to your abbey. You had horses—we needed them. We were not expecting resistance."

Carlos made a mental note to research French companies leaving for the east. From the description, Ramon's men were not part of the main force that left Venice in October of 1202 but perhaps part of Bishop Martin's companies.

"I am sorry for that, my son. But you must know, if you had come to me with open hands, the horses would have been yours. They are worth far less to us than the men you killed. The lives of your...companions as well."

"Well, I will keep that in mind for next time, then. Should I have occasion to need something of you, I will simply ask for it."

Carlos allowed himself a small smile. Frances had returned a touch of laughter to Ramon's shaking voice, even as the man damned himself as a deserter.

"Of course, my friend. We will care for you for as long as

you are with us. Please, continue if you can. The road from Rome?"

Frances offered Ramon a cup of water, holding the man's head so he could drink. When he spoke again, his voice was much stronger, and he seemed renewed.

"I am aware of what you are doing, Frances. But I will answer your questions. Forty of us left Rome, and twenty-five reached the Brindisi shore in time to leave on a commandeered boat under a darkened moon. The rest slipped away in the night, never to be seen again. We landed on the far shore and pillaged our way through the Greek lands under cover of darkness.

"Oh, we were strong, priest. We were very strong. We carried the banner of Christendom high above our heads as we marched, driving all foes before us. Always we had the strength you so revere wrapped around us, and always it carried us onward to our goal."

Another cup of water, and another fresh page. With each pause, Ramon's description of his journey gained power, and Carlos could almost see it play out before his eyes as he recorded the words.

"Twenty men arrived at Constantinople, and it was there we learned what true strength was. We laid siege to the city for months, raining fire and death over their walls. They surrendered neither their faith nor their city to us, and occasionally they launched back volleys of ruined gold and shattered jewels simply to spite and demoralize us.

"We scoured the countryside for stragglers, torturing, maiming and worse. We displayed our strength on pikes held high, all in the name of the one true God and his Faithful. Yet still they did not yield."

A rattling cough shook Ramon's body, and this time Frances allowed Carlos to assist. The two monks undid the bindings on Ramon's wrists and helped him to sit up. Once he was upright, his cough eased, and Carlos returned to his parchment while Frances rubbed the man's back.

Frances looked up from Ramon when Matthieu pushed aside the curtain to deliver some fresh cloths and a basin of cool water. Carlos mouthed silent thanks, but his brother did not withdraw immediately. Instead, he held out a hand to someone behind the curtain, and when it returned it held a stack of fresh parchments. Carlos' smile widened as he took them, and as Matthieu backed away Carlos thought he heard a muffled protest from Robere.

This is not for you, apprentice. I have done this many times, and still am not sure I'm capturing the essence of the interview properly.

"Can you continue, my son?"

"Yes, thank you, Frances. Where were we?"

"Constantinople."

Now that the man was sitting up, Carlos had a much better view of Ramon's face, and it seemed that his skin was darker than it had been before. But all the life seemed to drain from it at the mention of the city's name, even though he'd said it several times himself.

"The captain…he disappeared for days at a time, returning only to check on us and our positions. He would take men with him on patrol, diminishing our original company until only a dozen were left. They were replaced by other men—dark, hard men from some other part of the line.

"They were like him."

There was a long pause in the conversation, and Carlos used it to search Frances' face for some clue as to his mentor's feelings. Ramon's words seemed to wash over the Abbot as he picked his way through the man's memories. When he did speak, Frances' words were still calm, but no longer warm.

"Go on, my son."

The Abbot's voice had not lost any of its power, but something in it made Carlos nervous, and in his unease he allowed ink to gather on the record. He raised the dulled quill quickly, dabbing at the spot with his sleeve. There was no need to hurry though, as Ramon seemed unwilling to continue until Frances prompted him a second time.

"What happened, next, Ramon? We need to hear it all."

"No, you don't. But I will tell you anyway, Frances, and you will curse my name for it long after I'm gone.

"Eventually, our strength proved greater than theirs, such as it was. Our armies broke through the gates, and they met our charge under a dark moon, fighting as if there would never be another sunrise. For every street we took, we left behind another piece of ourselves, until there were no more enemies to kill.

"We sacked that city, burning down engines of war and what we were told was heresy, though none could name the inhabitants' crimes or which blazes contained them. Inside the walls, what we found…it destroyed us.

"We lost that battle, priest, as surely as if we had died outside on the plains before ever passing the walls. And for our efforts, for our strength, we were rewarded appropriately. We are cursed men, ruined in body and soul."

Ramon leaned back, eyes fixed once more on some spot of darkness. Frances leaned down until his face hovered directly over Ramon's unseeing eyes, his voice a hard whisper almost inaudible through tight, pressed lips.

"Why do you say these things, my son? What makes you believe that redemption is lost to you?"

What had Frances left behind on the battlefield so many years ago? What deeds had he done before he put down his sword and donned the black cassock he wears today?

Carlos frowned at his unspoken questions. Not only were they out of place, but he wasn't sure he'd be comfortable knowing the answers.

But Ramon answered them for him, in a whisper even harder to hear than Abbot's. When he was done, Frances reached out shaking fingers and gently closed the dead man's eyes. He sat silently for a while, then rose and walked away without a word.

Carlos sat alone until the candles burned out. The ink was long dried by then, and he gathered Ramon's testament into a neat stack, placing it into a leather folio to review later. He was tired, so tired, and the Bishop could wait a few more hours to read the account.

Then Carlos the archivist became a doctor once more, calling for Robere and arranging for disposal of the body and the burning of his garments and bedding. He stood next to his apprentice with the folio clutched tightly to his chest, fighting the urge to throw it into the too-white flames. Dark smoke rose into gray storm clouds for the second straight day, signaling the inevitable return of night.

Carlos took no comfort from the fire. Even sheltered against the whipping wind behind a wooden building safely outside the abbey's walls, he was cold—much colder than the night when he'd run for help so long ago. Tonight he would find no warmth in his brothers' arms, nor would he be able to succor the half-dead boy who had become a strong, vibrant man as the seasons marched on. Who even now lay near death, for no other reason than that he had charge of horses more valuable than his own life.

When he finally returned to his cell, Carlos wished with all his heart that he could forget Ramon's last words. He prayed not for sleep but for ignorance.

Carlos prayed that the bandit would breathe and live again so that he might take those final lines back off the page, and wished that Ramon and his foul friends had never come to Sant Cugat.

But Ramon had spoken, and Carlos had heard, and it was the monk's duty as a witness to record it. Just as it had been that of the one who recorded the Muslim's tortures centuries ago. The record of that confession now lay nestled beside Ramon's, many yards away in the scriptorium.

In the lonely darkness of his cell, Carlos saw each word he had written as plainly as if they were made of the fire that had consumed the speaker's body. He tried to shut his eyes tighter, to block out the memory of his hand's movement, but to no avail. Inside his mind he heard Ramon read back each one in a rattling, emotionless whisper that seemed never to end.

"As we left the shining city with our prizes, we walked out not onto the plains, but into Hell. From nowhere came an army of dark and furious men. They walked as one, attacked as one, and each life they took strengthened their assault.

"And then, as if such things could not become worse, we saw others at the edges of our damnation. Not men, but the remains of life, clawing and biting with what natural weapons remained to

them. Our foes were set upon as thoroughly as we, and the stinking darkness overcame us all."

"There was no voice to the attack, no hatred or passion in their movement. There was no meaning or intent, just violence. The screams of wounded and dying men were the only things that made sense. The lives and spirits of friend and foe alike mixed in that foreign soil, and only a crop of bones will spring from that watering."

(Your Grace, Ramon clears his throat and asks for water, which I am grateful to give him if only he would stop his tale. The Abbot prompts him further, and he continues.)

"No my story does not end there. But I told you already what happened. The Captain's men. They were the ones! Their sorceries threw the defeated back into the fray over and over until all who were left ran and hid. We could not stay on that field and remain men.

"Those we left behind were torn apart, their limbs ripped and shredded by beasts. The unlucky were kept alive, and we could hear their screams for miles. When dawn came, we returned and found no bodies whole.

"None! Do you understand? There were arms, legs, but no bodies. The earth itself was darkened with shed blood and filth, but there were not enough bodies to account for either the fallen, or the foes."

Carlos prayed for the oblivion of sleep and the comfort of dreams he never remembered. Prayed that his imagination did not continue tormenting him with the things Ramon had described.

Massed armies…acting as one mind to defend the shining city.

The dead rising to fight the living.

Dark men picking through corpses, tearing life from the dying as they called for help.

Damned men indeed.

Ramon was dead, and with him and his tale had died a

portion of the archivist's innocence. But Carlos was certain that the bandit's last, terrible words would linger on forever in his memory.

"If this be the result of prayers and faith, o Father, please give to me the lie, just for a little while longer."

Carlos did not seek the lie with this soft prayer—the truth was far worse in the telling. He had betrayed a promise and recorded what he had witnessed inaccurately.

Or rather, incompletely.

The report of Ramon's confession was shaded, leaving out the physical description of the fantastical men whom the deserter described in some exacting detail, bearing a not inconsiderable resemblance to the one the Moorish Inquisitors had chronicled.

Dark-furred animal men, with teeth, claws, and tall pointed ears.

Ramon and his six surviving comrades had run from these monsters months ago, but if his words were truth, such things still existed in the world.

Carlos had recorded the date and place of the confession and affixed his name to the document. The twenty-fifth of February, in Sant Cugat du Valles, in the Kingdom of Aragon. Almost two thousand miles and nearly a year removed from the sack of Constantinople.

Some force stayed his hand from making a complete and accurate account, and Carlos was honest enough with himself to admit that the mere possibility of these animal men was a fact frightening enough to take to his grave.

But what had stopped his quill—what he could never record with ink and parchment lest it become an unalterable fact, was Ramon's claim that before that night, he and his men had all been healthy and strong.

And the former crusader's account of the skin of his arms blackening and itching in the morning sun as he fled the battlefield. The first signs of the pox that killed him, which if untreated killed in days and weeks—not months and miles....

THE JOURNEY NORTH BEGAN WITH A HEARTY FAREWELL and a southbound horse. No tears between friends, only good wishes and recommendations. Life in the abbey would continue without its archivist, with new healers from Barcelona to tend to the needs of Ruri and the remaining brothers.

Inside the walls behind him, Matthieu had assumed the bulk of Carlos' duties. As promised, the Abbot would continue Robere's training while his apprentice in turn cared for Alejandro. Ten days of preparation had given the monk confidence to leave behind a decade of service.

The Bishop's reply to his letter had changed Carlos' travel plans. Instead of proceeding directly to the abbey of St-Victor in Paris, he was to make an overnight stop in Barcelona to receive personal recommendations not only to St-Victor, but to Rome, where he was to receive further training regarding the history and structure of the Church itself. While traveling, he was also to stop at various hospices as time permitted to confer with other healers regarding their experience with the pox and similar maladies.

Still troubled by Ramon's final confession, Carlos was eager to begin both missions. Ramon's story had raised wrinkles in an already mussed tapestry. Such things he claimed—such impossibilities. Car-los' sin of omission weighed heavy on him, and as penance he'd set himself a third task.

As his duties permitted, in addition to searching for this "Karl" in Paris and Rome, the monk would look for traces of the good man who became the outlaw Ramon—to see what events led him into a life of banditry. Filling the gaps in that history would shine light on the dark truths related in his final moments and ease the burden his witness now carried in silence.

Duty. The word dispelled the doubts and self-loathing in Carlos' mind. Leaving behind his work at the abbey did not absolve him of promises to God, though by riding a deserter's horse into a chilly morning he gained new perspective on the villagers he'd known and cared for these last seven years.

His traveling companion was in far better shape than its previous owner, well cared for even without the excellent talents of Alejandro. Though recognizably the same animal Carlos had led to the kitchens the night of the attack, the scars of hard riding were nearly faded, the damaged hooves treated and prepared for the miles of road to come. Carlos had seen to it himself—Alejandro would expect no less.

The stable master forbade the use of bits and spurs in the abbey, and over the years all its riders had learned to make themselves understood with no more than slight pressure of the legs and a simple bridle. Now part of that stable, the raider horse took very quickly to this method of riding. The saddle on its back was worn, but serviceable; and under it was a soft blanket, rather than a heavy coat of mail. And though Carlos' riding experience was limited, he did know he would be spending equal time resting on this precarious perch and walking alongside the big brown horse.

In the center of the village was a well with both a cup for Carlos and a trough for the horse. Although both had quenched their thirst minutes before at the abbey, the horse was quite insistent and refused to be moved back onto the road. Carlos laughed at his fickle companion, reminding himself to tell Matthieu of it when he wrote tonight.

Though the French monk would be staying behind, he'd arranged a journey of his own, sending word ahead to all the towns and hospices he could think of on the road to Paris. Carlos was to write to Matthieu of his travels, giving the collected scrolls into the care of the monks he met at each stop along the way.

How he had known who to contact and by what means he'd arranged this network so quickly were questions Carlos did not ask. His friend's forethought was gift enough on its own—one he would make full use of in the weeks to come.

Dismounting, Carlos felt the village under his feet and became part of its world. There was the home of Master Jonas, the carpenter who helped build the xenodochia, and who even now labored to repair the abbey's stables. There was the home of Consuela the midwife, who scolded Carlos the first time he held a newborn child in his hands.

When he and Matthieu had first come to Sant Cugat, the community of Ruri seemed puny viewed against the backdrop of nearby Barcelona's wonders. Leaving as a grown man, he saw how both had matured over seven years, and how fully each depended on the other.

Without the village, the abbey had little purpose beyond the spiritual and only those supplies it could produce itself. Without the abbey, the village had no refuge, options for education, or access to medical care. The grain from which both communities made bread, and the grapes that grew at the abbey's direction, prospered with the sweat of Ruri.

The horse chuffed beside him, large head and brown eyes regarding the monk before dipping a thick neck to the trough. The animal was far too great a possession for a simple man like Carlos, another gift accepted with no questions. In the past few days of preparation for the road, he had come to know its moods and surprising intelligence. At times, he felt as if somehow it was communicating with him in a language Carlos had not yet thought to master.

The horse snorted and pulled away from the trough. Carlos assisted its tongue in cleaning the surface of its mouth, careful not to get his fingers caught inside. He had treated enough bites and missing fingers to know that horses did not care to have things there besides food.

It took no special powers of communication to sense its impatience. The monk's feet were similarly anxious, but Carlos had stopped to regard Ruri one last time. When the Romans had come, Barcelona's buildings had been much like those of the village. Simple, efficient and plain, occupied by similar people attracted by dreams of a better life.

To reach the Castrum Octavium which eventually became Sant Cugat, the Romans did not follow their usual practice of building their road in a straight line. While such a thoroughfare would have made for easy marching, the steep incline would have precluded the safe transport of goods.

Instead, they followed the contours of the land, using the same logic that placed their soldiers here in the first place. They used what they had found, building up from the foundations of the past. Looking down that winding path, Carlos remembered his first views of Barcelona as the sun set over the water and cast reflected fire on walls and buildings.

Carlos came to the city's gates as another splendid sunset began. He and the horse walked through them unchallenged and began searching for a place where they could rest for the night.

The horse led the search for lodgings, reinforcing Carlos' opinion of the animal's intelligence. Its nose brought the pair to a small public house with space for them both, within sight of the cathedral holding the Bishop's offices.

The hostler accepted a coin from Carlos' small supply and offered to brush down and feed the animal while Carlos continued to his appointment, but the monk insisted on doing it himself.

Alejandro would expect nothing less.

WHEN HE WAS DONE CARING FOR THE HORSE, CARLOS exchanged his dusty cassock for a fresh one and walked over to the cathedral. Carlos' years in the city were spent elsewhere, and he had to admit it seemed a fitting place to meet his patron.

Although the Abbot had the authority to send Carlos on this journey, he drew that right from the Bishop of Barcelona, Berenguer de Palou. Carlos' previous meetings with the Bishop had taken place in Sant Cugat, and entering the structure brought him into another new world—a higher patch of sky he had not known to look for. It was an excellent specimen of Barcelona's resurgence, fully remade in the Gothic style after countless reconstructions over the centuries.

The soft slap of his sandals against the flawless stone floors carried up and away from his feet, and Carlos felt a sudden desire to lift his voice in song and hear it echo and grow as well. But the purpose and history of the cathedral stilled his tongue.

Carlos announced himself to a clerk, who waved him forward and led him up a small stone stair into a richly appointed room containing more wealth than Carlos had seen since leaving Toledo.

The Abbot had offered Carlos the sword he had wielded during the attack—that amazing blade that seemed so right in his hands—but it was not a thing to carry openly or from which to draw pride. Carlos left it behind at the abbey for the Abbot to do with as he wished.

Here in a room dressed in rich velvet and silk, the sword's white ivory handle and shining blade would rest among equals. The wealth and riches in the Bishop's office could have fed and clothed the village of Ruri for years. A single candelabra of those on display was worth a team of horses—the complete set would finance all the chariots they could pull or cover the entire cost of Sant Cugat's reconstruction.

The collection was ostentatious but not unexpected. Carlos knew similar ones existed in Toledo—an accepted, if not generally endorsed, indulgence of the church outside the monastic orders. Most of these items belonged to the office, not the man, and were likely crafted specifically for and donated to the Church with no question of payment.

Of particular beauty was a manuscript bound and displayed on a carved mahogany prayer box, and Carlos moved to examine it with a critical eye. The leather binding was rich and dark, a single thick hide selected and stretched to hold a book of rare quality.

The open pages showed the beginning of the Gospel of Mark. Rich colors applied with love and faith and framed by gold pounded into leaves so thin they clung to the parchment as they did to one another.

Carlos' skills in binding and calligraphy were well regarded, but the hand that had illuminated this volume was a true master of the craft. He had never seen the words look better, and their record of the Savior was just as eloquent in the Greek letters as they had been when Carlos first read them in Latin.

Carlos reached a hand out to reveal the previous section, but stopped short of touching the pages. The candles flickered, casting a red glow across the words. Leaning closer, shadows seemed to dance across the page, almost as if...

"I see you have discovered my secret, Brother Carlos."

A strong voice filled the opulent chamber, dispelling the illusion.

Golden light seemed to spring from each lit candle, and Carlos turned to see Berenguer de Palou, resplendent in robes worthy of both his spiritual and physical office. Here in his true element, the flashing of the big man's rings and the gilt crucifix around his neck were all the more dazzling by scented candlelight.

"Yes, your Eminence. This volume is a master work—a testament for the ages."

The Bishop moved through the room until he stood beside both the monk and the book. He more floated than walked, a casual glide that never quite touched the tightly-spaced couches and pedestals as he passed.

In close proximity, he noticed one of the Bishop's eyes was clouded. Carlos had heard nothing of it, and scars from healed blisters on the Bishop's cheeks were further evidence of a sickness that must have occurred in the last three years, as he was sure he would have remembered it when last they spoke.

"I appreciate your praises, my son, but my humble hands are nothing compared to the one who inspired its creation. What must it have been like, Carlos, to hear the words of the Messiah as he discoursed on the mount? To remember them so clearly, so precisely that they could be conveyed perfectly afterward to any willing ear?"

Carlos felt the answer to that question in his heart, as he recalled forming one very much like it weeks before. What indeed could be revealed if one had perfect memory of such an important event? But before he could respond, the Bishop continued.

"In Mark, I find that question echoed, although the truths he reports are clear and evident. In my mind, no closer account can exist save one recorded as the words themselves were spoken. His is the first of the written gospels, and by far the most accurate."

This was a familiar topic—one Carlos had visited frequently with Matthieu and the Abbot in the early years of their association. The opening the elder priest gave him now was a philosophical door he was happy to pass through once more.

"But what of Matthew? Or Luke? Surely their experience is more correct?"

To his delight, the Bishop wasted no time in replying.

"Certainly, they are more are direct, and different accounts of the same event. But the Book of Matthew interprets, rather than reports, casting a certain light on the events to make them more palatable to his audience. Luke does the same, but instead of resolving for Jews, it speaks to Romans in an attempt to educate those not schooled in the culture that spawned our Savior.

"What happened is incontrovertible, but the presentation differs, and thus the message is changed. This chronicle speaks most plainly to me, Carlos, and enhances all the records that follow."

The Bishop had a certain way of speaking, ending each statement with an unspoken question. Carlos was more than willing to answer each one, and their conversation wandered freely from manuscripts and Gospels on to Carlos' work in translation and then on to the meanings of parable and prophecy.

Carlos had never held an office like that of the Bishop and was surprised by the demands on the older man's time. Even after the sun set, their conversation was frequently interrupted by both priests and laypersons, each with some problem only the Bishop could solve. He handled each with speed and efficiency—traits Carlos valued highly.

A meal was served: simple fare but with a wine such as Carlos had never sampled. It energized him, sending a rush through his body that was not quite intoxication but also not familiar. Definitely not a local vintage, though Carlos' palate was not skilled enough to place it.

Regardless of its origin, the food and drink were welcome company to their conversation. Pushing back from the table, Carlos saw just how far the candles had burned down. The Bishop's voice came to him as if from another place, and it took Carlos a moment to process the words. At first it seemed as if they were not spoken in Catalan or Latin, but in some older, simpler language common to both. Carlos found himself nodding even before he fully comprehended.

"It is late, Carlos. The *Matins* is upon us. Let us raise our voices unto the Lord. A room has been prepared for your rest afterward."

As the plates were cleared away, the Bishop seemed almost spry. Following him from the opulent chamber, Carlos wondered if Matthieu had ever had occasion to meet with their patron like this. His Brother visited the city often, working with and on behalf of the people of Ruri and at the same time interacting with their cousins and partners in Barcelona.

Carlos thought Matthieu and the Bishop would get along well. With the backing of such men, he would surely prosper in the Church hierarchy. And with a faith even half as strong as theirs, he could live forever in the love of God.

The Bishop left Carlos at the base of the stone stair, to take his place at the front of the cathedral. Carlos moved to join the city-dwelling priests who had gathered for the office, and though none remained from his three years in service here, enough friendly faces were present that Carlos felt comfortable and welcomed by their smiles. He watched the Bishop lead the assembled men through their faith, a service different from the relaxed but still precise method the Abbot employed.

The Bishop commanded respect and obedience without ever needing to speak the words. Perhaps it was the unfamiliar setting, but there was an energy in the room very much like that Carlos had sensed while eating. As he sang, he was transported, almost as if he had never heard the words before or experienced their true meaning. A transformative experience, even for a man who had spent his entire life among men of faith.

Following the conclusion of the office, the Bishop was met by several of his staff and departed with a nod and a smile to Carlos. Cathedral priests showed Carlos to a cell not unlike his own at the abbey, and he was asleep almost as soon as he laid his head down.

The darkness of the cell is cool and comforting. Far better these cold prison stones than those over which he was dragged through town. Most of the grace given to him is now scattered across the streets with his blood, but some yet remains. Enough to leave a message…but for whom?

His wounds heal, his strength returns. Now comes a vision of what is to be, seizing his sight in the near blackness of his captivity. A thick rope fastens around his neck, and he is dragged once more. He dies, and his spirit rises into the Kingdom of Heaven. His abandoned body is thrown onto a great fire, but the sky splits with the passage of his soul bringing wind and rain to scatter his oppressors like dust.

His friend, his teacher, had been right in all things. The cup they shared brought the spirit to dwell in him, and the life he lived was never again truly his own. He will accept the martyr's crown gladly, earning the right to sit forever at His side.

Here, now, it is hard to differentiate between the end of the journey and its beginning so long ago. All the events of his life seem as if a story told to a stranger. Some have the semblance of memories, others the fulfillment of prophecy—a cautionary tale meant for those who dare to reach too far.

Though he might fall, three score and ten stand in his company.

The word will spread; the spirit will survive and grow in the hearts and minds of all who come after.

A new beginning—a new journey—this time one taken alone. None can follow where he goes, but perhaps they will understand the steps that brought him here.

Now, at the end of all things, he is ready. They will come for him soon, take him from this prison and make him truly free. The pain and troubles he has known will pass, and the rewards promised but unsought will be his.

The stones cannot confine him, the spears are not a fence, the ropes bind nothing but flesh. All the troubles of life are without meaning or lasting effect.

The message remains. Now and always.

Darkness becomes light—a shining, golden glow warming the cold places of his confinement. As the shadows are banished, his spirit rises until no limits remain. He is no longer alone, and something once thought lost is his again. The words he leaves behind are inadequate to record the joy in his heart, but after today, he will have no voice.

Words will have to do...

CARLOS WOKE FROM A DREAM, BUT AS ALWAYS, RE-membered none of it. All that remained was a sense of great joy. If anything, his faith was stronger now than before he lay down to rest. For the first time since the attack on the abbey, he was at peace.

Eager to speak with the Bishop and be on his way, Carlos walked from his borrowed chamber across the cathedral proper. The quarters he'd been given were not close to the Bishop's chambers but still inside the building, and as he walked Carlos received acknowledgment from faces he recognized from last night's chorus of faith.

Climbing the stone stair, Carlos felt a strong sense of familiarity. Though it was only his second ascent, the act was as practiced as the path he'd walked every day for the last five years from his cell to the abbey's scriptorium. After each step his body filled with energy until at the top he felt stronger and more alert than ever.

The door opened before he could knock, and in the entrance Carlos saw one of the silent, smiling priests who had served their meal the night before. The Bishop was behind his desk, and waved a bejeweled hand at the chair Carlos had occupied during their discussion the night before. When he sat, the energy in Carlos' body seemed to flow into the chair, until Carlos wasn't sure where he ended and it began.

"Good morning, Carlos. I have prepared letters of introduction for you. One set for Paris and another for the Council in Rome. These will assist you in your research, and in other things. I find myself in agreement with Frances—you have done good work at Sant Cugat, and we are very happy to confirm you in your new duties."

"Duties? Your Grace, I do not understand."

Carlos' mind raced at the implications of Berenguer de Palou's words. After his journey, was he to be reassigned—sent away to another community? Or had the journey itself been canceled?

"Certainly, my son, you must see that we cannot have a simple monk roaming about the roads of Europe on his own. Such freedoms are not seemly and would lead you into temptation. Therefore, we have decided to change your status, so that you might not fall victim to such things."

There was a twinkle in the man's unclouded eye, some joke he knew but would not share. When Carlos opened his mouth to voice a question, the Bishop silenced him with a glittering hand, indicating he should rise.

Confused, Carlos pushed himself up from the chair, and the rest of his extra vitality melted away to be replaced by a cold feeling in his gut. He was not at all comfortable with the implications of the Bishop's words. This sudden change in their renewed relationship was troubling, and as he followed Berenguer de Palou out of his office and down the stone steps, he had a feeling that something was about to happen that he would not like.

All such doubts were banished as he turned the corner at the base of the stair. The open, empty church he'd crossed before his brief audience was now filled with familiar faces. The Brothers of Sant Cugat stood before the altar, and at their head was a smiling Father Frances.

Filling all other spaces of the room were the men and women of Ruri, who did not have Carlos' compunctions regarding silence in God's house. A cheer rose from the assembly, and wide smiles grew on the faces of Matthieu and Robere.

Carlos stumbled, briefly stunned by the sound. A strong hand caught his arm, and he looked up to see an equally large smile on the face of the Bishop.

"You name me as your patron, Carlos, but it is I who am

in service to you. Every face you see today is a friendly one, and they all ask of you that you continue to lead them as best you are able. To this end, we must change your name to something more fitting."

Carlos stared into the large man's face, searching for some signs of deception or possibly some derangement. A familiar cough came softly from behind him. Turning, he saw that Father Frances had left his place of honor and come to collect his senior medicus.

"You need not look so surprised, Carlos. You knew this day would come eventually, and the Bishop and I have known for some time that you were ready to succeed me. Your journey is beginning, but mine is nearly at an end."

"But, Father, you are a well man. Surely this is not necess..."

Carlos saw the warm, knowing look in his mentor's eye that both admonished and forgave his impertinence. Chagrined, he swallowed the rest of his complaint.

The ceremony was brief, but exhausting. Carlos was taken to the front of the Cathedral, which was temporarily pressed into service as the entrance of the abbey. He walked barefoot through his community of friends and brothers, then prayed for wisdom at the altar while accepting the introductions of both the Bishop and Father Frances. His brother monks then advanced to embrace him as their Father.

The Abbot of Sant Cugat du Valles.

"This is a provisional appointment, of course." Frances' smile did not diminish during the investiture, and his first words to his successor were as honest as always. "I have much life left in me, and the journey ahead of you is a long one. But with this office, you will be accorded greater respect in your travels, and carry with you a reminder of your true self.

"You are responsible now not only to God and your conscience but to us as well. Before you can lead these men, you must know why we trust you as we do. Take the time to see the world, Carlos. Don't let it slip away before you realize how beautiful it all is."

Carlos accepted his Father's instructions as they were intended, noticing that Robere heard them as well. Seeing his eyes shift, Frances winked at him in agreement.

Matthieu's one-armed embrace was strong and emotional. "My Brother is now my Father. I do not want you to go, Carlos, but you must. You must go and bring back an improved world so that I may share it with you upon your return."

Carlos had trouble finding the words to answer his oldest and truest friend. What he had thought was their goodbye yesterday paled in comparison to this moment, and taking Frances' advice, he resolved not to let it pass unremarked.

"Matthieu, we will never be parted, though long miles of road may lie between us. I am still the boy you helped up out of the dirt, and I will always be your friend." Neither man wanted to leave the embrace, but others were waiting to congratulate the new Abbot.

Almost an hour passed before he saw the Bishop again. Carlos' new direct superior was called away after the formal investiture but surprised Carlos as he collected his horse from the hostel.

"Carlos, I hope you will remember this day always—the day your Brothers reaffirmed their love for you. You are the youngest in your abbey, but all agreed that you were the best among them. Do not forget that trust, and keep Sant Cugat du Valles inside your heart."

Carlos nodded, letting the words sink in. He did feel the weight of their expectations but also a lightness of being. The journey he had planned was nothing compared to the one he was now starting, and he owed a great deal to the man standing in front of him.

"Thank you, your Grace. This is an honor I did not seek—at least not quite so soon. I shall not forget your words, and I promise to comport myself well in all things to show my gratitude and love of God."

Berenguer de Palou smiled and rested one of his many-ringed hands on Carlos' shoulder. Carlos felt a rush of warmth at the touch, and when the Bishop spoke, he felt the words not with his ears but his entire body.

"Then let us part, dear Abbot, and in that parting let me give you one last measure of wisdom. When you arrive in Paris, do not let the power of the city overwhelm you. At its heart, it is a village just like any other, just seen through a larger lens. The same will be true of Rome, but by the time you reach it, you will be prepared.

"You will encounter all manner of persons in your travels, and sadly, even within your order there are those who would seek to suppress whatever truths you might uncover."

At the Bishop's words, Carlos felt a spike of fear. He was himself guilty of this crime, concealing information from the bandit Ramon's confession. He had buried the description of the "animal men" deep within his mind, and wondered if the Bishop would believe—or forgive—Carlos if he shared it now. But the Bishop was not done speaking, and Carlos tried to keep his doubts from showing.

"Have a care, my son, and guard your Faith well. It is your strength—your armor against assaults on your inner self."

The Bishop's smile had faded, and his one good eye studied Carlos intently. A ray of sunshine found and illuminated that half of the man's face, and for a moment the image seemed very familiar to him. But before he could place it, the Bishop pulled his hand away and took a step back. Both warmth and light were gone, and Carlos found his mouth working without any prior thought.

"I will, your Grace. My time here has been all too short, and some-day I would appreciate any more of yours that you might spare. In memory of our discussions, may I call upon you as just a simple monk when I return? There are many things I wish to learn on this journey, and I think you are the one who can make the most use of them."

Carlos was surprised by his own statement. The Bishop had made no formal overtures of friendship, but the words seemed right.

No, no seeming. They are the right words—the only ones worth voicing.

The Bishop smiled, and Carlos felt a bit of the light that had framed the man's face touch the back of his neck.

"Yes, my young friend. I would appreciate another visit. I will have finished Mark by then, and your assistance with Matthew and Luke will be quite useful. Go with God, and return clothed in his truth."

Carlos nodded, a wordless combination of thanks and

goodbye. The flush of life he felt upon awakening this morning now threatened to burn his skin from within, and he had many miles to cover before he reached the first of the hostels on Matthieu's itinerary.

With his meager belongings stowed on the horse, the new Abbot walked beside it through the gates of Barcelona and onto a road promising much more wonder and discovery in the weeks and months to come.

I will return, my friends. And when I do, we will celebrate my journey, and yours, as we begin our new lives together.

FRANCES DELAMONDE STEPPED OUT OF THE SHADOWS once Carlos passed through the gates. He wanted so much to call his young friend back, but Carlos' fate had been set for many days now.

After many years of working with Berenguer de Palou, Frances had learned to detect the large man's nearly silent approaches and was not surprised when the Bishop's voice came from behind him.

"How much does he really know?" The Bishop's words struck to the core of the matter, and Frances wondered whether his response would help or doom his favorite son on the road to Paris.

"Enough. Not all of it, not yet, but certainly more than he lets on. If we'd let him keep looking, he'd have discovered the rest for sure." Frances turned to look at his superior, trying to keep his face as neutral as possible. One word from the Bishop and Carlos' journey would end tonight, in a most ignominious fashion.

The Bishop nodded, closing his dead eye while staring at the tall walls of the city with the other. Frances had the distinct impression that he was still watching Carlos walk, but the other man spoke before Frances could wonder why.

"I thought as much. He'll get there soon no matter what we do, I think, but you've done the right thing in sending him away. If he stayed, he'd reject the truth out of hand, and we both know what would have to happen next."

It was Frances' turn to nod, wishing events hadn't turned

out quite like this. He and the Bishop had been preparing Matthieu as their emissary, but Carlos was too smart, too insightful to keep sequestered any longer. And as the Bishop said, after the man Ramon's unfortunate confession—in particular the parts Carlos had chosen not to record—it was only a matter of time before he started asking questions that neither man wanted to answer.

I just wish…there's so much more I could have taught him…

The Bishop smiled, and spread his arms wide.

"Do not grieve for him, my friend. Young Carlos is embarking on a glorious adventure. You and I were no different when we started seeking the deeper truths, and we managed to survive them."

If you can call it that…

Frances pushed away a memory of fire and smoke, of borrowed strength singing in his heart as he fought against foes the world had forgotten long ago. Of men and monsters from another age, and the terrible truths that sustained him in his darkest hours.

We are not alone in this world, and not all who share it with us are interested in peaceful pursuits.

"Yes, we survived, though there are times when I'd rather set aside this burden and be an old man again. What we're asking of him—do you think he's ready? He's still so young…"

The Bishop's smile faded, and the grim expression that replaced it sent shivers down Frances' spine.

"It's too late to wonder about that now. What I—what *we* have set in motion cannot be stopped. Carlos must walk the world for a time, and hopefully come back to us a changed man. If not…"

Frances nodded, remembering other seekers they'd sent forth over the years. Few had returned, and fewer still had been able to bear the things they'd learned. Sooner or later, most descended into madness.

Or worse.

And there are only so many more fires we can set before people outside our circle start asking questions we can't ignore.

"But enough of such thoughts. Come, drink with me old friend, and let us speak of happier times. I understand you've come into possession of a most unusual weapon?"

Frances nodded and described the sword—Carlos' sword, for it truly belonged to no other—as he followed the Bishop back to the cathedral. Both men kept an eye on the shadows, offering silent prayers that if they were attacked, their opponents would be of the mundane variety.

Because we are never, ever, alone....

SPRING

Matthieu,

Today's journey ends in a pleasant hostel, in the company of other travelers who honor this poor pilgrim. The sea breaks against the cliffs below, and on the morrow I am promised a sunrise that will lift me to Heaven's gates.

Such things I have seen already! Many sights both different and new. We spent much of our first journey to Barcelona talking about the past, but after only a few days my mind is alive with the possibilities of the future.

My last day among you was remarkable, and I have taken the lessons I learned from the Bishop to heart. There is a fountain inside me, a re-invigoration of my Faith, and an appreciation of the Holy Spirit in all things around me.

I start this chronicle for you so that you may share this journey through my words. Please give to the others what you deem appropriate—my words are meant for you, and your gifts make them possible.

Tonight, I feel restless, as if my feet still yearn for the road. With dawn, I shall satisfy their urges, along with my duty to the Father, Son, and Holy Ghost...

1 APRIL, YEAR OF OUR LORD 1205

M ATTHIEU SET THE LETTER DOWN UPON CARLOS' simple desk and smiled. It seemed right to read it here, in the place that had been his brother's.

The first of his network of couriers had received and transmitted Carlos' dispatch with great speed, but Carlos had been many days and miles gone before these words began traveling toward Sant Cugat. As his brother moved farther along the road to his destination, the messages would be more and more delayed, but Matthieu's contacts in both the church and the world would collect and direct them as Carlos traveled.

And through their efforts, I can hold on to my friend for a little while longer...

It was hard letting go. But not as hard as admitting that Carlos had left him behind long ago. Everything Carlos did, he did well, and such confidence was a trait Matthieu wished he possessed in himself rather than one he pretended to.

Though his brother was only a few weeks gone, Matthieu could still feel his absence in every part of the Abbey, see it on the faces of the other monks, hear it as they sang their devotions just a little louder to fill up the space where Carlos had been.

The accounts Carlos left behind were a confused jumble— one Matthieu could make little sense of without assistance. It had been so long since he'd had to read on his own, and without Carlos to help him he couldn't be sure what were words and what was "other." No one here knew his secret, and when Matthieu had been asked to assume the many duties his friend had performed, he had known he could not hide the truth for long.

Father Frances knows—he has to. But can I trust Robere?

A problem for another day. Outside, the sun was burning away the last patches of snow. The abbey in Winter was a place of preparation—the abbey in Spring one of renewal. As the year progressed, he would oversee the fields and vines, instruct and direct the laborers as they continued the construction, and manage the xenodochia as best he could.

Another gift from Carlos he could never repay. To help his fellow man had been his dream for as long as he could remember—one Matthieu had realized on the day the he first arrived at Sant Cugat and made possible through the diligent study and efforts of another.

Carlos.

Before Matthieu met Carlos, the Academy had been a place of bluster and sufferance. Their fellow students had been the spoiled children of Spanish nobility, interested only in themselves. From them, Matthieu had learned to fight and laugh but little else. His strength, speed, and size protected him from the worst of their cruelty, but he could not join in with them to bully the others.

Especially Carlos. Back then Carlos had been even more awkward than Robere, and Matthieu could not bear to see him suffer under their fists and feet. On the day he took a stand against the other boys on Carlos' behalf, Matthieu's world became a larger place. And though he took his own share of abuse from students jealous of their friendship and afraid of their own shortcomings, given the option, Matthieu would stand before Carlos against the entire world.

But Carlos no longer needs my protection. Though he will never admit it, he is the protector now.

Matthieu said a small prayer for his friend's happiness and left the rolled parchment behind in Carlos' cell. As long as the abbey stood, no matter how long it might take for their brother to come home, there would be a place waiting for him.

Matthieu moved down the cold hallways of the abbey, giving and receiving nods of respect. He tried to ignore the looks of judgment and comparison in the eyes of the other monks, but it was on too many of their faces for him to deny.

I am not Carlos. Just a poor copy.

In the courtyard, workmen from Ruri were unloading a

wagon of sturdy planks Carlos had arranged for by selling the swords and spoils left behind by the bandits who had invaded their home. Each shipment that arrived was destined for the new buildings growing from this ancient soil, a future secured by a selfless man traveling farther away every day.

Alejandro moved with the laborers, slower than Matthieu liked, but finally standing on his own feet. Another result of Carlos' care and skill, a better recovery than they had any right to expect. The angry scar on his head was healing well, and seeing it reminded Matthieu of the lingering pain in his own shoulder.

Another secret I will be unable to keep for long...

A LEJANDRO SEARCHED FOR THE WORDS BUT COULDN'T form his lips around them. Rather than stand with his mouth open, he motioned to the stack for another heavy beam and assisted the burly workman in hefting it into place.

Carlos' plans called for a double wall backfilled with loose stones and sand. This time, the stable would stand strong against both the weather and the flames, and the horses would be safe.

He would not fail them again.

Holding the plank against the frame, he concentrated on the nail in his hand. How did it get there? It was hard to remember—hard to focus for very long. Someone handed him a hammer. What was he supposed to do with that? Why were they asking him these questions when he did not know the answers?

He should know. The desire to know was a fire inside greater than the one that...that...

He looked at the hammer, and the nail, and felt something shift against his shoulder. Something large was falling. There was a grunt behind him...

Plank. It's a plank! Carlos' plans call for a double wall of planks, backfilled with loose stones and sand.

This time, the stable would stand strong against both the weather and the flames, and the horses would be safe...

ESPITE ROBERE'S BEST EFFORTS, HIS HANDS CRAMPED and the heavy board threatened to slip. The pain in his chest was not from the unexpected impact, but rather a hollow feeling that no amount of medicine could address. Face to face with the person he'd become, it was hard to look at Alejandro and not remember the man he had been.

Given enough time, the scars would heal. Perhaps it was too soon for Alejandro to be up and around, but there were no more excuses for keeping him isolated. And until new records arrived for translation, Robere's sole responsibility was supplying full-time care to the Abbey's sole remaining patient. Better to be out here doing some good than waiting for the stable master to "wake up."

If only he would…

"Alejandro. Please…help me with this. It is very…heavy."

Robere spoke slowly, only partially because of the effort necessary to hold the plank. Catalan was a hard language to master, but it was the only one Alejandro knew. Since Carlos' departure, Father Frances had insisted that no other be spoken within the walls of the abbey. Father Frances had even forbidden the brothers from using Latin, save for their daily prayers.

The burly man turned, recognition dawning in his eyes.

"Carlos! That p-p-plank is very heavy—let m-m-me hold it for you."

Robere surrendered his burden, wiping his brow to hide tears. At least the strength in Alejandro's arms had returned. The plank rose easily from Robere's shaking hands as Alejandro balanced it high across his broad chest.

"Carlos, let me show you how well the b-b-building is going. Once I p-p-place this p-p-plank here…" Alejandro returned the plank against the frame, easily supporting it with both hands, "we can use the…use the…"

Robere sensed Alejandro's focus shifting again, and motioned some of the workmen from Ruri to nail the plank into place while he occupied the big man's attention.

"That is…That is excellent work, Alejandro. With your… help, we will be finished very…soon."

Time. Time is what he needs. In time, he will remember. Who he was. What happened to him.

What we've lost.

Across the courtyard, Matthieu stood eying the both of them with cool confidence. Robere wished he could feel even a portion of the big monk's strength—that never-wavering, steadfast resolve. And he had always been envious of the older man's lifetime of friendship with Carlos.

After studying with the master for but a few short years, Robere had a much deeper respect for Carlos than for his uncaring, distant father. Here he had a real life—one worth living. *If it's one not entirely of my own choosing, is that so bad?*

FRANCES EXITED THE XENODOCHIA, WELCOMING THE cold rush of air on his face. Days like this reminded him of the glory of life—how each moment was worth living. The broad courtyard was filled with his successes over the last few weeks, the lives he'd returned to their proper courses.

Matthieu stood reviewing the abbey's construction projects from the side while engaging in thoughtful contemplation. He was settling in nicely to the place Carlos prepared for him. Not so far a stretch for the young man and a role he was more than ready for.

Alejandro worked as hard as ever and showed little outward sign of his injury. He laughed and smiled while preparing a new home for his beloved horses, lifting the spirits of all around him.

Robere worked by his side, finally standing tall in his own light rather than in Carlos' shadow. The boy would eventually outgrow them all and lead them into uncharted waters.

And in the same fashion, Sant Cugat will grow and prosper as well. Together, our linked hands will build a testament to withstand the ravages of time. Long after we are dust, the memory of our deeds will survive in these stones.

Overhead, a cloud passed across the sun, hiding its warmth for a moment. In that cold heartbeat, the years behind Frances tugged at his soul. Long, moonless nights framing thousands of bright shining days and uncounted journeys that had led him to this place.

Shadows and Light.

All my sins remembered...

THE RIDER SLUMPED LOW AGAINST THE WITHERS OF a lathered horse. Reins trailed low from a bitless bridle, frayed and worn against the ground. Wild-eyed, nervous, the animal had been pushed hard recently, but there were no immediate signs as to why.

A chill wind blew past the travelers, cooling the remnants of a morning rain that soaked them to the bone. The rider wore a simple black robe and seemed out of place on a horse so large and powerful. Though he gave no direction to the beleaguered mount's unsteady steps, it moved forward eagerly as if returning home after a long journey. The animal carried the man on its back without complaint, but both looked as if their travels were about to end in an exhausted heap.

Ahead of the weary pair stood a small grouping of stone and wood structures. The rude buildings were the only sign of life for miles of surrounding grasslands. Not even a proper road defined the extent of its domain. No matter; the smell of pooled water drew the horse ever onward like a moth to a candle's flame.

The two travelers did not go unnoticed.

"Mother...come quick! Another one—a rider from the south."

The speaker was a young boy, fresh faced and smiling in the heatless afternoon sun. His words initiated a flurry of activity. Women appeared from around corners carrying long-handled tools designed for pruning trees, though there were none nearby. A handful of tradesmen hastily covered their goods, and all eyes were drawn to a tall, thin woman striding purposefully through the center of the gathered buildings.

She moved with confidence, kind eyes smiling a response unlike that of those wielding the improvised weapons. Her simple black garment hung loosely on her spare frame, snapping in the breeze like the wings of a low flying bird.

The years had been kind to her but had left marks as they passed. Pleasant wrinkles covered her face and hands, the skin of which were tanned like soft leather. The rest of her was covered in rough, dark cloth, her only ornamentation a simple thong of leather around her neck from which dangled a wooden cross.

"Do not fear, children. This man is no bandit—he does not come bearing arms. And after our last visitor, there is little in this place to interest armed men. The traveler presents no threat to us, and we should offer none of our own in return."

As if to support her statement, the horse changed its direction, continuing past those watching it into the center of the village. When it reached a crude well defined by a low circle of stones, it shrugged, easing its sodden burden into the arms of two nearby women.

The rider's beardless face was covered in an angry rash, skin nearly the color of his wet hair. His eyes were swollen under blistered lids. A weak, whispered plea escaped lips burned by wind, sun...

And fever.

"Un...Unclean. Qua...Quarantine. For sa...safety."

His message relayed, he relinquished what small hold he had on consciousness. From limp fingers fell a simple string of cloth not unlike the ones several of his attendants held. The woman didn't have to read it to know that on it was written a prayer—a song of God to ward off the evils of the world.

"Another, indeed. Sisters, take this man quickly from here, lest he suffer further. And call for Marie Angelique—we need her skills.

A whinny and a long exhalation marked the horse's collapse. First to its knees and then to one side. More women came forward to assist it, working with the boy who'd announced its arrival to quickly remove its packs and saddle.

From the former, a packet of parchment fell to the stones and was nearly swallowed by the open well's mouth before the tall woman snatched it up.

The documents bore a pressed wax seal she knew well. The Bishop of Barcelona had sent a messenger their way, and Maria of Treve, Abbess of the Blessed Stone, wondered what such a message as this would mean for her tiny pocket of the faith.

CARLOS AWOKE IN DARKNESS WITH HIS EYES, WRISTS, and legs bound. He was lying on something soft, and as far as he could tell his weight was fully supported. His mouth was dry and his thirst almost overpowering. But given the very drastic change in his circumstances, he kept his mouth closed.

I can safely assume I am no longer in the hostel, as I purchased no cushion from the hostler, and if this weight on my chest is a blanket, it's of much better quality than my own. So where, then? The why I can deal with when I have more information—or perhaps someone to talk to.

Carlos relaxed his body, letting the warmth of the room surround him. He didn't feel anything holding his neck in place but tried to remain perfectly still as his other senses brought him information about the space surrounding him.

The left side of my face is warm, and there is a touch of smoke in my nostrils. A brazier, perhaps?

Carlos let his breath out slowly, listening carefully for any other sounds. The slight hissing of burning coals confirmed the presence of a brazier, and to his left there was a soft sound, followed by the smell of…flowers?

It's too early for fresh blossoms, or at least it was when I went to sleep. An essence of some kind, most likely on someone, rather than something.

Carlos flexed slightly, testing the limits of his bindings. Something scraped across a hard surface…a chair, perhaps? Then came a rustle of cloth, and the floral scent came closer.

Roses? No. Something else but similar.

The odd smell was sharp and crisp, and Carlos couldn't remember perceiving any other thing so clearly. He was almost lost in the scent, when a cool cloth touched his head and something pressed down on his chest.

Definitely a someone, then.

"Wh…where am I?" Carlos' voice sounded alien in his own ears, weak and thready. His tongue was too dry, and when it touched his teeth he tasted the memory of some road not seen, heard, or felt.

The dust of the trail would pass soon enough, though he had no idea how it had gotten there. But now that he could feel the cloth on his head, he knew the warmth on his face was only partly from the brazier. It seemed that his entire body was made of heat. And then the pain came.

Though he hadn't moved, Carlos' head started spinning. The constancy of the cold cloth and whatever was touching his chest helped keep him centered, but he had difficulty timing the pulse and pause of his heart. It seemed faster than normal, and though there seemed to be a cloud in his head slowing his thoughts, he knew what had happened to him.

I know these signs. I've treated enough patients to recognize the symptoms of pox in myself but have they? I need to warn them, in case…in case…

"Please, take care. I am…not well. There is a sickness in me, and it can spread…." The effort of speaking drained Carlos of whatever reserves he had left, and before he could tell his attendant the proper steps to take, he was spent.

"We know, Brother. We treat it often enough here, as best we are able. Rest. You will need your strength in the days to come."

The voice was that of a woman or a girl. Warm, comforting words, with the affect so lacking in Robere's bedside manner and a hint of Matthieu's accent. The cloth on his brow moved down his face with light patting motions, and Carlos could feel each blister and aberration on his skin as the cool cloth soothed them. When it paused over his lips to deliver a few drops of water, Carlos sucked at them greedily.

The coals hissed as something splashed over them, and a

rich cloud of scented steam filled his nose and mouth. Carlos detected a hint of anise and several other common herbs. He inhaled, drawing the cloud into himself and letting it strengthen his lungs.

After a few breaths, he felt recovered enough to try speaking again. This time, his words were offered in Matthieu's northern dialect, rather than the Provençal he had spoken and heard on awakening.

"Where are we? Is this your father's house?" The few words Carlos had heard from her didn't indicate great age, and the hand that pressed him back against the soft couch was small, like that of a child.

"In a sense. It is the house of your Father as well, Brother. I am called Sister Marie Angelique. You are here in our enclave, the Abbey of the Blessed Stone."

Not quite Matthieu's vowel sounds. Perhaps too far south for those but surely a related dialect. Her reply is slow but deliberate. Familiar with the language but not practiced. The words, while precise, are oddly accented, as if she swallows her tongue while speaking.

"You were near death from your ride when you found us. What purpose kept you on the road? With these symptoms you should have been resting, not riding. And through these winds and the coming snows? You invite sickness in many forms, were you not carrying it already."

Carlos accepted the rebuke with a smile, though the expression split his tortured lip. The pain was manageable, and he was more interested in the puzzle of her speech than anything else. He didn't hear anyone else in the room, so whoever they were, the leaders of the Blessed Stone knew enough to both isolate him and keep him warm against the inevitable chills.

Definitely a southern variant. Which means I'm likely not too far from the hostel. I just wish I could remember....

"If this is a sanctuary, then I was coming to see your Abbess, though I am not familiar with your community. However, if your manner of comfort is any indication, my mission was and is to confer with healers like yourself. I am Carlos de Roja, late of Barcelona and the Abbey of Sant Cugat du Valles."

Carlos coughed after speaking, and a wet cloth dabbed at

his face. A moment later he felt a cup against his lower lip, and he raised his head slightly to drink. When he was finished, he smiled and continued.

"I see you have received my news of the spreading pox. Although I had not expected to share my knowledge in quite so personal a fashion."

"Yes, I imagine you did not."

Soft laughter betrayed the presence of a smile, and he adjusted his estimate of her age upward to accommodate knowledge of sarcasm.

Though the odd accent makes the accuracy of any guesses suspect.

"Still, you are here now, and your mind seems intact after your high fever. We have leeched some of your poisonous humor, and the worst of your blistering is passed. You stand a far better chance of recovery than most who come to me. If you are a healer yourself, your general health explains much of your strength."

"Thank you for your kindness. Sister...? I must ask. My eyes?"

Carlos remembered the Bishop's dead eye and the rare cases of blindness he treated but could not cure in the village. If blisters and sickness sat in or upon the eye, they could damage or steal vision. Her mention of leeches was somewhat troubling as well. Was he in the hands of surgeons, rather than healers?

The bandage on his face was now far more relevant than the restraints on his wrists. As prescribed by Hippocrates, he had used similar measures to stop his charges from aggravating injuries, as well as to avoid any unconscious scratching of infected blisters.

"No damage that we discovered. As a precaution, we protected you while you rested. These last days have been very taxing for your body. You should have stopped before it got this...before your disease progressed to this state."

"Yes, it would have been prudent. Wait...days?"

When, exactly, had he contracted the disease? The last exposure he was aware of had been weeks ago, and after treating the sickness revealed by the bandits' attack, no new cases had been reported in Ruri. Frances and Carlos had been quarantined for a week after Ramon's death, and he had seen no signs or sufferers in the city, along the road, or at the hostel.

No matter. I am clearly infected now, and despite the leeching, my nurse seems knowledgeable and competent. Clearly they have both experience with the disease and the resources to treat it. But the severity of my symptoms is not a good sign—nor is my lack of memory. Both need immediate attention.

Marie Angelique had mentioned days of convalescence, which gave him at least some idea of the progression of his symptoms. But they, and he, would need to know more to devise an effective treatment.

Carlos reviewed what he could remember of his last day of travel. After arriving at the hostel, he'd shared a pleasant meal in good company, and then written a message for Matthieu. After entrusting it to the care of an eager messenger, he remembered lying back on a cot, then…nothing. At some time after that, he'd risen and traveled down roads unknown, to…

To…

hours, miles, days, riding, riding, heat rising, up from the road, out of his skin…

wind, rain, night, stars, swaying, clutching at clumps of coarse black hair, leaning low, the world shuddering, staggering…

"Something…something kept me going. I had to get away—had to come here to rest. I cannot explain it any other way—it makes no sense."

Carlos' memory of the journey was little more than disjointed images that felt as though they had happened to someone else. He couldn't string the experiences together with any certainty, nor could he fix the countryside to anything he'd seen on a map.

And there was something else dancing on the edge of his memory.

Someone…

"The Horse! Is it…did it survive?"

Carlos tried to sit up but Marie Angelique's hand pressed against his chest in just the right place to steal his breath. He fought to breathe, each motion of his chest trapping more of the scented steam in his lungs. Before he completely lost consciousness the restraint on his right wrist came undone and a firm hand helped him turn, holding his head steady before he choked.

Carlos didn't know what was worse: the pain in his lungs and chest or the shame of a mistreated mount. What madness had possessed him to endanger not only his own life but that of an innocent beast? It defied explanation, especially following his time discussing the merits of humanity with the Bishop.

From somewhere behind Marie Angelique, a second woman spoke with the same accent as his nurse, but none of the strange vowels.

"The animal will live, though it will not soon carry a rider. It too is in need of much rest. Like yourself, it is and was quite strong and survived where another would have been lost to the elements."

The words were clear and strong, from far enough away that Carlos expanded his mental picture of the chamber to include a doorway some four paces away from his couch.

Marie Angelique's chair is several feet away, within arm's length of the brazier. Somewhere nearby must be a table with a container of water. Beyond her must be a larger fire, since coals alone are insufficient to warm a chamber large enough to admit the...Abbess?

Marie Angelique's hand shifted to guide him back to a position of rest, and a sliding fabric sound accompanied Carlos' mental picture of her turning to regard this new speaker.

Definitely someone in a position of authority. And while this is an undignified introduction, the coughing has at least cleared my chest.

Carlos turned his face to where he believed the Abbey's mistress stood, so that he might show his own respect.

"My lady Abbess. My deepest apologies for not standing to greet you. As I was explaining to Sister Marie..."

A flush of embarrassment added to the warmth of his skin, and Carlos pressed his lips together to stop his words. What could he say to this woman about actions that defied logic and reason. There could be no explanation, and yet he wanted to give one.

It was then that Carlos heard another voice speaking. Not in the chamber but from the past.

"Never hide the truth, for in doing so you only show the lie."

Father Frances would never accept such a half-hearted apology, and there was no reason to believe that his equal here in the Blessed Stone would either.

For that matter, "Father Carlos" should not even try.

Marie Angelique released his other bindings, taking his silence for a signal to proceed. Carlos was working on a more properly respectful apology when he noticed she was having difficulty untying him.

"Yes, I heard, Brother Carlos. One would think that St. Benedict's follower would have more sense, but the fever can do strange things to us all. Rest now. We will speak again in the morning. I understand you have your letters. Some of our residents would appreciate the use of your hands and eyes once you regain them."

The bindings on his ankles came away, though the cloth wrapped around his eyes remained.

"Of course, my lady Abbess. It will be my pleasure to serve. Assuming that my attendant allows me such activities. She ties an excellent knot, and I should hate to be out of her favor."

"It is Maria here, Carlos. We are less formal than in the cities—the world you left behind."

Marie Angelique laughed as she adjusted his blanket, and a brief cool breeze on his legs revealed another aspect of his treatment.

My cassock has been removed, and I've most likely been washed at least once.

"But I will need appropriate clothing fi...first."

There was another hissing sound of water meeting coals, and a fresh cloud of steam filled the room. This time, it smelled of some burned compound Carlos did not recognize. The pain in his joints lessened, and his head spun away into...

"Carlos?"

The Abbess' voice came from far away, and he couldn't hear the other woman...what was her name?

Where am I again?

"Carlos, I have other questions for you, when you are stronger. There are things we...reasons why we are not on the main roads. When you are ready, I very much would like to know why you are here and on what mission the Bishop has sent you."

The last sounds of her voice trailed away, and Carlos' dark world lost the definition of sound around its edges. As he floated off into a deeper darkness, his last thoughts were of the unseen Abbess and her odd statements.

What is so special about this place? And why would the Bishop need a messenger?

The fires on the water burn brightly, red stars flaring and rising through clouds of black smoke. There is no moon tonight to obscure their diamond counterparts above or to reveal the men's location as they approach the rock spire near the walls.

Somewhere above them, a ball of pitch explodes against the stony hillside. The observation tower is a valuable target, but one proving invulnerable to their continued assault. The high perch sees for miles out to sea and over land. If they could gain it, or if it fell...

To the left and right, wooden engines strain in the darkness against Ascalon's barriers and thick gates. Each impact shakes the ground, and the knights feel it deep in their bones. Tonight they will break the siege and prevent another year of war. The banner of Jerusalem's king will fly above these walls, and the constant threat of the Egyptians will fade into memory.

A line of fire shoots from the tower, followed by another and another. Flaming bolts impact the top of a siege engine, igniting the thatch and creating a new sunrise. The Knights of the Temple deal with it quickly, passing pails of water and cutting away the affected sections while the men below continue their slow, pounding attack on the walls.

The assault group pauses, not wanting to betray their position to the enemies manning the walls. Everything rides on their objective, and these men know they are expendable. If only one of them reaches the tower, those who wait out beyond bow and catapult range will gain a great advantage over the much larger force inside the city.

All eyes turn toward their captain, who moves one hand down until his palm is inches above the ground. In the other is the relic, gripped so tightly that slivers of the ancient wood pierce his skin.

He watches the nearest engine to time their attack, but a fiery missile explodes against the scaffolding with a roaring, splintering sound. One of its axles breaks and the massive ram swings back, pausing briefly before dragging screaming men with it as it twists and slams into its own supports.

Cheers from the enemy observers drown out the panicked cries of crusader engineers as the collapsing structure pitches forward and breaks against the walls.

Setting them aflame.

Days, weeks, and months of constant assault resolve in an instant as the wall breaches. Cheers turn to shouts as the tower barks orders to the defenders inside. None of the knights speak the language, but the meaning is clear. With no immediate threat from outside, the advantage of numbers will see the breach repaired before a single crusader can set foot within the fortress.

"NOW! Press the advantage—the Lord is with us!"

The Captain commands, and the knights obey. He has molded them for years into an elite force that has never known defeat.

Taking the tower would have robbed the defenders of a forward observation post. Taking the fortress city of Ascalon will rob Egypt of its advantage in the holy land and protect the shining city for a generation or more.

Charging fearlessly through the breach, the Captain holds the relic high above his head, swinging his sword before him. One man, then two fall before his flashing steel, and for the first time in generations a follower of the cross stands within the city's walls.

The knights run after him, taking no time to marvel at the sight of fire bending away from their leader and the weathered carving coated in his blood. Opposition melts before his relentless

*charge, and as the knights fight through the streets they spread
chaos before them.*

*Their lives are over—none of them have any illusions. This
is their last night on Earth, made glorious by their heroic deeds.
Thirty-eight voices lift in song as they battle, and as each man falls
the others increase both their volume and their resolve.*

*Seven singing men reach the sanctuary, and five enter the low
structure. They ignore gold and jewels, following a trail of faith
toward their goal: a simple shelf on which rest three iron nails and
a stained strip of rough cloth.*

*A shaft of starlight pierces the gloom and then is gone. Four
hands rest on the shoulders of the Captain, then fall away into the
darkness. A fire rises, burning away the night as one man faces an
army of hundreds pressing in from all sides.*

*The light of the flames is reflected in their eyes, and dark smoke
and soot stain their faces and hands. The route back to the breach
lies beyond this wall of soon-to-be-dead flesh. Claiming the relics
required the sacrifice of thirty-nine lives.*

Keeping them will require hundreds.

*A grim smile grows on the Captain's face as he lifts his sword
and begins to sing…*

HEAD POUNDING IN TIME TO HIS RACING HEART, CARLOS
woke to the lessening of some great weight within
his chest and a whiff of pitch-heavy smoke teasing
his nostrils.

The soft hiss of burning coals was a warm reminder of his
location, as was the cloth binding his eyes tight. A whisper of
shifting cloth and a familiar floral scent alerted him to Marie
Angelique's presence.

Carlos took a breath to calm himself. Whatever unremem-
bered dream had set his heart to pounding was finished, gone
as always when he awoke.

*It must still be night. Were it morning, Marie Angelique would
have wakened fully and given some comment on my condition.*

A lifetime of prayer had trained Carlos to sleep in stages
so that he might sing the offices each night with his brothers.

Far away, in another place, his brothers were most likely singing now. Carlos moved his lips without breath, speaking the words in his mind and leading his memories in prayer as he would when he returned to the Abbey.

Careful not to rouse his nurse, Carlos sang the Psalms as quietly as he could, to remind himself both of his faith and of the sacrifices of those who had gone before. Each subdued verse settled his mind further until, with the final lesson, he was at peace.

He dismissed the community to their rest and walked the corridors of his imaginary home past the bowed heads of his brothers and back to the simple sleeping shelf in his cell.

The couch he occupied was a more comfortable resting place than that of his imagination. It was an odd feeling to sleep on something soft but one he would get used to in time. This community was not one of men dedicated to service. Though it had an Abbess and at least one Sister, its rules and routines were different from those he'd spent a lifetime learning.

But there still must be a structure and hierarchy to their days. I will need to learn both during however much time I spend here. Time enough for that tomorrow, though, when my head is clear.

Although the worst of his fever might have passed, Carlos was still far too weak for physical activity. Rest was the best advice he could give himself.

Perhaps whatever dream moved me will return and soothe my sleeping soul as prayer has done for the waking mind.

Carlos settled back onto the couch, waiting for the darkness to come.

TELL ME MORE OF YOUR PARENTS, SISTER. THEY SOUND very wise indeed."

Three days in darkness had done much to assuage Carlos' curiosity regarding his attendant—almost as much as the young woman had done for his health. And though both processes were ably assisted by the kind words of the Abbess Maria de Fuentes, there was still much he wanted to know about Marie Angelique.

While both women were skilled healers, the younger of the two had little formal training. Marie Angelique's talents stemmed from a knowledge of plant and herbal remedies—a discipline Carlos knew little of from his books. She'd learned this healing lore from her parents—though she had chosen the name Marie Angelique to honor the Abbess, her family had named her Qin Yee, and she was equally comfortable with either.

"There is not much more to tell. When the fire took them, they were not much older than I am now. I remember my father's devotion to our family, my mother's stories of the road, and the litany of herb lore we practiced each day. Our *cland* was once very famous in our province because of the great Yee Hero. My father spoke often of the Hero's legacy and our need to reclaim it."

Even without his eyes, Carlos could tell his new friend easily from the abbey's other novitiates who came infrequently with food and fresh bandages. Partly because of her odd pronunciation of sibilant words, but also because like himself, she was speaking a language that was not her own.

Out of respect to those around them, Carlos and Qin Yee primarily conversed in the same language everyone else used—that bizarre blending of Matthieu's northern words and the longer sounds of Catalan. Carlos suspected it was Limousin, which would place his current location a bit farther into France than he'd originally thought. The Abbess had been noticeably reticent to tell him, and Qin Yee had come to the Blessed Stone as a child with no knowledge of geography.

Her speech has other peculiarities as well, such as her use of the Celtic word for "family," rather than the local equivalent. Both Provençal and Latin have equivalent terms, so there must be some greater sense of the word in the musical language of her ancestors.

However she came to the service of the Lord, Qin Yee's peculiar faith crossed the gulf between her and "normal" people. While she honored the Trinity, she also venerated her ancestors and their place in what she described as a "Celestial Bureaucracy."

I certainly have no complaints regarding her beliefs. Without the lessons of her forebears, I would certainly have left this world very soon after the end of my ride.

In a private moment, The Abbess had told Carlos about the night she'd discovered a mob of villagers chasing a man with weapons and torches. Qin Yee's father had been ambushed on the street and defended himself too well for their liking. After killing several of the attackers, he ran for home, only to find it engulfed in fire and his wife beaten to death while protecting their daughter from looters. He died trying to pull them both to safety while their neighbors looked on and cheered.

The Abbess had rescued the child from the fires of hatred and fear, but she had been too late to save the girl's eyes. According to the Abbess, Marie Angelique suffered extensive burns to her face and a withering injury to her left arm. Difficulties that kept her secluded even in this remote enclave.

Perhaps the greatest tragedy of her injury is that while she is more intelligent than many scholars I have known, because of her clouded vision she cannot learn the scripts and letters for the languages she speaks. Like Matthieu, she is not "literate"—at least not as defined by the Church.

In Carlos' opinion, the Church was the entity that suffered most from that lack. The Abbess had sponsored and raised Qin Yee in the faith, and although the girl had taken vows of service to repay that kindness, she was not a true believer. The fiction allowed her to live comfortably and practice her craft of healing without prejudice. And it was a vindication of sorts for the harm she'd suffered at the hands of supposedly "God-fearing" Christians.

"I wish that I could be of more immediate assistance, Sister. I recall no references among the records I have studied of Eastern artifacts. But in truth, my knowledge of France is not great. Perhaps if you could remember more?"

"I too am sorry, honored Brother. I have no tales that directly relate to them. I know only of our *cland's* great sorrow at the loss of the items and of my father's quest to return them to Shaanxi province. Once they are recovered, the Yee Hero will be reborn into the next generation and again will protect the people."

While searching the ruins of the Yee family home for other survivors after the fires died down, the Abbess had instead discovered a carved chest. It contained a set of scrolls documenting the herb lore Qin Yee practiced and a bound volume detailing her family's lives and triumphs, including the tales of the Yee Hero.

Carlos had felt the binding on the book, and it was of comparable quality to that which the Bishop had used for his masterpiece. According to Qin Yee, painted on its silk pages were hundreds of years of history, in characters too small for her damaged sight to make out.

The scrolls containing her father's herb lore were written in broader brush strokes, and were the same documents with which she'd learned to read. She was familiar enough with them that she could tell them apart in a brightly lit area, and by tracing the painted letters with her fingers she could consult them as necessary. But the fire that had claimed the lives of Qin Yee's parents also robbed her of the ability to read the history of her ancestors, a pain Carlos knew only too well.

As an orphan himself, Carlos had often thought about

what it would be like to have roots, but never how it might feel to have them taken away in a blaze of fire only to be set down once more in fertile soil. And unlike his fellow orphans Qin Yee and Matthieu, there were no dimly remembered parents lurking in his mind nor any lost relics tying him to his ancestors.

The one thing Carlos did have was Brothers. Or more accurately now, Sons. His life of service gave him both pride and something to look forward to, two things he suspected were lacking in his new friend.

"Sister, you have given me much to think about over the last three days. Your world is new to me, and there is much in it I wish to know better. If it is within my power, I will help you continue your father's quest, and restore the legacy of the Yee Hero."

It was another of the sudden promises he'd made this year, but whatever spirit moved Carlos to say the words he knew it was one he would keep someday.

"You are too kind to give such a gift to a stranger. You may not be so generous when you are well again."

Qin Yee's voice betrayed the scars not of her body, but her soul. Carlos imagined her child's memory of fearful villagers and the life that might have been before it was snatched away on a night of rage.

"It is not a gift. It is my duty to give aid and comfort to those in pain. I would heal your pain, Sister. When I am well and can care for myself, I will care for you and those like you who are not strong enough to fight."

"Rest now, Brother Carlos. Tomorrow, we remove the bandages on your eyes, I think. You are healing well, but your strength is taxed. You must stay with us at least a few weeks more, but in the morning, we will see if you remember how to stand. Then you can care for us weak women by carrying things and reaching them down from high places."

A hint of laughter, but tinged with something else. Sadness?

"There are others to whom I must attend. I will return later with your evening meal, and we can continue our discussions then."

Carlos listened as Qin Yee rose and left the chamber. He had become accustomed to the sound of her footsteps and the easy way in which she moved around the chamber. He never heard her stumble or use her hand to...

Of course. Carlos remembered too late the Abbess' words about Qin Yee's injured arm. How she was not able to handle tools or work the fields like the other women of the community. And in attempting to give comfort, he'd only reminded her of her pain.

Carlos could not apologize for his foolish words without betraying the confidences the Abbess had shared. Alone with his shame, Carlos resolved to apologize through deeds instead.

She is right, though. I do feel strong, much stronger than when we first spoke. But exerting myself before it is time could set back recovery by days or even weeks.

His head still ached—a throbbing, pounding pain that at times stole his concentration. The sisters drew down the heat of his body as best they could, but Carlos was drained and spent when he woke each morning. The strength he felt now had built slowly throughout the day at the cost of the cloud now occupying his thoughts.

"She really cares for you. I have not heard her laugh like that in a very long time."

Carlos sat up at the sound of the Abbess' voice, and his head spun a bit as a result of the sudden movement. She'd once again entered without announcing herself, and Carlos wondered just how long she'd been listening.

"I feel I have upset her needlessly. My careless words, *mi bravado.* Even after a lifetime of humility, I still feel the need for *machismo.*"

"She does not mind, my young friend. It is a pain she has lived with a very long time, and she has adapted well. Observing her with you, I hardly notice it myself. But she also has few friends here, and it gladdens me that she has found another."

Carlos let the statement linger unanswered for a few heartbeats. He did consider Marie Angelique—Qin Yee—to be a friend. Though before now he hadn't considered exactly what the relationship might mean to her.

"I seem to be making them often this year. For a man who could previously count them on one hand, I am somewhat unaccustomed to the practice."

Carlos smiled, hoping that the Abbess could see his genuine amusement. They had spoken often during the last few days, of matters both spiritual and temporal, and but for the half-remembered feel of a weathered hand on a painful, fevered night, the two servants of God had so far interacted entirely at a distance.

"And what shall we talk of tonight, Maria?"

"There are a number of topics we should cover, but the first should be your health."

"I am not sure I understand. I feel fine—quite...recovered."

"Your body is healing, this is true. And your mind seems quick enough. But each day you seem weaker on waking than the day before, and as the hours pass you become as strong as or stronger than any man I've known."

The Abbess' words were remarkably devoid of inflection, and Carlos struggled to interpret them correctly. Was she smiling? Concerned? He relied so much on reading people's expressions while talking that without his eyes he felt he might never know her mood.

Maria, on the other hand, must have taken his contemplation for uncertainty. Her next words were much more to the point.

"We have spoken of your Abbey, Carlos, and of your life as a healer. Nothing you've told me explains this cycle in you. And to find the proper treatment, I need to know my patient."

Carlos thought back over their earlier conversations. He didn't think he'd held anything back, even relating in detail the measures taken to avoid contracting this very illness.

"I am still not taking your meaning, my Lady Abbess. I have given as complete a history as I can. Are you unsatisfied with my answers?"

"No, you have been quite helpful. But facts alone aren't enough. If you would permit more questions, I believe I can make myself clear?"

"Yes, please. I want to assist in any way I can."

The Abbess paused, and Carlos thought he could hear

her sipping something. The sound reminded him of his own thirst, and he reached for the cup of water Qin Yee kept filled on the floor next to his couch.

"Have you always been a fast healer, Carlos?"

The question surprised Carlos, enough so that he swallowed awkwardly. He grimaced as he coughed to clear his throat, and tried to determine what it was about the question that bothered him. It wasn't the fact that she'd she asked it, but rather the immediacy with which the answer came to mind.

No. And also, Yes.

Carlos had suffered injuries as a child, as all boys do. Fists, knees, and elbows had always seemed to find him when the Brothers were not looking. Before he'd met Matthieu, those bruises and cuts had been reminders of how not to act and how to avoid his tormentors.

Lasting lessons—and slow to heal. But to Maria's point, he could never recall being sick, or occupying one of the beds in his xenodochia other than for quick rests between patients. After that frozen night years ago when he'd risked his life to save Alejandro, his damaged shoulder had mended before the snows lifted and Alejandro re-covered from his exposure.

True convalescence was new to him, and outside of his sheltered life at Sant Cugat, it was an experience with which he would probably become very well acquainted.

"I…I have not had much direct experience with sickness, other than to treat it in others."

The Abbess was silent for a moment, and when she did speak it was with a weary tone he recognized.

Frances spoke like this to us, when Matthieu and I first came to the abbey. We were always worried that we'd say or do the wrong thing, and each time he dispelled our fears with the truth.

"I must be honest with you, Carlos. You should not have survived your journey here. You were far past the point by which another would have died—not only from the pox we treated, but from the exposure you suffered on the road. We fear for your life each time you sleep, but you somehow manage to fight off whatever weakness comes for you in the night without any help from us.

"I am an old woman, and I have treated many patients. I

am good at what I do, as is Marie Angelique. But I have never seen someone recover as completely as you have—and in such a short time. I suspect our success may have more to do with our patient than our cure."

Carlos had no idea how to respond to Maria's statement. He felt a fresh blush of shame on the back of his neck, but could not name any specific act for which he needed forgiveness. All he knew was that he had no answers for her and that lack embarrassed him greatly.

The Abbess waited patiently for him to speak, and Carlos took the time to compose his thoughts. If he could not give her an explanation, he could at least give her the truth.

"I am not quite sure what to make of this, Sister. I have seen many people afflicted with this pox—and buried most of them. I helped those few survivors through their illness, and returned them to their lives and family as best I was able. No two patients were discharged from my care in exactly the same way, though the severity of their symptoms varied from case to case."

"We have seen the same here, Carlos. Many times. But your recovery is different from any other. Perhaps we should look at the problem another way. What about your general health? You mentioned walking—do you find that when exercising you are any more able than your fellows?"

Carlos thought immediately of his apprentice Robere, who could not keep up with himself and Frances on their daily walks. Robere was certainly weaker, but Carlos did not think himself superior to the boy in any way. Older, more experienced perhaps, but the boy's breathing problems were not something he could address through exercise.

"No, no more than any other brother. We all led a physical lifestyle, and there were too few of us for too many tasks."

"Then we must let the matter rest for now. As you have time, think more on this. I often find that I know a thing more fully than I suspect but do not immediately have the proper words to frame a response."

Carlos heard more questions in her voice, and pondered her words carefully. He did not think his recovery particularly rapid, but he also did not know the true extent of his symptoms. He'd made up his mind to ask her for a more detailed description of them when she changed the topic.

"I had also hoped to talk again of your mission to Paris, and whether it may be delayed a while. We have need of you here, Carlos. Not as a man, but as an instructor."

Maria took another sip of whatever she was drinking, then moved forward to refill Carlos' cup as well.

"Ours is a small community, consisting mainly of women and fatherless children who have no other refuge. There are some artisans who bring us goods to sell, but we have little in the way of practical wealth. Many of us cannot read even the simplest of letters, and as you know, Marie Angelique's vision limits her abilities."

An unexpected and very welcome invitation. And as I am in no shape to travel at the moment, it seems proper to accept.

"I have been released of my normal duties to pursue my studies, but I am expected at St. Victor. What you describe is a worthy endeavor, and during my recovery, I would delight in it. As soon as I am able, I will prepare a message for the University. Would your people be able to take it to a...regular enclave, that it may be transmitted?"

Are these roots, spreading beneath me? A seed grown in cold winter soil—what fruit will come from such a planting?

"It is possible, but not likely until the snows lift. You will be with us for at least a fortnight, if not a month or longer. But when it is possible for a message to travel, I will allow it.

"If you would, make no mention of this place when you write. Women come to us because it is safe and away from the eyes of the Church of Men. There are those who know of us and our mission, but the more who learn our secrets, the less safe we become.

"We have invented the fiction of Wellstone Village above to disguise our general identity; if you must give a name or location, let that be it. Otherwise, we can send your message through traders we trust."

Carlos nodded. He'd suspected as much from the lack of male voices outside his chamber, but it was good to know for sure.

"I understand. Shall I become simply Carlos, then? It may

allow your residents some greater comfort. Otherwise, I believe I can assist your mission. Indeed, I am required to, by my oaths to man and God."

"I am glad. We lead a simple life here, marking the turning of seasons with no fanfare or festival. Your arrival, improbable and unexpected as it was, is the most excitement we have had in many weeks. God brought you to us, Carlos. You have a place here—one neither you nor I knew was waiting for you before you began your travels."

"I thank you for your invitation, Maria. And I shall endeavor to return your kindnesses as best I can."

Carlos did feel welcome here, at least with those few women with whom he'd interacted. It was a different place from Sant Cugat, and even if he lingered here for a while past his recovery, there was little danger he would forget himself or his duties.

Different does not mean better, nor does it imply worse. It is simply new, and Frances sent me out into the world to embrace the new.

Thinking of his mentor allowed Carlos to connect several of Maria's earlier statements. That the Abbess was not telling him everything was a given, as he was still too much of a cipher for them to trust completely. But if she was willing to offer him a place here, she was also willing to share her secrets, if he knew how to ask.

"What happened last month, Maria?"

The Abbess' laughter was like music, and Carlos found himself wondering if any of the women here sang the hours.

I have spent my entire life listening to the voices of men; softer tones would be another new and pleasant experience.

"You came to us on the waning moon, during a welcome break in the storms. When it last waxed, a traveler raided our stores in the night. But Wellstone Village is haunted by strange spirits, and he did not linger after they began to wail. A storm came in later that night, and we found no traces of him in the light of day. Since then, we have been more or less alone."

Maria's tale of the night's visitor, while amusing, seemed somehow incomplete. It wasn't that she had left something out of the tale, but Carlos felt that there were other aspects to the event—a deeper truth that begged for discovery. It certainly explained some of the caution the other sisters exhibited around him—but not all of it.

He was about to ask another question when the Abbess changed the subject once again.

"Now, Carlos, enough talk of sadness and sickness. I was wondering about your thoughts on Ovid and his fantasies of *Metamorphoses*. Are men truly beasts within, or is there more to it than that?"

Carlos smiled, happy to comply. The Abbess was right: there was a place for him here if he wanted it. Paris, and the fable of Karl Outrikos, would wait. The dead might have their secrets, but all mysteries would be revealed in time.

"My lady, we are all as God made us, no more and no less. We be-come...closer to his love when the Spirit enters us, but I do not think we become beasts in form...."

T HE LIGHT WILL BE PAINFUL AT FIRST. YOU MUST NOT strain your eyes, but instead let them adjust slowly."

Marie Angelique sat with him on his couch, unwinding the bandage holding his eyes closed. The floral scent he'd come to recognize as so uniquely "her" was sharp and distinct in his nose, and along with the bandage, was one of two things that had defined Carlos' world over the past week.

Denied the use of his eyes, he'd become familiar with every sound, smell and object in the room. If need be, he could use this mental picture to walk around, but so far he hadn't needed to go more than a few steps to relieve himself, and even then he'd required assistance. This construct of his imagination was as real to him as the person whose dedication and skill had nursed him through the fever that nearly took his life.

"It will take some time for you to see clearly. First, there will be light and shadow, then outlines, then colors, and then finally clarity. We protected your eyes before the disease could spread—there should be no lasting damage."

Carlos was impressed. Though her voice was muffled for some reason, his nurse, his friend, had described the exact progression he'd read and transcribed many years ago.

In Arabic.

One of Avicenna's students had analyzed the process, and from his own experience Carlos knew the record was difficult to translate. Having observed the stages of recovery himself, he could doubly attest to her statement's accuracy.

But those words, those exact words, are the ones I wrote down as a boy. How has she come by them? And more importantly, who else here has read my work?

No matter the source, Marie Angelique's assessment was correct. His world went from darkness to light as she removed the last rounds of bandages. Only two squares of cloth remained, and as she gently plucked them from his eyes, there was no longer any barrier between him and the room he'd imagined so completely.

Slowly, his eyes adjusted to a spare and simple room lit by low candles, a reality altogether unlike the one he'd created out of sound alone. And like in Plato's cave, the differences between manufactured reality and truth were many.

The blurry walls at the edge of his vision were dressed in thick blankets, but from the few glimpses of simple wood he could make out Carlos reasoned that this building had been raised quickly. But he could not hear the wind outside, and given the Abbess' descriptions of the enclave's origin, Carlos would not be surprised if the structure was at least partially buried to give additional warmth in cold, Gallic winters. It was also softer in design and more comfortably appointed than his cell in the Abbey. He could see no other cots or tables like those in his own house of healing, so he decided this must be a private chamber or one set aside for visitors.

As his vision sharpened, a black-clad shape rose and retreated from the low couch. It flowed through the room, past the charcoal burner whose position he'd marked on his first day. From where the shape stopped in the shadows, Marie Angelique's voice was muffled but still recognizable.

"Now test your legs. If you feel well enough, stand using the furniture to steady yourself."

Carlos leaned forward to find his strength. While he brimmed with energy, his legs had forgotten how to use it after only a few days of bed-rest.

Marie Angelique's chair was much closer to the couch than predicted, and Carlos smiled at her preparation for this moment. Carlos pulled it closer, glad that his arms were in slightly better condition than his legs. He felt the coiled anticipation inside him flood throughout his body, giving him a brief boost of strength.

Viewing the room from his normal height, he added more information to his growing store. The couch he'd occupied for the last few days was comprised of a thick red cushion on a solid wood frame, covered by a boiled white sheet and a wool blanket. Another pile of bedding sat near a small fire contained in a low hearth to his left. At its side was a chest painted in bright colors and odd scripts that seemed somehow familiar.

He wanted to know more about it, but of more interest to him was his nurse. Marie Angelique stood in the room's only shadowed corner, outside overlapping circles of light cast by candles, an oil lamp, and the hearth. She was perhaps a foot shorter than himself—something else his mental construct had not predicted. But even that assessment was suspect, as the darkness seemed to swallow her up. Only the sound of her voice and her unique scent betrayed her presence.

Interesting.

"Sister, I thank you. Your skills have saved my sight and restored the strength to my body."

"Do not push yourself. No walking for today. Just stand and relax for as long as you can."

As his vision improved, Carlos looked closer at his friend. The shadowed corner she'd chosen was in fact a doorway, and as he focused on her face, he was surprised that he saw neither a badly burned woman nor the bright smile of his imagination.

The dark veil she wore explained her muffled words and made his thoughts of looking on her injuries moot.

If she wishes to hide from me, it is her choice. Better to let the matter rest and have her speak of it in her own way. I should use this time instead to learn more about Marie Angelique's other unique qualities.

"Sister, the Abbess has spoken to me of an opportunity—a chance to stay among you for a while and impart some of my knowledge to those who wish it. I intend to do so, and was wondering if you would assist me further during my time here."

"What is it you would have of me?"

Her voice behind the cloth sounded uncertain—almost

frightened. In the dim light, what he could see of her body language suggested she was about to flee, so Carlos hurried his request.

"Your family's quest—the search for the Yee relics. I wish to assist in it, but to do so I should speak the language of your ancestors and read it as well. Will you let my eyes be your eyes, since you have worked so hard to preserve them?"

Have I lost her? Are those tears behind the cowl?

"What is wrong? Have I offended in some way?"

"No. No you have not. But you will need much training before you can read the histories or even the simpler forms in the herb scrolls. Unless you stay a season or more, your kindness is wasted on me."

Laughter, perhaps. But there is a catch in her throat—a hesitation not there before.

"I will be staying and teaching those who would learn. I may take no payment for doing so, especially from those who cannot offer it. But if tomorrow we might speak in your language, I would consider it a great gift. As much as I have heard it of late, Provençal can be tiresome, and I do believe it will be wholly inadequate to the tale of the Yee Hero."

Drawing on his time with Frances, Carlos tried to inject a warmth into his words that might set her more at ease. Marie Angelique spoke a word he did not recognize, a multisyllabic wonder that indicated even more complexity than he'd suspected in her language. Whether he was successful at calming her fears he couldn't say, as she turned away and seemed to walk through the wall.

A moment later, a heavy curtain fell back into place and the unseen door became a wall once more.

So that's how the Abbess does it. Maria of Treve has one fewer secret now, and I another mission to perform. One far more rewarding than my research would have been.

Carlos eased himself into the chair, sad that his weakness forced him to rest so soon after regaining his mobility. But his mind was also occupied by the implications of Marie Angelique's exit. He was not in an isolated building after all, but in a chamber set aside within a larger structure.

Carlos stared at the thick rug under his bare feet. It was knotted in the Persian style, and the chair he sat on was of a type he'd seen in Toledo. It was hand carved of heavy oak, a tree that grew in northern forests. The couch on which he had rested for so many days seemed puny in comparison, and was of a much lighter wood and rougher construction.

Looking around the room, Carlos cataloged the various pieces. None seemed to match, but they clearly had not been constructed here.

And where is here, exactly?

Carlos rose from the chair, only to kneel on the intricately constructed rug. There was a bit of padding to it, but years of kneeling on stone floors told him that not all was as it seemed. Searching with his hands, he found the edge of the rug underneath the couch along with the cool stone beneath it.

Blessed Stone, indeed. Where have you brought me, Lord, that my saviors hide underground?

Underground...

Carlos stood, careful not to rise too fast. His attention was riveted on the low hearth that heated the chamber, where a small bed of charcoal marked the remains of a much larger fire. Looking up, he saw no smoke curling overhead, and his curiosity deepened.

Slowly making his way to the hearth, he listened for sounds from the passage Marie Angelique had used to leave. His footsteps were silent as he crossed the room, so he didn't expect to hear much from beyond the heavy curtain separating him from the rest of this hidden enclave.

The hearth was deeper than those Carlos was used to, and the stone was smooth and unmarked. The coals were too warm for him to do a more thorough inspection, but when he used an iron tool to poke at them, small sparks and a bit of smoke rose directly up and out of his sight.

There must be a natural chimney of some kind. One more mystery of the Blessed Stone for me to solve at a later date. For now, I should rest and decide what I can share about this place with Matthieu.

The rhythms of Carlos' body told him it was at least afternoon, if not later. It didn't seem like it was time for the Vespers, but Carlos ran through words of the office anyway to settle his mind.

When he was finished, he reviewed his exchange with Marie Angelique and wondered what, if anything, she was sharing of their conversations with the Abbess. He'd made his first decision as a Father of the Church, and he hoped it would be remembered as a good one. But more importantly, he'd accepted responsibility toward students he'd never met, and that made him very happy indeed. It had been some time since he'd taught children, and the thought of learning a new language had its own appeal.

Tomorrow will be a good day, I think—the first of many. I hope I'm equal to the Abbess's expectations, but something tells me that if I'm not, I'll know soon enough.

After all, where else do I have to be?

Matthieu,

Today, I learned the tale of the Yan emperor, known as Shennong, and the personage credited with inventing both farming and pharmacology in the lands of Huixia. On certain days, Shennong would taste over seventy different compounds, identifying each and the plants from which they came. Along with his counterpart, the Yellow Emperor, he created the culture from which my friend Marie Angelique came to us.

After a month of effort, I have barely mastered the characters and concepts presented in just this one volume. To become a student again, after so long as the teacher, is refreshing beyond belief...

LIFE IN RURAL FRANCE WAS MUCH DIFFERENT FROM Carlos' experiences in Barcelona. For one, there was more snow. A thick, heavy blanket of white that did not lift as the sun rose above twisted and bare trees each day. Had his horse not brought him here, the pair might not have made it to Paris through this frozen landscape.

However it found the path, whatever trail or impulse it had followed through the storm, his equine companion had known precisely what was necessary to bring them here. And here it would stay, to enjoy a well-earned retirement from a life of hardship and war.

You are the wiser of us by far, my friend. You wait out the day in the warmth of the caves below, while I must trudge along this path to earn my keep.

The crunch of snow under his feet was a cruel contrast to the gleaming sun overhead. While it did little to dispel the chill, it shone down and filled the cold air with miniature diamonds. Carlos paused to shade his eyes, scanning around him for his duty.

In Sant Cugat, an additional layer such as a cloak was usually sufficient to keep away the worst of chills. The winters he knew as a boy in Toledo were uniformly mild, and apart from the occasional cold spell, no other protection was necessary for the students other than to come inside out of the rain.

Here at the Blessed Stone, he'd traded his cassock for more practical garments, including sturdy, oiled boots and wool stockings for his feet. After so many years in sandals or completely unshod, Carlos found the sensation of something covering his toes a strange one.

The rule of Saint Benedict allowed for this change in dress, just as it allowed him reasonable expenses while traveling. Carlos had rejected offers of warmer clothing from a grateful tailor in Ruri, and that lack of foresight had nearly been his undoing. Now free from the need to purchase lodgings for a time, Carlos gladly exchanged some of the coins he'd saved over the years on new attire.

As expected, Maria de Fuentes refused them until Carlos reminded her of the additional supplies he would need to establish a school.

Three weeks of lessons had been beneficial for the timid, cautious residents of the Blessed Stone. The recovery chamber that Carlos had mistaken for a private dwelling was but one underground space in a cleverly hidden complex of caves and had now been retasked as a classroom.

The rude walls were merely a facade constructed around a fortuitous natural flue that permitted fires to burn safely and carried away smoke. Several such chambers existed in the enclave, and the one he briefly called home was mainly used for newcomers of another kind.

The small community housed over a hundred souls: women cast out by intolerant men or villages who were unwilling to help families without support or unions not blessed by the Church.

While Carlos himself had never known physical love, union of the spirit was easy enough to understand, and he was very cognizant as to the results of both. It had been some time since he had given instruction to children; Robere had come to him already educated and prepared to learn. Smiling faces and laughter filled his mornings and afternoons—a significant departure from his former routine of transcription, devotion, healing, and prayer.

Today, Carlos walked above ground in deep snow, and his new boots were very welcome indeed. His small charges replayed imagined battles, lobbing missiles of cold, balled snow at one another, keeping score in a game seemingly without rules.

Carlos enjoyed this time as well. The boys at the Academy were never so happy, even when led by Matthieu's unquenchable spirit and laughter. He had never known this kind of life—such freedom to simply...be. It was a good feeling—one that brought laughter to his heart.

And, as the children who ran with him were fast learning, his healed arms and legs were very strong. Carlos never missed with one of his throws, and as large a target as he presented, he was even faster moving out of the path of their tosses than he was in returning them.

Over hours of practice, he'd mastered the feat of catching and returning the very same frozen missiles aimed at him, bringing a new level to their game that delighted the children to no end.

Perhaps it was the contrast of this new life, but every breath he took these days seemed sharper and more effective. After an afternoon with the children, he did not feel winded, and his renewed heartbeat hardly ever quickened with exertion. This was his Physical Faith now, and he felt his body grow stronger with each passing day.

Carlos' senses were also more acute and directed since his recovery. He at first took it to be overcompensation after being without the use of his eyes, but this new definition to his world had not faded in the weeks since his recovery. His ears caught sounds so soft they were almost imagined, and with each breath his nostrils thrilled at the discovery of new and different smells.

There. Pierre and Louisa, conspiring to attack me from behind a clever wall constructed of snow. The faintest memory of summer still clings to the pressed flowers she carries with her everywhere, the scent mingled with sweat and dirt and anticipation. Soon another mad hunt through the afternoon snow will begin.

Jean-Claude and Magnus approached in similar fashion from the left, whispering. Carlos imagined the sound of their hearts beating madly as they tensed to attack.

Wait. What is that?

Carlos walked past their ambush with arms held loosely at his sides, sniffing at the air. There was an odd smell on the wind—something familiar, but still foreign. He'd caught small tastes of it in the past few weeks, and still was not certain what to make of the strange odor.

He slowed his steps, seeking some clue to the source of his unease. A cracking branch drew his attention to a stand of trees many paces ahead of the children's snow wall.

In hills surrounding Barcelona, winter would have given up its hold on the countryside long before now. The trees were probably already producing leaves, his vines ready for the care that would reward the abbey with grapes later in the season. Even in the worst of years, the snow would have burned away under clear skies and coastal sun. It was as if time had stopped while he and the Blessed Stone waited beneath the earth, starting up again when he and the children began their frozen battles.

But no child armed with weapons of ice had made that sound.

From a frozen bough fell a dark form, and the odd smell came from the same general location.

As he moved forward to investigate, four cold, wet impacts exploded against his head and back, finding the inside of his warm coat.

Carlos fell back into the snow, signaling his surrender to

the leaping and laughing children while keeping a portion of his attention on the broken tree.

"I am vanquished. A moment, my young friends, while I recover."

Carlos hid his concern with a smile. There was something very wrong about this place, and he needed to get the children away from here. Luckily, they were only too happy to turn on one another and run in the opposite direction when he shooed them away.

Listening to their happy screams and laughter, he rose and approached the dark shape he feared would require the use of his other, more spiritual skills.

Settling into the snow at the base of the tree were the remnants of a man. Or the beginnings, depending on one's point of view. This was no more than a boy—a youth not much older than the innocent children playing behind him.

The corpse was definitely the source of the smell that had distracted him from the games of his charges. It was musty, earthy, like a pile of mouldering leaves. Soiled clothing was frozen to cold, dead skin that clearly showed signs of infection. There was something tantalizingly familiar about the face, even mottled by angry red blisters on black-blotched white skin.

But the things that most drew Carlos' attention were a golden crucifix around the boy's neck and a soiled tabard clinging to his wasted body, upon which was the white and black design of a Hospitaller.

A follower of St. John—a knight of the Crusades. The war has claimed yet another victim, even now robbing the world of light many months after its end.

Sometime in the night, this boy had gone on to his reward, not knowing that there were friends beneath his feet.

Or perhaps earlier? Carlos turned the body, which was heavy and solid. He could not remember how long it took to freeze a body all the way through, but he also didn't know how cold it had been in the heart of last night's storm.

Had I not reached the Blessed Stone when I did, this fate would have been my own. The pox did not kill this boy, but winter took advantage of its invitation. His face seems far too young to have gone to war, and yet there is something about it...

Looking back to his charges, Carlos knew what he had to do. Covering the body with snow, he marked the tree in his memory and made a further record upon its bark. The ground was too cold for digging, but he would return here later today with the Abbess to tend to the knight's soul. The man's effects could wait until a thaw to be interred, but if wood might be spared, the body should be destroyed sooner, rather than later.

The children should not be exposed to this sight. Their lives are moving fast enough at present.

"Come, children. We have finished our exercise for to-day. Gather your things, and we will see who can run fastest though the snow."

A fusillade of ice and laughter met his suggestion. He dodged all of the children's missiles, drawing even more screams of delight. Then he started running, hoping the chill air would carry away the smell of rot.

Several more balls of ice and snow sailed after him, but they were much slower than his feet. As he sailed around a corner, he thought of the cold corpse—of a life ended so close to its beginning.

The boy should have had more time. So much more...

When he could no longer hear the children's laughter, Carlos slowed his steps so that they might catch up. Turning, he was surprised to find them nowhere in sight and only his own light footprints marking a path down the hillside through the snow.

Carlos tensed for a dash back up the slope, worried that the children's curiosity might have drawn them to the tree after all.

Then: "Faster!" came Magnus' cracking voice. Snow flew as one child, then two, pushed through the snow at the crest of the hill.

Not lost, just slow. Their smaller legs must have had trouble moving in the deeper snow on the other side.

"Carlos, Carlos! Wait for us!" Magnus tripped and rolled down the frozen hillside. The others delighted in this new game, throwing themselves down the slope after him with abandon.

At the base, Carlos helped them up and brushed snow from smiling faces, all the while thinking about the boy he'd buried under a blanket of ice and what games he might have known in his too-short childhood. Looking into the eyes of his students, he hoped the knight had at least found some peace at the end.

30 APRIL, YEAR OF OUR LORD 1205

"THIS WAY, MARIA. I MARKED THE TREE."
Carlos indicated the stand to the left, but did not mention what had drawn him unerringly to this spot. It was hard enough to rationalize in his own mind how he could follow the dark, spoiled scent of the dead body through still air to the resting place he'd made under a thick barrier of snow. Explaining an otherwise undetectable smell to his companion would take a skill at deception he neither had nor wanted.

"Very good, very good. The coming storm will not wait for us to finish, and unless you carry me, I believe our return home will take longer than our ascent."

The Abbess was a fit woman, but the lingering chill did not sit well on her. And though Carlos carried kindling on his back and pulled a sled of dried wood behind him, the much smaller burden Maria carried still slowed her considerably.

Carlos looked up at the gathering clouds and had to agree with Maria—they would stay neither calm nor distant for long. Already black and heavy, they promised another week of intense cold weather, during which the Blessed Stone would hide underground and dream of the open sky. Today would likely be the only one in the near future when Carlos and the Abbess could deal with the knight's corpse.

Carlos set down the bundle of straw and kindling beside the sled, and moved beneath the bare limbs of the tree. Guided by memory and his sensitive nose, he chopped at the packed snow with his hands, remembering fondly the more powdery variety with which he'd covered the body.

The last brush of his hand uncovered the head and face of the corpse. The skin was black and shrunken, as if already exposed to the fire in which they planned to dispose of it. The smell was nearly overpowering now—not the scent of a corpse but something more earthy in nature that reminded Carlos of grapes too long on the vine, or vat leavings after the wine had been casked and moved away.

The corpse's face no longer spawned pity in his heart. It was little more than a wrapped skull now, its sad blue eyes replaced with dull white orbs. A shadow moved over the body, and it took Carlos a moment to recognize it as that of the Abbess.

"This child will suffer no more. Thank you for bringing me, Carlos, as I thank God daily for bringing you to us. In these past few weeks you have done more than just teach our children and their mothers. You have brought back hope—hope that there are men such as yourself left in the world who believe in honor and kindness."

"Thank you, Sister. But I am not the exemplar of such virtues. This man here who fought for the church might have been one such, but he also was no saint. These men, all men, whatever their faults, are still possessed of God's grace."

"This is not the time or place for such a conversation, my friend, but as you travel, you will find that grace in ever shorter supply. Let us send this soul on to its reward, and then we must make haste back to the Blessed Stone."

Carlos had a definite sense that she disapproved. She'd offered him a compliment, and instead of thanking her he'd allowed his experience with bandits earlier in the year to color his response.

Another transgression for which I can offer no apology.

While Carlos excavated the body, the Abbess constructed a bier. Carrying the corpse over, he swallowed his shame and focused on the man they both wished to honor.

Carlos tried to arrange the body in some semblance of calm repose, but the frozen arms had contorted during the days since he'd covered it in snow, and clawed hands caught and tore at fabric of his clothing.

It took a moment to disengage himself, during which the golden cross he'd noted the previous week slipped from around the knight's neck and landed in the snow, followed by a small iron dagger which fell from somewhere inside the boy's clothing. Carlos bent to retrieve both items, folding them carefully in a square of white cloth before placing the bundle in his coat.

Standing, he took a deep breath more from habit than need, and a rush of the body's cloying odor entered his nose and mouth. Carlos stifled a gagging cough as he draped a worn sheet over the remains, but the smell clung to him as he stepped away as if it had somehow leeched into his skin.

Carlos looked down at his hands. They were clean and unblemished, though a bit pale from the digging. He reached for the clay pot at his waist containing the embers meant to light the funerary pyre. It warmed his fingers, but that feeling did not penetrate to his soul.

Carlos coughed again, and his head spun with momentary dizziness. The world spun with it, and Carlos felt as if he was being dragged down a long, dark tunnel.

From somewhere far away, Maria speaks over the dead knight, asking forgiveness for his sins in life. It is a benediction Carlos knows by heart, but the Abbess imbues every word with a certainty he is sure he could never offer a stranger. Whoever this boy was, whatever he has done in life, he is no longer their responsibility. He is ready to move on to God.

Someone who looks like Carlos moves forward, removing the lid from the pot and touching the embers inside to the dry straw. Hungry flames spring to life, rushing around the bier until it is fully engulfed.

The two watch the fire rise and consume the body. Black smoke rises into the sky to merge with the storm clouds overhead.

The scent was stronger than ever, and as the body and its soiled trappings burned away Carlos shuddered, almost collapsing until Maria, mistaking his discomfort for emotion, rested a hand on his shoulder for support.

Carlos was glad she did. Whatever was affecting him was

entirely outside his understanding. The pox had been the most traumatic and damaging experience of his life, but he at least knew what had caused it. An enfeebling smell was on another level entirely from the sickness they hoped to eradicate by burning this body.

The moment passed, and with it his weakness. Carlos turned to regard his companion, and though his mind was racing he could find no words to say to her. She smiled, squeezing his shoulder.

A gust of wind sent ashes and sparks flying from the bier and whipped the flames into long fingers reaching for the slumbering trees. Carlos stooped and gathered a large arm-load of snow—an uncontrolled fire was a danger far greater than some phantom smell.

The fire flared, and instead of yellow-orange flames, a cold blue light erupted from the bier as the knight's body collapsed in on itself. Carlos had little time to wonder about this, for even as he deposited his armload of snow, Maria charged after errant embers before they could start secondary blazes. The monk added another armload of snow, and another, until a foul-smelling cloud of steam surrounded him completely.

Coughing, Carlos staggered back, stars forming in front of his closed eyes with each hacking breath. A heavy cloak fell over his shoulders, and wiry arms embraced him until the fit stopped.

"Come, Carlos. Our work here is done, with no permanent damage to these trees. We can return here when the snows lift and remember this man with a more permanent marker."

The Abbess' voice was rough, and Carlos opened his eyes and saw tears streaming down her lined face.

Nodding, he was able to stand with her assistance, but the motion made his head spin and he nearly fell back into the snow. Maria was a rock, supporting his weight and keeping him on his feet. Carlos could not help but laugh at the thought of how they might look to an observer, though it tore his throat and chest.

"And here...you thought...I would...have to...carry...you back."

The clouds choose that moment to release their own burdens of snow, and as the air filled with soft white flakes the two servants of God trudged back to their hidden enclave sharing a single dry cloak.

Carlos spared one last look behind them and was surprised to see how quickly and completely a blanket of white had covered their tracks. Only a single patch of blackness remained above a refilled grave, high on the trunk of a barren tree where a branch had once been.

CARLOS HUDDLED IN HIS CHAMBER, A HEAVY BLANKET draped across his shoulders while he sat on his couch and inhaled deeply of the herb-scented steam Qin Yee favored for recovery. Although filling his lungs with something besides air seemed foolish, he'd had extensive experience with this particular treatment since his arrival and couldn't argue with her choice.

Candles burned around the room, and a fire was burning merrily in the hearth. Maria huddled beside it in a blanket, sipping broth.

Carlos' hands and feet were still cold even after many hours of rest. The familiar folds of his cassock were meant for a much warmer climate, and he had no other dry clothes here in the Blessed Stone.

Upon their return, Carlos and the Abbess sequestered themselves, taking care to avoid unnecessary contact with any of the enclave's residents. Both healers knew that exposure to the elements allowed sickness to attack an otherwise healthy body, and the mounds of snow dumped on their backs while they walked had done them few favors.

Plus, while the sight of two community leaders shivering after a foolish romp through a storm was an excellent reminder of why not to do so, it was hardly a dignified public appearance.

And dignity is something of which I have short supply these days.

Ever since the bandit attack on Sant Cugat—no, since

the mystery of Karl Outrikos first fired his imagination—
emotion, not reason, had selected his actions, often with no
thought to those around him.

To date, there had been no penalty. In fact, he had been
rewarded for each transgression.

And while my faith is unaffected, my fidelity is in question.

In his hands was a solid reminder of why he must hold on
to it at all costs. A golden chain from which dangled a shining
cross. It was a simple, unornamented symbol, nothing like the
gaudy displays the Bishop of Barcelona favored.

With no home, no coins, and no food, the knight had kept
this reminder of his Faith and devotion until his death, when
at any time he could have exchanged it for comfort and ease.

Carlos thought of the knotted leather cord around his neck
which supported a cross of simple black wood. He'd made
both during his first summer at Sant Cugat, and wondered if
it was worth more or less than the one in his hand?

*Faith is a commodity not measured or traded between men,
and what little there is in the world cannot be replaced by coins.
I have met many men without it, and the former knights who
attacked my home had surely abandoned theirs long before they
began raiding.*

*Where did their Faith go? What happened to them out here in
the world, where temptations are subtle and so numerous? Did
their fall from grace begin with a surrender to desire, by following
the impulses of the moment?*

"Something occupies you beyond simple contemplation,
my friend. It is a beautiful piece."

The Abbess left her place by the hearth and dragged her
chair with her so she might sit by his side. Carlos had heard
that tone in her voice before, and in similar words spoken by
Father Frances. It was an invitation to speak freely, without
fear or judgment. An offer of counsel, from one accustomed
to listening.

Carlos hesitated before speaking, focusing instead on the
feel of the chain as it slipped over his chilled fingers. The gold
had absorbed warmth from the chamber when he had not,
and Carlos let a smile crease his lips at the irony.

"This cross was his life. It meant more to him than a night

in a bed or a full belly. More than family, companionship, or the clothes on his back. He was sick, with the same illness that I survived, that I have treated in so many others."

Carlos stared at the gold necklace in his hand. It was shadowed from the hearth by his palm, but the candle flames shed enough light so that it danced as if made of liquid fire. The Abbess offered no comment on his statement, waiting for him to finish.

"His fate could have been mine. I still do not know how I came to be here, my lady Abbess. A month has passed, and I can remember no more of the journey than I did in those first moments after awakening.

"I do not remember leaving the hostel, or what caused me to do so. But for an accident of fate, the man—the boy who held this cross—could have been the one you brought back to health. He could be here in my place, holding my wooden cross in his hand."

Maria tutted, and leaned forward to catch his eye. Carlos lifted his gaze from the cross to her weathered face and found himself unable to look away from the intensity in her eyes.

"Why does that bother you, Carlos? You are here—that is enough for us. You are alive—that should be enough for you. If I were asked to choose between you and him, I would choose you. No, do not object, I say it without prejudice or doubt."

The Abbess fixed him with a stare. He searched her face for a rebuke, but found only the same kind smile he had come to know so well since regaining his sight.

"Your life has meaning, Carlos. Beyond your service to God, more than your skills as a doctor or as a teacher. In you is the best of us—the qualities to which all men and women should aspire.

"And in you is the worst of us. The same feelings that drive men to hate, to hurt, to kill. To live is to feel. Good, bad—all of it has meaning and weight.

"Since you have been here, you have shown us all of the good in you, and none of the bad. I know it is there—I know how you labor against it. I have watched you struggle with the dreams you cannot remember. I have seen the pain on your face when you confront a sick patient you cannot help.

"You are a good man who takes responsibility for others— but you often forget that your first duty is to yourself."

"Why? Why do you believe in me, when I continue to disappoint?"

The Abbess shook her head and reached out a hand to rest on his knee.

"Oh, Carlos, you do not disappoint me—not in the slightest. You are as God made you, as are we all. Your arrival was no accident—you were sent here. You were the man we needed, whether we knew it or not. Had this boy shown up at our door, we would have treated him as best we could and assisted him with travel to another place.

"But we would not have asked him to stay and become one of us."

Maria's words were powerful and went far beyond a simple declaration of faith. The fire burning in the hearth behind her surrounded her face with a halo of orange light, almost equal to the joy in her eyes.

And it would seem she is not finished adding fuel to that fire.

"Carlos, do you recall your first words to me?"

Carlos shook his head, still unable to look away from her face.

"I am sorry, Sister, I do not."

"You arrived in our midst quite unexpectedly. Both you and the horse that bore you were near death, lashed by the elements far worse than we were this afternoon. You fell into the arms of the Blessed Stone and told us to send you away for our own safety.

"And then, upon awakening, you asked after your mount with such forceful concern that you nearly choked. We huddle here now against the chill because you wanted to give a man you had never met a proper burial before he could be savaged by animals. You charged at a burning fire with an armful of snow so that service did not burn down trees, an occurrence that happens daily across the world with no help or assistance from anyone.

"Do you think that your penniless crusader would have

done these things? Be honest with yourself, Carlos, as I am with you. For without your example I would not have done them, and I am far wearier from the world than I appear."

The Abbess' hand came up from his knee and closed over both his fingers and the cross. At her touch his hands finally felt warm, and he drew what strength he could from her. He breathed slowly, thinking about what she was saying and the things that he had not.

His life kept changing, and he was ill-equipped to face it. The Bishop had warned him of this before he left Barcelona, but Carlos had thought it a caution about the temptations of Paris. He'd thought he understood his patron's words at the time, but only now could he truly appreciate them.

My friends keep offering me their support when I stumble, regardless of any self-perceived faults. This is my life now, for better, or for worse. The abbey of Sant Cugat du Valles is behind me, and before it can be mine again I must come to terms with the world.

And with the help of my newest friends, perhaps I will succeed.

Carlos was surprised to find himself lying down, with Maria's hand still closed over his own. The hard shape of the crucifix in his palm was a reassuring reminder of who and what he was, and the woman sitting next to him was an example of everything he wanted to be.

His breath came easier, and he felt comfortable and welcome by her side. Closing his eyes, he set aside his burden for a time and slipped into oblivion.

The night is cold, but the chase keeps him warm. The stars light his way, outlining a countryside he will never see by the light of day. There is no moon, but he does not need its witness to his end.

They will catch him soon, and he is glad of it. He has been running too long, too far. He is not even sure where "here" is, but moving forward means staying alive.

Behind him is a terrible but well-deserved end. The others have found him—as they always do—after chasing him for so long through the hills in which he has chosen to die.

He is the last one now, the youngest, the fastest, the recipient of the wisdom and experience of the rest of his company. The rest met their end easily, in the hands of gentle captors. They cheated the others of their revenge, and now he has inherited all of their fury.

His eyes see well enough in the darkness, but theirs are better. They can track him forever and never tire. They will have their vengeance for what he and his brothers have done, for what they have taken. As long as he keeps running, keeps fighting, they are focused in one direction: his. And that works out well for everyone.

Everyone else, that is.

A dark shape from the left draws his eye, a group of tree standing tall in an otherwise bleak landscape. He senses life within them, waiting for the warm sun he will never see again.

His feet pound the ground, and his ragged boots do little to absorb the impact as he runs. His armor and sword are long gone, abandoned in a foreign land as he and his brothers fled the field.

Traitors, Cowards, Deserters. These are the names with which they were branded. Those who did so do did not know the secrets they guarded—what sacrifices were made to complete their mission. The prize was delivered, but their mission—his mission—will not end until the others were satisfied.

It won't be long now. The hunt is nearly over.

The long miles had other consequences. They became that which they fought against; blended into a background of thieves and murderers that painted the lands they had once walked as free men. They robbed and raided, trying to minimize the damage caused by their less enlightened companions, but there were always casualties.

The war continues, even now.

His nose finds a hint of water ahead. If he can smell it, so can they—and to take a drink, he will need to evade his pursuers temporarily. The trees offer that chance.

He slows his pace, circling widely up the hillside. The boots are the first thing discarded, followed by his tunic. The others will not be fooled for long, but he dresses the tree in his unneeded clothing, then rolls and scrubs himself in the sparse grasses and earth at its base.

He feels them, closer now, but still far enough back that his plan might work. All he needs is a taste of that water, enough to keep him going for a few more hours. After that, he can end this chase and complete his mission.

He can die.

The dim landscape flies by under his liberated feet. He has taken nothing with him save for a golden symbol of his devotion he could not bear to leave that behind for the monsters. He follows a winding, scrambling route toward a faint taste of moisture wafting on dry air.

It is not a spring—it is a well. A circle of low buildings surrounds it, and he realizes the fullness of his folly. They will follow him here, and these people will suffer for his sins.

There is no time to drink. They will not be fooled any longer than it takes to discover his clothes, and then they will come looking for him.

Here, where he has led them.

There is no doubt they will find the distant heartbeats he hears. The sounds are distorted, as if echoed from under water or through a long tube. He cannot count them, nor can he place them in these structures. But even one innocent life is too many to endanger with his presence. They will probably be found anyway, given time, but if he delays that discovery with his life, the light of day will protect them.

One of the buildings has a base wooden door. It is not locked, and yields easily, if noisily, to his pull. Inside are tools, hand implements, and empty baskets. This community houses farmers—far more valuable members of society than himself.

There: a knife. A poor weapon against the others, but better than bare hands. Picking it up knocks over a loose stack of wood, and the noise is enough to wake any of the farmers he wants to protect.

There. There is a cry from below, a howling, wailing sound. It is close—too close. He needs to start running. Clutching the knife in his fist, his other hand raises the cross to his lips for one last kiss.

He prays in silence for the souls he has endangered but not his own. Never for himself. He gave his life over long ago into the hands of God so that He may act through him.

He runs, touching lightly with each step, leaving as small a trace behind as possible. His presence here, this place, must remain hidden. When he is far enough away, he steps hard, marking his passage and announcing his flight plainly.

He no longer runs away, but toward. He will run the others down, hunt the hunters until they can find no hiding place from His light. He knows where to start, and if he is to fight the final battle of this hidden war, he will do so wearing the colors and honor of his order.

He will die as he has lived: in the service of the Lord.

Thy Will be done...

7 MAY, YEAR OF OUR LORD 1205

Matthieu,

My study of the life of the Yee Hero continues, and Marie Angelique is most helpful in the translation of that work. It feels good to again return to my duties as an archivist, although the stories of far off Huixia and Shaanxi province are too fantastic for mere words to relate. I fear that my simple retellings are wholly inadequate to the subject matter, and more is contained in the original text than can ever be translated.

The language of her ancestors is laid down in pictures, much like those of Pharaoh's Egypt. We have gained much from our associations with other cultures over the centuries, and my hope is that someday, I can adequately present the stories of Qin Yee's ancestor to a world sorely in need of such hope...

ANOTHER WEEK PASSED WITHOUT THE WARMTH OF the sun, and Carlos found the diversions of the past welcome ones. The renewed snows brought a flux, and the Abbey's healers were hard pressed to keep the younger children alive after a bout of *morbus*, the "child's pox." But then a debilitating wracking cough and accompanying fever stole strength from parents and children alike, disrupting life throughout the enclave. As the subterranean days passed, their tiny island of humanity lost a dozen members.

As the only healthy adults, Carlos, Qin Yee, and Maria had assumed nearly all duties in the Blessed Stone. Tonight's meal was almost prepared, and Qin Yee would be here soon to assist Carlos in serving the simple gruel that fed the enclave in lean times. He was cooking it now in a large cauldron suspended over a merry bed of coals on a heavy iron frame.

Oats and dried fruit, fortified with goat's milk and what spices remained in their supplies. Save for the lack of wine, bread, and cheese, it was very similar to the diet on which he was raised—excellent for filling empty bellies and sustaining a healing body.

The worst of the sickness was behind them, and soon Carlos would put down the cook's ladle and take up again the mantle of instructor. Already the warm laughter of happy children filled the cold stone halls. They would not soon forget their friends, but children were resilient and able to heal the wounds of spirit far better than the adults who loved them.

Death was a function of life—one Carlos knew well. In these last weeks, he had come to love the people of the Blessed Stone as if they were a part of his own soul, a deeper and more intense relationship than he had ever known. The loss of even one part of himself was evident, and he ached to be whole again.

His lifelong friendship with Matthieu was the closest comparison he could draw. But Carlos felt a different connection with these women and with all the lives he tended here. It was as if there were no secrets or lies beneath the earth—only truth.

If this was the Abbot's intention in sending me into the world, it has succeeded beyond all measure. As hard as these losses are to me, they are far worse for Maria and Qin Yee. Where I have been among them for weeks, they have lived here many years, bringing some of those we've lost into the world with their own hands.

Not yet to his twenty-fourth year, Carlos was painfully aware of how few moments in his life stood out from the rest. The Abbess had opened his eyes to the struggle inside him and all men. Here at the Blessed Stone, he'd learned the true meaning of the values he'd tried to impart to his student

Robere.

"Be a good neighbor to your patients. Suffer with them, and through suffering, bring them the grace of Christ our Lord. Let their ills be your own and healed by means of the perfect faith."

These were lessons he'd learned as a child and practiced as a healer, but had never truly understood until now. A man of winter, soul laid bare to the white ice above.

This is what Matthieu feels—it must be.

His brother loved all mankind. Even threatened with the loss of his arm, he'd worked tirelessly to save the lives of those who'd placed an arrow in it.

Matthieu's smiles and laughter would be a better fit here than my silent brooding. If his mother had lived, would she have found her way to Maria de Fuentes? Did the sickness that took her life after his father died in a foreign war rob him of the happiness he would have known here?

Carlos knew only fragments of Matthieu's life before the Academy, but one thing he was sure of was how much his friend missed his parents. It was another way in which the two men differed—Carlos had no memories at all before the Church. The only life he'd ever known was one of service and faith.

What sort of man would I have been, if I'd known my parents? Would I be kind, or cruel? Would I still love learning? Would I still love God?

Carlos could speculate as to other paths his life might have taken, but he could never truly know another person's mind or feelings. And no translated words could bring him that knowledge—even a history as detailed as that of the Yee Hero was missing details. It was up to the imagination of the reader—or in the case of an oral history, the listener—to supply the missing parts from their own experience.

Qin Yee. Matthieu. My closest friends, and both have known much hardship.

He had not spoken much of his Brother to his Sister, not wanting to betray either of their confidences. But they were related now—connected through his life. Both had helped him and given him hope for a better future. Neither asked for anything in return, but if they did, he would offer them anything he had without reservation.

Perhaps this is what being part of a family truly means.

Carlos had always been a private man who led a sheltered life. After arriving at the Blessed Stone, he'd started to come out of that shell, even as Qin Yee withdrew into her own.

He could certainly understand her choice; giving his strength to so many at once was draining. Though the duties here were little different than those at the abbey, the toll they took on him was far greater.

Long hours on his feet and long days in forced isolation left Carlos with an aching head and slow reactions. Not only was he cooking for the entire enclave, but he also carried wood for its fires, washed those too weak from fever to care for themselves, and carried those who would walk no more to their final rest.

With each death, a part of himself was wrapped in a shroud to be laid down in catacombs below. And his next choice was sure to make his heart as heavy as his arms.

When the snows lifted, he must decide whether to continue his mission to Paris and Rome or abandon it in favor of a life here. Faced with so much real suffering, his search for the truth about Karl Outrikos seemed foolish and petty.

The pages of his folio were nearly filled with translations of herb lore, and there was no more parchment with which to record a letter. In any event, a request for guidance sent home to Sant Cugat would arrive far too late to affect his choice.

And some things are best said in person.

It wasn't that Carlos' faith was wavering; his place in the house of God was assured. But the needs of communities such as this one were far more important than advancing his career in the church. The more he thought about it, the more Carlos was sure that such things are best left to men like the Bishop, who counseled popes and kings and might be one himself someday.

Carlos wanted nothing more than to be a healer and a devotee of St. Benedict. To teach, and tend his vines. His investiture was important to him, and he did feel a responsibility to his Brothers in the sunlight world. But there was another life here—another way to exist.

Is this, then, the temptation the Bishop warned against—one of longing and regret? Can I sacrifice the happiness of one community for the future of another? How can one ever know?

The histories he'd studied since childhood wrote that the choice benefiting the largest group was the preferred one, no matter how difficult. His training as a monk offered much the same guidance, but also stressed humility and service. His brothers trusted him—named him as their Father. But could a man have two families? Was such a thing even possible?

Every community needs a leader, and here that leader was Maria de Fuentes. Despite his location, Carlos was still Father Carlos, the next Abbot of Sant Cugat de Valles, and unless he renounced that honor could never be more than a visitor in this community.

Maria said I am the sum of all the good and bad within me, and the result is the man they needed. But how can that be possible, when the greater part of me is pledged elsewhere?

The Bishop had warned him to keep his faith as an armor against those who would challenge it. Frances delaMonde had encouraged him to find truth in the larger world and bring it home.

And Alejandro...

Alejandro...

Alejandro had asked but one thing. That Carlos live without regret.

The rising smell of spice and dried apples signaled that the evening's meal was ready. Carlos added a pinch of salt to balance humors and then covered the cauldron, swinging it away from the heat.

With his hands protected by folds of cloth, Carlos lifted it from the frame and carried it to a nearby table where he and Qin Yee would portion it into smaller containers and distribute it throughout the enclave. Carlos turned to bank the fire for the morning's bread...

The bread...I have not yet made the dough! Where is the flour for the loaves? Brother Tomas carried it in just yesterday...

Where...

The heat of the fire made working in the kitchen a favorable duty in these cold winter months, and...

And...

...it hurts so much to breathe...to move. The sheets are soaked with her efforts to rise, but today she cannot do it. This is the end of their journey, and her heart aches at the thought of her son living without her.

Or his father. Everything they owned—everything they had left—is here in this room. He has been gone so long—so many months serving the command of his captain.

She can still see him smiling in the sun on top of his magnificent horse.

She sees his back retreating down an ancient road to fight an enemy she does not know in a place she has never been.

She hears his promise to her, to their child.

"Wait for me, Marie. My heart and my love. I will come back to you when our campaign is finished and the righteous rule the Kingdom of Acre. Every night when the sun sets, I will look West and see your love looking back at me. In the mornings, I will wake with your name on my lips and turn my head to see your face bring life back to the world.

"When I return, my swords will rest, never again raised to war. My fighting will be over, and I will dwell forever in your love."

Her head burns, her heart flutters and fights to keep beating. Her arms are black, wasted and thin. Her love waits for her on the sea to the South—she need only to reach him in time.

She has to rise and join the rest of the wives as the caravan travels to meet the swords of the Faith, home from their war.

If she does not rise, who will be there to love her son?

If she does not rise, who will be there to bury her husband?

Who will, who would...

The light outside grows, and her love comes back to her, even as the blackness rises. The door opens, and footsteps approach the bed. Hands press a cold cloth to her head, and she feels love in the darkness.

"Jean-Paul? You have returned to me—to us? They told us... you were..." The breath leaves her, rasping and final. She is lifted up to a place of no more pain.

There is only love.

"Maman? Maman!"

"Carlos? Carlos, are you well?"

Far away voices. Are the angels speaking? Perhaps after a brief rest...they will...they would...

"Carlos, please, please stay with me now. You have struck your head, and you are not well. Come with me now—you must be cared for."

Small hands pulled at him, lifting him from the warm stones. The scent of lavender, roses, sunshine, and love filled the air.

Of friendship, and of family, and a welcome voice heralding the dawn.

Marie.

No, Marie Qin. My angel. When did she grow so strong, to carry me so? And how can we fly so fast without any wings...?

Beyond the fires, he hears the others moving. Within the circle of light, as many as can be protected are huddled around the flames, grasping at each other for some semblance of security. There are too many—far too many—judged "clean of life and limb" for an effective perimeter.

Yet here they stand. Set in their places by the priests, handed spears and shields, with no discussion about what to do next. Everything of relevance was said before the sun set fully over the horizon.

Before they put out the unclean and infirm.

Brothers, sisters, fathers, and daughters alike. To survive in this place requires hard, unpopular choices. Everyone within the circle prays silently for the others to survive the night.

Everyone at its edge prepares themselves to kill their fellow pilgrims if they attempt to breach the camp, in defiance of the Word.

He tries not to think of his brother, unable to stand on a broken and splinted leg, back raw and bleeding from the overseers' whips. He did not complain, offered no comment other than one last look up as he was set down in the most secure spot available. A rude knife and a skin of too-scarce water were all they left him to battle the darkness.

The spear in his hands is heavy. If he could, the sentinel would cast it aside and find his brother in the night. This is not right, no *matter what the brothers say. This place will be their undoing; this madness of segregation accomplishes nothing but to divide the tribes further.*

Where can they possibly go from here? Back is not an option.

Forward is nothing but sand and sun. This land has no promise, and whatever place the setting sun finds them tomorrow will be no better than today's landscape. This feeling the brothers follow, the call from the wilderness they alone hear, is forcing the people ever onward over blasted and barren earth.

The wood of the shaft is dry and cracked from the hot agony of day. Honeyed drops and smoked fowl do little for the men asked to hold vigil, and his throat is as parched and splintered as the weapon pressing into the skin of his palms.

A knocking sound beckons from the darkness. Ears straining for another impression, his eyes find no difference in the night—nothing not imagined there before.

The demons were not left behind with their chains. They followed the people out of captivity, eating away at their lives no matter what precautions they take.

To his left, Matthias watches his own patch of blackness but gives no indication that he hears anything amiss. To his right, Benjamn shirks his duty by staring back into the camp, hoping to catch sight of fire-haired Rebekah. The boy is as much a danger as the darkness, but every able body must stand watch.

There. Something moves beyond the firelight. Friend or foe is not a distinction he can make from this side of the line. Something scratches against the ground in a darkness stars do not penetrate. A murmured whisper calls to him for assistance.

Which of them is it? Is it his brother crying out from the pain of his wounds? One of the women, whose only fault is the moon overhead? The lepers, whose bodies betray them with every breath?

Does it really matter? This boundary they enforce is nothing more than a line in the barren sand drawn with words by two mad prophets.

The true danger to the tribes lies inside the circle, not out in the night.

He can have no more part of it. This madness must end.

There is no land of promise beyond the next hill of sand. There was life back by the river—one where families were not separated by ignorance. Hard, sometimes brutal, but each day had a measure of safety to it, however scant.

Certainly no one was advocating a return to slavery. But they'd traded sanity for security. There were places that could support life here in the sands—places passed by and abandoned once the landless nation slaked their thirst. There was more than enough to support those they'd cast out, so why had they been denied the light and warmth of the fires at his back?

Benjamn and Matthias are occupied with their own thoughts. He cannot depend on their assistance—they have no loved ones to care for beyond the line. Nothing calls to them, asks them for release from this second exile.

One step over the line, and he is committed. The spear is lighter in his hands, his spirit cleansed of doubt. His head held high as he searches for the sounds of suffering. A second step, and he is surrounded by the darkness, removed from the influence and "protection" of the brothers and their mad quest.

He is finally free.

Freedom is cold, a bone-deep chill that comes on too suddenly to be explained by leaving the circle of light. It is as if spring were regressing to winter, rolling back the passage of days and repealing the sentence of unending, burning sunlight.

One last look back to the world he leaves behind. But darkness swallows it whole leaving no trace of light and life. Two steps should not have been enough to erase it completely; there is something wrong. Something missing.

Something…moving.

He spins, spear held at the ready as his eyes frantically scan the black night. His mouth moves to shout a warning, but no sound comes forth. He moves back—is it back?—but his sandals are covered with a heavy weight of sand.

Impact. Lines of fire rip down his spine. Wet warmth replaces the cold for an instant, then becomes a river of ice.

The spear seeks but does not find his hidden attacker. It grows heavier with each swing, slicing and stabbing away at the air as it thickens around him.

Another strike finds its way past his shield, and he falls. When his back hits the cold sand, iron claws seize his ankles and begin dragging him away.

There is no time left. No hope for rescue and no one to follow him outside the line.

And when they find his body, no one else will question why.

He drives the spear hard into the earth, holding on with all the fading strength he can muster. With each tug on his legs, the wood splinters in his grasp, until one last, tearing motion yanks him away into the night.

His dying scream freezes in his chest, but through the darkness the sounds of Benjamn's last words echo in his ears.

"Matthias, help me! Help me, Ma..."

MATTHIEU!" THE NAME ERUPTED FROM CARLOS' throat, a desperate cry from the depths of his soul. A firm hand pressed his head back as he tried to rise. His chest pounded, heart racing in an attempt to escape from...from...

Another dream—another life I cannot remember. Oh, how I wish that I could, if only to make sense of nights like...like...

"Rest, Carlos. Sleep. You are safe here—nothing can touch you."

The hand at his brow was small and warm and the words reassuring. A hiss of scented steam filled the air, and the pain in Carlos' chest eased.

"Sleep."

The warmth of the hand spread through his body, as his heartbeat slowed and the world spun away.

Sleep...

10 MAY, YEAR OF OUR LORD 1205

IN THE DIM LIGHT, MARIE ANGELIQUE REFILLED A BRASS censer with dried herbs, then splashed a bit of water over the coals. The steam seemed to help, calming Carlos as he slept.

This man deserves peace. His...their God should offer some assistance. But if he will not, this smoke will have to do....

There was a sound at her back, and Marie Angelique smiled. She knew those footsteps as well as her own, though one blurred shape was much like any other to her.

"I heard. This is worse than the last one, isn't it?"

The Abbess had sat this same vigil many times in the last few days, witnessing with her the trial of spirit the young monk faced. Marie Angelique nodded in agreement.

"He may not see another morning. When he is awake, he barely speaks, and when he does it is in no language I understand. The fire in him burns so hot...but he fights—still he fights."

"He is strong, my child. We have seen it before, and he is still with us. I will not give up on him—not now. He is a part of us, and without him, we are diminished."

Marie Angelique's right hand traced the outlines of Carlos' face, her left resting on his chest to time his heart. She wished she could do something more for him. Even now, his muscles tensed for some great effort only his nightmares could name. After several minutes, she added another handful of herbs to the coals and spoke.

"I have not your faith, but I hear your words. I will sit with him until he no longer has need of me."

"I understand. I will bring more cool water, enough for the both of you. And for myself—for if you will fight with him, so will I."

Marie Angelique nodded again, and as the Abbess' feet retreated she noticed a patch of light on the floor. At first she was afraid it was a coal that had somehow fallen out of the burner, but then she realized what was really bothering her.

It wasn't so much that she was worried about something burning, but more that she was surprised to see anything at all other than the shadowy outlines that defined her life.

She reached her right hand down and found a sliver of cool metal connected to a thin chain. She held it up close: the shadows defined it as a cross, the symbol of Maria and Carlos' martyred faith. She turned it, marveling as it caught the light of the fire in small flashes of bright colors she hadn't seen since childhood. The chain fell across her fingers, flowing like a stream of water.

Carlos moaned, and she leaned closer to listen to his breathing. As she did, the chain brushed against his bare skin, and his heart slowed. She moved the cross away and it sped up again, racing wildly until she placed both hands against his chest, with the cross over his heart.

Heat rose from his skin, traveling up Marie Angelique's arms and racing through her body. She bent her head until it too touched his skin, letting her tears fall onto his chest as prayers she'd learned long ago from the Abbess came softly to her lips.

She mouthed the words, hoping either Carlos or his God could hear them. She prayed until she no longer heard herself speaking but rather felt the words resonating throughout her body.

A second voice joined her, and a wrinkled hand came to rest on top of her own. The Abbess knelt beside her at Carlos' side, her strong voice moving in the same cadence.

"Pater noster, qui es in caelis: sanctificetur Nomen Tuum..."

They call him Mad. They fight against his rules and the Word. They receive proof time and time again until he despairs of ever delivering them from their own mistakes.

Down below lies the valley he promised them. Across the river, they will be safe, for a time. The journey has been long, and keeping them together was a task no other could have accomplished.

And still they resist, even in the face of the greatest proof of all. He has kept them alive. Most of them, anyway.

His successor will carry on what he'd started. Changing the boy's name is the first of many steps necessary to continue life for the tribes. He'll take on more as the years went on; names are of little worth, and during a lifetime a man collects and discards many according to his needs.

Prince, Warrior, General, Shepherd.

Husband, Son. Brother, Patriarch.

Madman. Murderer.

Priest.

Prophet.

None of them touches the whole of his life, nor does he desire one that does. Names aren't necessary for the next phase of the journey.

This land will shelter them—of this he is sure. It is free from the madness, for now. Years of careful attention have removed all traces of it from the people, or at the very least pushed it aside—contained it.

Here on the hill, those touched, but not taken fully by that power gather behind him, continuing their preparations for the dawn.

He is glad of the end. With each passing season it has been harder to keep them all in line. To keep them safe from the others, who even now search the sands, following false trails laid down with blood and pain.

The dark hunger that drives the others is too seductive—too destructive. It corrupted the river people completely, blinding them to their own power and light until they performed acts that made even the others take pause. So few knew the real reasons why they'd fled; so few were willing and able to learn the truth.

That will change. Must change. But not today.

Today is for goodbyes.

The mountain still calls to him, ever singing from the rising dawn. He has resisted the pull long enough, and it is past time to go into the East.

To the source.

Let them think I am gone. Let them think themselves free of my tyranny—of the rules that protected them in their ignorance.

Let them believe they are safe for a time.

He turns to regard his true followers. The radiance he cannot hide, horns of light arrayed around his brow illuminate an army of true faith, one thousand strong. They believe in the message. They share in the power and have remained pure and free from dark temptations.

In the eyes of the people below, they have been dead for many years. This is his true legacy—his gift to the tribes. Guardians of faith. One among them will return here to this place to see what crop grows from the seed they have planted. A Protector—a Shepherd to guide them through the coming darkness. Perhaps someday, he will return himself in another guise.

Arms raised high, he holds the rod of dark metal before him. It pulses once, sending warmth throughout his body. The power is his again, and with it, the responsibility to lead.

"My children. Are you ready to do what must be done?"

The words are barely above a whisper, but they carry clearly to all assembled.

One thousand heads nod in agreement. These men and women have accepted the Truth and are prepared to hold back the darkness with whatever sacrifices are necessary.

"Then let us be away. We are already dead, but let no man below know the place of our resting. Let us rejoin our brothers in the sands and then begin our true journey."

No more words are necessary. Turning his back on the river, on the reward denied him by his calling, he walks. The army of light moves, not waiting for him to stand at the fore.

They know the way. For they too hear the call of the mountain...

The skin beneath her hand was cool, and the movement of Carlos' chest free and calm. Whatever battle he'd fought in the realm of dreams had ended, and his strength had carried him through.

Marie Angelique said a silent prayer to Carlos' god, while Yee Qin thanked the memory of her ancestors.

In the dim light of the coals and candles, his face was alive with color. It glowed as if lit from within, and though she marveled at the sight, she feared it as well. The fire within his body also burned in hers, and there was no longer any need to sit beside him.

Careful not to disturb his rest, she moved his blankets back into place before returning to her own pile of bedding by the fire. She needed its comfort more than the warmth, though she doubted she would sleep any time soon.

Nestled within her blankets, she counted her too-fast heartbeats as they marched in time to the flickering lines of light dancing on Carlos' brow....

MASTER YEE REFUSED TO YIELD COMMAND OF THE allied forces following the battle with the demon lord. A short time of healing was all that was required, during which the hunters were ever vigilant against threats from below. They had seen the face of evil and would not abandon their duty.

"The Peace of the Garden eased the pain of memory—the battles of yesterdays past.

"'No more,' the warriors proclaimed. 'No more will die in this place...'"

Carlos looked up from his translation and saw small faces peering around the corner. More and more children were coming to hear the tales of the Yee Hero, even though they were supposed to be kept away from the monk during his recuperation. Qin Yee and the Abbess seemed immune to the effects of his affliction, but for safety's sake all three had voluntarily maintained seclusion.

But the tales of Master Yee and the Witch Hunters were compelling, and the sound of Carlos' voice was no threat to any willing to listen. Qin Yee's ancestor was an enigmatic figure, sometimes described as a noble and at others as a farmer. The current passage he was working with told of a series of battles against "The Great Crab"—a demon sorcerer who commanded lightning and thunder.

The children knew the tales of the Judges and the battles fought by the tribe of Israel. That faraway time and place was as wondrous as the Eastern tales he and the young healer had translated, but these stories were new, fresh and exciting.

As much so for Carlos as for his students. The words and concepts found on these pages were so precise in their meaning that once Carlos established a basic vocabulary, translation was an almost organic process.

Almost as if the stories "want" to be read.

All of his parchment was gone now, or rather, filled. There would be no scraping or recycling of this record. The language and customs of Huixia would be preserved in the West. And needed to be, if the children were to remember.

Over long weeks underground, Carlos had witnessed a change in their perceptions both of himself and of Qin Yee. While Carlos had had the advantage of laughter and play to win their hearts, it was not until the younger residents of the Blessed Stone had seen the "dark sister" tirelessly attending to their mothers over the last month that they'd gained a measure of respect for her.

Seeing Carlos fall prey to the same sickness that took away their playmates, their family, and then "revived" once more by the veiled healer, the children now wanted to know more about their neighbor.

And her ancestor.

The life Master Yee had lived was not one they were likely to know or experience, save through the stories Carlos read. Far away Castle Kakura, the fall of the cherry blossoms… these tales were as real as Daniel in the lion's den and the walls of Jericho. The pages he had filled with translations—and notes on how to continue once he had access to more parchments—would keep them alive.

Carlos' head ached, and he raised a hand to massage his temple. Speaking like this for extended periods was tiring, but his companions made it worthwhile. He owed these women his life—making their days even the tiniest bit happier was the least he could do.

Thanks to Qin Yee and Maria, his skin was smooth and free of scars. The blisters from the pox never burst, nor had those from his recent bout of spotted fever. He was now completely recovered from both afflictions, save for an occasional cough.

And the headaches.

It was as if stones were being raised against his skull. A continual, dull pounding that never seemed to go away, increasing as he read but lessening as he spoke.

The Abbess broke the silence. "I believe that is enough of the Yee Hero for today," she said, speaking louder than necessary as a warning for small legs and hands to be about other tasks. "Tomorrow, we will talk more, I think."

The laughing echoes of bare feet on stone indicated that her message had been received and understood.

Rising, the older woman spoke now to an audience of two.

"I shall prepare a broth for us, I think, that we may remain healthy and hale for tomorrow's efforts."

When the Abbess turned, Carlos saw a smile on her face— one that remained as she moved past the tapestry separating them from the rest of the Abbey.

Even though there was little he could have done to prevent it, Carlos still felt somewhat foolish for allowing himself to fall sick. The signs had all been there: fatigue, weakness, and trouble sleeping, but he'd assumed he would be immune to any "child's" malady, since such ailments were common and widely spread at the Academy.

But the countryside of France was not the streets of Toledo, and apparently he'd never been exposed to this one. He'd pushed himself too far for his body to compensate, and once again Maria and Qin Yee had taken care of him.

This simple chamber defined the Blessed Stone completely in his mind. The three healers spent much time together here, and the close confines strengthened their friendship greatly. Carlos knew every sound, smell, and tiny air current in the space from his time without sight, and his second recuperation had only served to deepen his understanding of it.

After only six weeks, The Blessed Stone was as much his home as were Barcelona and Sant Cugat after as many years. He no longer had trouble resolving the two; there was room for both in his experience. His moment of doubt, brought on by exhaustion and depression borne of illness, was over. He would continue on to Paris when the snows lifted and then on to Rome as planned. This place—this family—would travel with him, nestled with and equal in reverence to his memories of home.

"Carlos?"

"Yes, Qin Yee?"

The two spoke in *Hanyu*, the spoken form of the *Wenyan* in which the Yee family chronicle was recorded on pages of fine silk. The practice increased Carlos' fluency, and was invaluable to his translation efforts. When Carlos and Qin Yee were alone they spoke almost exclusively in *Hanyu*. And despite her sly misdirections, Carlos was aware that the Abbess' frequent absences were arranged so that the two could do so.

But this time, there was a quaver in Qin Yee's voice—an undertone Carlos had not heard there before.

"I want to thank you again for giving me my family's legacy. More so than the lost relics, these stories are a treasure found—a happiness I will never forget."

What is that sound, that extra emphasis to her words?

"As I have said before, Sister, it is the least I can do. These are more than just stories—they are a testament of a way of life that all can learn from. Your father was right to bring them along on his search. When I more fully understand that life, I should be of far greater assistance in recovering your clan's legacy."

Qin Yee was silent for a few moments, and Carlos thought he saw a smile forming behind her veil.

"You have also reintroduced me to my mother's language and my father's words. These are kindnesses—things of great worth. Thanks to your diligence, my family lives again.

"You...you make a lonely woman happy."

Carlos made no effort to hide his own smile.

"Then it is I that am happy, for you have no need to be lonely—not here at the Blessed Stone. When I move on to Paris, I will be forgotten, but you will be a reminder to everyone of the bravery of the Yee Hero. I will send back materials so that you and the Abbess can recopy the histories into forms that are easier to read and remember. I think that when you become the storyteller, these tales will be much more entertaining."

"I...I am not worthy of this."

Qin Yee rose and made to withdraw. But before she did, she paused to place her right hand on Carlos' shoulder. For a moment, he thought her comforting grip a bit too firm, but the lingering effects of the disease were still stubbornly affecting his perceptions. Then she was gone, quickly retiring to an adjoining room that she and the Abbess had been using for sleeping.

He heard the makeshift door shut behind the cloth covering, perhaps a bit louder than usual, and imagined he could hear a similar tapestry installed on the other side to mute the sounds of a crying newborn fall into place.

"I don't know what you speak of when I am not in the room, Carlos, but the words sound pleasant enough. And before you say it, I am far too old to be learning another. The dialects of three countries, along with Latin, are enough for me."

The Abbess had slipped into the room unseen at some point, holding a tray with bowls full of the broth she'd promised. As was their custom, Maria addressed Carlos in the tongue with which she, and most of her charges, was most familiar. It was similar enough to one he'd been speaking for almost twenty years, and every time Carlos heard it, he thought of home.

So very much like Matthieu she is. Always smiling, never too tired to offer friendship. Theirs is a language that makes anything sound pleasant. I wonder if some part of the Gallic soul is always happy.

"Yes, Maria. It is, as you say, a difficult language. One based on formalities and apology. I am no expert in it, and in many ways, Marie Angelique is learning it at the same time as I. Were she able to see as we do, it would be easier."

"Many things could be easier for her, Carlos. Her damaged eyesight is not so much of a barrier as it could be, but certainly one to keep in mind. Despite the difference in our ages, you and I are closer in temperament and experience than we can ever be with her. We were born into a different world—a different place."

The Abbess handed him a steaming bowl containing the last of the winter vegetables and a touch of wine. The rich scent was invigorating, and almost distracted him from the older woman's next words.

"Marie Angelique is many things, Carlos. She certainly is the most important thing I have ever done, and I love her as much as if she was the child of my own flesh and blood. In another life, in that world we do not know or imagine, she would be more respected and revered than either of us."

She's leaving something out again. We have had so many conversations directed by these things unsaid, beginning on one topic and ending in an entirely different place. It's yet another language for me to decipher, but I could spend six years here and never get the full story from her.

Unless, of course, I ask her directly.

Carlos sipped gratefully at the broth, enjoying each fragrant mouthful and composing his thoughts as best he could. Maria was a much different conversationalist than Frances— and by extension, Carlos—and he'd need to pay close attention to the words she *did* say to uncover those she did not.

"Now it is I who does not understand, Sister."

"Have you not guessed by now, Carlos? Or are you still too *macho?*"

The Abbess balanced the tray holding the remaining bowls in one hand and with her other, brushed aside the covering that led to Qin Yee's bedchamber. The door behind it was closed, and Maria's mischievous grin became pure sunshine.

Instead of knocking, she crossed back to the outer passage, pausing with her back to Carlos. Her head turned slightly, and he saw a flash of light reflected in her eye. The years fell away, and in that moment she was no older than the children who'd been hiding outside earlier.

"My very young friend, it is clear to me in every story you tell that the Yee Hero, 'Master Yee' as it is recorded in those strange letters only you two understand, was a woman. Someday, if I am very lucky, I think I would like to see these lands of Huixia for myself and discover if I too am capable of such things."

Carlos' laugh built in his chest, banishing all traces of his lingering cough until his smile could no longer contain it. His voice filled the room, echoing back to him his embarrassment and wonder. He reached for the volume of tightly pressed silk pages, resolving to read it again. Whatever witness had recorded the Yee Hero's chronicle had been a master of misdirection.

This time, I will look for the truth within the words, rather than the poetry...

一二零五年五月二十零日，甲子月

Master Yee came late to the study of the sword.
The way of the warrior is a hard one.
Better suited to life at temple,
Surrounded by scrolls and songs.
One song rises on both paths;
Duty to the Clan before all else.

YEE QIN MARIE NEVER HAD A FRIEND BEFORE HER PARENTS were killed. That night was burned into her memory as indelibly as were the marks it left on her body. The sounds of angry, ignorant men breaking down the door. Of her mother screaming and of how she'd died covering her child's body against blows and boots.

Of crunching, breaking sounds, a pain in her arm, fire, and smoke.

Of Treve Fuentes Maria beating the flames away from her face and shouting in a barbarian tongue.

Of darkness.

Her world after the fire was one of mists. Of remembered colors overlaid on the pale shades that had come to replace them. She'd learned to twist her tongue to communicate basic concepts, and eventually how to hide her real beliefs inside the fiction of Christ.

After she'd taken the black robes to honor the Abbess, she'd come to this place so that she could help others who'd also suffered losses. And when the children came, she'd added the veil to her wardrobe of lies.

For ten years, she'd hidden her true face from the world, and had only recently come to regret that choice. Women whose husbands used fists and feet to communicate instead of poetry understood the scars left by hatred. Children who had known only love could not, and should not, understand those that would never heal.

Santos Christ Carlos cannot understand them either, though I wish he could. His scars are inside, where he thinks others cannot see them.

But Yee Qin saw them all too well. Even now they called to her and haunted her days and nights. Her hand on his brow had quelled his demons, but his dreams—the secret words he spoke in his delirium—could not be unheard.

In his loneliness, the isolation of his youth, and his doubts and fears for the future, she'd seen the beauty of his spirit clearer and sharper than anything else since the fire. When his body burned, hers burned as well. But when he healed, she diminished.

Not out of shame, but once more from necessity. Part of his healing involved his return to a life of duty, including teaching the children of the enclave she avoided to protect them from her very adult pain.

When the fevers came, the Blessed Stone needed them both. Working with Carlos was a pleasure, as his skills complemented and enhanced her own. And the Abbess healed in other ways, setting the spirits of her patients at ease while she fortified and strengthened their bodies.

Together, the three had struggled against an unbeatable foe, with a predictable outcome. Some of the children would grow up without their mothers, others without their friends. But for every life lost, their treatments saved a dozen others. Those who survived would grow stronger and wiser. Many mothers would see their children become adults because of their efforts.

Because of him...

When she found Carlos unconscious on the stones, she feared that she had again lost a part of herself. Finding life within him still, she'd acted without thinking, picking him up and hurrying him back to the chamber where their time together began.

Despite his condition, she'd enjoyed the opportunity to spend time with him once more, away from the others. Hearing Carlos speak the words of her fathers and mothers, she'd been transported to another place, and had begun to believe anything was possible with him by her side.

When the visions started, she knew that day could never come.

Each story of the Yee Hero the monk recited evoked a terrifying memory in her: one subtly similar but more real, more accurate than the stories he read aloud from her clan's history.

The visions centered on her ancestor, the brave woman Carlos' words brought to life. It was the greatest gift she had ever received, and she'd repaid his kindness with treachery of the worst kind.

For though he'd learned the language of her ancestors, he'd yet to grasp the true meanings of the histories he read.

Histories that included monsters with incredible strength, elders with the power of prophecy, witches that could heal from any wound, and demons with sight granted by the lords of the underworld.

As was her practice, she'd secured the doors to her chamber before removing her outer garments for the night. It would not do for another to come in unexpectedly and discover her shame.

No one can ever know...

The veil was first. The dark, coarsely woven wool that hid her deformity from the world was wet with tears as it came up and over smooth and unblemished skin. Her long, black robes fell off her left shoulder to expose a strong arm, assisted by a left hand with a full range of motion and ability.

All of these things she saw clearly, with wide eyes brimming with tears. She could hear Carlos' heart beating in the next room, feel his blood flowing throughout his body. And now when he healed, so did she, growing stronger every day.

I am the worst kind of demon. The Betrayer, who takes on another's form to gain advantage. Each day that passes makes my hidden evil more terrible, my lies more cruel. This secret life, this temptation, can only end badly.

Through the heavy door and the thick cloth hangings on either side of it, she heard Carlos sound out the words of the first tale of the Yee Hero as if she was still sitting across from him. And as the words passed into her, the room around her drifted away, only to be replaced by a scene from another lifetime.

Honored ancestor, forgive me, for I so very much want to share this secret with the man I love...

CHAO-XING WAS A QUIET GIRL BY NATURE, AND HAD always been so. Her tutors found her an apt pupil, but one who did not make many friends amongst the other students. She learned her lessons quickly, and her ability with a brush was sure and precise.

At an age when most young women turned their thoughts to young men, Chao-xing was instead dedicated to the tasks set for her by her Lord uncle, Yee Shou. He had been her companion and protector since the day of her birth, and she had pledged her life to his example of service. She was prepared to assist the clan in securing a trade contract through arranged marriage as had her cousins—her "sisters"—before her.

She was also quite unaware she had become a particularly beautiful woman, and that news of that beauty had spread far.

Lord Shou entertained many officials, and in the Spring of Chao-xing's seventeenth year, his house was graced by the arrival of the Sui Emperor's personal guard. They had traveled far spreading the new philosophy throughout the empire and were grateful for his hospitality.

Chao-xing was entranced by these strong, serene visitors. They were the ideal warriors: noble, proud, and wise. They were everything she had read about—excellent ambassadors of the Western thinking embraced by the Emperor.

Their bravery was well known, and in addition to explaining concepts of enlightenment and karma, the emperor's guards put on an exhibition of sword techniques that matched their other teachings perfectly. Honor, dignity, and respect were foremost among the precepts of the warrior, and a soul that could embrace all of these notions—become one with both the hard mountain and the soft valley—could not be defeated.

After seeing the relics they'd brought as gifts for her uncle and other provincial officers, Chao-xing felt the philosophy they invoked blossom inside her, and she composed a poem about them.

Her uncle was delighted by her interest in their visitors, and when he read her composition for the warriors, their captain was similarly impressed. After speaking with her uncle and her instructors, the swordsman asked for a private audience to speak with the author about what she'd written.

And other things.

Chao-xing was honored by his interest, but did not wish to offend. To be a wife, his wife, she would have to leave her family behind, and the potential advantages her union could bring to the clan. Marriage to a warrior, however well regarded, was not the same as a match to prosperous lord or merchant.

When they left—when *he* left—she returned to her chambers, selected a fresh sheet of paper and began to write.

A heart cannot have two masters; duty to the clan must come first.

She drew those words many times in the days that followed, each stroke of the brush moving more of her soul through the bristles and onto the paper. Each time, her hand was inadequate to the task, and the words went into the coals, becoming a white puff of memory.

The pattern repeated without pause until Lord Shou came to check on his niece and inquire as to the reason for her absence from his side. When he looked at her characters, he was overcome with emotion, and his tears fell upon the paper to mingle with her own.

Lord Shou gathered his ward into his arms and led her through the garden to a table set for two. As he spoke, for the first time in her life Chao-xing heard the sound of her own heart echoed in the words of another.

"My sister, Shumei, was a beautiful girl, gifted with a kind smile and graceful hands. Her music called the birds down out of these very trees, and visitors to our house would wait on the other side of that stream for hours hoping to hear even one note from her flute.

"Many suitors came to speak to our father, and your honored father Makuo was but one of them. He was my friend, my companion. The son of a poor noble, whose voice was pure and unsullied by anger.

"He loved my sister, and when the birds looked into his eyes, they were ashamed to land close to her. But though his love was great, his means were small, and our father promised Shumei to a business partner who had already taken and discarded three wives without producing a son.

"The joining of our houses was arranged by imperial decree before any of us were born. And though there was no love in it for Shumei, she agreed to go to him as was her duty.

"Makuo begged her to reconsider, but she said the same words to him that you wrote down today. She told him that though her heart dreamed of a different world, their love could never be. When she left, Makuo fell to his knees and cried, and the sky wept with him.

"Months later, she wrote to us that she was with child. At first we rejoiced, but then we received a message from her husband, the Honored Haknu, that a fall had ended it.

"As I have said, Makuo and I were friends. He spoke often of his love for Shumei and his pain at her absence. But when we received that second message, he stopped speaking altogether. The next day he left without a word to myself or his brothers.

"Weeks later, he returned, bloodied and wounded from some fight. He did not tell us where he had gone, gave no words to his father as to why he abandoned his duty.

"As soon as he could stand again, he was gone.

"Three times he came back to us, each time more wounded than the last. He would not speak, offered no explanation for his injuries, but even the most inexperienced healer could see the slice of a sword or the marks of arrows that had pierced his skin.

"During his last convalescence, he burned with a deep fire that could not be quenched. His wounds were terrible, and remnants of dark metal lingered inside his body from barbed arrows. Still he gave no complaint, and though we feared him lost, he rose again the next day, still burning but still strong.

"We begged him to stay, to tell us of his foe. His brothers and I wanted to fight alongside him, but he was too fast, too driven for us to follow his feet as he ran. We saw only his back, rising up into and then above the trees. When we returned with horses, his trail had gone cold and dark.

"Whatever quest he attempted, whatever battles he fought, we did not know where he pursued them. But I knew, deep in my heart, that Makuo was either seeking Shumei or some way to forget her.

"We did not expect him to return a fourth time. We certainly did not expect him to return with a small, sobbing woman that had once been my sister.

"She had been beaten, and Makuo was in worse condition than ever. Terrible wounds scored his body—not only the slashes and punctures of weapons, but the marks of long curved claws that had torn through his flesh. He spoke to me for the first time in many months as we watched the healers work to save your life.

"For she was still with child, my beloved. It was you she protected, and you that Makuo sought and fought for again and again. I will remember his words forever, just as you have written them so beautifully.

"'The heart cannot have two masters.' He said them with such passion—such raw need that I could not look him in the face. I could only look at his torn, bloodied clothing and the worn sandals on his feet.

"His hand rested on my shoulder, and I could feel the fire still burning under his skin. He had become Fire itself—a being of power that walked in a man's body. I raised my head to see his face, and saw light burning white and pure in his eyes.

"Your first sounds pulled me away, and then he was gone. As I held you in my hands, Shumei left us as well. I have been your protector ever since, and if I could do for you one tenth part what Makuo did, I would.

"The heart cannot have two masters, my daughter of spirit. The clan will survive, but only if you live as that heart dictates."

After his tale, Lord Shou left Chao-xing alone in the garden. She heard his words repeated in the songs of the birds, the whispers of the trees, and the soft sounds of the stream.

When she returned to her room, the paper was gone.

A month later, a scroll arrived from the capital. The Emperor would allow his most trusted warrior, his nephew in fact, to marry. But the Emperor demanded that he serve for one more year before the ceremony could take place.

The next day there was another scroll, and another on the day after that, and Chao-xing read each one with eager eyes. Though they mostly exchanged news of duty and honor, as the seasons passed the messages grew longer and more personal in nature.

In the spring of her eighteenth year, Lord Shou prepared his household for the journey from Shaanxi province to the capital for the ceremony. The Emperor himself was to perform the joining of their families, and in addition to managing her new husband's affairs, Chao-xing was to join the imperial court as a scribe.

Movement of a clan took many weeks and was not always along well-traveled paths. While the house of Yee moved south, a messenger rode north with a scroll that would have stopped all travel, as well as the motion of Chao-xing's heart.

When they arrived at the Imperial city, a tall bureaucrat met the clan at its boundary and informed them there would be no wedding.

And why.

He spoke of a sick and ailing emperor, whose skin was black with poisons and death. Of the Emperor's retainers, locked in their chambers with skin similarly blackened, or dead by faster, self-inflicted poisons.

Of a suspicious assassin.

Of the capture—and imprisonment—of the Emperor's Guard for their failure to prevent it.

Entrance to the palace was forbidden to all but the most loyal retainers. Lord Shou had been one such, but his motives were now suspect, and he was asked to take residence in the River House while the council debated the fate of Chao-xing's heart.

None would admit to complicity in the attack on the Emperor. Chao-xing was passionate and eloquent when speaking for the guards' release, although the council would not listen. Similar petitions from her uncle, the Prince-Heir and his bureaucrats, and from other housed nobles also did nothing to sway them.

The facts of the day were plain. The emperor was dying, the result of a cowardly attack while his guards slept easily a stone's throw away.

Stories surfaced. A passage unguarded, a shadowy figure beckoning to dark forms, terrible demons in the night. Tales of loyal soldiers paralyzed and impotent, some sleeping while standing, some with faces frozen in fear.

Other stories had no shadowy figure. They told not of demons but men whose clothing matched the darkness of the stricken ruler's skin.

The cruelest stories of all made Chao-xing weep long into the night. Of loyal and noble guardsmen kept in cells below the city, beaten, starved, and stripped of their honor.

But not their pride. That died softly in the night with the Emperor, and with the setting of the moon all appeals were dismissed.

Sentence was proclaimed swiftly. The execution was to take place at the Emperor's hour, third after dawn.

The guardsmen were washed, clothed in the white robes of mourning, and led into the light of day. They were made to kneel with the sun in their eyes, while they asked forgiveness of their ancestors, of the Emperor, and of the assembled noble clans.

One head dared turn to face his accusers, and the soft morning air carried one whispered message for a sobbing girl.

"It cannot be."

Seven swords flashed, and seven heads left their bodies.

One heart broke, never to be whole again.

Chao-xing would not be moved from the courtyard, even long after all others had left. She stared into the past at the love of her father Makuo and her father Yee Shou. She stared into the future, a bleak landscape bereft of either.

She was still standing there when the moon rose, and Lord Shou came to her bearing a message from one no longer able to deliver it himself. Carrying a pair of thin swords, he knelt before the girl, offering both up to numb fingers and dead hands. Shoulders braced, back stiff and wooden, she accepted them without a word. The noble rose and looked into his niece's eyes.

"You will never forget what happened here today. I would have spared you this if I could. But you must always remember the reason why.

"Your heart died today not to save his honor, but to protect the Empire. To save your life and the lives of all of us. By taking responsibility, he absolves us from blame. The Empire will remain whole, united behind the Prince-Heir. There will be no war among the families.

"We need not fear nameless demons in the night or mystical poisons. We need fear only men and their black hearts.

"It could be no other way."

A crack filled the cool night air, echoing off the empty walls of the courtyard and returning to the lonely man with an imprint of a small, fast hand on his cheek.

Lord Shou stared into eyes wide with shining fire, set into a white mask of anger. His eyes were fixed to hers, locked together in one thought until the older man dropped his gaze and gave in to his own grief.

"I am sorry."

The sunrise saw a new warrior walk away from the capital wearing brocade robes and the symbol of the Yee family on her back. Paired swords rode on small hips, and her close-cropped hair hidden beneath a simple cap.

The Emperor would be revenged....

AS THE VISION FADED, THE MEMORY OF YEE CHAO-XING and the sacrifices she made tore at Yee Qin's heart. *Is this, then, my future? How long can I hide my true self from Carlos and still remain true to her memory?*

Carlos could never know the heart of the Hero—see her

soul as did Yee Qin. He would never feel the pain in her heart as she walked away from the clan—could never understand the true bravery that went beyond the words on the paper.

He cannot, for he has never had a family. When he recovers, he will leave us—leave me—behind. His life awaits him in the world above, and I...

Yee Qin closed her eyes, as if willing her dreams away could stop them. She knew she could join him if she wished. Her face was whole now, her eyes were clear. Away from the Blessed Stone, none would know her shame.

But my soul is tainted, touched by some demon's hand. How could he ever love me without seeing that evil? Or look at me without remembering the tiny bodies buried in the catacombs below. He would know, somehow he would know, and then he would leave me, never to look back.

In the dawning of her twenty-fourth year, Yee Qin replaced the veil and cowl, becoming again Marie Angelique. She wrapped the heavy black robes around herself, binding her left arm to her chest lest someone else discover her corruption.

I will bury my heart in the catacombs below and remain at the Blessed Stone until Carlos is a distant memory, gone far away like the faces of my parents. It would be better if he had never come here. Better that he had died on the road than to discover my lies.

My love.

A vision of Lord Shou rose up and mocked her from the past. A kind and gentle face, with the light of the rising sun revealing a red palm print as he watched his heart walk away.

The heart cannot have two masters.

Duty to the clan before all else.

4 JUNE, YEAR OF OUR LORD 1205

Matthieu,

I am once again recovered from a sickness I fought long to treat in others. My healers are very much my friends, and I think you would find comfort here among a community that values truth, honesty, and compassion.

This will be my last record of my time here, cribbed as it is atop a salvaged fragment of parchment discovered under a forgotten crate of blankets. Were there more time, more space, I would record all of the truths I have learned.

Perhaps someday I will tell you of them...

CARLOS LOOKED UP FROM HIS COMPOSITION. HE WROTE out of habit more than any other need, as these messages would not reach Sant Cugat for many weeks, if at all. The back roads of France were neither well-traveled nor often maintained. The Abbess founded the Blessed Stone here not for the caves, but the isolation.

Packing his possessions had been easy. Apart from the writing kit open in front of him, all that he owned fit into a small travel bag—the very same container he'd carried from Barcelona. Paris lay somewhere to the North and East, but over what roads he did not know. His arrival here was pure chance, aided by a thirsty horse and some agency he still could not name.

A season in this place had shown him a different kind of life. In Sant Cugat du Valles, time was structured—controlled. Hours of devotion, days of service. Here, the days were full of laughter and friendship.

It was not at all what he had expected to find when he set his feet upon the path. Were he given a score of years to spend as he wished, he might do so in a place like this.

But the course of my life is fixed, not open. And though the length of the journey is easily adjusted, the destination remains certain.

Paris. Rome.

Responsibility.

"Carlos?"

The voice was familiar, but the face of the woman speaking was not. She had smooth skin and almond-shaped eyes, and the words had a strange, somewhat familiar rolling sound to them. She was dressed in simple, handmade clothing suitable for traveling, topped with a heavy black cloak adorned with some flowery design he did not recognize but felt that he should.

Who is this woman? I have seen and met every...

No. Not seen.

Not everyone.

Qin Yee.

"Carlos, there is something I must tell you, before you go."

Where is the veil? Where is the cowl?

"What...what is it, Sister?"

Where are the scars? The burns she hides from the world?

"I do not want you to leave. I want you to stay. Here, with me."

Her voice was almost a whisper, but Carlos was trained to listen to pain. There was much of it in her request.

"My...I have need of you."

Carlos' mind raced, trying to classify the sight before him. He had never seen her face—Qin Yee's face—before. He hadn't heard her voice clearly for many weeks, but it was unmistakably hers. And he saw no defect in the person before him—no flaws to hide from the community.

Only perfection. An alabaster angel, walking on earth among men.

"I...I do not understand. What do you say?"

"These months with you. They have awakened in me...I...
Something lives in me that was not there before you came."

The perfect face turned away, her sobs swallowed by the
walls and candle light. But Carlos' hearing had grown as acute
as his other senses, and even with her face hidden behind
shaking hands her next words were as clear as if she had spoken them directly into his ear.

"I...I want you. To be...with me."

These words. These are the words that cannot be spoken.

"Sister, I cannot. We...cannot. This...this is a common feeling when people are in extraordinary circumstances. When
they care for one another. This...this is not what you think it
is."

Carlos moved to comfort his caretaker. Not thinking, his
right arm reached out to take her left in friendship. Before he
could stop himself, his fingers closed on her damaged limb...
and found a soft, full arm.

"How...how has this happened? This gift? *C'est un Miracle!*"

Qin Yee turned to face him, and Carlos stared into brown
eyes flecked with gold. Small hands grabbed his face, and with
a desperate, unexpected strength they pulled his head down
to hers. Soft lips pressed against his mouth, and his muffled
objections were stilled by both surprise and a rush of energy
from the kiss that filled his body.

Carlos tried to pull away—to disengage without hurting
his friend any more than necessary. But she was too strong—
stronger somehow than he was after a season of hardship. He
felt his feet leave the floor, though there was no strain on his
neck or head.

Carlos looked down. Both his and Qin Yee's feet floated
above the knotted rug. He tried again to break her desperate
embrace. There was a flash of light, and Qin Yee's hands no
longer held him fast. His body sailed across the room into the
crude wall he'd stared at so often from his couch, and then the
couch itself crashed into his chest.

The second impact stole his breath as he watched the room
spin, blinking madly as spots of light danced in front of his
eyes. From miles away, he heard a voice growing fainter and

fainter as the darkness pressed in from all sides.

"Non, c'est un horrible cauchemar! I am touched by darkness. I do not...I do not deserve happiness. Or this life. This evil in me only brings pain."

Carlos heard footsteps running from the room and objects crashing to the floor in their wake. He had a feeling—a not-memory—that filled his heart and mind until...

The morning sun rises, illuminating the shining blade in her hands. The ground is white, matching her robes and the stack of folded paper in front of her.

One breath, two, then she pulls at the blade, splashing red across the canvas and staining...

The scene was alien, but somehow more real than the room around him. The air held a hint of blossoms, a mixture of roses and lavender he knew as well as the smell of his own sweat.

He feels the wind blowing a strand of his long black hair across his eyes, the yawning emptiness inside him, as he aches for a man he can never have.

These feelings were not—could not be his own, but though Carlos didn't know where they came from, their meaning was clear.

Qin Yee is about to take her own life.

He knew it, believed it, as if the action had originated in his own thoughts. Carlos pushed the couch away with a strength born of desperation. He steadied himself against the wall until his head stopped spinning and then lurched for the faded cloth that separated him from the hallway and his friend.

The passage on the other side was blocked by additional obstacles of a previously harmless nature. Baskets, boxes, and splintered crates hastily thrown behind echoing footsteps.

He quickened his own steps as best he could, weaving past and leaping over each hurdle as if chased by slavering hounds. He was vaguely aware of calling for help, rallying others to stop her as she ran, but the words were of little import.

He had to be faster. There was still a chance, as long as she kept moving.

If I can catch her before she reaches the surface...

His chamber was deep within the caves of the Blessed Stone, located far enough down twisting passages that any sound from a baby's lungs would not betray the world of women to the world above. But today, every turn and rise of the natural passages slowed him further.

Carlos' feet knew the way back into the sun, how far he had to run, and how far he was behind his quarry when the entrance to the world above came into view. Though he could no longer hear Qin Yee's footsteps, she could only have gone in one direction, and he burst out from the cave entrance with all the strength in his legs.

Carlos pushed himself, each step propelling him faster and farther, hoping to catch his friend before she carried out her plan.

It is a sin to do what she intends. Not only will she be denied her place in the Kingdom of Heaven, but she would be rejecting the miracle that has given her back her life!

From both his training and experience, Carlos knew that of all the gifts given to mankind, life was the most important thing one could possess. Qin Yee had given him back his own, and he couldn't let her squander whatever grace had come to her now.

The sweet, fresh smell of new grass whipped by Carlos as he ran. Spring was finally here and with it the promise of new life. But even after long weeks underground, he could spare no time to take in the sights and smells of the new world around him.

He had to save one more life.

My latest, last, and possibly most important patient of all.

The circle of buildings that made up the Blessed Stone's upper facade came into view. At their center was the well—the beacon which had drawn Carlos' horse through rain and exhaustion months before.

And kneeling before it was a tiny form that slumped to the ground as he approached.

"NO!"

Too late, too slow to stop her, Carlos' objection was wasted as his foot caught a stone and he tumbled to a halt. He scrambled on hands and knees toward her, but all he could do was cradle his dying friend.

The first rays of the morning sun shone full on her perfect face as she bled onto the hungry earth, and the dark knife in her chest was a symbol even Carlos could understand.

"Car...Carlos. You have come to be with...with m...me?"

"Yes, Qin Yee. I am here with you. I will not leave you again."

"I...m...must a...polo...gize again, Brother Barcelona. It is I who will...do the leaving. I am...sorry...to cause you...pain."

No, not yet. Not now.

"Stay, sister. Stay with us here. We need you, oh so much more than you know."

Carlos tasted tears on his face, a bitter, salty counterpart to the smell of flowers that represented Qin Yee in his mind, mingled now with the heady scent of her life's blood.

He felt it staining his hands, and the skin there itched as if unseen insects swarmed over it. He held her tighter, afraid to remove the dull iron knife from her chest lest he do even more damage.

"You must stay..."

I must leave. There is no place for me here.

The words were so faint, Carlos wasn't sure he heard them at all. More like a whisper on the wind, if the wind had somehow learned to speak *Hanyu*.

"I am...impure. I have become what I cannot be and must be...reborn. Pl...please, please keep your promise. Please d... defeat the enemy—the monster within. The people...must be defended...the Hero..."

The Hero must rise again. Must be reborn. Use what we have learned.

Her last breath trailed away into the air, one last pulse shuddering through her body as the sun rose over the center of Wellstone Village.

Carlos did not watch the dawn. His eyes were fixed on the knife, and he wished he could reach back through the last moments before his arrival and destroy it before it ever came into her hands.

When the warmth of the sun found his face, Carlos opened himself to it, an empty vessel desperate to be filled. Heat pulsed through his veins with each beat of his heart. He tried to will that energy into the woman in his arms, but she was gone. The long, sunless spring was finally ended with the death of a friend. Her blood was on his hands, and her last words were etched in his soul.

The Abbess found him there, still holding the small, empty thing that had once been a vibrant and intelligent woman. His tears were dried, and the thirsty ground had taken its own record of her life.

MARIA OF TREVE, MARIA DE FUENTES, MARIA OF THE Blessed Stone placed the wrapped body on a bier constructed of salvaged wood. The night air still had a chill to it, the last memory of a season that refused to yield its influence. The moon, long absent in the memories of the assembled community, shone pure white light over her burden while shadows cast by torchlight gave color and life to the crowd.

It was hard to believe Carlos' account of the morning, even though she knew his words were true. That her friend, her daughter, would cast away her life so foolishly. He had barely spoken since her death, sitting silent and alone at the edge of the well for many hours after she eased the body from his shaking hands. There was something unsaid—a sentiment dancing around the edge of his silence that the Abbess feared she knew all too well.

Qin Yee had not been a Christian, but had lived as one for many years. She spent her life in service to others, seeking to repay a debt that did not exist. A life of women, and here was a man who understood. One who cared but could not care. One who grieved for a thing he knew but would not know.

He will be many days in healing this latest sickness, and this time, Qin Yee cannot assist him. For she is the cause.

Though her heart ached to do so, the Abbess could not speak words for Qin Yee. Her death was tainted with sin, and she could not be laid to rest with those friends recently passed in the catacombs below. But it was within Maria's power to arrange a different parting—one that neither required words nor offended her faith.

She stepped back and bowed her head in silent remembrance of her young friend, wishing she had thought to explain to her those things mothers gave to their daughters. The words her mother had said to her, many years ago, in a world she no longer called her own.

Fighting back her tears, she backed away from the bier. Other women stepped forward, each bearing a gift of their own. Small things, items of personal worth. A carved icon. A painted relic. A golden ring. A wooden crucifix.

One hundred women and children came to the bier and left behind one hundred memories. A century of gratitude never voiced directly to a woman who lived among them but always apart.

When they were finished, Maria walked forward and laid her hand on the body, no longer able to hide her tears.

One hundred and one offerings. One more to give, and it will be done.

Maria took a thin branch from the piled wood and carried it to the silent monk whose eyes still burned red from long dried tears. Numbly, he accepted her offering and set it alight with a nearby torch. Shuffling forward, he held it against the pyre.

The straw and pine nettles caught quickly, and the stacked wood raised a beacon into the night sky. Carlos stood in that light, a slim silhouette outlined by fire. Both the man and the corpse shone with white moonlight, as if painted in silver outlines by a hidden brush. After a time, he walked away, skin flushed from the heat of his offering.

Without speaking, he walked toward the caves, down into the earth and away from the light.

6 JUNE, YEAR OF OUR LORD 1205

"YOU DO NOT HAVE TO LEAVE, MY BROTHER. YOU HAVE A place with us for as long as you need it."

A day and a night had passed, long hours of silence during which the cold of winter returned for one last day, if only as a reminder of their loss.

I am old...so old. Marie Angelique and I brought this community together out of the dispossessed and the lost, only to have it find its true identity in an unexpected fashion.

Of her friend Carlos, the Abbess had worry. It was not right to keep this pain inside. It could tear away reason and eat at the soul. What acts he might take next were unknown, his destination uncertain. But she knew that if he didn't learn to forgive himself, his pain might well destroy him.

Carlos shouldered satchels meant for the horse he rode in on and then picked up the pack containing his meager belongings. Along with his cassocks, sandals, and a sadly depleted case containing worn quills and empty inkwells, he now carried away a roll of scrolls copied from a very old, very foreign book, as well as two volumes of lore from a distant land inside a painted wooden chest.

Not seen, but definitely present among his belongings were the heartache and loss that should be left behind, but Maria could tell by the sound of his voice that Carlos might never let them go.

"My feet must walk a different path, Sister. I have set them toward a goal and a task that must be completed. I have promises to keep and a legacy to continue."

His voice is no longer the strained politeness of mourning, but he is far from whole. Carlos is choosing to ignore his pain—to bury it deep inside—and I cannot fault him for it.

But at what cost, Carlos? At what cost?

"Then go with God, my friend. Should your feet bring you back in this direction, the Blessed Stone will always welcome you. You take with you the best of us, and I know that you will see it to its destination in proper fashion."

Carlos gave no reply, nor did she press for one as the pair ascended into the brilliant light of a new day or as they crossed the half mile to Wellstone Village over a fresh blanket of white covering the ground.

Winter's last gift had covered walls and thatched roofs with drifts of shifting ice. A low mound was all that indicated the well in the courtyard. There was no sign of either the violent red end of her daughter or of the blazing fire that had taken her body into the sky.

Carlos did not look at the well as he walked past nor back at Maria. He simply walked on to the north, his leather-wrapped feet breaking a path in fresh crusts of snow and setting his tracks where none had gone before.

He did not see her fall and rest her burning head in the cool snow....

SUMMER

Matthieu,

The past months have shown me things that I cannot describe. Though I have not written in some time, know that our friendship has been much on my mind of late, especially after my arrival here in Paris.

Please inform the Abbot that the messages you sent earlier in the year were in fact here, having arrived during my extended stay at Wellstone Village. They were opened somewhere between Sant Cugat and Paris, and our private script was taken for nonsense and the letters were discarded. It was pure providence that I discovered them while cleaning old parchments, and I have instructed that any similar correspondence be brought to me immediately upon delivery.

Your account of Alejandro's recovery gives me great joy, and your kind wishes, and those of Robere, are greatly appreciated.

Paris is certainly not Sant Cugat, or even Barcelona, and I have not found many here who share our interests. It is an older, harder city, and the people here do not easily trust. There is a dark undercurrent to all their dealings, one centered on the advancement of self above all others.

Please convey to all my great love for our community, and know that in spite of the difficulties I face, I am adhering to the precepts of our brotherhood.

I have written to you before in regards to the Yee Hero, who lived in faraway Shaanxi province. Today I read a passage regarding a journey not unlike that of our beloved Benedict, in which the Hero faced a test of faith. Accompanying this dispatch, please find a record of the hunt for the Witch King, along with my poor attempt to reproduce the illustration that accompanies it.

In answer to your other query, I have regretfully found no more news regarding "dark" Karl Outrikos and the nature of the anomalous records we have studied for so long. Whatever secrets he had have been buried with him, and I might search forever and find no more than we already suspect: that he was a criminal of some kind who was shunned by the church, and the details of his life have been lost to time.

There are many such anomalies here in the university. And although so much is yet to be seen, I cannot tarry here any longer.

It's time to move on...

JOSIAH SAT BETWEEN THE CANDLES, AN ISLAND OF reality in an unreal place. Their flames combined to surround his hands in golden light—a reddish-orange outline from the right, a bright white glow from the left.

The chair was uncomfortable, but comfort was the least of Josiah's problems right now. The rhythm of his breathing, punctuated by his pounding heart, betrayed his fear to the accusing darkness. The heat of the candles was not nearly enough to explain the sweat running down his face, and Josiah wished he were somewhere, anywhere else.

Why am I here? They didn't tell me it would be like this...

His tongue moved, breaking the lines of his dry mouth. How long had it been? An hour, two? Despite his aching back and legs, the candles seemed not to have burned at all. Josiah wanted to measure them and know for sure, but to do so would require moving his gaze from the cup at the edge of the light—and the hand that held it.

The rumors had started as soon as the "Sword of Rome" arrived in the city. At first he had dismissed them as idle talk. The man across the table from him was not ten feet tall, nor did he have knives for hands. He was not bathed in blood.

Or is he?

"Are you ready, Father?"

The hungry darkness swallowed up Josiah's words, and the response he received made him even more uncomfortable than the chair.

"Yes...Constable. Bring them now. You will stand...silent.

Witness. Reflect on...what you learn."

The voice was made of gravel, each word clawing its way across the table and sending his heart racing even faster. The hard man across from him hadn't spoken since growling instructions to remove the torches and brazier that would normally light the room. When Josiah returned from that errand, the impossible candles were already burning.

He didn't remember why he brought the jug of wine, or what had become of it. He could smell it in the air—thin, watery and bitter. But where was it? The cup had not moved since Josiah sat down, nor had the hand holding it.

By now it must be soured in this heat. If only he would raise the cup and soften his rough throat.

If only I'd thought to bring my own goblet, or perhaps some bread...

"It shall be as you say, Father."

Each word Josiah spoke cemented him in this reality. Each heartbeat pushed him further back into his chair, making the world outside the candles' light seem far away. He thought of fresh wine, full of rich notes and body. Of the moon and stars and cool summer breezes. Anything but the cup.

And the Voice.

"Of course. There is no...other way. You will see...things. Hear things. You will...learn."

"Yes, Father."

Josiah hoped whatever lessons the priest meant for him would be over quickly. Each minute he spent here was an ordeal, one he could only escape by...

"Constable?"

The sweat on his face and neck was suddenly ice cold.

"Yes, Father."

"Your first...lesson. Addressing...men...of Faith. There is but...one...Father. And...we all...serve...at his will!"

The unseen chair shifted, and from darkness emerged a face as angry as the words. The cup was forgotten, replaced by a cold, dead stare framed by a twisting white scar. Light from the candles clung to the sharp edges of an otherwise clean-shaven jaw, pulling shadows high onto his forehead.

Josiah felt something scraping across his soul as the priest spoke. All he could see were the man's hard eyes, even as his ears registered the sound of unfamiliar words. Each one stabbed deep into his mind, and the more he tried to understand them, the more they slipped away like sand in a glass.

When the words finally stopped, Josiah was sitting in his chair with tears streaming down his face. The candles were as unchanged as ever, but the cup had moved and was unattended on the table.

"Bring in the...first one. You have more...to learn. Bring more wine...when you...return."

The words were hardly louder than a whisper, but from the deep blackness on the other side of table they sounded like an avalanche.

"Yes...Brother."

More wine.

The words echoed in his mind as he stole another glance at the empty cup. It was a simple thing, hardened wood turned on a lathe and lined with some dark coating. It drew him in, welcomed him as if there were room enough to crawl inside and never be frightened again.

More Wine!

The needs of Josiah's feet triumphed over those of his soul. He stood, careful not to jostle the table and upset the priest further.

If I am to be witness to an inquisition, I should take care not to become the object of one. The girl first, I think. Her account is incomplete, but more reliable. She is the best source for the answers he seeks.

IT WAS DARK, I DIDN'T SEE MUCH, BUT I SAW THAT MONK. I ain't never forgetting that!

"He was dressed like you. He even looked like you, a little. Our part of Paris, we don't get lots of traffic from University folk. He was always coming by, walking and looking at things. Moving like he belonged there, but just didn't fit right. Like he wasn't part of things, but almost was.

"No, I don't know his name. He never stopped to talk with anyone, all the weeks he was here. Always looking so sad. That ain't normal for folks like you, right?

"Oh, I didn't know that. But it was more than just sad that evening. It was...dreamy, sort of. Like he was listening to something none of us could hear.

"We was all closing down our stalls. It was a good day, lots of students wanting flowers for the festival. I had some coins—too many I guess, and someone noticed. A man grabbed my arm, took my bag of coins. Another one put his hand over my mouth. It smelled like bad fish.

"How did I feel? Worried, scared. I know what happens to women ain't got no protectors. All I can think is maybe they'll go quick, maybe no child comes from it. Maybe they won't kill me after.

"How many? I think there were three, maybe four men. I couldn't see so clear, they dragged me into the shadows. Maybe I saw one man.

"Yes, yes! He was dark, like his skin was burned. How did you know?

"Everything was frozen in place like one of them paintings hung on a wall in some fancy room. I felt cold, like maybe I was frozen too. The other stallholders was just staring, standing still. There weren't really nothing they could do, so I ain't angry or nothing.

"Thank you, that means a lot to me. You're a kind man.

"And that's when I saw him. None of us was moving, just him and the men. He was moving fast, fast like a horse, running around the corner kinda blurry-like. The hands let go and I fell on the ground. I couldn't move or turn my head, but I could still hear things. There was shouting, lots of it. I didn't understand the words.

"I think he got one of their knives, then drove the others away. I never knew you men of God was strong like that.

"No, I don't think he was hurt. I never heard his voice before, so I guess he could have been one of them yelling behind me. I just don't think he was. If someone was getting hurt, they deserved it more than he did.

"Does it make me a bad person? That I'm glad he was hurting them, punishing them for what they did, or was going to do?

"Yes, you're right. It's all right to be happy. Thanks for saying that.

"No, I ain't thirsty at all. It's not so bad, talking to you like this. I feel better than I have since...well, you know.

"The fight. Yes, that's it. Like I said, I really didn't see all that much. The light was fading. Just like I was hoping for, it was over quick.

"After they was gone, after it ended, things was moving again. I felt something wet on my neck. When I could move my arm, I touched it and felt the blood. It wasn't my blood, but I saw one of them on the ground, with lots of blood all around him. Your friend put my coins back in the bag and tucked it inside my dress.

"Oh, I'm sorry. I thought you knew him. You *are* a lot alike.

"He lifted me up and laid me back against the cart. His hands was

kind, gentle. Like my mother's, when I was a little girl. Helping me when I fell.

"Yes, it was exactly like that. He touched my arm here, and here. He put his head on my chest, and placed a hand on my head.

"I think he weren't hurt at all himself. There was some blood on him too, but he was moving fine. Not as fast as before, but in better shape than the other one.

"When the others came crowding around me, he just slipped away. Except for me, and the blood, and the man on the ground, it was like nothing had happened.

"No, I didn't see where he went, but if you find him, you thank him for me. I owe him my life, and more.

"That's it, I think. That's all that happened. I hope I helped you. I like talking with you.

"Yes, thank you. You go with God too."

W HAT HAVE YOU...LEARNED?"
The hard voice from the darkness caught Josiah by
surprise as he closed the door, but he at least knew
how to answer the priest's question.

Josiah had given quite a bit of attention to the woman as
she spoke. The light of the candles framed her face, revealing
sores on her cheeks and brow and dark discolorations on her
neck that were most likely healing bruises.

Just hours after the attack she had been frightened and
near tears. Her story had been hard to understand, and there
had definitely been something odd about it. Several days later,
her second account was detached, describing the events almost as if they had happened to someone else. Her chief concern had been for the identity and location of her rescuer, the
man who now...

"What have you...learned! Collect your...thoughts. Quickly. Impressions. Meaning. These fade with...time. Speak your
mind...while you can."

The darkness was intent on an answer, and Josiah gave it.

"I...things are not always what they seem? This third version of her story is different from the other two. She said she
could remember nothing, but when you asked the questions,
she did. More and more as you went on. How..."

"You do not...question. You stand as...witness. She heard
what...she needed...to hear. What else?"

Josiah was sitting now, with no memory of how he came
to be across from the scarred man. Somehow he had walked

to the table, pulled out the chair, and filled the cup in front of him.

I am so tired, as if I've been standing for a hundred years. A drink, a cool drink of wine will...

"Constable! What else?"

A chill passed through Josiah's body, replacing the impossible heat on his skin with ice in his heart.

The cup was forgotten.

The Voice was all.

"The things she describes, the light, not being able to move, the speed of the attack. These are things she did not tell me before. But when you asked, when she answered your questions, I knew the words were true. I do not know how that can be possible, but it is."

Josiah's racing heart slowed as he spoke, as if voicing his thoughts were the most important thing he could be doing. In this newfound calm he noticed an odd smell, a scent of flowers that must have come with the girl and lingered in her absence.

How long did she sit here, to leave behind that part of herself?

How long have I sat here before noticing it?

As the silence deepened, Josiah felt other questions bubbling up inside him. How had the priest known exactly what to ask, or even what the right questions were? No witness had ever spoken to Josiah with such honesty and certainty, yet the scarred priest drew information out of the girl as easily as...

As...

The candles still refused to move as they burned. Josiah no longer feared them, though sweat still trailed down his face to gather at his collar. His mouth was dry and pasty. If there was water to be had, or better yet wine, he would surely feel better. He would...

"The next...witness...Constable. Little time...remains... for us. Much to learn. Much to...accomplish. Go. Now. Bring more wine."

The candlelight flickered, and to Josiah the unexpected change seemed every bit as violent as the crime they investigated. No wind had stirred the flames, and the room's other occupant was too far from the candles for his breath to move them. And outside the island of light there was only darkness, untouched by the sweltering heat. It was if the warmth and light outside the chamber's door was forbidden to enter that space…

His space.

"Do not…tarry. And do not…forget…the wine."

Josiah found his feet, and in the act of standing his spirit soared. Each step he took toward the door brought him closer to the world of light on the other side.

His hand closed on the handles of a wooden bar he did not remember securing, but he paused before opening it, his churning thoughts at war with his desire to turn and look at the priest.

When he did look back, all he saw was the cup, now dry and empty like his mouth. Josiah didn't know how long he stared at the cup, but fearing another breathy rebuke he fumbled with the bar and slipped outside to fetch the next witness.

I SAW EVERYTHING! IT WAS AMAZING, SIMPLY AMAZING!
"We were all packing away our stalls and carts, and some
dark men grabbed Anne-Marie. We all wanted to help,
but for some reason, none of us could move. There must have
been at least six of them, all dark.

"Dark like Gypsies? We don't like their kind, but I don't
think so. Their heads weren't covered.

"Really? Jews? I didn't know that. I thought, what with all
the scarves...

"Sorry. Yes, dark like that. Like they were covered in shadow, like something was between them and a bright light.

"Anyway, these men were dragging her away, back into
the corner. It was hard to make them out back there, almost
like the sun set early just in that one spot. They must have
knocked her out, because she weren't screaming or kicking or
making any fuss.

"Then, from around the corner, on the far side of the
square, the monk came. He was running like the devil himself
was on his heels, and he charged right into them.

"It happened so fast. Half of them ran away, but the ones
that stayed attacked him with these long knives of theirs. It
was still dark in that spot, but right around where he was I
could see everything clear and sharp, like a white light was
shining on him.

"No, now that I think about it, there were still shadows—
but I saw him really clearly—he seemed to be the only one
doing anything! I was trying to move, but all I could do was

watch him.

"He was so fast. He disarmed the first man, threw him against the wall like he was a feather. Another came at him, and their blades flashed. I guess it was lighter over there than I thought, because the knives was rippling and shifting like the surface of a river.

"Oh, sorry. Yes, two men fighting him. They weren't all that good. I seen a few knife fights in my life, enough to know that the monk was better than anyone I ever seen! Lots better than the two fighting him. He must have been a soldier or something before, he was so good.

"Right, sorry. You're right, I got no way of knowing about that, I was making that part up. But like I said, he was much better than other people I seen, and he didn't shy away from any of their attacks. He just...he just...

"One went down almost right away, with a long, bloody cut on his arm. I think the monk said something then, but I couldn't make it out.

"No, no I'm not thirsty, thank you. You should have seen him fight! He was down to one opponent now, and he danced and spun like an acrobat. All the while it looked like he were saying something—something that made the other man laugh. But then I saw he weren't laughing, he were angry.

"Now that you say it, yes, it did seem like singing. I couldn't make it out though...

"Yes, Yes, that's it! Those were the words. What is...

"I never...I...oh, yes, the fighter. He went a little crazy, and started swinging wild at the monk, and it looked like he had an opening to really hurt him. But then he slipped, maybe on the blood. I didn't think the first man was that badly hurt, but there was lots of blood on the ground.

"Anyway, he went down hard. The monk stopped...singing, and he looked surprised. There was lots more blood now, but none of it seemed to touch the monk. He bent over the man, said something, and then moved his hand over his face.

"Yes, like that, exactly like that! Then he bent over and picked something up. He took Anne-Marie over to her cart, and I think he said something to her. I couldn't hear that either, but I saw her smile.

"We could move again then, and we rushed over to help. I lost track of him in the shuffle, but I remember what happened for sure. If you see your friend, let him know that we all appreciate everything he did for us. No-one's had any trouble since then.

"Oh, I'm sorry, I thought you knew him, from the way you were talking. I guess I was mistaken. Yes, yes, thank you. I feel a lot better now that I've talked to someone about it."

WHAT HAS HE...SAID...CONSTABLE? THAT THE GIRL...
did not?"

This time, Josiah was ready with an answer. After ushering the merchant out, he'd started arranging his words in anticipation of the priest's question. Josiah had only heard the man's account once before, but even though it had grown in the telling it was still recognizably the same.

Nudging the door closed with his shoulder, he set down two jugs of sweet wine and slid the bar into place as he spoke.

"He had an excellent view of the attack, but his account is suspect. That part about the light. His own lack of action, his failure to help the girl—it makes the rescue seem more heroic."

"You forget...something. Something...important. The girl's story. How does it... differ... from his?"

"I...I can't think of anything else. I'm sorry."

"Think on this...as we go...to the last...witness. Both spoke...truly. They had no...other choice."

Though Josiah heard the priest stand, he could not tear his eyes away from the cup in front of him. The candles were little more than stubs now, and their light only covered half the table.

The cup danced at the edge of their glow, half in light, half in shadow. Its edges were blurry, but the dark interior still beckoned him in to warmth and comfort. He reached a trembling hand toward it, but his arm was too heavy and sank back onto the arm of his chair.

Chair? How did I...what...?

He knew the cup was empty. He knew he had filled it, and that three jugs of wine were now dry on the floor at his feet.

But he did not remember...

Three?

Josiah looked down at the unfamiliar jug in his hands. His mouth was dry, sour, and the smell of wildflowers still lingered in the air.

"Are you quite...finished...Constable?"

Josiah turned to find the priest's scarred face a hand's breadth from his own. There was something in his eyes, as if something...more...was looking through them than a man.

Something old.

"Brother?"

There was a flash of red light as the left candle guttered and died, and a rustle of black cloth moved away from the table. Josiah wanted to follow it, but he had to look. Had to know.

The cup was gone.

"Brother?"

"Yes? Something you...remember? Something you...want to say?" The priest's voice came from somewhere behind him, and Josiah's Eyes were drawn to a dark shape silhouetted in the doorway.

Without waiting for an answer, the priest turned and moved down the hall. Josiah hurried after him, stumbling over the empty jugs as the second candle went out.

He caught up to the inquisitor when he stopped at the top of the stair leading down to the lower levels. The priest's scar seemed like a living thing, framing the cold eyes of a man who had seen and heard too much.

"Ask it then. What you want...to know. Hurry. There is not...much time."

The heat of the room was a distant memory, and Josiah shivered as the torches flickered and died. There was much he did not understand about tonight, and as he searched through his memories of the questions, he settled instead on a set of words in a language he did not understand, but were still somehow familiar.

Ask your question.

"Brother, what was that phrase, those words you spoke to the merchant? I've never heard anything like it before. But when you said them, it seemed...right."

The scar twisted as the priest pressed his lips together, then turned away before speaking.

"It was...The Matins. We sing it...when the night...is blackest. We do it...to remind...ourselves...there is still...light...in the world."

Josiah followed the priest down the curving stone stairs, the sound of his boots chasing the much softer impacts of the other man's sandals until the world above was all but forgotten. When the dark priest spoke again, he nearly stumbled the remaining distance to the next landing.

"He was...praying...Constable."

I BEG OF YOU, SIR. DO NOT GO IN THERE. THERE IS A FOULNESS, an evil surrounding that man. Let him die in the darkness, as he so well deserves."

The corpulent jailer stood fast in the archway, barring access to his small domain. Deep underground, the bowels of this urban stronghold so thoughtfully supplied by the Templars had been turned into a dungeon, and he was its sniveling master.

"Always...there is light. You profess...this is...untrue? By my...office...and my...order...you will let...us pass. Attend your...other charge. We see him...soon enough."

The fat man still refused to stand aside, and in a flicker of torchlight, the priest was on him. The dark-robed man's eyes flashed as he seized the jailer by the shoulders, leaning in close to his ear.

The priest's scarred lips whispered too low for Josiah to make out the words, but with each wheezing syllable, the jailor's face drained of color. Josiah's memory of his own earlier lesson was terrifying enough to turn his attention to the room around them.

There was indeed light around them, from flaming torches on the walls and a bright fire burning in a tiny hearth across the room, the blaze contained by an iron grating and fed by chunks of white wood and dark lumps of coal from a nearby bronze pail.

The heat from the fire dried the air, warming stone walls, heavy wooden doors, and the heavy iron traps securing them.

But though it warmed Josiah's face and arms, it did nothing to melt the ice in his veins.

The priest's whispering stopped, and the jailer stumbled. He pressed a ring of iron keys into the constable's hands, then ran shivering up the stairs.

But Josiah's attention stayed on the hunched back of the inquisitor. After his encounter with the jailer he seemed smaller somehow. But whatever it was the priest was feeling passed in a few heartbeats, and his thin shoulders squared once more as he turned toward Josiah.

For a moment, Josiah considered running up the stairs as well. The smile on the priest's scarred face had nothing to do with pleasure. The man's eyes were entirely untouched by the movement of his lips, and whatever words were fighting their way from his ravaged lungs died in his throat as a muffled voice called to them from behind a solid door.

"Hey, you out there! If you sent that fat pig running, I say come in. I would meet any man who can inspire such action in so great a wasted space."

The voice was weak, but confident. At a nod from the dark priest, the constable moved forward, fumbling with the cold keys until he found the proper one.

The trap came free, and as he opened it the door scraped to a halt on the uneven stone floor. The half-opened panel blocked the warm yellow light of the fire, and in the torches' red glow the dirty flesh of the man sitting in the cell beyond appeared almost black. A gaping wound ran along his right arm, and the stitching on his tattered tunic spoke to better days long since passed.

The prisoner squinted at the torchlight, trying to make out Josiah and the priest. When the nature of his visitors finally registered, he laughed.

"Another priest. What luck, that I should be so attended twice in one week."

"Take care...brigand. I am not...Fortune. I am...Truth. And I am...Justice. You live for...my answers. You will speak...the truth. Only then...will you know...peace."

The priest's pronouncement did not faze the prisoner, but to be fair, all he could do from his position on the floor was shrug. Josiah saw weeping sores on his hands, and also through bloody holes in his pantaloons.

Perhaps he has no strength for anything else.

The priest flowed forward, and it looked to Josiah as if his robes swallowed up the red light. The prisoner's eyes widened as the dark presence eclipsed his face, and all Josiah could make out of the man was the rattling of his chains.

The priest took hold of the door and pulled it toward him. One eye and the tip of his scar regarded Josiah from the narrow opening. In the torchlight, both appeared carved from the stone walls around them and painted with blood. The next words the priest spoke sent a charge along his skin, as if lightning had struck in the room.

"Remember what you were told."

Then the heavy door slid closed on the cell already crowded with one prisoner, leaving Josiah alone with his thoughts. He had been told many things tonight, but foremost in his mind were his superior's last instructions before the rest of the constables left the building.

"Carry out whatever orders he gives you as if they were my own, and God help you if you question the man or impede him in any way."

But there was another voice in Josiah's head, speaking words he only now recalled.

"After I enter, lock the door, and no matter what you hear do not open it again."

Josiah's hands came up, and part of him wondered why they were shaking. He watched them reset the iron trap on the door, and lock it with one of the keys. He closed his eyes, and when he opened them he was standing next to the hearth.

The torches were nearly burned out, as was the bed of coals. Josiah's heart hammered in his chest, but he made no move to replenish either. He could just make out the door in the dying torchlight—the light from the hearth skulked around his feet as if afraid to go any further into the room.

Josiah understood that fear all too well. Shadows danced around the door in time to the low murmuring he strained to hear from the other side. Then there was a sharp cry, and nothing more.

The door swung all the way open, slamming into the wall. The dying torches flared to angry life at the touch of an unseen breeze, revealing a dead man in rags slumped on the floor. The chains still hung over his body, but his arms were now free and his face was fixed in a child-like smile.

Josiah's mouth worked, but no sound came out. He couldn't tear his eyes from the dead man's expression, so unlike the scowl he wore in life. Then the fire in the hearth went out, and he turned to see the priest standing next to him, holding an empty cup and a ring of iron keys.

"Ask."

Darkness hovered in the lines of his cruel face, and the scents of sweet flowers and sour wine rose from him. Josiah tried to remain true to his promise, but the compulsion to speak was too strong.

"What...what happened? What did he tell you?"

"The truth. There was no...other way...to respond. You must not...you will not speak of this again. To anyone."

The torches died completely, taking with them the sight of those cold, dead eyes. One last ember popped in the hearth, sending up a spark that revealed the edge of the priest's scar before burning out and leaving him in darkness.

With the Voice.

"Go. Now. I have the...proof I need. You are...released."

Josiah needed no further prompting to turn and stumble for the dim sanctuary of the stairway. He was halfway there when the heat on his skin disappeared, and his feet refused to move.

"Josiah."

Josiah strained against unseen chains of ice binding him to the floor and walls. Hints of red teased the blackness around him, and slow footsteps crept toward him from behind.

"Do not leave...the city. We are not...finished...you and I. There is more...service...you will give. Answers...to extract."

Josiah closed his eyes and offered up a prayer for strength, then he ran, bouncing against the cold walls and tripping over his feet as he scrambled up the stairs. He hit the ground hard, and the smell of garbage and urine and musty wood was everywhere.

He opened his eyes onto a dimly lit alley and scrambled back until he collapsed against a solid wall, staring out at the foggy streets he'd walked too many times to count.

Outside? How...

The last bit of warmth inside him drained away, leaving him hugging the stone wall in a futile attempt to capture even a portion of the previous day's heat.

He heard the city wake up around him, the people of the night giving way to those who worked the dawn with sounds of laughter and creaking cart wheels. The cold morning sun burned away the mists, banishing them back into the last shadows of night.

A shadow moved at the corner of his eye. A black doorway formed, from which came a thin, hard man. Josiah stared, a scream rising in his throat as he recognized the place his feet had brought him.

A cold smile pulled at an angry scar, and a low chuckle escaped the priest's lips. Abandoning the wall, Josiah kept his eyes fixed on the man as he descended three low steps to the street. He stumbled away on torn palms and bruised boot soles until he felt the solid wood of a cart at his back and a soft, colorful avalanche of wildflowers took it away.

Josiah raised a bloody palm to wipe away petals from his eyes, pushing back against the cart and rising with the assistance of a sweet-smelling, delicate hand. When they were clear, he found himself looking into the face of the flower girl, now covered in angry red blisters.

Josiah ran, trusting no sense but survival. He had to escape before madness swallowed up what was left of his soul. Before he spent his life in a darkened room, drinking forever from an empty cup.

He ran as the city woke around him, leaving behind its true self and donning its beautiful disguise.

Until all he could hear was rasping laughter echoing off the warming stones, growing louder with each step he took.

C ARLOS...DE ROJA."

A splash of foul-smelling water woke him to darkness and pain. Carlos' dry, cracked lips parted, but a hacking cough was the only reply he could offer. The bucket that woke him for each session of questioning was all the refreshment he'd had in days, and a second helping was never offered.

The coughing reminded him of the grating in his left wrist and the cracked bones in his chest. As the shock of his awakening passed, the agony of Carlos' situation returned, and with it the memory of a smoking censer exploding on his skin and filling the room with the smell of frankincense and burning flesh.

The wounds from the coals would be long in healing, though they were the least of his difficulties. Stripped of his dignity as well as his cassock, he kept a record of each of the inquisitor's questions on what little flesh still hung on his bones.

"Carlos...the Red. You are...accused...of dark deeds. Brought here...so we may...cast out...your demons. Do you dwell...in God's light? Or has the...Beast...taken you?"

Carlos' memory supplied the face, though despite the pain he was glad his sight had failed him again. His last vision of his tormentor was of the man's perpetual sneer and twisted scar glowing in the light of heated irons.

Somewhere in front of him was Brother Paulo Rodrigo. Special Inquisitor for his Holiness, Pope Innocent III.

His second attempt at an answer was not as painful, although it could hardly be counted as success. Nothing that brought such agony could be thought of as a desired outcome.

"Accuse though you may, I... I confess only that I do not yet dwell with the Lord. I am no demon, Ro...Rodrigo. I am a man, as much His servant as you. You can do no harm to my soul, only to this vessel."

The words were more painful than expected. More coughing, more blood, precious life he could ill-afford to spill onto the reeking straw covering the floor of his prison.

"Have a care...Carlos. You presume...much...with such words."

"I am no northern heretic that I should fear you. I am God's servant, thrice ordained in Faith and Sacrament, and he may call me home at his leisure. I have no fear of this world or the next."

Nothing matters now but my failure.

The beginnings of a pained smile danced on Carlos' abused lips. His arrival in Paris had not been the spiritual awakening he'd hoped for, but no-one could have predicted that an act of kindness would land him in chains.

"Enough! Your...heresy...is clear. You serve...evil...or are... possessed. Did you not...record...such things...in this book? Or in these... heathen scrolls?"

Without his eyes to inform him, Carlos assumed that Rodrigo either referred to the legacy bequeathed to him by his friends in the south, or the rough volume Matthieu gave him to document his investigations into Karl Outrikos.

Sewn by hand, it was a gift of love meant to share experiences as those scholars before him had done. This tiny vanity was no blasphemy, though it did contain a copy of the record that started this journey so many months ago.

'Knowing what manner of demon it contained, we threw back the shutters, and the cleansing light of day shone full upon his face. He would kill no more.'

His search for answers led him to Paris, and though his journey was surely over, Carlos' thirst for knowledge was as deep as ever.

"Shall I read...these words...to you? Or perhaps...you to me. These lies…sent to your...cabal...confirm your...guilt."

Rodrigo must have intercepted my letters. That is how we come to this.

Carlos had known many men like the inquisitor over the years, men who saw only those facts they sought in the words on the page. His life was dedicated to uncovering truth, but he never thought truth would lead him to this ignominious end.

"Confess...Carlos. Release...Satan's tail. Embrace...again... our Savior."

Would it be so bad, so wrong to confess? To tell the madman what he wants to hear, so that I may rest? The Lord knows what is in my heart, and words not given to him mean nothing.

They would stop the pain. Stop the questions.

But not the Truth.

Carlos could not turn his back on truth, after chasing it so far. He had made promises, commitments to his Brothers that would die unfulfilled with him if his life ended here. But if he died alone, with his honor intact, his soul would be safe.

Though his reputation would be ruined.

His life was over either way, all because one man could not think outside his own experience. Afraid of a conspiracy that does not exist.

Lies sent to my cabal, he said. But I never…can Rodrigo even read?

If he'd had any breath to spare, Carlos would have laughed at his tormentor's uncovered ruse. Fear drained from his wasted body, and his last doubts slipped away like leaves on the river.

If Rodrigo cannot read the journal, he couldn't read the dispatches either.

"You mistake facts for fiction, Brother. You have only a portion of the record, rather than the whole. Shall I tell you a tale that you may carry back to Rome? Had you allowed those missives to travel south, they would have been answered by now, and with any reply would come facts compiled by my apprentice that even one such as you could not ignore."

Another solid truth Carlos was sure the inquisitor would reject. His apprentice Robere had continued Carlos' research since he'd left the Abbey of Sant Cugat du Valles, augmenting the records Carlos assembled before his departure with some unexpected analysis of his own. Some of them had been waiting for him when he arrived in Paris and, should he ever leave this place, he was eager to speak to his student about what he'd learned.

But first I must survive Paulo Rodrigo.

The actions of Rome's special inquisitor made no sense. Carlos had done nothing wrong, yet he had been imprisoned and beaten. Rodrigo seemed less concerned by the events in question than uncovering Carlos' supposed sins against the church and his fellow man.

And all the while, Rodrigo's rasping voice commanded him to confess dark intent. The questions were not in line with what Carlos understood Rodrigo's mandate to be, and even if he were inclined to give one, there were no witnesses to hear his confession.

"We are...aware...of your...ridic...ulous...fictions, Carlos. Monster men. Strange...diseases. Dark plots. Your claims...are madness. Your stories...are lies. You have...taken...the power... of darkness...for your own.

"Repent...Carlos. While you can."

Rodrigo's words were honey sweet, but there was no mistaking the malice that lay behind them. The last time Carlos had seen his face, there had been a touch of madness around Rodrigo's eyes.

But when he spoke just now, his anger was cold and calculated. What, if anything, has changed?

Carlos could hear Rodrigo's labored breathing from across the room, and when sandaled feet approached across the floor, he steeled himself for another blow.

Instead he heard a new voice, and almost wept.

"Carlos, do you truly believe what you have written? Do you still assert that that the Moors fight against Satan's corruption as do the faithful? That the healing light of the Lord will combat dark forces if commanded by our enemies, as well as it would serve us who dwell in His love?"

To have an audience at last, after so much pain, could only mean that the end was at hand. But in contrast to Rodrigo's harsh barks, something about the new speaker's voice was compelling, and if Carlos was to die, he wanted first to speak to at least one person who might listen. Pain, hunger, cracked lips, bruised ribs, all could be ignored if it meant his last words might be heard with open ears.

Teeth clenching tight against the pain, he responded to the questions voiced by this unseen and unknown witness.

"The only blackness here is that which Rodrigo has brought. I have none to offer—only truth. Offer it to you I do, and gladly. Both my research and my faith are valid and pure. All that I have said, all that I have written, and all that I have done are correct and true to God's teachings. I have no use for witchcraft or sorceries. I have no power on this Earth not granted by the Holy Father we all serve."

Carlos' spirit soared with each word. A new fire burned inside him, and though he could not see his witness, the desire to tell him everything grew with each breath he took.

"The truth is known and has been known by others through the years. I am only the latest to embrace it, and though I die today, I will not be the last."

Carlos heard something metallic jangling to his left, and for a moment imagined the room as he'd last seen it. In the dim red light of the coals, the outlines of three figures co-alesced into one, which shone with a bright light that rivaled the sun.

After so long in darkness, even the imagined light was enough to make Carlos turn his head away. But the vision passed as suddenly as it came, leaving him blind once more.

Darkness is my life now. Never again will I read a history, or write a manuscript. And even if I knew where the parchment was, there's no point in holding a quill. Rodrigo has done worse than kill me—by blinding me he's taken away everything I love.

The jangling continued, and fresh pain flared as his injured wrist was lifted. Metal scraped against metal, and when the cuff fell away, the pain shifted into a wave of ecstasy as his arm came down.

The right cuff came free next, and for the first time in an eternity of exhaustion, his arms and shoulders no longer supported his weight. Strong hands caught him as he collapsed, sending fresh agony though his chest as he was laid back on the straw floor.

Free. For now, at least. I am almost finished. Welcome me, oh Father on high. Your child returns home.

"Father Carlos de Roja. Of Toledo, late of Barcelona, late of Sant Cugat de Valles and the Blessed Stone. By my authority, and by decree of His Holiness the Pope, you have been examined and found blameless of the charges laid against you."

Blameless. Innocent?

In another place the words would have meaning. Here, they were strange music accompanied by a smell of freshly baked loaves.

"I...am released?"

This must be some cruel jest. No one is ever set free after this level of questioning.

"Yes, my Brother. There is no taint within you that we can find."

Thank you, for believing me. Please tell them that I...

"Stay with me, Brother, we are not done here. You will tell them yourself, in time."

You will rise again, and carry a sword of Truth against the gathered darkness.

A cool cup was placed to his lips, and Carlos drank down sweet water tasting of blood. The memory of flowers on a hillside carried him down into oblivion.

16 AUGUST, YEAR OF OUR LORD 1205

Who will climb the mountain of the Lord?
Who will stand in his holy place?
The one who is innocent of wrongdoing and
pure of heart, who has not given
himself to vanities or sworn falsely.
He will receive the blessing of the Lord
and be justified by God his savior.
This is the way of those who seek him,
seek the face of the God of Jacob.

FOR CARLOS, RECOVERY WAS A PROCESS DRIVEN BY WILL more than any other factor. After the trials of body and soul he'd endured over the last few months, he refused ever to give up again.

If his friends could see him now they would hardly recognize the man walking the streets of Paris. Although his robes hid much, they hung on his too-thin frame like a collapsed tent. The flesh of his face was drawn tight across angled cheeks, and his hands sometimes shook with remembered pain.

There was little padding left on either face or hands, and his months in the hidden enclave of Blessed Stone had already cut away any extra tissue surrounding the core of his faith. Though the bruises and burns had faded, the true pain of Carlos' ordeal was still with him.

Putting the memories of that persecution aside would be a long and arduous process—one much less certain than recovering from his physical wounds. His wrist was completely healed after only a month, with only the occasional twinge to remind him of the grinding ruin it had been. The vision in his left eye had returned, but the right side of his world was defined by haze and too-sharp sounds.

To aid in his recovery, his medicus—a visiting scholar named Luther Welmach—suggested that he resume his walks through the city. Carlos was happy to comply, but had been unprepared for the assault on his senses. Aside from the partial blindness, his time in the torture chamber had sharpened already acute senses to unheard-of levels. Each breeze carried smells to him from across the city, and sounds no one around him could hear.

A flash of memory came at him from the right, of ill-dressed robbers with foul breath assaulting him as he attempted to give aid to another according to his vows. The image disappeared when he turned to look at it with his left eye, showing only an empty alleyway.

More often of late, an errant breeze or isolated sound triggered a memory like that one—a picture painted of what was, and sometimes of what could be in the gray shadows seen through his previously dominant eye.

At times he pretended it was but a shadow cast over objects in his field of vision, a temporary darkness that would soon dissipate. Then a turn of his head brought an unspoiled look, a splash of light and color.

In a city as large as Paris, this was a blessing accompanied by a curse. With each smell came a great sense of nostalgia, and he sometimes had problems placing the exact reason why he could describe places he was sure he'd never before visited. But the feelings—the memories—were there in his mind, lack of context notwithstanding.

Of the months he'd lived in the city, half had been spent acquiring—or healing from—injuries. And despite the confusion it brought, it was good to leave his borrowed bedchamber for a while and walk the streets like a man without fear.

They looked different now, as summer moved on. Like his too-short spring, this season was almost over, and the cool days felt more like those of fall. The shadows were longer and the light warmer, though the rising wind promised new chills in the night. Further north than the Blessed Stone, the university schools of Ste. Genevieve and St. Victor were known to see snow quite early in the year. Cold fogs embraced the Seine at dawn and in the preceding hours—mists that often brought sickness to the unprepared.

Another experience I have no desire to repeat. Too much of this year has been spent as a spectator. And if my sight does not return...

Since there are no vines to tend, and few patients to see with more than enough skilled hands to see them, Carlos was little more than a curious visitor who could not read for long without assistance.

Far worse than his inability to serve was the isolation. Despite the Bishop's most excellent introductions, his time in the custody of Paulo Rodrigo had made him an individual of suspect motives, verdict of innocence notwithstanding. As the days moved on, he spent more and more of his time alone. Tonight he would reaffirm his faith along with the other monks, but without the warmth of spirit he had felt singing alongside Matthieu, Father Frances, and the brothers of Sant Cugat. It was hard to find a harmony with men he did not know. Rather than disturb their worship, he often stood in the back using only a portion of his full voice. The lack of friendship was palpable but survivable.

The continuing construction of the Cathedral of Notre Dame meant workers, labor, and noise. The construction kicked up dust, tickling both his nose and his memory and bringing to mind happier days in Barcelona.

Perhaps it is time to move on.

Rome still waited for him, and if any of his missions were to be completed, it would be there. Apart from his delayed search for records on both previous disease outbreaks and the elusive Karl, his duties back home—and whatever future he may have in that place—took precedence.

Perhaps, by then, I will be of some use.

It did not feel right to leave Paris before finding any evidence here of his theories, but researching with only one eye had proved more difficult than the painful exercises necessary to rebuild his body. And if his blindness persisted all the way to Rome...

Only time will tell. For now, back to my cell. Physical Faith has concluded, and Luther Welmach is waiting for me.

And with the coming of night, I will lift my voice again, alone in a choir.

"I MUST BE HONEST, CARLOS, THESE VOLUMES ARE REMARKABLE in their descriptions. This Yee healer you met was truly a master of the craft."

Carlos smiled at Luther Welmach's words, hiding the pain in his heart at the mention of his departed friend. Luther was referring to Carlos' efforts to transcribe her manual of herb lore, now spread across his shelf and desk.

"Yes, Qin Yee was remarkably skilled." Carlos winced at the deception, but the pain was still too raw, and if Luther thought "Master Yee" to be a man, it was a mistake Carlos could well understand, having once made a similar one.

If the books' previous owner were present in his spare cell at the Abbey of St. Victor, she could provide no more clarity than the words Carlos had laboriously deciphered during the cold months of spring.

Luther's smile crinkled his eyes. He was a stocky man, whose face and hands were tanned from a life spent travelling across Europe. Although he'd never asked, from things he'd said Carlos estimated Luther was fifty years old, possibly even a few years older. While Carlos' mentor Frances delaMonde was even older, Carlos found it amusing to have a "student" almost twice his age.

Luther had come to Paris to make copies of the very work that had inspired Carlos to become a healer, Avicenna's *Canon of Medicine*. While not a Christian himself, he'd bartered his own knowledge and made a sizeable donation for that right, and the two healers had begun their association weeks before

Carlos had found himself accused and Luther's more practical skills had been required.

Luther's knowledge of forestry was extensive, and combined with the knowledge of Avicenna, his skill as an herbalist was remarkable. His mission to bring back a more permanent version of that lore would certainly be enhanced by the contents of the Yee text.

And while Luther had been willing to assist his colleague's recovery for free, Carlos had insisted the man accept instruction in the herb lore learned during his time at the Blessed Stone as payment. Few others had been so inclined, and Carlos was also thankful for Luther's help during those times when his vision clouded.

Of late, only one other man had been so helpful, the nameless Judge who ended Carlos' torture after hearing his true confession.

But that was another life. My act of charity may have ended my career as an archivist.

Carlos had returned to a monastic life easily upon his arrival in Paris, and this sleeping chamber was a near duplicate of the one he'd occupied in Sant Cugat du Valles. A small writing desk, a shelf for sleeping, and a stool for visitors, occupied now by his doctor. Here he had no window, but the candle's light was an acceptable companion to the daylight streaming in from the hallway. As the hours of the day progressed, it would no longer be merely a supplement, but the cheapest and best alternative.

There was one other difference of note—the brightly painted chest holding the family records of the Yee clan.

"The other volume is the key, I think. The Yee family contained many learned masters, some of whom were capable of incredible things. Among their acquaintances were such men as the Yan emperor, who compiled most of the herb lore of their culture. The smaller book is full of facts and applications, but the larger contains knowledge I can only guess at."

"I wish I could read these words for myself. I have not your gift for learning new languages, my friend. German and Latin are all I can wrap my head around, and I am not the fastest reader of either."

Luther was certainly literate—his persona as a simple man from the country was one of convenience rather than actuality. In the last two months, Carlos had heard many of his stories, and all had a lesson of some sort to impart that revealed his great intelligence. Like Aesop before him, Luther had found a way to make difficult concepts acceptable to simple people, using humor and a kind smile like the one Carlos had buried with his friend Qin Yee far away to the south.

"Carlos? Are you still with me?"

The question brought Carlos back to the conversation.

My mind wanders again.

His inattention had already cost him much, but while recovering from Rodrigo's tortures, Carlos discovered that his memory had become as sharp as the rest of his senses, so much so that he now processed the world around him on a constant basis and could instantly review it after one of his mental wanderings.

Luther was asking for more information about the Yan emperor and the Yee family. But before Carlos could answer that question, the German doctor had one more of his own.

"Your head is still troubling you, isn't it? You should give renewed consideration to the patch I suggested. I believe the vision will return fully in time, but it is your mind that causes you these difficulties. Trying to adapt your perceptions to overcome the defect is the source of your pain. Once you can master it, your troubles will fade."

On days when his vision was particularly affected, words on a page were blurry, almost doubled, as if the words were trying to re-arrange themselves into new patterns. It was an eerie echo of the problem with which his friend Matthieu had struggled his entire life.

Each time it happened, Carlos felt a dull pain behind his eyes. Closing his right eye against the pain stopped the sensation, but not the problem. The image of the doubled letters stood out in glowing red outlines in his mind and refused to be ignored.

The written word, copied or composed by the hand of a man, was almost uniformly affected. Certain texts were clearer than others, but some nearly guaranteed one of these strange fits. No particular information seemed the cause of the difficulty; established church texts and lay records awaiting translation were equally afflicted. Strangely, carved signs on buildings presented no problems, nor did words inscribed on marble statues and plaques.

Like patients suffering symptoms of the same disease, each volume presented differently, though whether in Hebrew, Arabic, Latin or Greek, the effect was the same. Certain books just seemed...wrong.

Carlos moved his gaze from his translations to the brightly painted silk pages of the Yee manual. The pain in his head returned with a vengeance, only lessening when he closed both eyes. The letters of red light were waiting in the darkness for him with a message of caution regarding excessive dosage that was not present when he'd first looked at the page months before. Opening his left eye, he saw the commonly known properties of Valerian root explained in fading brown ink and his own handwriting.

But from the right side...

Carlos slowly opened his other eye. Whichever Yee master had drawn that page, they had not thought to include cautions against the envy of elves, instructions to a groom as how to ward them off on a wedding night, or how to combine it with ground toad skins to cause a death-like slumber.

And yet, I know that he knew them all.

"It is hard, Luther—very hard to separate the world I see from the one I do not. To hide from it is a surrender I am not yet prepared to make. A denial of truth that makes my ordeal less real."

Carlos had tried the patch, but placing an artificial barrier between him and the world did not seem right. However strange this impaired perception, it was now part of his life. He must adapt to these new circumstances, and with luck would learn ways to continue his re-search despite the red letters.

If there was ever anything to find.

"You are the only one who can make that choice, my young friend. I can only advise you from my own experience, which tells me that you need time as much as medicine. Your recovery so far has been remarkable, and only some of it can be credited to me."

This was a fact Carlos could not dispute. Despite his wasted appearance, he felt strong, more and more so each day as he walked the University grounds. The Abbess of the Blessed Stone would likely have even more questions for him, were she to observe this latest return to health—questions he could not answer, but for which he very much wanted an explanation.

"You underestimate the value of your company, Luther. Your words—both before and after my injuries—have been quite helpful to me. If you could but store your charm in one of your potion bottles, I am quite sure that all men everywhere would heal as I have."

A deflection. Not a lie, but also not an answer. Luther was an intelligent man, and Carlos knew he was not fooled by such wordplay. And while Luther gave no sign of annoyance, his eyes searched Carlos' face for any signs of discomfort he was unwilling to share—a technique Carlos had used himself with non-responsive patients.

Luther smiled and indicated the translations with a broad wave of his hand. "With the information in these pages, they just might. Tell me more of what other things you have read. Are there even more unknown uses for the plants and materials around us?"

Carlos attempted another deflection, while at the same time hearing the voice of Frances delaMonde chastising him for not telling Luther the whole truth.

"The nature of science is to experiment, to discover. There are possibly many additional uses for the plants we know and cultivate. I have only begun to understand the full intricacies of Wenyan, the script in which these books are composed."

"Is there no hint, no thread of insight that you have uncovered?"

Why yes, of course. White Cushion Moss can be dried, ground and powdered. When cured with a tincture of Anise and introduced in grains to food, it renders the subject extremely susceptible to suggestion, and...

"What I have uncovered relates more to my obligations

than my passions. I made a promise to complete a quest, a mission of discovery for the Yee family. I do not know how long that task will take, but I must do my best to complete it."

She deserves no less, after...

"You are pained again, Carlos. I should withdraw, and allow you to rest. May my team and I continue copying what you have translated?"

"Certainly. I am sorry that I have not copied over the illustrations, but your assistant's hand is quite adequate to the task."

Carlos gathered his parchments into neat stacks, ordering them according to the date of their translation. Looking at them with both eyes, he saw text of his first sheets as a blur, with flashes of red light throughout. His later, more recent efforts were clean and unblemished, and he set them aside, no longer sure of their accuracy. Until he was, he couldn't pass them on to Luther and his assistants.

And yet part of me wonders if the stack I hand to my learned colleague is the correct one.

"There is quite a lot of information in the descriptions you added, more than enough for us to work with. If your translations of the other volume are as complete, you do your friend and his quest great justice."

"The memory of the Yee Hero's fight against dark forces is a story we can all learn from. Bravery, Honor, Loyalty. These are all qualities to emulate."

Honesty. Carlos was again perpetuating the myth of the masculine hero, rather than the truth that he knew. Someday, he would keep his promise and compile a fully accurate and unbiased record of Huxai Yee's life.

And that of her descendant.

"What you have shared so far brings to mind the Argonauts. The scope and content of the stories are similar. When you are refreshed, we will speak more on this."

Luther rose and gathered the parchments, then walked out and closed the simple door that allowed Carlos privacy.

Carlos knew he had several hours before he was due in the library for another session of transcriptions, and thought about what Luther had just said. The two men had spoken repeatedly regarding his difficulty with both reading and seeing the world through his right eye, but Carlos had never mentioned the letters of light that could not possibly exist, or told him how much easier reading and understanding Wenyan had become than scripts composed in other languages.

When Carlos looked at the text of the Yee records, the characters had a greater meaning than his translations could communicate. He could "see" the multitude of concepts represented by each one, and his problem now was not in extracting meaning, but in finding the proper words in Latin to represent them. The language of his education was nearly incompatible with the concepts in these ancient books, and preserving their truth was a promise to a friend that he could not set aside.

It was a process neither easy nor fast, but he refused to write down what he did not see, and feared to include all that he did.

Carlos reached under his shelf and pulled out a thick bundle of parchment. Translations of the first third of the heavy volume were complete to the best of his ability, and he was certain that any failing in translation was in the transcription, not the source.

And I have just enough time to attempt one more story of the Yee Hero's bravery.

With the door closed, the candle was barely sufficient to light the cell, but another benefit of his enhanced senses was a reduced need for illumination—in fact, it was easier and less distracting for him to read in dimmer places.

Carlos opened the Yee family chronicle to the section he wanted,

sharpened a fresh quill, and closed his eyes to prepare himself. When he opened them, the world was both yellow and soft and sharp-edged red. He looked down at the chronicle, and began to work.

In the time of planting, The Hero came upon the village of Dancing Water.
The land was dry, the season warmer than expected.

No signs of sorcery were on the people, or any dark works that would explain the lingering heat.

On the fifth night, the Hero returned from searching the hills for the minions of the Witch King.

The Center house was aflame, the village alive and moving toward it.

There was no question of the next steps. The Hero's duty was clear.

Protect all life, no matter the cost.

Carlos' hand shook as the pain in his head grew, and he pulled the quill away before marring the precise lines of his translation. Images of fire danced in front of his right eye, and shutting it against the light had no effect. Rolling smoke rushed in through the walls, and the sound of the building collapsing around him made him duck his head.

The flames lick at the family crest on her back. Her clothing flutters as she flies through the air. The air pushes close, never touching, always seeking to burn fair skin and smooth silk alike...

The chains bite deep into his wrists, slick with his own blood and the filthy water used to signal the start of each day...

Confess...Carlos. Confess!

Help us. Someone, please, help us!

Carlos felt the heat of the fire on his skin, and pain in his arm from falling beams and debris. He was blinded by the smoke, but somehow could still see. And what he saw was impossible.

I may have been released from the torturer's chamber, but the lingering effects of Rodrigo's attentions run far deeper than any wound Luther Welmach can treat.

And no herb I've read about in these books can cure a man of madness...

...I find that while writing my vision is not so afflicted as when I read the words of others. Especially when I compose words in the fashion which we determined works best for you, or in that strange script of the East, the Wenyan, that expresses concepts rather than single words, represented as pictures. Indeed, the family history of the Yee Clan is one I can read now without difficulty...

C ARLOS LAID DOWN THE QUILL AND RAISED HIS HANDS from the table to massage his right temple.

"Carlos?" Luther Welmach's question was whispered, but in the quiet of the university library, it was as good as a shout to the Carlos' sensitive ears.

"I am fine, Herr Welmach. Another headache, but it is passing. They are frequent, but less troubling than they appear."

"I wish that I could do more for you in this matter, my friend. Is the light troubling you, or is something else?"

Luther set aside his parchment and slid closer on the long bench the two men shared so that their words would not carry. Around them, sure-handed students worked at their transcriptions, applying ink to vellum in precise patterns that had not changed since Carlos himself was a student. With each page the acolytes filled their skill grew, as did their understanding of the Vulgate they transcribed.

Carlos could not bear to look at their pages, or the volume from which they worked. He was surrounded by a sea of red light that flared in time with his beating heart, and the knowledge that the legion of students around him might be perpetuating lies as they copied and recopied sacred texts tore his soul to pieces.

Instead, he lowered his head and looked at the surface of the table. He knew Luther was waiting for a response, but Carlos needed a moment to collect himself.

The dark wood of the table had been polished smooth by centuries of use. The grain told Carlos a story of patience and strength, one that helped center his mind. The pain behind his eyes faded from crippling to merely uncomfortable, and after a few breaths he was ready to talk.

"You have done so much already, Luther. That I have any portion of my life back is a testament to your skill. The light here is tolerable, and the pain—the pain is a part of life that I must accept. As you have said, it will fade with time."

Deceiving his friend like this bothered Carlos. Hiding the extent of his pain from Matthieu was easy with hundreds of miles between them. Luther Welmach was here, now, and did not seem convinced by Carlos' evasions.

"Still, you are my only patient at present, and this allows me to obsess a bit in regards to your treatment. Is the pain constant, or is it triggered by certain stimuli?"

"It..."

Would it be so hard to tell Luther the truth? To confess the extent of the problem and the consequences of his recovery? Carlos had thought often about doing so but feared the results of admitting the nature of his difficulties to another person.

As a doctor, Carlos knew that delusions of this kind presaged madness and death. The afflicted were often locked away, and after his encounter with the inquisitor Rodrigo, he feared attracting any additional attention.

Even now, the ill-concealed looks of the other monks proved he still bore the stigma of his interrogation. To offer them actual proof of his supposed "powers"...

No, it is too much.

Luther Welmach was a man of science and facts. He might accept what Carlos saw, but his quest for understanding would not be a silent one, and the brothers of St. Victor would not—

could not accept glowing letters of fire, senses more acute than those of any man, or strength beyond measure.

At least, not from one already accused of witchcraft.

And if the monks here condemned him, could those of Sant Cugat receive back into their company a man so afflicted?

"It is a passing thing. Brought on by different things at different times. Light, motion—I cannot say what truly causes my problems. I am learning to deal with it as best I am able."

Their continued conversation was attracting the guarded looks Carlos had hoped to avoid. He lowered his voice further, raising a hand to stop Luther's response.

"Perhaps we could address this topic later, my friend. I do not wish to disturb the others as they work."

The German doctor answered in an equally soft voice. "Such evasions do not assist in your treatment, Carlos. I do not wish to badger, nor shall I press for responses you are unwilling to give. But this problem will most likely not address itself."

Carlos met Luther's gaze as best he could, unwilling to either budge from his position or reveal his secrets to the other man. The light from the high window over his doctor's shoulder limned his head in a sparkling, dancing halo, causing additional pain behind Carlos' eyes. Clearly his evasions were not effective—he had to give Luther some kind of medically relevant response.

Taking another breath, Carlos looked down at the table again for strength. The red letters, the halo, and pain in his head all faded, causing him to wonder if blindness was so terrible a fate after all.

"The light pains me at times, primarily from the right side. It takes

me longer than it should to perform simple tasks, and… this frustration is new to me, and it is a difficult adjustment.

"I am sorry if my pride injures you, Luther. It is not that I do not wish assistance, but rather I do not wish for you too to be frustrated. You do more for me with your presence and support than any potion, tincture, or treatment the two of us might devise."

Carlos chanced a look at his message to Matthieu, completely free of red letters. But then another set of text emerged beneath it, and another—remnants of whatever records had been scraped away by others before the parchment had come into his possession.

Images formed in Carlos's mind of a traveler's account of the holy land, and also of a farmer's need for additional feed for his animals. The world spun as the lives of other men took shape in his mind, and he closed his eyes tight to shut them out.

Too much…

A hand on his right arm dispelled the visions, and even with eyes closed Carlos saw the smile in Luther's kind eyes. Carlos places his free hand over Luther's, and the two sat silent for a time.

If words are my problem, perhaps silence is all the treatment I need.

"Carlos, what is it you write here?" A slight shifting sound accompanying Luther's words brought Carlos to attention. He opened his eyes to see Luther's fingers adjusting the letter he'd been writing.

"It is a message to my Brother Matthieu. I hope to send it through the Church road tomorrow. I have not written in some time, and I do not want him to worry overmuch. My earlier writings were…"

Fire, exploding against his skin. The mocking, rasping voice of the shadowy inquisitor, darting in and out of the light.

"Confess… Carlos. Confess!"

Water sluices over him, but offers no relief. It washes the fire on his back, spreading it farther along his nerves until he can stand no more.

He will not break. He will not give the satisfaction of the lie merely to end the torment.

"Tell me what… you have… written. Your… heresy… will be… revealed… for all… to see."

Dull, unfocused pain comes to replace the phantom knives of heat. A blow rocks his head, and before he can recover, fingers seize his hair, forcing his head back and his swollen eyes open.

An angry white scar looms large in the darkening room. Some great hand grabs his chest, squeezing and forcing the air from his

lungs. The scar glows red, and the Rodrigo's mad eyes flash with anger. Far away in the black shadows, a bell tolls, low and long.
"You will... confess. You have no other choice..."

"...delayed by my recovery."

Carlos fought to contain his fear, to keep his heart from racing at the touch of the gentle hand on his arm and the comforting closeness of the man who helped heal him.

"If it is not too personal, might I examine this page more closely?"

Luther's whisper conveyed real interest in the letter, and Carlos was glad of the change in topic.

"Not at all. It is, as you might imagine, a summary of the last few weeks, concerning the very difficulties of which we speak. The Abbey receives news from all parts of the faith, but that information is filtered by Barcelona, and contains little of a...personal nature."

"The script is fascinating. In what language do you correspond?"

Carlos smiled, and remembered two Toledo schoolboys filling, scraping and refilling countless scraps of parchment while developing their "secret" language.

"It is Latin, but not of a sort you might have encountered. Matthieu...he and I have written this way since we were boys."

"I had not seen it applied to Latin before. It is an interesting adaptation. I see it now, the way you have shifted the letters. Truly remarkable."

Carlos stared at Luther with his mouth open. The warm nostalgia he'd felt drained away, leaving a cold chill in its place. Many years had passed since two young wards hid their compositions away from frowning instructors, secreting their "pointless, nonsensical scribblings" from old men with older temperaments. They felt no shame in what they did—it was a necessary exercise so that Matthieu could exist in the world of letters. But in the two decades they had employed this private script, they'd shown it to just two other souls. Neither had been able to decipher or learn their private letters.

Luther Welmach had looked at the page for less than a minute.

"Luther, you...you say you can read this page?"

"Yes, although as I said, this is a very clever construction. You have applied Jermid's basic structure and style to the Roman letters. I had not thought it possible, but you have done it very well.

"You relate here, I believe..." indicating the second section of text on the page with his finger "...how you are having little difficulty reading that foreign script, the Wenyan you showed me. Why did you not say this when I asked?"

Carlos' mind raced, trying to make sense of Luther's statement. He and Matthieu had used no guide to create their hidden letters save for Matthieu's ability to read them.

And who is this Jermid?

"This—this is not a formal script, my friend. I—we developed it so that my brother could better understand our lessons. It is freer, looser than the texts we had to use, easier on the eye and faster to transcribe."

"Yes, I can see that. Jermid must have come to the same conclusion. But I do not recall anywhere in his commentaries any attempts to apply it to Latin, or any other of the Western derivatives."

Jermid. That name again, spiking daggers of ice into his chest and a renewed pounding in his head. Before Carlos could ask about the name, Luther continued.

"Although I see now how it is possible. I wonder why his commentaries and translations did not reflect it. Latin is awkward and overly complex. It is both durable and inflexible, with countless rules for how words may be introduced and derived. Within that rigid framework there are holes and gaps that can contain volumes."

"I do not take your meaning, Luther, What are you saying? Who is this Jermid?"

"Carlos, you of all people should know Jermid. I—oh, I am sorry. I have forgotten where we are. You know him as Jerome, he who translated your holy book."

The Vulgate. The very text the acolytes around them copied. Unchanged and regulated by the Church for a thousand years. Saint Jerome, who collected, established and defined the scripture that Carlos and all other Catholics venerated, while at the same time commenting on the Tradition that all men should follow.

The man who composed and wrote in Latin so precisely

that it supplanted Greek as the language of scholars throughout the Faith.

The language Luther declares insufficient to relay a complete truth...

"Perhaps it would be easier if I were to show you, rather than tell. Will you walk with me to my lodgings, Carlos, while I attempt to ease your mind?"

It took Carlos a heartbeat to find his voice. His mouth had gone dry, and he had to swallow several times before he could speak. When he did, it was little more than a whisper.

"Yes, yes that would be acceptable."

Carlos did not want to walk. He wanted to run, as far and fast as he could. Luther's statements intimated inaccuracy in the most revered of documents, then indicated similarities between the hand that compiled it and that of two orphans trying to find answers in a world of jumbled chaos.

The pain was back, severe enough to force Carlos' eyes shut. With trembling fingers he reached for the parchment, gaining confidence when he felt the familiar irregular surface. He stacked it with similar pages, then placed them carefully into a leather folio he had used since childhood. His quills, inkwells, scraping blade, and blotter he then stored in a wooden kit nearly as old.

The routines of a scribe were familiar and comforting, but did little to salve the uncertainty caused by the smiling man at his side. Thinking of Luther's face brought his words back to mind, and Carlos saw letters of light swimming behind his eyes in time to match his thoughts.

Inflexible. Gaps. Holes. Volumes.

Freer. Looser. Faster.

Hidden. Volumes.

Inaccurate.

Wrong.

"Carlos? Carlos?"

Carlos's hands went slack as he fell, surrendering at last to the whirlwind in his head.

Carlos walks first through hallways, then down paths made by his feet over the weeks of his stay. He follows as they lead him through newly familiar streets in an unfamiliar city, watching the shadows shift and move along stone buildings and wooden walls.

He follows his feet along paths seen not with his eyes, but with his heart. He moves through the city like an arrow, fixed on his destination with unerring accuracy. He looks not at the journey in front of him, but the one unseen by his fellow travelers. Carlos watches what they ignore, feels the city move around and through him, hears its heart beat with each sandaled footfall.

There is history at each corner as two paths meet under and away from the eyes of men. Centuries-old buildings rest in their foundations, waiting to tell tales not easily read.

He has walked silently among them since his arrival in Paris, making no assumptions as he looks at painted signs and bare bricks. Each new day takes him on a fresh journey down the same path, focusing his vision tighter and tighter on the smallest of objects, then expanding it to include the whole.

With each pass he learns more, memorizing and reviewing each component of his journey until it is as familiar to him as words on a page. Such a manuscript is commonly read at arm's length, not from across a crowded and bustling street.

For Carlos and the senses he has developed, there is little dif-

ference between the two viewpoints. So precise has his vision be-come that he can not only make out fine details at a distance, but also reinforce his observations with scent and sounds.

Up close, the stones tell a tale of cutting tools and a mason's skill. Each piece selected for a specific place in the structure, then laid down carefully in that pattern as if eased into a jeweler's mold. They were shaped by one person, carried and placed by an-other—each hand leaving distinctive marks. The bakery near the street of flower sellers has the most interesting stories of all, and is the end of his journey.

Carlos has marked in his mind the efforts of eight stone-cut-ters and a team of twelve masons. Such care and practice indi-cates great importance, suggesting that it was once more than just a humble bakery. It seems larger, more real than the buildings around it, drawing him like a lodestone each day.

The stones of the walls are tightly mortared, a mixture of lime and powdered granite much like that used by the Romans and Egyptians for their great works. It is as out of place on a street of lesser buildings as is Carlos wearing his black robes among the brightly colored garments of the merchants he passes.

It carries something straight to his heart, a tale of security, sta-bility. As if the men who assembled it were standing around the walls, daring all who approached to attempt and fail to destroy that which they had made. It is a tower, a beacon of strength, and those in its shadow laugh and feel at ease.

Carlos is more comfortable in this place than at any time since leaving Sant Cugat. Winter is long past, and spring soon will join it in memory. Thoughts of what he left behind shadow every step on every walk he takes through the streets of Paris, until each day he arrives at this very spot. He wears those months on his face, much like the stones before him mark the passage of years.

There is a noise, low and dull at the edge of perception as he passes. Carlos tries to ignore much of what his ears tell him. The confusion and distraction of so much life is too much to deal with all at once, and each day he works harder to minimize its impact.

This sound will not be denied. To disregard it is a choice he can no longer make; the world around him narrows, receding from the fore. Down a long, dark hallway is a single point of light. The sound comes flowing across some surface and reaches ears-his ears—like stone sliding on stone. A chill washes over a body-his body-and a foul, heavy scent fills a nose that does not belong to him alone.

The Smell. Dark, rotting, putrid. The smell of dying bandits and frozen knights. Of bodies and bonfires, and smoke.

The smell of Violence. Of Anger.

One small image far away resolves into two men, then three, holding dull and rusting blades to the throat of an unresisting woman. It comes rushing at him, and his feet remember from where...

C ARLOS! CARLOS, WHAT IS IT?"

Carlos let out a ragged breath as the stars dancing in front of his eyes faded into the warm glow of the late afternoon. The scent of flowers lingered in the air, and Luther's strong arms around him were the only thing keeping him from joining his supplies on the floor.

Carlos looked around the room, trying to find any place that did not stare back. Even the shelves and racks of scrolls accused him of dark deeds from their red, glowing depths.

Luther was asking him questions and waving fingers in front of his eyes. Carlos shook his head in response, trying to figure out what his senses were telling him. Something felt wrong, but what?

His eyes locked onto the wall next to a table of startled apprentices. It wasn't occupied, but the stones there seemed too close together, too rounded. A portion of that wall did not belong to the library.

A portion the height and width of a grown man.

Carlos tried to stand, but his legs were made of water. He tried to raise his arm to point, but neither did his shoulders answer to his will.

A hand moved in front of his face, and Carlos saw a flash of light. He could move again, and his head snapped back violently enough that Luther's arm nearly released him. The flash resolved into a shining gold band on Luther's finger, and when the hand moved away, the wall was just a wall.

"Carlos, you must answer me. You must look at me now

and respond to my voice. You must tell me..."

You must...tell me...what you have...done...

"I...Will...NOT!"

Carlos' voice was a thunderclap, chasing all sounds from the room.

"Carlos...?"

Ignoring Luther's half-formed question, Carlos bent to gather the scattered remnants of his life. His message to Matthieu was ruined, obscured by a wash of black, red, and green inks pooling and swirling into dull gray on the stone floor. The text was obscured, but Carlos could still see it in glowing red letters bright as the noonday sun.

"Carlos, I..."

"It was a memory, Luther, something that happened once to a man you never met. A person who was, but can never be again."

"My friend, I did not mean to..."

"It is nearly time for the evening prayer. We will speak tomorrow, when we meet again. There is no time for this now, I must be away."

With the belongings of a stranger, Carlos left the library with his eyes closed, trusting his feet to follow well-traveled paths back to the stone comfort of his cell. He heard whispers at his back as he walked, but nothing the monks and visiting scholars said could keep him in the library for another second.

Everything he worked for this last year—all his efforts to become a part of this community after his ordeal in the chamber, his research, his patients—all were undone. Swept away by a memory and a moment of anger. His failure was written in letters of fire, hidden within the lines of every volume he had ever transcribed.

Incorrectly.

Even with no proof, he knew Luther was correct. But the German could not understand the magnitude of his revelation and what it meant for the Faith and the men who walked these halls.

St. Jerome was the most precise and diligent of translators, the author of commentaries, confessions, correspondence, and controversy. The writings of Jerome shaped the Church, bringing its scattered shards into solid reason and order after the persecutions of the previous age.

Jerome had condemned inaccuracy and incompleteness in the works of others, the additions and revisions that changed and diverted the message of the Gospels. Had himself been accused of forging the book of Genesis, for the sin of including passages left out by others to serve political needs.

These thoughts and more chased Carlos back to his cell. He set down his ruined correspondence and sat down on his sleeping shelf, still afraid to open his eyes.

The whispers continued, but muffled by the door and walls they were no longer a constant assault. Carlos tried to shut them out completely, withdrawing deeper and deeper into himself until he was an inviolate atom of Faith.

In his mind, he reviewed the all the volumes of the Vulgate he could remember, including the illuminated work of Berenguer de Palou, Bishop of Barcelona, who maintained that Mark's account was superior to that of Matthew and Luke—a viewpoint that Jerome had shared in his lifetime.

Carlos could see each book clearly, plain white pages covered with sharp, regular letters. His memory was free from any defect, and more importantly, contained no letters of red or phantom additions to what Jerome set down and Carlos had transmitted through his copies to the next reader.

Gripping the cold stone of the shelf, Carlos opened his right eye and looked at the small table on which rested the *plenarium* into which he'd copied the gospels upon his arrival in Paris.

It was a violent jumble of red.

Carlos turned his head and closed both eyes tight, but the glow did not fade. Carlos prayed, using the litany to calm himself. The slow cadence of his voice filled his room and covering the voices still speaking beyond his door.

And still the glow does not fade.

Carlos sat at the center of a storm, no longer sure if there was anything real in the world. No shelf under his hands, no walls of faith protecting him from uncertainty. Tossed about by forces unseen, he saw a chain of glowing red leading the way back to reality, a solid, unchanging line that promised answers if only he let go of everything he believed.

Somewhere far away, bells tolled and sandaled feet scuffed across smooth stones. Carlos did not need his eyes for this journey, and his heart yearned for something—anything—familiar. The storm raged on around him, but having a destination other than the red line of lies offered him hope.

He stepped out into the hall and into a procession of monks, orienting himself by the sounds of their feet and the smell of their sweat. Each man moved in silence, but the sound of their heartbeats was almost deafening.

Carlos had walked alongside them for many weeks, but until tonight's Vespers he'd never asserted his rights as a visiting abbot and taken a place at the front of the assembled monks, as was his due. He knelt, placed his hands on the railing, and joined in the chant, letting the words resonate in his chest and chase away the maddening sounds of the world around him.

Carlos bowed his head as the cantor read from the book of Matthew. As he heard the words of the Savior on the Mount of Olives he wondered if Berenger de Palou had begun his copy of that text.

The Bishop had not chosen Matthew's gospel as his highest truth, judging it to be of lesser quality than that of Mark. But in Matthew, there were accounts, facts found in no other place.

Carlos knew the story of how Jerome had searched for years until he found one copy written in the Hebrew alphabet and not already corrupted by Greek scholars hoping to gain favor with their landlords and creditors. A copy which he used to create a clear, concise message for the ages.

And if the evidence of his senses was correct, the words Carlos now heard, the voice of the Son of Man carried down through the ages could be...could have been...

Wrong.

To know, he had only to open his eyes and look down. All he need do was read them with the Grace of God illuminating each passage.

Eyes shut tight, Carlos gripped the railing in front of him with shaking, white-knuckled hands. He heard his brothers raise their voices in the *Magnificat*, Mary's praises of the Lord contained in Luke.

And in no other place.

A splintering sound echoed around the room, and the monks to Carlos' left and right faltered briefly in their song. Only when the pain in his hands registered did he realize he'd stopped singing, and his face burned with the shame of disrupting the evening's worship.

Carlos relaxed his grip and his blood flowed past the wooden shards in his hands and over the railing. Despite the sounds of faith around him, he heard each drop as it exploded against the cold floor, smelled the coppery scent of his life spattering in front of him. He wanted to run, to leave the university and never return. But he could not avoid the results of his madness any more than he could avoid the emptiness in his heart.

The office continued, and for the first time in his life Carlos did not rise for the Blessed Sacrament with those around him. There was no strength in his legs, and only when strong hands took him under the shoulders was he able to stand.

"Brother, if you can hear me, please be strong for us for a few moments longer. Your fervor lifts us up, and we will not forget your love of the Spirit."

A gentle touch of wetness on his lips signaled the end of his worship for the day. Carlos couldn't bear to open his eyes for fear the others might see his hypocrisy. He followed numbly as they led him from the chamber, trailing blood and splinters and hushed whispers. The pain in his hands was nothing compared to the agony in his soul.

Carlos marked his steady progress from behind closed eyes as the monks led him back along a glowing red path he desperately wanted to escape. Only when he was laid back with care onto his shelf and heard the door to his chamber close, did he finally open his eyes to the comforting darkness of night.

And the red shadows demanding attention.

Sometime later, a voice called softly from the other side of the door.

"Carlos, please allow me to enter. I am told that you have injuries requiring treatment."

The concern in Luther Welmach's voice was clear, but Carlos did not answer him. As the door opened, the light of a candle came in ahead of his doctor, bring with it just enough illumination for Carlos to see the anguished expression on his friend's face.

But whatever pain the doctor sought to relieve was nothing compared to the glowing red outlines of Carlos' collected manuscripts, pulsing to the beat of his heart.

The wood is cool and dry against his hands. They are coming for him, unable to resist the temptation of his life. Even diminished as he is, removed from the larger events of the world, he is too great a figure. He hears the trumpet sound far away, and prepares for the coming task.

He pushes hard against the handle, driving the stone wheel as it pulls the basket higher and higher. They have loaded it more heavily than normal at the base of the cliff, but he gives no complaint.

The limit of a day's production is not his ability to raise the loads of ore from the mine entrance far below, it is the thick, braided rope of jute twisting and creaking as it winds around the central pillar of fire-hardened wood. The cord is as big around as one of his arms, but unlike him, it has limits, though it is easier to replace should it break.

With each revolution the ore climbs the height of a man. With this system, the miners can work longer and harder, and he contributes to the community that assisted his recovery. He measures progress by the sound of the catch falling into place, the notch in the stone that holds the basket fast once it reaches the top, or in the unlikely event he requires a rest. No one would begrudge him a break in effort—in a day he lifts the same amount of stone as the team of ten men below. Twice, since he loads it into the travel carts after it reaches the top.

When he first joined the pullers there were five other men working at the wheel. As days and weeks passed, strength returned to his body, and the others made their way down the winding path with picks in hand so that the miners could keep up, leaving their sons behind to assist him.

He hears the boys at play, acting out traveler's tales. Strangers come often to the camps, following rumors of the "Lion of the Sun," a title he never sought or approved. He is just a man like any other. He has known great success and great tragedy, and better men than he are accorded far less respect.

These pilgrims of adventure stare at his reality and find it not to their liking. They carry away stories of visiting his grave, not believing the scarred, blinded man they met was once a great hero. Better to mourn him than to remember the price he paid for their freedom.

He hears the children hunt a mighty lion, taking its skin as proof of their courage. He hears them fighting legions to avenge the virtue of a kidnapped woman, chasing torches through the fields of the enemy, raising clouds of smoke and destroying a season of growth.

The blind man accepts these fantasies. If that is what they want, need to believe, who is he to correct them? It is a far more pleasant fiction than the wanton impulses of a vain and vengeful man. A man who ran from his obligations to live among a foreign people, using his gifts not to protect, but to destroy.

The lion was true, an act meant to impress a woman whose name he cannot even remember. At least he had loved her, after a fashion. Fighting his way through an army to reclaim her? That was true as well. But her virtue was never in question, for it was gone long before they met beneath his blanket. It was pride he avenged, the shame of being deceived by the enemy within his own home and hearth.

They came for him then as well, and his mighty arms put a nation to the torch to remove their dark stench and corruption.

It is his duty, after all. No matter how far he runs, or to where, they always find him.

The last time, he almost found the release denied him by all previous foes. The very people he protected cast him as the villain, and in the confusion their settlement was surrounded by an army as black as the night that spawned them.

The "innocent" ran, leaving him bound in heavy chains and partially buried. The sounds of their deaths brought him little pleasure. Their choices were theirs, though the consequences were certainly not to their liking. He avenged them to the last man when he escaped, and was left burned, blinded, and powerless as payment for his efforts on their behalf.

Better men found him as they rode hard to discover the source of a towering column of black smoke. Spent, weary, he waved the sound of their feet away but offered no complaint when they lifted him up and carried him home.

Home. The word is a lie, another fiction tolerated without comment. These are not his people, this is not his function. Now that he is recovered, the fire inside him calls out, responding to the pull of a setting sun he can no longer see, drawing his enemies closer with each breath.

The two-hundredth sound of the wheel stop dropping into place is the end of the ascent. It will be some time before the miners arrive at the top; their path up the rock wall is twisting and narrow, much longer than the more direct route taken by the fruits of their labors.

The sound of the basket gently swaying in the breeze is all the reckoning he needs to navigate his workplace. The rope is tight and strong, and he grabs it in both hands. One pull twists the scaffold joint, swinging the load onto solid ground. He hears it settle, then releases the line so that it lies slack beside the basket.

The children are far enough away, and young enough to have little concept of distance or rate of lifting. He raises a dust covered hand to his dry mouth, and whistles for them. If he does not allow them at least the illusion of helping, they might tell the next travelers the truth their fathers helped him conceal.

One hand reaches into the basket, finding rough-cut stone just beneath the lip. They worked hard in the mine today—this is the most ore they have cut in some time. The wagon is nearly full already, and this load will strain the backs of both horses and men as they guide it back down the trail to the foundry. It is easier to move the stone down the hill than to haul fuel for the fire necessary to liberate its contents here. And more convenient for him, since lifting the basket over his head with one arm as he does now would be very difficult to explain under the watchful eyes of the village elders. His sandaled feet sink slightly under the weight—he will need to smooth the impressions of his steps before the miners arrive from below.

Emptying the basket is a careful process as well. He has to leave small stones inside for the boys, but not enough to tax them overmuch. The horses are the only witnesses to feats of strength that once made the world take pause, and they are not likely to reveal his secrets.

His task complete enough, he dampens his long, flowing hair and garments with vinegar before drinking some to soothe his throat. The smell is sufficient to simulate the exertion he does not feel, and the taste is refreshing, more so than the water contained in the mouldering cask the others favor.

The rule, the Word, is a discipline he keeps still, as he has done for more years than the elders in the village below have drawn breath. It keeps him strong, renews him after each battle with darkness, and prolongs his life.

And his suffering.

Shuffling and dragging his feet, he reclaims the sturdy crutch "necessary" to make his way through the world without sight and uses it to lever himself into an uncomfortable seat against the heavy stone. Stooping, with a rough and patched shift draped over scarred shoulders, he presents as a man several sizes smaller. Those who work the stone with him are not fooled by his clothes, but the disguise allows the village to perpetuate a system that sustains them in this time of need.

The air cools—clouds passing as an unseen sun ends its journey across the sky. He imagines a white, full bank lit orange from behind.

Countless thousands of sunsets have passed in his life, and with every one he has prepared himself for the long vigil of night. Whether or not he ever calls this place home, the people below have no defense against the darkness.

No Protector.

He pushes back an errant lock of hair, remembering days when women lined up to perform this task for him. When men waited for him to speak, asking for judgment on their actions, for leadership and protection from the night. He is no longer that man, has not been since he left his true home to follow the call of the mountain.

When he returned, the women all sounded false, and the men were empty and weak. Among the tribes were others who could perform his duties, and he left them to it gladly to make his own life. To serve his own needs, responsible only to his own whim and desire.

But always they found him.

The wind brings a faint scent to his nose. One from the past, signaling change, violence, and pain.

A dark, rotting wetness that follows him wherever he goes, touching everything around him.

Eventually.

CARLOS, I DO NOT KNOW IF YOU CAN HEAR ME. I AM going to speak anyway, so that there is a sound here other than your breathing. This prison you've built for yourself is too dark, and lacking in those things a man needs to live."

Luther Welmach was determined not to let his friend die. After assisting in Carlos' recovery from the barbarism of his fellow priests, he could think of no greater failure than to let him simply waste away.

Following that ordeal, Carlos had healed with remarkable rapidity. With each passing day, muscle came back to wasted limbs, and burns and cuts faded to unbroken skin. There was no precedent for such a recovery in any of Luther's books, and he'd restricted his friend's treatment to himself only, not even recording it in private journals.

Then—and now—the monks of St. Victor's were of no use in determining what was wrong with him—in their eyes, he was simply touched by the hand of their god, and would be fine on his own. They hadn't even wanted for him to sit by Carlos' side, but in the end the brothers relented to his repeated requests.

Luther pressed a damp cloth to Carlos' head, but like the last one he'd applied it did little to address the fever. Just sitting so near made Luther sweat, and the stale air in Carlos' cell had a sour taste to it that seeped into his soul.

But what else can I do? He is my patient, and my friend. And no one should die alone.

"It is not easy for me to see you like this, Carlos. You have not moved in three days. I know you are alive, I know you are not physically injured. Your hands are clean and healthy, and the cuts have closed without scars.

"But you must listen to me now. You must not give up on this life. You are young, and too many days remain to you. If you leave us now I am not at all sure what I will do in this place."

Luther reached for the cloth, now dry and warm to the touch. Setting it aside, he closed his eyes and tried to remember the feel of the sun on his face.

"I do not pretend any understanding of your life, my friend. I know only the man you were before your incarceration, or at least the one you allowed me to know. There was so little left of that man afterward, and until those few minutes before you collapsed in the library I despaired of ever seeing him again.

"But now you lie unmoving with eyes open and blank. You do not eat, do not drink, and soon all my work will be undone. I would listen to you, if you wanted to say something. I will stay here for as long as I can, and I will even pray a little for you, though I do not know the words to say."

Luther thought he heard something, but when he opened his eyes Carlos had not moved. Perhaps it was some echo of the monks at their prayers, or one of the other rituals that occupied their days.

"Whatever happened to you, whatever memory has stilled the light in your eyes, I am sorry for it. If the cause were here in front of me, I would wrestle with it until it agreed to free you.

"But these are just words, Carlos. I say them so that there is life in this room. If you would listen to me a while longer, I would think of it as a kindness."

The only answer Carlos gave was the slow, steady rise of his chest. Sighing, Luther poured a bit of water over a fresh cloth, and laid it on his friend's head before speaking.

"I am a teacher, and I instruct my charges to the best of my ability.

But I am growing old. What I know is growing older yet, and there are few opportunities to reverse this trend. You are young, and what you write is young and alive. Your words are like a beacon in the darkness, and I fear that if it goes out the world will lose something it desperately needs.

"Before I came to Paris, my students and I thought ourselves learned men. We had access to libraries—books and scrolls and illuminations preserved for us by men we did not know.

"My home in Prag is a cold place and a hard one, shaped by centuries of conflict. Very few of my friends can read, and fewer still have the ability to teach. But in the history of that place, there were men of vision who cared not only for their fellows, but for their sons and their sons' sons. They left us a gift, and asked only that we share that knowledge as far as we could.

"Years ago, my own son followed my example and became a scholar, an instructor, and a doctor. He took what we knew and he shared it, bringing life with him wherever he went."

Luther paused and poured himself a cup of water. The air in the cell made his throat dry. What he had to say was difficult for him to share, but Carlos needed to hear it.

"My son lived apart from me, his mother, and his sisters. He was a man, and a man stands tall on his own. One night, he was at my home, teaching his students alongside mine. He also had a fire in him, and it showed in his eyes as he told us of his successes treating a sickness of the lungs among the river men.

"He laughed, he danced, and his fire warmed us. When he went home that night, he walked strong and proud.

"They came to tell me the next morning. Of how he came upon dark men taking things that did not belong to them. Carlos, my son was no soldier, nor a man given to reckless acts. But witnesses told of him charging hard into many men, swinging his cane and books about him to protect a bloodied woman and her child. "They told me of his last actions, how although bleeding from many wounds, he was still swinging a broken shard of wood about him as the king's men came in relief with swords and manacles.

"I looked at my son's body, lying peacefully in a merchant's parlor as he slowly died of his wounds. He was smiling at the end, Carlos–happy in death as he was in life. He had been true to himself, and to the memory of his family.

"My boy was a hero, and when we buried him I looked at a crowd of faces I had never seen before, and have never seen again. They were his children, his patients, his friends. They were people worth dying for, even if their names were not known to our family."

Luther paused for another sip of water, and to collect himself. He hadn't talked about Miklos to anyone but Anna in some time, but the words kept pouring out of him. It was almost as if the story was telling itself. He removed the cloth on Carlos' head, dry and stiff from contact with his burning skin, and replaced it with a damp one.

Stay with me, my friend. There is still more to tell...

"My son is gone ten years, and sooner than I would like my daughters will be leaving me, to become wives and mothers and the center of other men's lives. Anna and I will be older then, and we will leave Prag to spend the rest of our days in the north with her family.

"I wish you could have met him, Carlos. He was a good man, the man I have always wanted to be. You would have liked him, I think. I know that he would have liked you.

"I have few things worthy of remembering that I have not given to my students. But to you I give you the memory of my Miklos, of his courage and his honor. I want you to remember him as I do, so that many years from now, when Anna and I have gone and my daughters have forgotten the people we were while he was with us, you will know that there are things in the world worth holding on to."

Carlos gave no sign that he acknowledged Luther's words, but it made Luther happy to say them. Knowing that the vigil was far from over, Luther poured himself another cup of water, and sat back in the wooden chair that he'd occupied for so long.

"Carlos, the candle has burned low. I will replace it with another, if you would like. I have brought a story to read, and I was wondering if you would like to listen to a tale not so dreary.

"I have always liked the way it sounds, a beginning full of energy and mystery. It begins as follows.

"It was a dark and stormy night..."

The cart rolls on down the hill, flanked by the miners and their sons. He follows them, using his walking stick and a practiced limp to slow his progress. They'd offered him a place on the cart as they did every night, but the habits of a lifetime kept him on his own feet.

This is a journey he needs to make himself. The road is short enough that he can make it down before the last light of the sun fades, were he still to mark time in that fashion.

Were that his destination.

Without sight, he relies on his other senses. The fading touch of warmth on his skin, the taste of the breeze, the smell of cook fires as the villagers prepare evening meals.

The sounds of the night creatures as they stir from their hiding places. Rustling, scrabbling, inching forward over rocky ground just behind the receding sun. The sounds of their passage are a counterpoint to the wheels of the cart and the feet of the villagers.

Far enough. This is as good a place as any to start. The wind is cooling as it rises, and the children's laughter fades as it passes down around a corner.

It is replaced by a slow hissing, and a smell that travels through centuries.

Not long now at all, but still too close to the village.

He kneels, setting aside the staff that defines an injured old man. His pack goes next to it, then off comes the shift, exposing his broad back to the night air and freeing his thickly muscled arms from their disguise.

He takes a deep breath, and then another. With each expansion of his chest he feels stronger, younger. The smell is stronger as well, and he feels it on every inch of his skin.

Inside the pack are the items he is never without. A jar of ointment sealed with a heavy layer of resin and inscribed with the symbols of his old life. A smooth tube of bone, carved carefully during long months of recovery. These are his armor and his sword, and finer weapons a man could not ask for.

He places both palms against the ground, feeling its solidity beneath fingers still sensitive under a heavy layer of callus. Forming a fist, he knocks against it, hearing the impact with his arm. The fist opens to become a blade of fingers striking the ground.

His smile is unseen and his laughter unheard. Past battles replay inside his head as the smell of the night rises.

The seal crumbles beneath his grip, and a scent of life replaces that of death. He places the waxy fragments in his mouth, and the sharp flavor sets his mouth on fire. His heart beats faster, carrying the warmth throughout his body each time he chews. The fruit of a hardy tree, the contents of the jar are worth a fortune greater than all the shining metal inside the rocks rolling down the hill.

The oil inside he applies liberally over his body and hair. It seeps into his pores, clings to every fine hair on his broad chest. Once a small army of priests and supplicants performed this task, but they are as unnecessary for what is to come as his ruined eyes.

Tonight, he needs no help to find the battlefield. He defines it with his very presence. The foe comes to meet him, and he is ready.

He stands taller than he has dared to in years. No more hiding, no more running. Carved bone in one hand, empty clay pot in the other.

His right arm draws back, and a scented missile sails into the air. The last drops flying out leave a trail of life up the hill, one easy enough for his nose to follow.

One step, two, and the path is set. He raises his weapon to his lips, and blows a summons meant for different ears.

Far away in the cooling night, it is answered.

How many will come? How many died while he lingered here? Hands that now play a song of life have brought death to tens of thousands. Some, most, were like those screaming and leaping toward his chosen ground. Others were their allies, misguided men with darkness in their hearts.

Theirs are the most tragic of deaths, lives spent and lost not for their own purposes, but as pawns in a war ancient as the world itself.

The sounds of his instrument fill the unseen places in the landscape. Each rock sings in response to his summons, each stone calls out the passage of twisted, scrabbling feet.

The wind blows back over the cliffside, carrying more of his enemy to his nose.

Come, then. It ends for us all tonight.

The flute lowers, its purpose served. The time of waiting is over, the time of war has begun.

His mighty chest fills with air, and he releases a challenge into the canyon below, filling it up with decades of remorse and solitude.

Down the road, down the hill, another world exists. One of light, warmth, and community. The arrival of the ore cart is greeted with smiles and laughter each time it rolls in.

Women find their men and welcome them home. Torches come alive to hold back the night, ringing the village with fire and smoke.

All heads stop at the sound, a faraway howl of pain. It starts somewhere beyond the fire, then is answered from all sides by fading echoes.

Men find their families, gathering them together and hurrying them inside to safety and warmth. No one spares a glance for the road, or the last member of their company. Night has come at last, and with it ancient fears and selfish acts.

Shame is for survivors. And there is plenty of night left to come...

A ND SO THE HUNTSMAN WENT ON HIS WAY, NEVER TO be seen again. The girl returned home to her family, and they all lived in peace for the rest of their days.

"What do you think of that story, Carlos? Is the huntsman a good man or a bad man? I find his tale to be cautionary, a warning to those who might want to touch the darkness and run with the wolves through the night. He leads them, but at the same time he runs from them. He is both Hunter and Hunted, and can never stop running, lest he be overcome."

Luther paused for some response from the stricken man, any sign that the sound of his voice was reaching his patient. At least it was cooler in the cell now, a small mercy for which he was thankful. Pouring himself a cup of water, he filled a second for Carlos before continuing.

"There are many tales like this in the forests and mountains of my country. We are a nation of many people, collected and classified by the Romans a millennium ago. Someday, we will be separate and unique once more, just as the lands of France now stand apart and distinct from what was once Gaul. Germania has become Germany, and blends further with the Low Countries into the Holy Roman Empire.

"But the people are as they always have been, and the Wild Hunt knows no borders. Somewhere in the night they still run, although I have never seen them. On nights when the moon is dark, when the air is cold and the dry leaves crack underfoot, I have heard sounds that put ice in my belly.

"But that, my friend, is a story for another night. I find

my throat quite dry, and I must take a drink to wet it. Shall I pour you one? It has been some time since you have had sustenance, and I would be a poor guest if I did not share this refreshment with my host."

Luther sipped lightly at his water. He had sat this vigil before with Miklos, whose decline was slow and silent until finally he slipped away on the fourth day. Carlos was quickly approaching that same milestone, but Luther refused to give up hope.

Please, Carlos. Grant me another of your miracles.

Though the monk's wounds had long since healed, there was nothing Luther could do for his young friend's mind but wait, engage him as best he could, and pour his own life into a slowly emptying vessel in hopes that its unseen crack would seal itself.

Watching his friend's unmoving form, Luther felt so very tired. Just a moment's rest would do no harm, closing his burning eyes against the flickering shadows playing across Carlos and his slow, steady breathing. The guttering candle created the illusion of motion on the monk's face, as if his mouth was moving and his too-hot skin was...was...

Luther leaned forward, examining Carlos' face and trying to make out the whisper escaping his lips. He knelt at the monk's side, bending his head until his ear was just above Carlos' mouth.

But his eyes were fixed on the now-empty cup that had not moved since he'd filled it.

"Where...did...Jermid...live?"

Luther swallowed a shout of joy, only allowing himself quiet words in response.

"In Rome, but at the end of his life he lived in your holy city of Bethlehem."

He reached a trembling hand towards the dry cup, afraid to touch it and dispel whatever magic had emptied it. A light touch at his wrist became Carlos' thin fingers, and Luther turned his head to meet a fierce, determined stare.

"What...did...he...write?"

The candle flared in the cold, dry air of the cell. Luther's mouth was dry again, but his heart leapt at the knowledge that his vigil was ended.

"He wrote many things, Carlos. But this you know already."

"No. Not...all of it. Not what you do not speak of. Tell me of the hidden volumes."

The fierce energy behind Carlos' eyes was something new in their admittedly short acquaintance, but to Luther it seemed a very old thing. He felt compelled to answer, but wasn't exactly sure what Carlos meant.

"There are none that I am aware of, my friend. I am not a man of words, despite my father's wishes. I know only what he meant to our people, what he introduced to us."

"Tell me. I have to know. I must know what you meant to show me before...before..."

Carlos' light grip on Luther's wrist tightened, a drowning man's desperate hold on life as it slips away; a madman's terrified strength. This fervor was unhealthy so soon after Carlos' ordeal, but as long as his friend was talking, he knew he had to answer. It had been days since their last real conversation, but the need in Carlos' voice brought it back to mind.

"I can tell you the tale as it was told to me, and as I taught it to Miklos. It is not as entertaining as that of the huntsman, but I will try if you want me to."

"Please...I must know. Leave nothing out."

Luther nodded, adjusting himself as best he could with Carlos holding onto his wrist. While kneeling was appropriate for checking on patients and stoking fires, to tell a good story one had to be comfortable.

"There are many kinds of men, Carlos. Many nations, histories,

and traditions. It is hard to know all of their stories, especially those that were never written twice, but I will tell you the tale of our people, as it was once told to me.

Farther back than any of us know, there was a tribe of great men. As empires formed and fell around them, their stories traveled the world, becoming the basis of many legends.

"There was a time when my people—driven west by conflict—tried to abandon their stories and disappear into the shadow of Rome. Most arrived with nothing, and stopped speaking in the languages of their fathers."

The words flowed from Luther like a river seeking an end somewhere behind Carlos' thirsty eyes. He could not look away from the last spark of candlelight living there, fed and fanned by the sound of his voice into something...else.

"One of those men was Jermid—Jerome. He believed as you do, that stories must be told with nothing held back. And though the emperor accepted his translations of the four gospels, his successor wanted a different kind of history, with heroes it could control.

"For each text he translated, corrected, and updated, he offered reasons for his actions. His words endure, and you know them well."

Carlos' hand squeezed Luther's wrist, and for a moment Luther considered pausing to extricate himself from his friend's iron-hard grip. But the fire in Carlos' eyes burned brighter than ever, and Luther wasn't entirely sure what he would do if he won free. When it was clear that Carlos was not going to release him without hearing the rest of the story, Luther swallowed and started again.

"But just as he wrote for you, he wrote for us. He worked to create something else, a way to make the stolen histories live on. He designed letters that could preserve ritual and tradition, with which a dispossessed people could speak for themselves.

"These letters were not the ones the Romans used, nor those of the Greeks. They were shaped around different references, easier to adapt and understand than the rigid lines of the West.

"I learned to recognize those letters as a child, just as I learned those of the west and the harsh runes of the North. My father was like you, like Miklos, and he knew them all.

"When I saw your letters, Carlos, I was a child again, sitting at his feet and tracing words in the dirt as he spoke them to me."

Luther watched fire flare in Carlos' eyes, even as the candle burned ever lower. They captured and magnified each movement of the flame into a blazing brand.

Then both were gone, and Luther found himself without words. The iron grip on his wrist slackened, and from the darkness he heard a strong, clear voice. It found all the hidden corners of the cell, filling them up until there was no room left for anything else.

"Why do you come here, Luther? Why stay here, when you could leave me in the darkness?

"Why?"

Why?

"You are my patient, Carlos. You are my responsibility, my duty, and also my friend. I made a promise long ago, as did you, to offer aid when needed, and it is needed here."

Need?

"I think you know better than I how to address whatever ails you. Whatever memory drives you, keeps you apart from the rest of us, it is yours. We can help, if you let us."

We?

"I, then. I can speak for no other, but your confidences I will keep as dearly as my own. I am certain that whomever you trust, whomever you feel can share your burden, you would find them willing."

Whatever presence had invaded the cell left as suddenly as it had arrived, and the darkness was warmer, less total than before. All he could hear was the sound of his own heart beating, and the slow, steady rhythm of Carlos breathing upon his shelf.

Luther felt for the chair with one hand while massaging the muscles of his legs with the other.

When Carlos spoke again, a memory of Miklos' smile came to mind.

"How do we know, Luther? What is real and what is not? What defines imagination, separates the mythic from the mundane when there are no longer any boundaries of sense or reason? What makes one thing a fact, and another fiction? How are we to tell them apart, when truth is among those things most suspect?"

Luther considered his friend's words, but instead of an answer, all he had was another question.

"Is that not, my young friend, what constitutes Faith?"

The words seemed to hang in the still air for a long time, and Luther wished he could see Carlos' face. There were no more candles, and no fire with which to light one. But darkness magnified the silence between the two men, making time irrelevant.

When Carlos finally spoke, Luther nearly fell off his chair.

"Luther, I have a tale for you. One I do not quite understand myself. If you would listen, I would speak for a while."

Nodding in the darkness, Luther had the distinct impression that Carlos was smiling, and had followed the motion with his eyes.

"I will, Carlos. For as long as you wish me to hear."

Atop the broad stone, he stands and waits. The wind blows stronger now, carrying the scent of myth away from him. He breathes deep, and with each beat of his heart the power within him grows.

There is no more need to hold back. Every rock he's lifted these last few months, every revolution of the wheel waits to be freed from his body. Tonight, it will all be let loose, and then his trials will end.

The bone flute warms against his lips as he forces air through it. Each note speeds the pursuit, drags the enemy through the years until their own myths are heavy and thick in the air.

They are a forest of flesh, planted by his presence on the unforgiving rocks. Their massed heartbeats are a drum chorus, a rumbling, flowing sound like water rushing over sand.

He lowers the flute, holding his left hand by his side. Another challenge erupts from him, quickly answered by throats too numerous to count. The stone rumbles under his feet at the sound, and he smiles.

He releases the strength in his legs, and his leap carries him high above the tide of flesh. At the top of his flight the flute becomes a whistling missile announcing his path through the air.

There is one less howling voice, and the hard soles of his feet remove another as a coarse, fur-covered form smashes into the ground.

They are his weapons now, extending the strength of his arms until—broken and limp—he discards them in favor of others un-

til there are no spaces not filled with flying fists or slashing claws. Where he ends and they begin are the only boundaries as they battle up a path beaten hard by his feet.

A wide swing, and his portion is cleared and made larger. The broken thing flying away from his left hand is of no matter once his fingers close around the wood of the wheel's handle.

The sound of the great column shattering splits the night. Shards of wood cut deep into his back, joining scored lines left by his passage through the sea of enemies. The weight in his hands is little more than that of the air rushing ahead of it as he brings it down on a weaker, no longer screaming patch of blackness.

The ground shakes with the impact, surrounding every moving thing with a fine coating of earth. Far away under his feet, something shifts, and the corners of his mouth turn up in satisfaction.

Rising, standing, shouting, the answering howls are larger, louder and greater in number. His smile widens, and he stokes the fire in his belly, sending flames along his nerves and limbs.

One foot rises, then slams down hard. Claws lose their footing, blown back by a wave of force as solid as the shaking stones. Another step cracks the hard surface and launches him into the sky.

Higher, higher he rises, his destination fixed and sure. His legs spread wide to avoid the remaining wood, and a notched circle of stone becomes two broken moons as he returns to earth.

One foot shoves, and one half of the moon shoots forward and clears a path. One hand grabs, and as he runs he swings the second.

Knives tear at his left side. He swats them away. Deep under his skin darkness takes root, a corrupting fire warring with the pure source within him.

With each step, broken bodies fly, and more wounds appear on his own. The enemy growls and spits beyond the reach of his arc of stone. Their howls are disoriented, almost afraid. He pushes on, soaking the ground with blood and crushing bones beneath his feet. Free of enemies for a moment, he puts down his weapon and takes up the heavy line of jute, feels the weight of the broken column at the near end as he loops it around his waist and right arm. His left reclaims the discarded wheel to meet their next charge, which ends as he brings it down with all the strength in his shoulders.

The earth screams with each blow until its cries are answered by his own throat. Each swing is harder, faster. Something tears loose in his arm. The stone shatters, filling the air with sharp edged daggers.

The ground shakes and does not stop. His skin burns, sizzling the last drops of oil from his chest and back where they are not covered by thick rope studded with knives of rock. An animal growl erupts from his chest, and he charges over the shifting earth and jumps.

The air blows his hair back as he falls, and he imagines rocks and trees rushing past him as the canyon floor comes closer.

The rope tenses and jerks, slowing but not stopping his descent. The tortured crane above gives way with a screech and a crack, and joins him in the air.

The ground arrives first, a hard, jarring impact that batters but does not break him. The smell of the beasts is everywhere around him, and he laughs, truly laughs for the first time in years. He is alive again, here at journey's end. On three sides of him are a swarming mass of cold claws and reeking fur. On the fourth is a tower of cracking and rumbling stone, with a long tunnel cutting deep into its base.

He staggers towards the mine opening he has never seen. They follow, wary of his legend. Fresh to the fight, these ones, but also aware of the outcome above.

He spreads his arms wide and presses his palms against the shaking rock walls of the entrance. He strains with what life he has left, pushing harder and harder until the rock cracks over his head.

"What are you waiting for, you bastards? Come and get me!"

For the first time in his life, he shows his back to an enemy. He moves as fast as his tired legs and arms allow, leaving a trail of his life behind him as his laughter fills the spaces ahead.

The passage fills with shouts and snarls, and then all sound not made by falling rocks is irrelevant.

FALL

Matthieu,

Thank you for sending me a list of the new births in Ruri. It will be some time until I return to greet these new faces myself, and it pleases me to know that this past year has been a good one for you all.

With the changing of the season a new fever has come to Paris. The brothers here have embraced proper health practices since my arrival, but the people I work with outside the University are not so enlightened.

We lost three more yesterday that we know of, although there are many who visit Luther Welmach for treatment and do not return. Out in the city, in the homes and hearths of the poor and disadvantaged, we fight a battle that we cannot possibly win.

I shall stay on here a while longer, as I do not want to chance the road if there is any chance their sickness has passed to me. It was foolish of me to set out as I did into the Catalan hills last spring, expecting their fair climate to continue through and past the Pyrenees. This aspect of travel is one that Father Frances left out of his descriptions, and be sure to remind him of that omission.

Before his departure on a personal errand, Luther Welmach suggested that I might continue working with him as he travels back to Prag. You would like him, Matthieu. He is much like our Abbot, and I have learned a great deal from his example....

CARLOS ADJUSTED THE PATCH OF CLOTH COVERING HIS right eye and laid down his quill. Writing to Matthieu remained easy enough, as was reading those few messages he received in return. The invented script they shared was still fast and free of confusion, unlike all other things that were tainted by his second sight, the delusion of hidden Grace that tormented him still.

The temptation to use that sight was strong, and as the days marched on Carlos deferred to Luther's suggestion and covered his eye. It was easier to look at but half his world than to walk past angry red secrets no one else could see.

In the dim candlelight of his cell, even the neutral, inoffensive documents with which he surrounded himself made Carlos question his perceptions of reality. His translation of the Yee family records was complete, yet the deception regarding the Yee Hero's identity was a glowing red reminder of a lie perpetuated for generations of chroniclers and continued by his own hand.

It pained him to shield his abilities—and his difficulties—from Matthieu. Even Luther did not know the full extent of the changes that had come upon him, only his ability to find hidden meanings in any written document, and the visions that resulted from those buried truths. Until he could come to terms with this new existence, in which he could not trust his senses and perceptions of the world around him, he also could not articulate the depth of his fall.

The other monks here in Paris thought his most severe

episode to date was a display of great faith, rather than an assault on his soul.

Some accounts Carlos had heard whispered in the hallways ascribed to him a halo of light while he had struggled with his doubts. While he had certainly burned with shame during that evening's worship, he gave that rumor no more credence than he did the one describing wings of blue fire reaching out from his shoulders.

They were only words, harmless and without effect. His brothers would have far more to talk about if they knew the truth of that night, of the pain Carlos still carried in his heart, and why he had not returned to communal worship since. As a titular Abbot, he was accorded the freedom to pray as he saw fit, as long as he complied with the other aspects of the Rule of St. Benedict.

Another lie of omission, one perpetuated in his messages to the Abbey. If asked today, Carlos would reply honestly that he was no longer fit to lead a community of brothers. There were many men who held that office without faith, but Carlos could not be one of them.

For surely he was now completely of out of favor with the Lord.

Enough introspection. Putting away his personal message for later, Carlos rose and left his spare cell. Brisk, long strides through the cold and misty morning brought him past the respectful nods of his fellow scholars to doors of the University library. The other monks now offered him the kind of assistance he'd expected on his arrival months before, but with the summer over and the days of fall numbered, it was too little, too late.

Carlos wished he could return to his time of ignorance, when he could look with both eyes at an unbiased world. When he could believe honestly, without fear of discovery.

But that had been before his faith had suffered the dual blows of

Inquisition and Doubt.

The patch he wore over his right eye was a shield, his armor against the world. It was both a refuge and a crutch; a constant reminder of his fear.

Even working alongside Luther Welmach had its perils. Wounds told stories as did words, and few of them were good. If he chose to, and though it pained him, Carlos' visions could confirm a fatal diagnosis with just one look. Qin Yee's remarkable poultices could do nothing for most of his patients, but at least they increased the chances of survival and recovery of a merely sick individual, even those in the critical period of the pox Carlos had chased across Europe. A tincture of garlic, a touch of spoiled grains, and a handful of tree moss gave hope where there was none, and saved many lives.

Luther was traveling now, making preparations for a mission into the East that had a place for Carlos if he wanted it. Joining him would necessitate a change in his travel plans, and another, longer delay on his journey to Rome. He might not find the answers he sought along the road, but if the records here in Paris were any indication, the mystery of Karl Outrikos went far deeper than he'd originally suspected.

The monks and probationers looked up and smiled as Carlos entered the library. As it was every day, Carlos' preferred corner of the library had been tidied during the night, and some person had left a stack of clean parchment sheets to aid his efforts.

Luther. Again you prove yourself the best of friends.

The parchments were fresh, not remnants scraped and bleached clean. No record of discarded words would stare at him with accusing red letters, daring him to cover their truth with his own. Whoever was acting as Luther's accomplice, Carlos owed them a debt even greater than the cost of the parchments. Though they could not know it, they spared him the worst of the headache he would develop as he worked.

Carlos sat and prayed for a moment. He no longer joined the brothers in song each night—he could not worship alongside them without thinking about a great number of things that were best left unexamined. A silent, personal request for forgiveness was all he allowed himself now, the last ember of his once-blazing faith.

At his back was a glowing reminder of where the rest had gone, and the main reason Carlos still used the patch. He'd once thought the library at the University of Paris to be a fortress of unassailable truths, but with his new abilities he found there were very few volumes and dispatches of relevance left to examine in this place. All had been heavily edited during centuries of transcriptions, until the unrecorded stories only he could see were more numerous than those between their bindings.

Two months of anticipated research completed in two weeks, and for what result? His was not so noble an endeavor as that of Jermid, St. Jerome. No one would ever read Carlos' commentaries. They would not be debated, interpreted, or taught to novices after he was gone. No young monks would copy them and gain enlightenment. He was no longer a scholar in the strictest sense.

He was a grave robber.

The words in previously examined records referenced other accounts that should have been present in the archives, but those documents were strangely absent—not just the dates of the records, or what was contained in those he could find, but a pattern of omission. It was what he was not finding that bothered him.

Any mention at all of Karl Outrikos.

He should be here, if only in passing. Copies of the very records that had started Carlos on his quest from Sant Cugat were absent the words that had fired his imagination all those months ago.

Those words, but not the words that surrounded them. Before he was a Bishop, before he was counselor to kings, Achard of St. Victor had been an archivist like Carlos. He had trained here, had possibly worked at this very table.

And the records he left behind were amazingly bland and empty of content. Fifty years after his departure from Paris, they held no sense of the man at all, or any hint of the man he would become.

In fact, even the words Carlos had transcribed into his personal journal last year were absent, as if Achard had never written them.

"Yet another pair as the Bishop described were discovered to-

day, bodies torn as if by a beast. No hints as to the nature of the attacker were found with the corpses, only a thick, cloying scent, such as that described in the matter of dark Karl Outrikos."

The record in question had come to Carlos from a private collection to be translated, dated and confirmed weeks before the canons regular of Séez elected Achard as their Bishop.

Once he was confirmed by His Holiness Pope Adrian, St Victor's master archivist left behind the dusty shelves and pages of his youth for others to copy and recopy. Pages like the one in front of Carlos now, describing deaths along the river Seine, and of a blistering sickness among the poor. A near identical twin to the record resting now in Sant Cugat, but one which ended in an entirely different fashion.

"It is deplorable that conditions here do not permit a more aggressive approach to healing this taint. But as long as there are those who turn away from the light of the Lord, there will always be those we cannot help. I pray for them whenever I raise my voice to Our Father."

Whichever record was proved accurate, the other must become false. Either the words he had thought true and worthy of exploration, or those he feared were true, would undo his last year of research.

Putting the lie to Carlos' beliefs, and the truth to Rodrigo's.

His translation of Achard's words was still among his papers, one of the few sheets not destroyed by ink, weather, and the rough searches of a scarred maniac. He could lay them here on the table next to their near twin, and cast aside his armor to face one knife-edged truth or the other.

But not yet. Not while there were still rational explanations to discover. Today he would determine what belonged in the holes outlined by his research. His feet would walk the library while his mind wandered, and carry him through the sections no other men visited. If the records were there, he would find them. If they were not, they would be elsewhere. In however much time he had left in Paris, Carlos was resolved to the task of at least discovering their content.

Carlos sat and regarded the empty tabletop that would soon be full of records too faded for anyone else to read. The left side of his world was full of possibility, and the promise of discovery.

The right was dark, and full of his shame.

Closing his eyes, he gave another empty prayer for the strength not to lift the patch.

As always, there was no response.

ORNING BECAME AFTERNOON, AND THE SUN ROSE high outside. Carlos' head pounded, the strain of reading with only one eye a hammer against anvil. The Patch was a chain around his soul, not just holding back the pain of discovery, but binding his mind and heart with tortures of his own design.

This section of library had been visited before. Not by him, but by another, and that passage told a story of a man.

Wazo of Liège, Bishop from 1041 until his death seven years later. Wazo led a life of controversy, noted widely for his commitment to justice and fair treatment of the accused. His stance called his loyalty into question many times, and his ordination at Liège, while unanimous from the congregation, was contested on many levels within the Church.

Here in Paris, his chronicles were missing. This was the clue that Carlos sought—an audacious removal of some thirty books, texts, and annotations. As a student in Toledo, Carlos had studied Wazo's friend and colleague Anselm's history of the man, and copies of Anselm's words were here.

But Wazo's words—the Bishop's own records—were gone. *Missing.*

There was no reason for their absence. There was every reason for them to be discovered, and the parchment he'd found tucked away in a battered folio indicated clearly the number and type of records transferred to St. Victor's one hundred years before. Seven scrolls indicating births and deaths during his tenure, a four-volume codex penned by

Wazo regarding the life of Carolus Magnus, Wazo's commentaries on the gospels, his missals, and many letters sent and received from Rome.

Gone. As if they had never been present. Only this one yellowed sheet offered witness to their existence, and no eyes but his own could make out the faded lettering, even in the bright light of today's noon. And if Carlos hadn't dislodged the patch slightly while wiping his face, he might never have found it.

It was the rolls of the births and deaths Carlos sought, but the other volumes' absence was equally significant. The missing texts were the mildest of documents, little more than vanities warehoused here by a former Abbot desperate to please wealthy patrons.

Carlos was not a man given to fanciful speculation, despite his recently wandering mind. In any other case, he would assume either that the records had been destroyed, or that they had been sold off to some collector long ago.

But this sheet had been deliberately hidden from view, folded and placed in a folio with no label, alongside others containing records of tides on the Siene. The crease was heavy, and fresh, and no librarian would have replaced a cured parchment with the hair side pressed against the flesh of another sheet.

No librarian would have scratched a single letter on half the lines of inventory with a dry quill, possibly ruining a document of value.

No archivist would have written such a crudely formed K.
K, For Karl.

Carlos stopped his hand as it moved up towards the Patch. He could not succumb now, in full view of all present. The fact of his temptation was troubling enough, but he feared another public vision might ruin any hope of discovering the truth.

The scratching of sharpened quills behind him offered a distraction from his inner struggle. Carlos turned so that his unobstructed gaze regarded novices copying selected texts under the watchful eye of St. Victor's head archivist, a thin and severe man named Henri Bouchard.

Bouchard was a stern master of the libraries, and one of the few staff that had accepted and accommodated Carlos both before and after Paulo Rodrigo had put him to the question.

Rather than the constant murmuring vocalizations Carlos remembered from his days at the Academy, where a student's ability to read was secondary (at best) to the steadiness of his hand, Bouchard insisted that all novices and probationers to the University learn their letters well enough so that they need not recite them aloud in order to verify their transcriptions.

At present, there were no requests for copied texts, else Carlos would gladly have lent his hand. Master Henri's charges were practicing against a faded and yellowing exemplar, much like Carlos himself had done with the almost illegible inventory.

A plan formed in Carlos' mind, one that would require a slight but necessary deception. Carlos raised a palm to signal his colleague as he approached. He managed to catch the older man's eye almost immediately, and the look of surprise on Master Henri's thin face made Carlos doubt the wisdom of his plan. As slow, deliberate steps brought him closer, he steeled himself for a whispered discussion with a man whose voice could shave ice.

"Brother Carlos, what is it you require? Is your station well and to your satisfaction?" The simple question made Carlos feel as if he were a boy again, fearful of reproach from a looming, black-clad instructor. It took several heartbeats to remind himself that on his best day, Henri Bouchard stood a full head shorter than he, and despite the menace in his tone, was among the gentlest of men.

"Master Bouchard, my station is as it always is, a gift and a pleasure to sit. If I may, I would like to ask a favor of your experience and your memory." His whisper was barely loud enough to move his tongue, but under the withering gaze of Henri's brown eyes, it sounded in his ears like an avalanche. Carlos could still recall the pained look on the man's face the first day he had returned to the library after lashing out at Luther after a vision, and did not want to see it ever again.

"If I can give assistance, I will." Henri indicated a space away from the novices where the two could speak without disrupting their efforts.

"Master Bouchard, I am ashamed to admit it, but I cannot locate the most recent transcriptions of Wazo. Do you recall the name of the brother who last made use of them?" Not quite a lie, yet, but Henri's mind was as sharp as his tongue, and Carlos needed to shield the true nature of his research from others for as long as possible if he was to be successful in his...ruse.

"What do you wish of those, boy? It has been well over a generation since we have had need of them, and even then it was only in support of a request for Anselm."

Anselm again. The only witness to whatever events were obscured by the absence of the records. Whose chronicles were either inoffensive enough to escape notice, or inaccurate enough not to matter.

"I read Anselm myself many years ago, Master. I transcribed his history at the Toledo Academy, but I have always wanted to see Wazo's words for myself. Either a recognized copy, or if I am lucky enough, his own hand." No deception here, Carlos had been fascinated by all the men described by Anselm, including Wazo.

And at this very moment, there was little in the world that he wanted more than to find documents written by the Bishop of Liège.

For that, he would set aside the Patch gladly.

Henri's reply was a throaty grunt, but the hint of a smile twitched the corners of his wrinkled face.

"Very well, boy, now you have put your desire into my head as well. As you are able, speak to Brother Michel, once he returns from the noon office. He would have been among those with access when the last full inventory was taken of that section."

"I thank you, Master Henri. I will certainly come to you with whatever texts I find."

Another grunt in response, then the thin man returned to his students, muttering something under his breath as he walked.

It was not Carlos' intention to listen to the man's softly voiced words, but his hearing was as acute as the rest of his senses, and the sounds came to him as clear as the notes of a bell.

"...entire generation of men with no interest in all things Anselm, then two in the space of four months. First Rome's man, now Barcelona's. Next will be his Holiness, most likely."

Rome's man. The words chilled Carlos to his core, while at the same time bringing to mind a memory of fire and madness.

You are...wasting my...time...Carlos. This is an...unneeded... distraction...from my...mission. Confess...your sins...and spare me...the fiction...of your...innocence. I have...other...deceptions... to which...I must...attend.

Carlos felt the wood of a chair compressing under his fingers, and relaxed his white-knuckled grip slowly. A one-eyed glance around him revealed no alarm on the faces of the library's other occupants.

Rodrigo. What other madness do you practice, that you would steal from both the future and the past?

The man's shadow was palpable—the unseen presence of an unseen opponent dogging his steps from memories he could neither escape nor move beyond. *Rome's man.* Two whispered words had placed him back in chains, and even though the blow had fallen elsewhere, he could feel the touch of the torturer's hands once more.

Carlos eased himself into the chair, remembering the network of scars he no longer had as they pulsed with the beating of his heart. He placed both hands flat on his legs, and tried to remember anything, any hint of Rodrigo's presence before his arrest.

Four months. The Inquisitor had already been in Paris when Carlos arrived, already weaving whatever schemes involved stealing documents no one else would want from the archives.

Documents that might hold the secrets he sought, the hidden story of Karl Outrikos. Or was this pride speaking, drawing a connection where there was none?

Rodrigo could not have known of his mission to search for the anomalous records. *Could* not, since he had been able to read neither Carlos' letters home, nor his journal. So whatever reason he had to remove them, it was not related to his arrest.

Carlos' fingers inched toward the patch. Touched the rough, dark cloth over his right eye.

No. Not yet. Please, oh Father, give me the strength to resist for just a while longer, that I may serve you with a clean soul, that my testimony not be tainted by madness, or further accusations of dark power.

He rose and eased the chair back into place, wincing at the screech of wood on stone that no one else could hear, feeling the fine grain of wood worn smooth by hundreds, thousands of hands as sharp in relief as the bristles of a horse's mane. He could smell his own nervous sweat and hear his thundering heartbeat, distinct from the dozen other heartbeats pounding in his ears.

Please, just a little while longer...

THE VOLUME OF ANSELM'S WORDS RESTED ON THE shelf before him. Without touching it, Carlos knew where the passages regarding Wazo lay, their number, and what they related. No special sight was needed to remember words he had read and copied so diligently as a student in a dusty room he could recall as clearly the archives he saw before him.

Inside this volume were Wazo's recorded conversations with Roger II, bishop of Châlons-sur-Marne, on the nature of Heresy. His conflicts with the Emperor on the nature and rights of the pontiff's chair, and how Henry was not meant to sit in it.

The words he had read and transcribed at the age of twelve.

Carlos had stood staring at the folio for hours, willing himself to look at it with both eyes. Five times his hand had reached for the patch, and four times it had returned empty to his side.

He could feel it under his fingers, just as he could feel the tight band circling his head, and the pressure of the thick fold he had sewn with such care to hold his eye shut against that which he feared.

The Truth.

He gently lifted the cloth, careful not to cause injury to the eye beneath. His other hand came up to unfasten the binding, and with both eyes closed, he stood silently and alone in the Library. The other monks had all gone on to worship, leaving Carlos to his own devotions.

There would be no other witness to his revelation, and what it would mean to his faith.

Opening his eyes, he saw a red, pulsing glow around the volume, one that intensified as he reached forth his hand. The heavy book slid easily from the grasp of its neighbors, who were trapped by the dust of years. It was warm to the touch, as if left carelessly in the sun.

He placed the book on the table, but did not open it. Was it enough to know that there was a problem? An omission of facts within? Need he cast doubt on the words of a man who had recorded the lives and deeds of twenty-five Bishops, including his dear and close friend Wazo? Carlos' personal torment had already robbed him of the wisdom of Jerome. Must he add another to that list?

Can I live the rest of my life knowing I had the answers in my hand, and chose the lie instead?

Carlos moved his hand across the cover, and the churning red light that surrounded his fingers became a blazing torch as he opened it. The parchment was strong and whole, the words sharply defined in black ink and red light.

The last rays of the sun warred alongside tallow candles with the growing shadows in the rest of the room. With both his eyes open, Carlos needed neither light source to see clearly. His memory supplied the contents, while his vision supplied what was missing.

Were there witnesses to his study, they would have thought him not an example of intense faith, but a madman. Furiously turning pages, each pair revealed for only a second, then replaced with another. Only minutes had passed when he came to the end, and Carlos closed his eyes as he turned the last leaf.

Anselm. Why? Why would you, why did *you, hide this from us?*

When he opened his eyes again, only candlelight remained in the room. That, and the red glow surrounding and condemning Anselm's book.

He pushed it aside, reaching into his folio for a yellowed, coarse sheet of parchment. Without looking at it, he placed it on the table before him, staring at the dark recesses of the vaulted ceiling. His other hand drew the Achard volume to him, careful not to damage the aged and faded page.

Twin bonfires shone through the tears in his eyes. Impossibly steady torches, red rays of sunset captured and enslaved by a forgotten quill.

One glance destroyed him, brought him that much closer to the edge of madness, dragging him down with heavy chains towards the jagged cracks his soul had bled through onto the page.

Carlos did not see Lies. Or Truth. Carlos saw a pair of bodies, torn and ripped with wide, spreading gashes.

He saw two thugs bleeding onto a pile of scattered blossoms, with a dull, wet knife in one of his hands and a listless girl in the other.

He smelled the smoke as the fire consumed the knight's body, watching his ruined face melt away to reveal that of Qin Yee as she died.

He saw two completely correct and accurate reports, penned by the same hand, on the same day. He saw the sun's last rays as the quill was laid down, and a scarred and weathered hand reaching for both.

I cannot do this again. I cannot see these things and remain myself.

Carlos flexed his arms, and the ancient table flew across the room. As long and as heavy as a wagon, it lay now a dozen paces from where he sat, small cracks too fine for any other to see accusing him and his childish rage.

Carlos' only companions in the room were the voices of dead men's memories and small, distant candles that paled in comparison to the burning red lies surrounding him. Priceless manuscripts lay scattered in the wake of his display, and the noise would bring someone soon.

Gathering the pages with closed eyes, he walked another two paces and found Anselm with his fingers. Eight to the left, he set them down on a station untouched by madness, then carefully replaced the table where its weight and history had kept it for two hundred years.

With eyes closed, he could pretend he had never come here. That he had not been touched by the darkness where

Rodrigo lived, or carried it with him when he left the chamber.

He could lie to himself, for a while.

But not to God.

There was one task remaining for tonight, and then he would remove himself from St. Victor. Better Luther did not return to find him like this. Better that he never return to Sant Cugat.

Wait for me, Qin Yee. I come to join you in torment.

Raising Anselm before him with open eyes, Carlos noted a change in the light. A small wind set the candles to fluttering, and in that moment the red glow of the room contracted and was centered wholly on the book in his hands.

It became a line, stretching away from where he stood.

Walking now, dreaming with eyes open, Carlos moved through the shelves and stacks, leaving the building to follow tendrils of red stretching out from the heavy, blinding book in his hands.

The monks parted before him as they exited their prayers. He paid no attention to their stares and hushed words. His whole being was focused in one direction.

Forward. To the end of lies and deceptions.

Carlos' black robes snapped around him in the growing wind, and his sandals slapped the cooling cobbles. The echoes of his passage came back across the empty courtyard, and the full light of the moon above all was no match for the blazing line of red outlining his destination, or the glowing strands stretching out from his hands and lighting the entrance to the crypt.

Carlos moved down into the damp, dusky ground, walking past history. In these caves lay the remains of St. Lazarus of Marseilles.

Of Cassian, Maurice, and Marcellinius of Ravenna.

Of Peter, and The Holy Innocent.

Before him in a humble, unremarkable alcove, light pooled around a relic not named or recorded by the world above. A shroud containing bones, dead now one hundred and fifty years, and falsely enshrined four hundred miles away in the community that bore his name.

He did not speak the words, did not question their accuracy. As sure as his feet knew the paths of his day, they had taken him down the paths of night, into a past he had read in pages flipped fast enough to rival the wings of a hummingbird.

This, then, was the man who knew the answer to his questions.

Wazo of Liège.

A red mist surrounded and defined the relics. Where there had been only bones and dust, there now lay a complete man, resting peacefully with the smile reported and admired by Anselm upon his face. Carlos leaned closer, staring at that which was not there, could not be there.

This vision. This apparition that called to him from beyond the veil.

The Truth...

Y OUR GRACE, HE...IT IS IN HERE."

"Thank you, Timothy. I will attend him now."

The Bishop followed the young acolyte down the hall, flanked by the two guards sent from Rome by his Holiness to "protect" him. These times were perilous, and although his office was elevated, there were those who sought to tear him down. Opposing the pope's political machinations had been the right thing to do, but exercising the dictates of his heart carried consequences—uncertainty, doubt in the faith, and schisms of belief spiraling out of control.

So many heresy trials now. So much anger, so much pain. And for what? The persecution of men and women wishing to know God? He had counseled, he had instructed that these people were to be left alone, to live their lives and find truth on their own terms. Again and again he had preached tolerance.

Again and again he had been called into a room such as this, to deal with the ecclesiastical excesses of those who had too much fervor and not enough faith. But this time, Timothy had called him in for something different. Something... dark.

The smell was the first thing. Foul, earthy. It was as if the man before him were already dead, and not from the burns and bruises visible on his body. The air tasted of grain too far gone to rot. One such pot turned could taint an entire store room, and being in this place, he could feel fingers of darkness trying to gain purchase on him.

In him.

The man raised his arms, rattling the heavy iron chains securing him to a ring set into the floor. The effect was like standing next to a collapsing building, watching it fall to the ground and feeling the impact of the stones deep in one's bones. He had ashen skin, drawn tight over sharp, angular features and further shaded by the torchlight. His ears tapered back to points, with tufts of fine, dark hair covering their surface. His eyes burned like the coals in the brazier behind him, and when he smiled he revealed a mouth of white daggers.

"What now, are you to 'save' me as well?" The man's voice sent shivers through Wazo's soul.

"No, my son. I am here to listen. My apologies for what has happened to you. It was done without my instruction, or my knowledge." A truth, this sort of thing did not happen at Liège. Should not happen, anyway. Tolerance extended in all directions, and remembering that moved Wazo to action.

"Release him. What harm can he do here, with all of us present?"

"Your Grace...that is...not wise. It, he...it has...killed."

The guard, a young man whose sad eyes had seen too many days, was uncomfortable with his statement, as if there was more for the telling. The way in which he and his companion gripped their spears told Wazo that story would be very interesting indeed.

"Yes, release me. I have suffered so." The weight shifted, and sarcasm was replaced by malice.

The man smiled, showing teeth that grew longer by the minute. Wazo took a step back from the sneering visage, looking to Timothy for confirmation of what he saw. The acolyte nodded, and Wazo swallowed hard before speaking.

"Perhaps we shall keep the chains on for a bit, then. A chair for these old bones would be helpful, Timothy. While I speak with...?"

"Kristoff. Kristoff Jäger, your Grace. He was captured outside the shrine, attempting to break into the reliquary. At the time, he did not...he looked different."

The relics? The longer Wazo stayed in the room, the greater the sense of wrongness around the prisoner grew. There was hidden truth here, but there was also madness.

"And what do the remains of St. Hadelin mean to you, Kristoff Jäger?" In the weeks they had shadowed him, Wazo couldn't recall hearing the voice of his second guard. But his words were like a ray of sunshine on a field of flowers, tossed gaily into the teeth of a thunderstorm. "What about the bones of a man centuries dead would cause you to steal, to kill?"

The prisoner twisted in his restraints. He snarled and spat curses in a language the bishop did not know, and his features shifted into an inhuman mask of hate. His skin went from dark to black, and coarse hair sprouted on his face. And on his hands were...! Wazo shrank back, horrified.

"You dare? You dare to question me so! I curse you, servant. My master will feast on your flesh. You cannot keep it hidden forever, and we will have it!"

With this final utterance, Jäger went from man to monster, too-long teeth becoming fangs and a too-wide mouth pulling back over his distended jaw. Muscles bulged, ripping his filthy shirt to rags. A pull and a scream, and the chains holding him burst as the iron ring tore loose from the stone floor.

Fragments of sharp metal flew around the room, and Wazo fell to the floor to avoid a swinging blow aimed at his throat. The chain whipped around, and something snapped in his leg.

A wash of pain blinded him, and screams, crashes, and metal echoes assaulted his ears as a battle raged over his head. There was a wet, tearing sound, and his first new sight as the pain faded was of the prisoner falling to the floor with the head of a spear protruding from his chest and foul, black blood gushing from the wound.

Behind Jäger, one of the guards held a broken shaft. A long bleeding slash marred his handsome face—the flesh torn by the impossible claws on Jäger 's hands.

"You fools...we will have it. In the end...we will win. Karl Outrikos...will prevail!" The last words of a demon, for clearly that was what lay on the floor before him. Where the spear protruded, the flesh burned, and a faint hissing accompanied the smell of seared meat.

He—it seemed smaller now, less threatening. Wazo leaned in to examine the body, but was pulled back by a bloodied hand on his shoulder.

"Your Grace, you must leave. There are things to be done, steps to be taken." The scarred guard seemed unconcerned by his wound, and the rest of his face was hidden in shadow. "It must be burned, so that its corruption will not spread. I can do this, but you must not be connected with this act. Go now, and I will come to you when it is done." The calm, warm voice was a soothing balm to Wazo's soul.

Yes, yes, that's what must be done. It was so clear now. It could be no other way. Strong hands lifted him, and Timothy came forward to help so that his damaged leg would not drag on the floor. Dazed, he stumbled through sweetly scented air as Timothy led him from the room.

Wazo heard someone speaking in low, melodious tones, and looked back to see the guard tear the spear free. He couldn't quite make out the words, but whatever they were seemed right. He called back to his savior as Timothy hurried him away.

"Thank you. Thank you for your service, Pa..."

Carlos fell to the ground with trembling hands, the book scattering the dry bones and the threads of the shroud that held them. Pain not his own receded from a leg not broken, and his pulse slowed.

Alone in the crypt, he wept for the remains of his soul.

Through his tears, he saw red, glowing threads wafting through the air between the bones, himself, and the other alcoves. He dared not give them more than a brief glance, lest their lives overcome him as well.

The patch was gone, discarded somewhere above as he walked in the night. Even if he still had it, he could never forget what he'd seen. Closing his eyes, he reached for the book, careful not to let even a sliver of that horrible light pass to him.

Slowly, carefully, he made his way out of the catacombs, never sparing a glance backwards until the cool night air blew across his skin.

Karl might be there looking back.

...at first it appeared that our friend would recover from the fall with but a slight limp, a far better fate than the horse he was riding. It was necessary for Alejandro to end the beast's suffering, and the two of us, along with Robere, felt it seemly to speak some words. The Abbot agreed, but as we finished the service, he collapsed. It was then we learned of his greater infirmity...

THE SHAKING OF HIS HANDS WAS NOT SEEMLY, AND Carlos was glad that he had chosen to read Matthieu's message in the privacy of his cell.

The first communication from home in many weeks contained the worst possible news, delivered just as he finished his preparations to join Luther's eastbound mission. On the road, at least, he could continue his search for truth.

For Karl. There was nothing more to learn here that he could not find elsewhere, not without losing what was left of his soul.

Carlos resisted the temptation to lift his self-imposed veil and look beyond his brother's words. He had not been wearing the patch when he opened the Bishop's message, sent weeks earlier but arriving on the same horse as that from Sant Cugat. Only a glance had been necessary, and in that flash he felt the Bishop's great sorrow, but also his respect for Carlos and the echoes of the friendship they'd established when the year was new.

Carlos had used his visions sparingly after the memory of

Wazo. Most days, he could not bear to know more than what was written on the page. Yet the patch was off as often as it was on. Would it be so hard, so wrong to look through the miles and see the truth for himself?

No, the patch would stay. His grief would remain real, and unsullied. Matthieu's words continued, but Carlos already knew what they would tell him. The Bishop's sharp, precise hand had been very complete in his summation. No omissions, no shaded truths to be revealed.

The facts were painful enough. Turning one eye, and one eye only, to the symbols he shared with his childhood friend, he did not have to guess at truth. It was there, as surely as if Carlos, and not Matthieu was the witness.

...a spotted fever was high on his chest, similar to that you report during your travels. For one as aged as our good Father, this would normally mean another burial. But as even as your words arrived and sat unread, we pooled our prayers. All the Abbey added their voices to ours, as did those we have helped in our ministry.

God granted us this gift, but took from him some of what made him such a man. His eyes are useless, his right side weak and lame, his strong arm is now withered and unable to hold your messages.

Robere and I sat many hours by his side, and spoke your words to him. We know he heard us, but it is your voice he wanted to hear. Alejandro adds his request to ours. Please return. As four, we will have the strength we lack as three. Your faith makes you the strongest of us, and there is not much time.

You must come home as soon as you are able, and become our teacher. Our Father. All is arranged, as the Bishop explained in his earlier communication. I speak for all of us here when I relay our love, respect, and desire for your return.

In his name,
Matthieu.

Numb of mind, Carlos set aside the letter with leaden fingers, while his unbiased eye saw again the instructions he had mistakenly read first. They confirmed his previous appointment as the next head of the Abbey at Sant Cugat, along with another honor he neither sought nor wanted. Upon his return, he was to be further ordained as a Bishop.

The price for this office was neither coin nor lands. No sacrifice of a worldly nature was required. He had only to abandon the mystery he had spent the year unraveling here in France, and renege on the promise he'd made Luther to travel with him to Prag.

Which would be easier to abandon, a promise made to God, or one made to his children not yet met on the road? He had not been ordered to return—the Bishop had made that clear enough. He was to act as his heart directed, and that part of him had been sorely tested since leaving Sant Cugat.

Behind him on the road he'd walked were his oaths and the brotherhood he had left intact and healthy in the care of Father Frances. Thrice ordained, he had not only a duty to Rome, but to those men who had called him Brother and now deferred to him as their Father. Were they any less worthy of his love than those souls he would touch moving forward, whose names and faces he did not yet know?

Was the Abbot? His mentor, his confidant, his confessor? *His Father?*

This then, was the final test set before him. Once he set a foot on either path, the other would be lost to him for all time.

What was it he had read in the chronicles of the Yee Hero? Carlos had completed and set aside that translation months ago, but the words were still there in his mind.

The heart cannot have two masters.

Carlos knew he could no longer search for answers within himself, the primary reason he was willing to travel with Luther for a time. The greater part of him was bound by duty to return home and serve his Abbey with a false face and a cold emptiness inside where his faith once dwelled. His heart was a small light on a faraway hill, beckoning him closer to the Truth, and to the secrets he would find if he faced the world with eyes open.

Carlos carefully closed the messages from home. They

could tell him no more than they already had, and that story was already causing distress. He stacked the parchments with care, and placed them on his writing desk next to a box containing Matthieu's other letters.

Upon his arrival in Paris, Carlos had rewritten the messages he had scraped away while compiling notes of herb lore at the Blessed Stone, and sent them along to the Abbey. Matthieu had used the same skins to compose his replies, and on his latest message Carlos recognized a tear caused by a too-sharp quill and a heavy hand from his first month in Paris. He had once placed a story of the Yee Hero on this page, of her time alone in the mountains seeking perfection of mind.

His retelling was abridged, but the original story was tucked away under his shelf in a brightly painted chest made to shield it from the passage of time.

All he had to do was open both his eyes to Chao-xing Yee's lessons, and draw strength from her spirit.

Carlos knew without looking that the orange light coming from the hallway was that of the setting sun. The noon office was long past, and after it was gone he would again be left alone to worship on his last night here in the University.

He pulled out the box, and felt the carved symbols on its surface. He did not need the soft light of a candle to read them, he knew the words as thoroughly as he did the songs of Zion, and the Gospels he feared to read with both eyes open lest his memory be betrayed.

Both the true blossom and the painted flower float down the river out of sight.

Carlos removed the folded cloth with one hand, and opened the box with the other. Orange reflections gave way to golden light, as he eased the book free with both hands and placed it on the low desk it had not occupied for many days.

His hands moved quickly to the painted silk pages containing the words he sought, and he bowed his head briefly before reading.

I am sorry, Qin Yee. You deserve a better remembrance than any I can offer.

Carlos was overcome for a moment, pained by the still

raw wound in his heart. He tried to separate his time with the searcher from his study of the search, but it was hard to find a balance in himself. He was no hero, and despite what the brothers here thought, he no longer found peace in prayer.

He was a drowning man seeking a hand to pull him out of the water. Like that man, he was dangerous. His desires might drag others down with him, never to rise again.

This was not the lesson of the Yee Hero, and if he was to learn, he must first be ready to listen. Swallowing his grief, he thought of happier times.

He envisioned both the terrible memory of Qin Yee's death, and the beautiful sound of her laughter. Images formed in his mind—two motes of light in a dark sky that moved toward him at the same speed until they passed beneath his feet.

They floated away down the river of memory, leaving behind gently fading ripples that settled into a smooth sheet of clear water. Carlos settled himself in its center, opened his eyes, and began to read.

"So it is written that in the twentieth year of the journey, the Hero left the paths of Men and traveled up the dark mountain..."

CHAO-XING WATCHED THE RISING MOON. THE OTHERS had passed into exhaustion, spent and weary from the day's battle. They slept, and in the light of the moon, their faces were calm.

Their victory had given them new strength, but it was a temporary balm. The long days of marching, the weight of the swords, the pain of burying friends—all had extracted a price yet unmarked on their skin.

It was one she would pay herself someday. So far her second life had brought only one inescapable consequence. Sleepless nights like this one, watching over her followers as they enjoyed their well-earned rest.

It had been years since she had done the same. Meditation and a focused mind carried her through the hours of the day and comforted her through the dark of night. It was all she needed, and all she had.

The years of night had introduced her to every star over her head. She had memorized their endless dance through the seasons, and they were the only map she needed to chase the Witch King and his minions across the empire. She had followed them, and him, for two decades.

The Travelers, the Chariot, The Dragons of Winter and Spring. The markers in the firmament were unchanged by thousands of years.

They were old, fixed.

Stuck.

She was tired. Not in her body, but in her soul. Nothing

remained in her life but the struggle, no change in the content of her days. Tomorrow would be the same as today and the day before. They would search for the enemy, and if they found it, they would fight.

After the graves were filled, there would be new faces asking her to lead them. Asking her to watch them die on some far away hillside, under an uncaring moon.

There was a new star tonight. Left of the moon, traveling fast through the sky. It passed across the map and disappeared over the eastern edge of night. Chao-xing felt something as it moved, a curious desire. A humming, pulsing need, her thoughts of better days and other lives manifested.

Low on the horizon there was a white flash, tinged with red. An answering flash appeared to the west, and Chao-xing felt a tiny shudder under her feet as the earth changed its song.

She stood, gathering her scabbard in a motion practiced on battlefields too numerous to count. Her sandaled feet moved out of the camp and down the eastern slope. A steady, effortless gait that carried her from rising moon to the dawn.

Her back saw the setting sun, though her eyes paid no attention to its passing. She chased a faraway sound not heard with her ears. Each step brought her closer to the source, and with each pace her heart beat one time in response until the mountain loomed above her, obscuring the Lion of the East. Silvery light from the round moon fell on its tall slope, illuminating her path to the sharp edge at its summit.

"Do you feel it as well?"

The voice was odd, slurred. Whatever man stood behind her was not born to the language, but had learned it well from someone raised in Liaoxi or the kingdom of Goguryeo. She turned to face him, and bit back a laugh at the sight of his ridiculous, over-sized clothes. If he noticed, his next words gave no sign.

"I have come here from far away, in search of the dark metal. This, this is the place. I feel it in my bones."

Chao-xing regarded the stranger with her warrior's eye. His light showed no traces of anger, but burned constant and pure around him in yellow satisfaction. There was something else—a patch of white tucked against his spine and carried from far away. It disturbed his otherwise balanced stance, causing him to lean slightly forward.

Into the mountainside.

"I do not know of this dark metal, but I have also come here from far away. This is a new thing, one I wish to understand." She continued her inspection of the stranger who as yet had no name.

Calloused hands, conditioned by some constant activity. Broad and powerful shoulders, barely higher than her own. One larger than the other, the right hand curled around a missing handle.

A sword did not belong there, though one would rest easy in his fingers. Her mind painted a hammer there. Tongs in his left, holding the metal steady against repeated blows.

"And what will you make with this dark metal you have come for? What will result from your sweat and strength?"

A wide grin flashed in the moonlight. A few teeth were missing, but the rest were strong and white. Lines formed at the corner of his eyes, and she suspected his bald head was not the result of a barber's knife, but of a long life spent in a hot room.

"I see you are an intelligent and observant traveler from the West. I forgive you your ignorance, as you have not yet been graced with the wisdom of my home. I am Master Wang."

"Well, Master Wang, I in turn forgive you your rudeness. Whatever wisdoms exist in your home, the courtesy of an answered question is not among them." Chao-xing saw no weapons, but she knew all too well that lack of arms was not lack of threat. Anger flared in him briefly, and its red light surrounded his hands and feet.

He intended some demonstration, but the source of his frustration was lack of recognition for his accomplishments. And she also knew how the vice of Pride distracted from Balance, and removed Satisfaction.

"My weapons are the finest a warrior can wield," Master Wang asserted. "They are far beyond the quality of the simple blades you wear, and when I remake them with the dark metal they will be unbeatable."

"This is true, what you claim? You have no dark metal of your own, and I see none of Master Wang's weapons here, save sarcasm."

The white at his back flared, and Chao-xing noticed it did so in time to the sound of the mountain. "Master" Wang had indeed carried a piece of it with him.

Had carried it home. She regarded him with half her being rooted in the Stone, while the other became the Wave, free and light.

When his hand snapped forward, she was ready for the leaf-shaped blade as it flew. Her heart beat once, and the arc of metal slowed under the light of a full moon. She did not look to her hands as they inched toward the hilt at her hip, nor did she instruct them to separate and position her blades in the knife's path. She moved into the attack and past the danger it presented with eyes closed, flowing across the space between her and the smith.

Another beat, and the right blade rung with impact as it deflected the missile into the dirt. The left rested at Wang's surprised neck under his widening eyes.

Chao-xing's eyes looked at neither, but her right hand was no longer balanced. Her foot shifted to compensate as she opened her eyes. A deep gouge had formed in the sharp, flexible edge that had met and repulsed a thousand attacks. It drew her attention for a just a moment as its twin pressed slightly into the smith's skin.

His light flared with each beating of her heart, until the small, lingering vibration in her scarred sword stilled. Both blades lowered, slower than they had in twenty years. Two were no longer one, and remained separate.

"My apologies, Honored Smith. I had thought you to lack balance, and to be in need of correction. I am Yee Chao-xing, and I do feel the mountain as you do."

The smith fell to his knees and bowed his head.

"You are correct, Lady Warrior. Balance is not mine, though I seek it both in this place and in myself. My hand moved unbidden, and my life is yours to do with as you please."

Chao-xing knelt in the strange, coarse soil, carefully placing aside swords which did not align for the first time since she had taken them from her uncle's hands. Her empty fingers enclosed the hard palms of the smith, and she felt the warmth of the forge in the lines of his hands.

In an instant she knew him, and in that instant cast aside all things not seen by other eyes or heard by other ears. She was a child once more, innocent and without pain. For that moment, she lived again in light, and not darkness brought to the world by the Witch King's evil.

"Then I choose life, and all that comes with it. These eyes have seen too much death to cast aside such a gift. You and I have come on different paths, but we are here, and we start anew from this moment."

Wang's head rose, and their eyes met for a heartbeat, a breath, a lifetime.

The silence ended when he picked up the ruined sword.

"Please allow me to repair the damage my pride has done. This defect is one I can erase, and return to you your gift to me. Go, and do what needs to be done."

Chao-xing understood now why she had walked away from her camp the night before. The mountain was here, was *her*, long before the star crossed the sky. The answer to her questions was not at its edge, but at the center of the summit that scraped the stars.

She removed her sandals and stepped into the dark soil. It gathered around her feet, cool and comfortable. Her coat was next, and the belt that fastened her robe tight around her waist fell away, joined by a drape of green cloth.

The smooth white silk of her shift caught the moonlight as she climbed, free of all burdens. Her hands and feet found purchase in small places, and the mountain welcomed her heartbeat home.

Wang watched the woman climb as he gathered her belongings carefully. Master Yee's life was his to care for now, and he regretted the action of his hand that might have ended it.

That hand would now be devoted to her lessons for the rest of his days.

The mountain was still in his bones, and he retrieved the ancient, leaf-shaped blade from its embrace. He stood up straight for the first time in many days, watching as Yee Chao-xing scrambled up the mountain as if she were walking down a garden path.

Wang walked around the base of the mountain, toward the cave entrance he'd passed by as the blade pushed him ever onward toward his destiny. He'd smelled a forge's fire earlier in the day, and as he approached a half dozen men surrounded him with hammers in their hands.

"Why did you attack the Yee Hero, stranger?" The question was the same one Wang pondered as he walked, and still he had no answer.

"I do not know. Our paths have come together here, and someday, the reason will be revealed to us both."

"You must not do so again. The Hero protects us from the Witch King and his minions, who no longer walk the lands around our homes. Though we have never met her, she is responsible for our safety."

"Then, my friends, you are now my responsibility as well. Please, help me to help her so that we may continue to live in balance."

Wang followed them into their cave, down into the earth and closer to the fire.

The sounds of a borrowed hammer rose to meet the moon, echoing in time to the beat of seven hearts.

Chao-xing moved over the crater's edge, and descended the wall of rock towards the center of its bowl. Her white shift was unmarked from her climb, and her lungs worked in time with the unhurried beating of her heart.

On her ascent she passed no plants, no record of life. Some long-ago fire had shaped the mountain, burning away everything not connected to its solid core. Hers was the only breath that stirred the ancient dust.

She saw this place echoed above her on the face of the

shining moon, larger now than she'd ever seen it. Plains of white on its surface rose into ridges enclosing circles of stone.

It was a bright candle casting the shadow in which she now stood.

Three bouncing steps carried her to a soft landing in the center. Her legs fell easily into a position of rest, and folds of silk settled around her, forming a white cone in a plain of black.

Her back was straight at first, then leaned slightly, aligning to some axis felt rather than known. Her breath slowed, no longer offending the untouched stone with motion. Her skin cooled to match the night's chill, but her core remained warm and alive.

One beat. Two.

A long, slow exhalation, emptying her lungs. Her legs settle and harden, matching the stone below. Her heart beats a third time, then stops as she becomes one with the mountain.

Free of her body at last, her mind moves down through the rock along veins of dark metal. It surrounds the cave carved out over generations, and resonates with each blow of the hammer. It moves deeper, beneath and below all places of air and light.

It touches the Other, cold and hard.

It rises, up through the ages, the wordless memory of fire, fluid, solid, fire, and flow.

Past the air, high above the spot of white at the point which used to be Chao-xing, and expanding outward toward the Void. Past the moon, slowly turning and falling past its blue-green lover below.

Past the boundary without limit, into the Place.

Into solitude shared by the one, and defined by the missing.

A fourth beat resonates deep along paths of darkness, continuing past perception until it is indistinguishable from the night.

There is another, slowly moving past at a distance inside. There is contact, a kiss shuddering through the world, deflecting progress down paths...

Down paths...

Chao-xing is elsewhere, in a place without light. It is not black—it is the absence of black, the sound of nothing reflected until it roars.

Chao-xing is too far apart, spread over innumerable angles by a brush with too many bristles.

Chao-xing is lost. Unfocused, without center.

Out of balance, too far removed from Fire, Wind, and Earth.

Chao-xing is One become all. Adrift.

Alone.

Adrift...

Yee Chao-xing is the Wave, flowing over, under, past herself in currents not concerned with distance or volume.

Pulled by the moon away from the shore. And back again.

She sees a golden line curving around the place she has just been, looping and twisting past everything, everywhen. She touches footsteps not yet placed on the road, and flows back toward a tiny white place that was her body.

Chao-xing opened her eyes and saw the last edge of the moon pass over the edge of the rock wall above her. The heart of the mountain beat a fifth time in her chest as she drew in a crisp, energizing breath. She leaned forward, legs unfolding until one knee rested under her opposite the one bent against her chest.

Her next step carried her to the crater's edge, where her feet found the places they had stood before as the mountain's heart beat a sixth time. In the white light of her eyes, the mountain fell away from her, until it flattened far below into a tiny mouth of fire.

One more, and white silk fluttered as it moved out into the air, following her balanced breath.

Down.

Rivers of sweat ran down Wang's bare chest, desperate for escape from the heat of the forge. Behind him on the shelf were loops of leather, pins of bone, and pieces of smooth, polished wood that once imprisoned the soul of the divided blade.

Wide-eyed men watched him work, afraid to speak lest

they break the spell of his motion as he hammered the white hot bar of metal until the two weak planes became one.

One beat. Two.

    one beat, two.

His sweat-soaked skin was a uniform red, and each pump of the canvas and leather bellows sent motes of fire toward him as the forge flared into brilliant light. Touching his chest, they were robbed of energy and vanished, unable to compete with his inner heat. The hammer fell again, and a pure tone rose as the metal realigned along new patterns.

It would not break again.

One beat. Two.

    one beat, two.

The air, the anvil, the floor and the fire responded to the final blow of the smith's hand. The tongs lifted a burning piece of the sky, and six men breathed sighs of relief, only to gasp in alarm as the bar was thrust again into the forge.

It glowed hotter and brighter than any piece they had ever seen, and they drew back from the Master who had awoken its spirit.

His strong arms closed tongs on a dark stone mold that had rested in the fire unattended while he worked. Twelve staring eyes could not see where the black metal ended and the stone began, and widened when Wang took the mold in his bare hands and broke it open to reveal a shining square ingot carved out of the sun's heart.

One beat. Two.

    one beat, two.

He took up the tongs, holding the ingot steady as the hammer lengthened it, extending its strength. Each blow of the hammer coaxed a different sound from the metal, until finally he judged it ready. It went back into the fire to rest among the burning coals that refused to yield to ash.

Wang's hand stretched out, and one of the smiths hurried to fill it with a bowl of polished wood lined with cold, dark metal. Into the bowl went the leather, the wood and the bone. Wang knelt, grabbing a double handful of black dirt, and poured it over the top as he set the bowl on the anvil. A shining knife appeared in his left hand, then sliced the palm of his right.

Blood poured into the dirt. The knife fell to the ground, forgotten as a line of fire leapt from the forge into the smith's bloody hand and coiled gently around the bowl.

One beat. Two. A flash of white light erupted from his palm, and a puff of black dust rose from the bowl. Wang set it aside, turning his attention to the pair of shining metal bars resting in the coals

He reached the tongs in for the first, longer bar, bringing it back to the anvil before tipping sizzling blackness from the bowl over its glowing surface. He laid the second bar over it, and poured the rest of the mixture on top.

The hammer rose, and when it fell the mountain shook.

Again and again the metal was caught between the ground and sky, flattening, folding, screaming a single pure note that repeated with each rise and fall.

A rush of cool air blew into the cave, and six men turned as one to see a vision of white crouched at its mouth with blazing eyes, while the seventh laid thunder into the metal.

The stone around her feet was rippled like a stone dropped into water, and tendrils of mist followed her as she passed by the stunned men without a sound.

One Beat,

One Blow,

One Step.

Two, three, and Wang and Chao-xing stood together next to the forge as the stone walls around them vibrated. They were alone with the sounds of running feet retreating into the night. The ringing of one last blow of metal on metal followed the footsteps, and rocks shook loose from the hillside as Master Wang laid the cracked hammer to rest.

Chao-xing's small hand reached for the white-hot blade, grasping it at one end and lifting it from the anvil. Wang's stubby fingers reached out for the other side, and the cave was plunged into darkness, only to be lit again as pure yellow light erupted from two pairs of eyes.

Pulsing in time to the beat of a single heart.

"After battling the sky, the Master returned from the place of no place, armed with a shining sword that knew the Witch King's servants in any guise.

"Two paths had become one, and never again did the Hero doubt the purity of the quest."

CARLOS OPENED HIS EYES, SHAKING AND SPENT FROM the heat of the forge. Behind him, at the mouth of the cave, he heard whispers of the others. Their hushed tones spoke of the purity of light from Carlos' candles, which remained cold and unlit on the desk to his right.

This cannot continue. Where do they end, and I begin?

Carlos placed the golden glow back into the carved box, and returned both to their place under the shelf. The lesson was learned, but he could not apply it to himself. Neither path before him would lead to the mountain.

There would be no smith for him to save, no moon to which he would fly.

He was the metal, waiting to be hammered flat and forged anew.

He was alone, adrift, and no hand would pull him from the river but his own.

His belongings were packed for either road. The dawn was hours away, and there was still time for Physical Faith.

His feet carried him through hastily emptied hallways as he settled the patch over his eye. There was no need for a cloak tonight, the last days of the season were warmer in Paris than the mountains of Shaanxi province. They were getting shorter, like the days of the past that assaulted him in unguarded moments.

The journey home would be an easy one. He would settle back into familiar patterns and duties, but there was one he would not resume. Robere would be the archivist now, if that was still a path he wanted to walk. Carlos would abandon the world of the past, and live only for the future. Only by complete abstinence would he be free of temptation. When he stepped off the road of discovery, he would never again look back.

The river was a silent witness to his deliberations. Its source was far away, nestled against the mountains on the plateau of Langres. Hundreds of miles floated past him, slowly moving toward the sea to the West. Centuries of memory at his feet.

Were he to walk its banks to the East, he would travel into the kingdom of Burgundy and the Western Empire. Standing at the river's mouth, two more roads would lead his feet east. Rome would be to the South, Prag to the North.

In Rome, he would find his future in the Church. In Prag, he would deliver Luther Welmach to his family, and find the answers he sought.

And echoes of Karl.

Carlos watched the dark water flow past him. It gave no advice as to in which direction his future lay. It moved on to its own end, merging with the great ocean that slowly devoured Europe's mountains over the long years of history.

He had read that the water on the northern ocean was green, and tossed men and boats like toys in the slightest wind. That great creatures swam in its depths, monsters of the deep that dwarfed even the titans of the Aegean myths.

Carlos would not see them. The wave of his future rushed ever faster toward the shore, and would dash him against tall cliffs sooner than he would like. He wished he could become a bird—a white-winged gull that would fly above the waves and the rocks, seeking only the warm sun on his wings and the freedom of the sky.

But he was just a man.

Imperfect. Small.

Alone.

Watching the water with both eyes, he saw the lie in himself. He was not alone, he only chose to live that way. The Lord, and his servants on earth, were there to listen to him, should he speak.

He had not spoken to anyone but Luther of his problems, and to no one of the things he had seen in the last year. In the Abbey, he had shared himself daily. At the Blessed Stone, his example was his testament, and all the lives that touched him knew his heart.

In Paris, he had been silent, even before Rodrigo's irons had stripped away his illusions. The red letters he had shared with Luther, but when the visions and memories of other lives came, they came to Carlos alone, and there they had stayed.

He was not cast out, he was merely incomplete. Without that sharing, a confession of his heart, he could not find the peace he sought, the clarity necessary to make this decision.

He could not be forgiven.

His sins were unheard, unredeemed. And had been since he began his travels.

He was no longer humble before God.

The road would wait until he received a sign.

Carlos turned his feet back toward the Church, walking with greater and greater confidence. His patch was back in place, and the left side of his world showed him the river as it flowed past him.

The right remained dark, absent memory and temptation.

A piece of the darkness moved away from the rest of the night as he passed, following silently behind the monk's feet.

MOTION BEHIND HIM BROUGHT CARLOS OUT OF HIS reverie—a soft, scuffing sound at the back of the oratory. The other monks had left hours ago, and none had come to him after the office ended. He was left alone to pray, kneeling then as he did now with eyes closed before the altar.

There was a familiar odor in the air, teasing both his nose and his memory. It was rich, earthy. Some part of the road he had walked before carried along on an errant breeze.

He heard a coughing, throaty sound, and the closing of a carved panel door. When his feet carried him here to the altar, he had not been ready to unburden himself. The other monks had come to sing soon after, but their voices were as inadequate to his needs as had been the example of the Yee Hero.

Both lessons were pure and honest. They promised enlightenment if he would give himself fully into their embrace, but Carlos' soul was divided cleanly in two, and no outside influence could bring him together before he was ready.

He was almost there now, and it would not do to keep his unknown brother waiting. Before rising, he replaced the patch. This moment was for men—honest men. No mysterious influence would aid in his confession.

The candles had burned low during his hours of prayer, but there was still enough light to look at the chamber around him. It was the simplest room in this otherwise grand house of God—a place for worship, and for healing.

He was ready.

"Forgive me, for I have sinned. It has been many months since I last shared myself and confessed."The cold, hard wood of the confessional's seat was a reminder of his place in the world. It was not made for comfort, but for contrition. It had been worn smooth by many years of use, by those that came before him seeking a closer relationship with themselves and with God.

The sound of sliding wood signaled the start of his redemption. An unfamiliar voice addressed him from above his bent head. It was better this way. There would be no shared time together to color his judgment. Carlos would offer his sins honestly to a stranger, and accept the guidance he received the same way.

"What is your name, young man?" The words sounded wet, as if the lungs labored against a hard weight. Too many priests neglected the body in this place, as he himself had neglected the spirit.

"Carlos de Roja, Father."This was an uncommon, almost unthinkable opening to the ritual of confession, but Carlos was used to strange and new things in France. Even now, as he prepared to leave Paris forever, he learned more about a place he had ignored for too long.

"That is not a name with which I am familiar. Where are you from, and how long has it been since you were there? Your Latin is the equal of any I have heard in many years, but inside it is something else entirely."

"I...I am from Toledo. In the Kingdom of Castile."

"Iberia! I have not been there in far too long. I spent time there as a young man, as a soldier. I remember the people, the women and the sounds of the night. Tell me, is there a woman for you, in Toledo?"

The comments of the man on the other side of the screen were disturbing at first, until Carlos realized his error. He had not fully identified himself to his confessor, something which must be done before his sins could be explained.

"Father, I...I am a monk, Father. I am here in Paris to study, seeking knowledge of a subject that...it is difficult to explain, but I will try."

"So, no woman for you, then?"

Snow fell lightly on smooth, cold skin as the sun's light touched them both. The cold spread of her life's blood froze them together, uniting them into a single...

"No, there is no woman for me. I am true to my vows, and to my Order."

"Hmm. So you are a monk in Toledo, who has not known a woman and seeks truths in Paris that cannot be easily explained. What possible sin could you have committed, with such lack of opportunity?"

Carlos could not find the words to answer him. It was as if this journey, everything he had seen and heard was now without meaning. He had denied sin, rejected it at every turn, but still there was this darkness, this taint within him. What had he done wrong, what crime against God had he committed to deserve his judgment? Before the questions, he had been sure of his course, yet two small sentences from a stranger had undone his resolve.

"How long ago was this sin then?"

"I am not sure, Father. I...I know only that I have become unworthy of what has been given me. I have traveled far in service, and for many months I have neglected this duty while pursuing another. A personal quest, which I believed was sent from on high."

The words of Frances DelaMonde sang back to Carlos' memory. *Confession allows Contrition.* The torture of his spirit laid it bare, all the worse that it had been his own hand wielding the irons.

Tell me of this quest. The voice of his confessor gained strength, and for a moment, Carlos thought he had heard it with his entire body.

"Why have you strayed from your path? What were these steps, that you must confess them to me?" The man's voice was so similar to that of his beloved Frances that Carlos fought back tears, some of which escaped his eye to soak the cloth he wore across his face.

"I do not know. Until today, I thought myself firmly on

that path. Father, I have killed, taken the lives of evil men to protect the innocent and felt no tinge of regret in the actions. I have healed the sick, I have helped pious women to bring forth new life and buried others taken by disease and age. I have lived my life in service, never knowing another. And yet, this day I feel..."

False? The word was branded in his mind, as if born there in fire. "Yes, I feel false. As if my life has been a lie, a blanket spread over a bed meant for a greater man."

"Where have your footsteps led you, if you are no longer following those of your father?" Carlos thought on the words of the priest he did not know, who offered him a hand to lead him back to the path. His decision was quick, urged by the heretofore silent spirit he now knew to dwell within him still.

Confess. Confess all.

Carlos spoke of his books and letters, of the Abbey. Of the attachments he had made which tempted him from pure service to God.

Of the disease that nearly broke him, and had claimed so many others. Of his secret fear that he had carried this pestilence with him as punishment for believing the words of foreign invaders. Of the sisters of the Blessed Stone, both living and dead.

The words came faster, easier as he talked, almost as if they were being pulled from him. He spoke of his trial, and then finally with relief, of his visions.

The whispered temptation of what was real and what was wrong. Of other paths his feet might follow, if he set aside his calling.

Of Wazo, of Anselm.

Of Karl.

When he was through, only Carlos' ragged breathing, and the wet gasps of his confessor remained.

"Carlos, you have seen a world few men can comprehend. You have shared it with me, but I cannot take your fear of it from you. I have neither the power to save you, nor to forgive."

Carlos sobbed openly, even this small grace was denied him. His honest confession had received an honest answer.

Truly he was lost.

"And why should I?"

A choking sob stopped in his throat. The sweet scents of roses and myrrh he had breathed throughout his confession now seemed stale and sour. Never had he heard such a response, but one such as he could expect nothing better.

"You have committed no sins. You have been given a gift, a promise to keep. You have these strengths, these strange perceptions. Use them as you use your hands, as the strength in your arms lifts up those that need it.

"You have within you the seeds of power, which cannot be given to the false, but only to those worthy of such...only those with a purpose." Carlos saw a flash of red, and the sweet smell of crushed blossoms returned. His confessor had refreshed the censor, fanned the coals with his hand, and set the resulting air in motion.

"You, Carlos. You are one who can grow...strong. Take the scales from your eyes, and become what you were meant to be. Go. Go and do as your heart dictates. Accept no other guide than your...your inner power. Use what you learn, what is shown to you. Become...more than just a man."

"Th-thank you, my friend. I am unworthy of these gifts, and of your wisdom. I will do as you instruct. I will share my gifts with the world."

Yes. "Spread your net wide, and collect the bounty of life. But guard yourself. There are many within the...many who have not heard what is in your heart. "You must keep your path to yourself. What we have spoken of is not for others to know."

Carlos' heart raced. Purpose burned within him, and his hand strayed absently to his face, moving aside the cloth that hid his sight for the final time. His eye opened, free from all obstruction.

Below his eyes was a carved wooden plaque. It was as worn as the seat beneath him, letters barely visible by the flickering candlelight.

The Latin phrase there was one he had heard and known before he could ever read the words, before he had taken Christ into himself. The words he read aloud now, in the silent presence of his confessor, in a place of grace, and pure faith.

"God, the Father of mercies, through the death and resurrection of his son, has reconciled the world to Himself and sent the Holy Spirit among us for the forgiveness of sins; through the ministry of the Church may God give you pardon and peace, and I absolve you from your sins in the name of the Father, and the Son, and the Holy Spirit."

The words were true, golden in his sight. He had avoided them for many months, and that fear was now the falsehood.

An intake of breath, an exhalation, sweet and wet, from a faith so like his own. "Do you believe those words?"

"Yes, Father."

Then Go. "Do then, what your heart instructs. Do not tarry in the garden, but stride boldly to meet your fate."

Carlos felt as if he could fly back to Barcelona. But first he must discharge his service as best he was able. He would write to Matthieu and to the others. Matthieu would understand—his faith was strong. The strength of it would hold them all together until Carlos could complete his quest. He was pure of heart. Like Carlos, like the man behind the screen who had allowed him to forgive himself. He rose, and gave respect to the man whose face he did not know, an anonymous river of faith whose waters refreshed and invigorated him.

Carlos' feet knew the way back to his cell. His eyes were fully open now, and took in the carved and painted images of the saints and their own confessions on the walls around him. This room gave them power, and granted it to others who would follow.

Behind his back he heard the wooden panel slide closed—a sound that marked not only the separation of priest from parishioner, but Carlos' passage back to the light of God's love.

Thank you, my unseen friend. I will work hard to follow your example on my journey.

14 OCTOBER, YEAR OF OUR LORD 1205

THE DOOR OF THE CONFESSIONAL OPENED, AND FROM it fell a soft, weak thing. It had struggled at first, but the priest had no real fight in him, no fire in his heart. *Really, the Church has fallen so far in my absence.*

The dead man's life was barely worth the gold and gems his killer now pried from lifeless fingers.

But his death—his death had been so very useful.

This new one. This Carlos. He is a man worth the effort.

The irony of that name was sweet, like the blood still wet in the killer's mouth. The hunt of an age, against a long sought—possibly worthy—challenger.

The killer's smile was cold and merciless, with altogether too many sharp teeth in a cruel face surrounded by soft black fur, below eyes like red pits of Hell.

Yes, this will be...interesting.

But then again, hunts always were. They reminded him of...

Of when he was alive.

AM 10 OKTOBER 956

EVERY BREATH SEARING HIS LUNGS, KARL RAN THROUGH the darkening streets as he tried to escape his fate. There was a presence, a thing chasing him that he could not name. People scattered before him like leaves before the storm, not wishing to anger him by delaying whatever dread task he hurried to complete. This was right and proper. Karl was their master—their better in every way.

They would stare without words, quaking with fear if they knew that tonight, Karl Outrikos was not the hunter.

He was the prey.

He, Karl the Killer, whose name was spoken in hushed whispers, fleeing from an unknown, unseen thing like a frightened child because he could not name his fear. He had no memory of how he came to be in the street, covered in cooling blood as the last rays of the sun faded away.

But he would remember the first words he heard upon waking forever.

"Well done, Karl. You are almost ready."

The words crashed like waves upon rocks. Smashing, pounding, Cyclic, echoing around him but not diminishing as he ran from the source.

He had heard the voice before, over the long months of his recuperation. But never like this.

Only in his dreams.

His dreams—the terrible nightmares which caused him to wake shaking as the sun rose.

Well done, Karl. You are almost ready.

The dreams began the night he drank that vile concoction tasting of ashes and death, and smelling far worse than either.

The Cure.

By day, life returned to his body. By night, it drained from him as if from a wound that would not heal. Karl called no man master, but in the darkness, the half-world of sleep, he had neither power nor strength.

He was nothing.

Tonight, he had fought to stay awake, fought to avoid even a minute of weakness. When he finally succumbed, it felt as if he were drowning in a black pool as he closed his eyes, only to discover himself covered in something cold and wet when he opened them again.

Blood. Torn from their hearts, their lifeless forms tossed to the cold street like dolls with their strings cut away.

"Well done, Karl. You are almost ready."

He rounded the next corner, seeking safety in an alleyway. In the darkness, he felt strong, again the master. No voice could rule him. No words in the dark could shake him.

The voice. Low and gravelly. Echoing from all places and none.

It is time.

Running, turning, following. Hunting. The images came faster—flashes, glimpses into his past. A piteous, shrunken man, body ravaged by months of illness. Sweating with the pain, shivering in the night and unable to draw a breath. A strong man, hands closing on the throat of a woman. A laughing man, carving his way through men at arms while a fire burned the building down around them.

There was no fire in this alley, no lover to betray him. There was only a shivering man with fear in his heart and stabbing pain inside his chest.

"Who are you? What do you want of me?" It took all the courage Karl could muster simply to speak.

When the answer came, he wished he had not. Darkness fell around him, stealing light and warmth. A wind called back from a winter's night. He had gone blind—no more torches held aloft by angry corpses too stupid to know they were dead. What breath he had was stolen by night no longer warm or welcoming.

The darkness moved, shifted, and folded in on itself. Before him stood the source of his nightmares, a terror given form, if not name.

The beast towered over him, with thick, matted black fur. Muscles rippled beneath its skin like those of a horse. Its red eyes glowed like fiery coals, framed by huge, bat-like ears and a gaping maw of horrendous fangs as stained and red with blood as Karl's clothes.

It radiated darkness, filth, rot.

Evil.

And the murderer who had strangled, stabbed, trampled and flayed scores of men quailed before a killer without equal.

It spoke with a voice like the wind through graveyard leaves, a rustling from beyond death.

"Who am I? I am Arthos. I walk through the cities of men and feed on their misery and pain. Their blood is my life, their dying gasps my screams of ecstasy. I am the Witch King! I am darkness."

I am Death, Karl. And it is time.

The beast glided toward him, its eyes pulsing fiery light in time to the terrified beating of Karl's heart. His limbs, weakened from illness, exhausted from his frenzied run, refused to move. If his mouth would open, he would scream. If his life continued for

Just

One

More

Beat.

Then came the blackness. And the kiss, soft like a lover's breath upon his neck.

The pain, as the beast's jaws found Karl's throat and bit deep.

Fire raged through Karl's body—his every nerve screamed—his blood was molten lead. The pain had no precedent, no equal among the images of his life replaying before his frozen, staring eyes.

Every drop of life, every measure of will was sucked from his body. Locked in a twisted embrace with his dark lover, his murderer, Karl was suspended across a great abyss, torn between the fires of Hell he so richly deserved and the hope of life that still clung to the ruin of his body.

I am Karl Outrikos! I will not die like this.

But no cry went forth. No warning, no last gasp.

Just one trace of his former strength remained.

Hate.

One last defiant act as dark tendrils wrapped around the shriveled remains of his soul. Anger drove his head forward. Rage drew a tortured breath and a stench like the cure that had "saved" him filled his lungs. Fury opened his mouth, then closed it upon his killer's shoulder.

He returned to life in two worlds, seeing himself through two sets of eyes. His own, and the surprised, suddenly startled red coals of his murderer as it shoved what remained of Karl from him.

Karl came away from Arthos with a chunk of flesh in his mouth, as if it could replace the one the monster had taken from him. Swallowing, a new fire rose in Karl's chest—a slow, cold burn that gave new life to dead arms and legs. Fresh strength thickened wasted limbs, and set his mouth in the cruel smile that had ended so many lives.

Karl's heart beat for the first time of his second life, and his lungs filled with the rich, heady scent of his prey.

"Now, monster. Now we will see who rules the night."

Their screams merged, and four arms twisted and sought a hold. More memories came to Karl, unfamiliar images of distant faces, forgotten roads and shadows.

Of a sad, frightened old man, with a charlatan's bag.

Of empires lost beneath the sands of time, and of fire in the sky.

Of Saracen conquerors, and a proud king on a shining white horse.

Barbarians burning a shining city.

Of men and ships.

Of pain. Of sickness.

Of blood.

The monsters circled one another in the darkness. Two killers, both dead and dying. Blood, black and hot running from their mouths, spilling out from ruined chests and gashed arms.

Another tight grapple. No seduction, no sweet, cold words passed when Karl bit at Arthos. Arthos bit back, and memories tore at Karl's mind—familiar faces he had never met. Fears not his own.

Victims not his own.

Bloodstained streets, a wagon of travelers. Resting his burden so light and weak, the perfect convert. Brightly-clad men with their jingling scarves and sharp knives. Stabbing, tearing, screaming.

No escape. No survivors.

A blood splattered knife, carved handle falling from bloodless fingers.

Fear.

Rage.

Where Arthos had centuries of accumulated power, Karl had his wits, a lust born in the streets, and a lifetime of struggle fueling his rage, his never-ending anger at a world where only the strong survived.

Of course, a knife came in handy in this sort of fight. Karl had none, but he knew where to get one.

The killers ran back over their own steps. Back through shuttered streets and moonlight. Back over empty cobbles, towards dead men and a pool of drying blood.

Karl's men. Karl's people, whose blood even now stained his face.

And lying beside them, Arthos' knife.

The killers made a desperate dive, and three hands reached for a sharp blade. One hand grasped a black-furred throat, an arm's length extending Karl's life until his fingers closed on a carved bone handle.

The killers rolled, snarling, biting, and stabbing at each other.

They came to rest with a whimper, and the wet, sad sound of escaping blood.

"Tell me, old man. Is it time? Are you ready?"

Karl's voice was a harsh, gasping whisper, a promise of pain. But with stolen blood running through his body, he felt stronger than he had been before his illness. Far stronger, and the dying flesh before him promised more strength yet.

"Show me, Arthos. Show me...Fear."

The scream brought a smile to Karl's cruel, bloody lips.

It was always better when they screamed...

ARE YOU ALMOST READY, CARLOS? IT IS TIME."
"Luther! It is good to hear your voice again, my friend. Yes, I am ready. Will you assist me with this case? I seem to have acquired quite a supply of parchment in your absence."

Luther's smile was a welcome sight after so much time alone. The road ahead of them promised many such smiles, and many miles of friendship.

"Is that a rebuke I hear, Carlos? Or perhaps you are complaining about something else."

"I am through complaining, kind sir. It requires an anger at the world that I no longer hold close."

"It seems then that my journey has brought even more benefits than I had anticipated. If I had spent longer on the road, who knows what might have happened." Luther laughed and collected the case.

The cell was nearly empty, almost exactly the same room Carlos had found when he arrived months before, though the monk himself was quite different. The cassock and sandals he'd worn in summer were now stowed in worn leather packs slung over his shoulder. They had once rested on a horse's back, but their weight was negligible on the man's.

He was again a traveler, dressed in trousers and heavy boots, with a cloak to fend off the rain and mud.

He lifted the painted wooden chest in his hands, and his departure from the Abbey of St. Victor was complete. No trace of his stay remained, and after a long delay, his journey resumed.

The two doctors walked down a hall of silent monks who watched their fellow leave with a mixture of regret and awe. Carlos met their eyes without fear, no longer ashamed of his personal demons. He fixed their faces in his mind, thanking them for their patience by remembering their devotion.

Carlos knew the world was far larger than those places he'd seen with his own eyes. There was more to discover, more to verify than could be found within stone walls and between the pages of a book or on faded sheets of parchment.

The man at his side would help him find it. The roads they would walk would uncover but a small portion, but the experience would be better shared than simply survived.

The light outside the university walls was warm and inviting. Carlos walked out into air rich with the scent of flowers. The pair moved down the broad steps to the wide avenue where the expedition was gathered, waiting for their leader to arrive.

Luther's wagons were packed with his own belongings and those he had collected traveling the north roads. His path wound down from the islands of the Britons, across a sea Carlos had imagined but never seen.

There was plenty of room for Carlos' meager belongings there among them. Quick hands relieved him of his burdens, and he stood unencumbered for the first time in many months. He looked back at the city that had been his residence but never his home.

He was a stranger to this place, no more a part of it on leaving than arriving. A part of him would remain here always, where he had lost and regained his faith, and renewed his belief in the spark of the Divine dwelling in all men.

He had discovered the touch of evil that lived there as well, the dark place from which the torturer's hand drew its strength, and in which his hatred, intolerance and madness hid from the light.

Where monsters dwelled. And heroes were born.

"Will you miss it, Carlos?"

Would he? Dark dungeons where bravery and selflessness

were rewarded with pain and fire. Cold rooms where faith became madness, then faith renewed. Dark, dusty tombs containing secrets and lies and stories from far away.

"No, Luther. I will not miss Paris. I take it with me. Every day when I wake, part of me will be here."

And when I lay down to sleep, the darkness will be waiting.

"Then let us be off. There are many Parises awaiting you, and we cannot reach them if we do not feel the road beneath us." Luther climbed up on the wagon and signaled the men behind to do the same. A snap of reins, and the journey east began.

Carlos walked along beside the wagon. Paris passed him by, its sounds and smells offering their farewells to the departing caravan.

For a moment—only a moment—Carlos felt himself rooted in place, though his feet moved on. That part of him he had spoken of to Luther was here on the street. It was down the next alley, around the next corner. It wanted to be seen—waited for him to come running, fists flying and blood pumping.

It was the rotting, dead remains of his childhood, finally cast aside during the seasons of his twenty-seventh year. His twenty-eighth now began, and the smell of it tugged at him, begged him to take it back.

But only for a moment. His eyes turned to the road ahead where tomorrow waited, and Carlos welcomed the changes each new mile would bring.

Behind him, the shadow of yesterday shifted and crawled further back down cold and twisting streets.

Scrambling to avoid the sun....

AUTHOR'S NOTE

This collected edition of *Seasons of Truth* is the end of a literary journey spanning half my life. It's been a long road from there to here, and I'm glad you could share the last part with me. Carlos' world is a large one, and I hope that in the years and months to come you'll enjoy it as I have over the last few decades.

Yes, I've been writing this book for over 20 years. These things happen. *Seasons of Truth* has seen a lot of drafts during that time, and is far removed from the half-coherent notes I scratched out in the early 90's. So first on the gratitude list is my friend Matt Forbeck (www.forbeck.com). His kind words and encouragement kept this project going when I was ready to stick it back in the shoebox forever. I'd also like to thank alpha/beta/tireless readers Jen West-Scholes and Peggy Foy, whose brutal honesty forced the second and third rewrites, which eventually led to the seventh that you've just finished

Or is it the eighth? I originally published *Seasons of Truth* as four e-novellas, hoping that the episodic nature of this novel would translate into serial sales. It didn't, but that same year I also had a major science fiction novel come out (*Homefront*, from Arche Press/Resurrection House), and another novella in the Foreworld shared universe (*Blood and Ashes*, from 47North/Amazon Publishing), having a dark/alternate/monster-y/superhero book series seemed like an awesome thing to run alongside them.

So after finishing the submission draft of *Homefront* I knew it was time to dust off *Seasons of Truth* and beat it into submission for the last time. To do so, I called upon the services of the Editing McKennas, three of the keenest publishing minds I know. With their help I was able to knock the last rough edges off and mold *Seasons of Truth* into the book it is today.

To prepare this collected edition, I tapped my boon companion Roberto Rodriguez Calas to not only transform the covers of the e-books into interior illustrations, but give me a print cover that would really light up store shelves (those of you turning your e-reader over and over will have to trust me on this one, or pick up a copy yourself).

My partner Lindsey has been with me since I started writing this latest version of *Seasons of Truth*, and over the years has suffered through many bad retellings of its central plot. She's been a light in the darkness for me, and I honestly don't think I could have finished this book without her support.

Similarly, Tony Rivera and Janna Silverstein spent a lot of time trapped in cars listening to me muse about Carlos and his many problems, and since I somehow left them out of all four of my previous Author Notes, I'd like to acknowledge their encouragement and friendship now.

And although this book is already dedicated to you, the reader, thanks again for believing in me. I hope you enjoyed my stories of Carlos and Karl, and I hope that you'll find my other offerings to your liking as well. If you can, please write up a review and post it online, or at the very least tell your friends. Writing is a lonely profession, and the only way we know if we've reached anyone with our words is if you tell us.

Let's do it again sometime.

Scott James Magner
January, 2015

AUTHOR'S OTHER NOTES

My official afterward to this collected edition is a mixture of the ones originally presented with *Winter* and *Fall* with a few additional words. But the notes I presented in *Spring* and *Summer* had more content than just the normal "thank you's," and since I already got your money I figured I could take up a little more of your time with some additional additions. So here we go, back down the rabbit hole.

From *Spring*:

One of the dedications to *Seasons of Truth* is "to my Brothers," which I feel might require some explanation. When I first wrote about Carlos and company, I was in a very different place than I am today. Telling the story of men without fathers seemed very relevant to the person I used to be, estranged from the only father I could remember and concerned that I'd never know the one that gave me life. I grew up alone, and when writing a superhero's origin story it never occurred to me that he should be any different than I was.

In 2013, I wrote a book about three brothers who had a very strong bond with their father, but still managed to form meaningful relationships with other people. (*Hearts of Iron*, from 47North/Amazon Publishing). While writing it, I found I wanted very much to speak to my own father, and also one of my "capital B" Brothers. I was very saddened to learn that both men had passed on, and even more so that I hadn't heard about their deaths until the very moment I needed both of them in my life.

It was not the best of days.

In 2014, while writing yet another book about people with Daddy issues, I resolved once and for all to find my birth father. I knew the odds, and prepared myself for the worst. I'd almost found him the year before, but didn't take the next step and solidify my desires. Now (then), understanding what I did and preparing to rewrite this book for the last time, I knew there could be no more excuses.

I found him, I contacted him, and the two of us are slowly working toward the relationship both of us always wanted. And better still, I learned that I have two brothers and a sister that I only dreamed about having when I was growing up. Like Carlos, I wanted more, but was satisfied with what I had.

Both of us were wrong. But through the written word I can address at least one of our problems, and I hope you've enjoyed our monk's journey so far.

And from *Summer*:

I am not a biblical scholar, nor have I ever wanted to be. I read and write books, and over the years have learned to appreciate a good story no matter its source. The events in Carlos' flashbacks are meant to entertain, not to mock any one faith's beliefs.

The second thing I'd like to mention is that am neither an atheist nor a Christian, though I did attend Catholic school as a child. (The same one my editor did, but that's a story for another time.) Carlos' faith is his own, but his ongoing struggle with the nature of reality is one I fight alongside him every day.

I was talking to a friend recently about this book, and I gave him my standard elevator pitch of "It's about 13th century superheroes." His smile and laugh were all I needed to know I'd made another sale. But my slightly longer pitch for the last few years has been "The Bible is actually a zombie apocalypse survival guide, but we've forgotten how to read it." That one takes people a little longer to process, but once it does the result is the same.

Biblical inerrancy is a real thing, but my highly fictionalized account of the *Vulgate*'s creation should not be taken as, well, gospel. One of the things Writers of Fiction ™ do is take a small fact and blow it out of proportion, just to see what might happen. St. Jerome was a truly fascinating man, and there will be more written about him as *The Hunters Chronicle* unfolds. I do not believe he intentionally gutted the Bible—in fact, I think his efforts preserved a lot of material which otherwise would be forever lost. But no one who wasn't there knows the full story, and that works out nicely when creating a fictional world for heroes (and villains) to play in.

Speaking of which, I believe our world doesn't have enough heroes in it, at least not ones we know about. There are a lot of things going on around us right now that paint the human race in a very unfavorable light. People who should know better are doing Very Bad Things. In our ratings-driven news cycle we often don't get the information we should, and shock value rules airwaves which used to be controlled by truth.

Thanks for your indulgence. And while I'm not done writing about Carlos and his world just yet, I'll try to keep my afterwords to a minimum from now on.

Or not.

Scott James Magner
January, 2015

ABOUT THE AUTHOR

Scott James Magner is an Author, Editor, Analyst, Designer, and whatever else he can reasonably get paid for. His work has appeared in games, books, and interactive media projects, and he once ran the largest tabletop roleplaying game in the world.

You can catch up on all things him at his website:

scottjamesmagner.com